Also

MADAME

SARA CATE

sourcebooks
casablanca

This book is dedicated to everyone who found a home at the Salacious Players' Club. To everyone who loved Eden from the start and knew the series wouldn't be complete without her story. And to the fighters.

And to the horny moms.

Copyright © 2023, 2024 by Sara Cate
Cover and internal design © 2024 by Sourcebooks
Cover design by Stephanie Gafron/Sourcebooks
Cover photo by dogbitedog69/Getty Images

Sourcebooks and the colophon are registered trademarks of Sourcebooks.

Published by Sourcebooks Casablanca, an imprint of Sourcebooks
P.O. Box 4410, Naperville, Illinois 60567-4410
(630) 961-3900
sourcebooks.com

Originally self-published in 2023 by Sara Cate.

Cataloging-in-Publication Data is on file with the Library of Congress.

Printed and bound in the United States of America.
LSC 10 9 8 7 6 5 4 3 2 1

Trigger Warning

Dear reader,

There are elements in this story that could be potentially triggering. Please be aware there are scenes of domestic violence and abuse on the page.

There is also cheating, neglect, and emotional abuse from parents, and childhood trauma.

With these, there is also recovery, struggle, self-doubt, and healing.

Like any book in this series, there are dark/heavy sexual themes, BDSM, impact play, rope bondage, and degradation.

If any of these story elements could cause you harm or distress, please continue with caution. Your health and safety is important to me.

Thank you,
Sara

Prologue

Eden
About seven and a half years ago

MY STRAIGHT BLACK HAIR HANGS OVER THE PORCELAIN BOWL AS I'm assaulted by another round of violent dry heaving. There's not a single thing left in my stomach, but just the whiff of pungent cleaning products from the restaurant's bathroom triggered this relentless sickness.

Will this misery ever end?

There's a tremble in my hands as I wipe my mouth and flush the toilet. I'm not sure if the shaking is from nerves or the lack of sustenance in my body. Maybe both.

After washing my hands at the sink, I reapply my red lipstick and black eyeliner, smudged from the tears that crept out during my heaving spell. Then, when my makeup is fixed, I dare to glance in the mirror again.

The woman who stares back is one I don't recognize.

She's bold.

Beautiful.

Fearless.

Smart.

She's standing in the restroom of a high-class restaurant wearing a brand-new tight black dress and about to go on a first date with a billionaire she matched with on a kinky dating app—and she's pretending she's not scared out of her fucking mind.

This woman is *not* me.

But I'm willing to pretend for tonight. I have to. If not for me, then for the life growing inside me. I have to pretend to be this woman because I refuse to go back. This woman is intelligent, sexy, and bold enough to seduce a rich older man for a one-way ticket out of her own life.

If he gets me away from my husband, I'll do whatever I have to.

And I might be afraid, but I'm not ashamed.

With that, I slide my clutch under my arm, toss the paper towel into the trash, and walk out of the bathroom. My head is held high as I approach the hostess stand. With as much confidence as I can muster, I tell her my name.

"Eden St. Claire."

"Oh yes, Mr. Kade is waiting for you," she replies. "Right this way."

Squeezing my small purse, I force my hands to stop shaking as I follow her. Instead of leading me into the crowd of tables in the classy restaurant, she turns toward the curtain that leads to a set of stairs. I follow her up the winding wrought-iron steps until we reach the rooftop of the building.

When she opens the door, I pause. String lights cover the rooftop of the restaurant that overlooks the bay, with the sound of waves crashing against the shore in the distance. There is one single table in the center, and a tall salt-and-pepper-haired man is standing next to it, staring pensively out at the dark ocean beyond where the moon shines over the water.

He turns when he hears the door opening and smiles at me with a warm, genuine expression.

"Eden," he says as he approaches.

As he gets closer, I notice how handsome he is, which I guess is good. It will make this so much easier. He had a photo on his profile, but I never fully trust those, so it's a relief to see he's just as good-looking in person.

"Mr. Kade…sir," I reply with a smile as he takes my hand and places a kiss on my knuckles.

"You look stunning tonight. Thank you so much for coming."

"Thank you for inviting me," I say.

When I notice the shake in my voice and the tension behind my smile, I keep reminding myself to be the woman in the mirror. Bold. Beautiful. Fearless.

"Please, sit down." With my hand still resting softly in his, I follow him to the table, where he pulls back my chair, allowing me to sit.

There is a candle in the center of the table and an ornate setting on each side. Something about the sight of two different-sized forks gives me anxiety. It reminds me I don't belong here. I'm not prestigious or wealthy. I've never dined anywhere that gave me two different-sized forks to eat with.

But tonight…I'm not me.

"I went ahead and ordered us a bottle of Château Lafite," he says as he sits opposite me. "I hope you like red wine."

My stomach turns, and my hands begin to tremble again. "I don't…drink, actually," I stammer.

His eyes widen in surprise before relaxing into an expression of understanding. "Of course. It's best to be sober and clearheaded anyway."

With that, he waves down the hostess before she disappears back down to the restaurant. "Please cancel our bottle of wine and bring us some sparkling water instead. Thank you."

"Of course, Mr. Kade," she replies with a polite smile.

Just as I'm about to apologize for being difficult, I close my mouth. The woman in the mirror doesn't say sorry for making her preferences known. She has nothing to be sorry for.

I square my shoulders as I stare across the table.

Ronan relaxes in his chair. "So, Eden…tell me a little bit about yourself."

"Well…everything I said in the app was true. I'm looking for a Dom—"

"I read your profile and every message you sent, but what I want to learn is who *you* are. Who you *really* are."

I have to force myself to swallow. "Who I really am?"

My cover is blown. He's on to my lies. Fear snakes its way up my spine, and it feels like each breath is a chore.

"Umm…" I choke out.

"Yeah. What makes you happy? What's your family like? Are you a dog person or a cat person? That sort of thing."

My lips part, and I stare at him in surprise. "Oh," I say.

When I don't speak for a moment, he leans forward, a wrinkle between his brows. "I'm sorry if you assumed this would be a quick hookup. I like to get to know the women I take to bed, especially if we're entering a Dom/sub relationship. And I figured since you said you were new to the lifestyle in your profile, we could take the time to get acquainted first. Is that okay with you?"

Technically, I'm in a bit of a rush to win this rich man over, at least enough that he might be willing to spend some money on me. If he buys me jewelry or designer clothes, I can pawn them for something useful.

Realistically…I feel more at ease knowing he's not a shallow, pussy-hungry creep, even if it does mean faster to bed and faster to cash.

After a deep breath, I look him in the eye, and then I *lie*. "Things that sparkle make me happy. My family is loving and humble, but they don't live as close as I like, so I'm often alone. And I'm definitely a cat person."

Lies, lies, lies.

Something in Ronan's eyes flickers with skepticism, which

worries me. If he doesn't believe I'm just a beautiful, lonely woman who loves jewelry, then my plan will fail faster than I'd like.

I can only afford so many more nights at the motel before I'm out of options.

"What about you?" I ask with interest.

"I—" he starts. Just then, we're interrupted by the door to the roof opening and a waiter approaching with a tray on his shoulder. "Oh, I hope you don't mind. I went ahead and ordered us some appetizers to get us started. The scallops here are to die for."

Just then, the waiter places a silver tray on the table, and my stomach clenches as the pungent stench of seafood wafts directly to my nose.

A cold, clammy sweat covers my forehead, and my mouth fills with saliva. I won't make it to the bathroom. I'll be lucky if I make it out of this chair.

Without warning, I burst from the table and sprint, stumbling in my heels as I fold myself over the rail lining the rooftop and dry heave onto the empty beach below. As I retch over and over again, my hair is flying with the wind, sticking to my face and neck.

The entire time I'm throwing up the nothingness in my stomach, I think about how humiliating this entire endeavor is. I'm faking a personality to try to con a wealthy stranger out of money, ready to sleep with him and do God knows what else. Now I'll have to walk out of this restaurant with my tail between my legs, back to the smelly, noisy motel I can barely afford until I devise another plan.

Then I feel something cool and wet against the back of my neck. As the heaving stops, warm, soft hands wipe my hair from my face, gathering it in a ponytail at the back of my head.

Wonderful—I just tried to con the nicest billionaire in California.

Good job, Eden. I can't take a dime from him now, not without feeling like the worst person in the world.

"Drink this," he says. A cool glass touches my lips, and I take the water from him, sipping it slowly so I don't anger my stomach again.

After a few sips, he takes the glass and moves the wet washcloth from my neck to my forehead. It's embarrassing but also…nice. I close my eyes as he softly pats my clammy face with the cool towel.

"Better?" he whispers.

I nod, but with each movement of my head, it's like shaking loose the tears I've held back since finding out about the baby. They slowly start to slip through my closed eyes.

"I'm sorry," I reply, my voice cracking with the words. The sooner I can get out of this restaurant, the better.

"Don't be sorry. I've had the plate removed."

"I should probably go," I say.

But I don't move. I let his tall frame shield me from the wind, and I allow him to wipe my face, soothing me so much I don't care about my makeup.

"Come here," he mumbles, and I instantly fall into his arms, not entirely knowing why or how I can feel so comfortable with a man I just met. But his arms are big, and they feel safe, and even if I know there isn't a dime in my future from this stupid, elaborate scheme, there's nothing wrong with enjoying one embrace before I go.

Maybe it's because he's not berating me or calling me stupid. He's not telling me that I only think about myself and that everything bad that happens is somehow my fault. Instead of slapping me across my face and spitting insults, he's caressing my back and telling me everything is going to be okay.

It's enough to have me crying in earnest now.

"I can't let you leave like this, Eden. Will you let me at least feed you first?"

I pull away with a sniffle. "Really?"

"Come on, have a seat, and I'll order."

———

Twenty minutes later, the table is covered with an array of random plates. There's a bowl of risotto in front of me. Then in the middle are a basket of French bread, a plate full of fresh fruit, and a tray with sliced chicken breast and sautéed vegetables.

My mouth waters at the sight of the fruit. With one of my fancy forks, I pluck a piece of fresh pineapple from the plate and put it in my mouth with a satisfied hum.

"Okay, what's with the fruit salad?" I ask with a smile when the taste doesn't immediately send me puking over the edge of the roof again.

"My first wife craved pineapple during her pregnancy," he replies nonchalantly. For a moment, I nod, caught on the fact that he was married and has children, but then I realize I must not be so good at keeping secrets.

"How do you know…?" I ask, frozen with my fork in midair on its way back to the plate of pineapple and strawberries. "I mean, I'm not—"

"It's okay," Ronan says with an easy smile. "I figured it out after you turned down the wine and lost your lunch over the smell of fish. I remember this phase well."

For a moment, I say nothing. I stare across the table at him, wondering what the hell I'm supposed to do now. What do I say? That I agreed to come on a kinky Dom/sub date knowing that I'm six weeks pregnant? That I was never planning to tell him that? Or do I just come clean altogether?

"It's complicated," I say.

He nods. "I'm sure it is, but don't worry about it. I don't need to know the details."

Ronan and I fall into a comfortable conversation. He tells me about how he lost his first wife and son in a car accident twenty years ago. And how he's given up on long-term relationships after having his heart broken time and time again. Which led to him investing in the company that runs the app with plans to expand in the future.

"So you're…really into this stuff then," I say, nibbling on a piece of bread. Eating slow, small bites is the only thing that seems to keep my queasiness at bay.

"By this stuff, do you mean BDSM?"

"Sorry. It's all still so foreign to me."

"That's okay. I read in your profile that it was new to you. Yes, to answer your question, I am really into it."

"You're not what I expected," I say with a shy smile.

"To be honest, neither are you. And I don't just mean the *situation*." His eyes glance down to my stomach, and I put my hand there, thinking wistfully about the new life growing inside.

"So tell me…" he says with an arched brow. "Were you honest in your kink quiz?"

My mouth falls open. "Of course! Why?"

He tilts his head downward and glares at me as he waits for me to be honest. He's too nice to lie to, and it's been so long since I felt this comfortable around a man (if ever) that I can't stand the thought of lying to him at all. So I fold within seconds.

"All right, fine. I wasn't *entirely* honest."

"Why would you lie? Why did you want the quiz to tell you were submissive?"

When I open my mouth, ready to argue that I didn't *want* it to tell me that at all, I realize…maybe I did. What if it was never about being paired with a rich Dom? What if I answered that quiz as a submissive for other reasons?

Suddenly, I find myself uttering the most honest thing I've said to him all night.

"I think I wanted it to tell me I'm submissive because that's the role I've been playing my entire life. I belonged to my father. I belonged to my small town and all the expectations put on me there. Then I belonged to my husband. I thought that's what I wanted because that's how it's supposed to be."

"Is that what you want?" he asks, his warm-brown eyes focused on my face.

With my next breath, I feel renewed. And it's not about sex or BDSM or anything like that. But for the first time in my life, I realize that I am not meant for the role I've been playing. The cards that were dealt to me were never truly mine in the first place. So with confidence and boldness, like the woman in the mirror, I stare back at the man sitting across from me.

"No," I reply. Then I add, "I don't know who I am."

"Hmm," he replies, reclining in his seat and watching me as if studying me. "As much as I wish we were compatible, I'm afraid we're not. But I'd love to teach you if you'd like to learn. I imagine you have one hell of a journey ahead of you, Eden—and I'm not just referring to the baby."

Emotion builds in my throat, stinging my eyes as I feel those words hit me. I expected to come on this date and hopefully wake up with a new diamond necklace or designer shoes. I never expected to give a second thought to the results of some kink quiz. But now I suddenly want to rush home and retake it.

If I want to start fresh now, I need to do so as the *real* me—whoever that may be. I won't go back to the woman I was before. I won't keep playing roles to accommodate others. It's time I put myself first.

"I want to learn," I reply with confidence.

Ronan smiles as he lifts his glass of sparkling water in a toast. I lift mine and touch it to his. It feels like the start of something big, and that's worth more than cash. This time when I picture the woman in the mirror, instead of imagining she's someone else, I imagine that woman is *me*.

Rule #1: Love is just another form of control.

Eden

"YOU'VE BEEN A VERY BAD BOY."

The whip flies with a crack, and the man currently bound to the cross hollers around the ball gag in his mouth. In his right hand, the red-silk handkerchief is still safely clutched in his fist. This is our nonverbal sign to communicate since his mouth is a little stuffed at the moment. The second that piece of fabric falls, I stop.

Once every sixty days or so, he comes in and pays me to take him to the extreme, pain-wise, and he loves a lot of degradation while we're at it.

For all I know, the guy is guilty of something, and he needs someone like me to punish him for it. Some people go to confession or say their Hail Marys—and some people come to me. It's not my business to know all the details. It's just my business to be his Domme for the night.

After our third round of six hits, I give him another break, letting him breathe, sweat, and cry.

"Pathetic," I murmur against his ear as he moans in agony. "A good boy would take the pain, but you're not a good boy, are you?"

He shakes his head.

"Are you going to be a good boy now?"

He nods. His eyes are clenched shut while tears, drool, and sweat cover his bare chest. And as gross as it is, I love seeing people like this. It's like a cleansing ritual or an exorcism. They come to me carrying baggage, guilt, pain, worry, and stress, but within a few hours—whether it be from pain or some time in subspace—they leave feeling refreshed and renewed.

I unclasp the ball gag at the back of his head. He groans again when he's finally able to close his mouth with an ache in his jaw.

"Say it, Marcus. Promise your Madame that you'll be a good boy from now on."

"I promise," he croaks. "Madame."

"I don't believe you," I reply in a cold, emotionless tone.

He whimpers because he knows what this means. I take another glance at the silk handkerchief, but he's still holding it tight.

"I think you need six more to be sure. What do you think, Marcus?"

His chest is heaving with each breath, and he looks like he's about to cry again. Then he nods. "Yes, Madame."

I'm not too concerned. He always gets like this at the end, looking like he really wants to stop, but he never does. I trust Marcus to tell me if he's at his limit.

"Give me a color, then."

"Green, Madame."

I lean closer, grabbing him by the hair and craning his neck until he cries out in pain. "You really deserve this, you know."

"I deserve this, Madame." His voice is strained and raspy.

"After these last six swings, you're going to be my good boy again, aren't you?"

"Yes, Madame."

"Good. No gag this time. I want to hear you count them out. And don't forget to thank me after each one."

He whines when I let him go and step away, and his first shout of pain nearly shakes the walls. The sound of it is beautiful. Doing this gives me purpose and control. Even when my arm tires and aches, I love it.

An hour later, after some much-needed aftercare, I spot Marcus coming out of the changing room, looking refreshed and lighter than he did when he first arrived. His shoulders are no longer hunched by his ears, and he's wearing a lazy smile. I'm unwinding with sparkling water at the bar as he leaves the club, waving to me as he goes.

Even though he's a regular and accustomed to the routine, he will still receive the automated email with instructions on caring for his welts, bruises, and feelings. Not everyone who leaves my sessions is hunky-dory happy, and I just like them to be prepared. Getting your ass flogged and spanked—literally and metaphorically—tends to bring up a lot of thoughts and emotions not everyone is ready to deal with.

All that to say, I haven't had any complaints yet.

As I sip my drink, I make a list on my napkin of the things I need to do at some point tomorrow or, rather, today, considering it's already two in the morning.

Pick up cupcakes
Order movie tickets
Write the sponsored sex toy review post
Make waxing appointment

Lost in my thoughts as I try to think of what else needs to get done, I look up from my list and see a man walk by in a dark-blue suit. He has longish brown hair swept back and a narrow, athletic build.

For a moment, I pause, waiting for him to turn around.

From the back, it looks like *him*. Although I'm not sure why I expect it to be *him*. *He* hasn't been here in months.

A beautiful woman scurries over to the man, who puts his arm around her, angling his face toward me. I feel a wave of relief *and* disappointment when I realize it's definitely not *him*.

With a mixture of unidentified emotions coursing through me, I turn back to my list. But now I can't focus. All I can do is reminisce on that night when I opened my door at the club to find Clay waiting for me. The night everything ended between us. When he uttered those earth-shattering words—*I just want you.*

Anxiety burrows its way into my chest at the memory. Not a night goes by that I don't wonder if I did the right thing. I keep reliving that moment, telling myself over and over that it was for the best.

But I'm never fully convinced.

In an effort to distract my brain from having the same conversation again, I wad up the napkin and shove it into my purse. Then I climb off the barstool and wave goodbye to the bartender before heading for the exit of the club.

I toss my workbag in the trunk of my car and climb in the front seat, mentally planning the order of events for the morning. The entire drive home, my brain is making a schedule. If I make it home by three, I can get six hours of sleep before I'll have to get ready for the day. If I order the tickets by noon, we should be able to squeeze in cupcakes and presents with Ronan and Daisy before Jack and I go to a seven o'clock show tonight. If I keep him out any later than that, he'll be a major grump tomorrow.

I pull into the garage at exactly two thirty-seven. Being as quiet as possible, I sneak inside. There's a kitchen light on, which means my nocturnal nanny is still up. Sure enough, she's sitting at the island, typing away on her laptop. When she sees me come in, she pulls the AirPods from her ears.

"Hey," she whispers with a sweet smile.

"Hey, you're up late. How's that paper coming?"

She rolls her eyes. "If I never have to write the words *child welfare* again, it will be too soon."

I laugh as I drop my purse on the counter. "Well, you might have to if you're going to be a social worker someday."

She slams her laptop shut. "Don't remind me."

"How was he?" I ask, changing the subject.

"Perfect as always," she replies. "We ate the leftover spaghetti for dinner and read four books before bed. He was out like a light by eight."

"Awesome. Thank you again, Madison."

"Of course. I love hanging out with him, plus it gives me somewhere quiet to work on this stupid paper."

She packs up her laptop and rubs her eyes as she yawns. I walk her to the door, grateful she lives with her parents just one neighborhood over so I don't have to worry about her driving too far this late at night.

"You're almost there. Just stick with it," I say with encouragement as I pat her on the back.

"Thanks, Eden. Tell Jack happy birthday for me," she adds. "See you on Thursday."

"See you on Thursday," I reply. I wait for her to get into her car and start driving away before I close the door.

I hired Madison three years ago when the club opened, and it's been working great. She's a college student who needs extra cash and time away from her parents. She doesn't mind the late nights and *adores* Jack.

The best part about Madison is that she knows exactly what I do for a living and thinks it's *badass*—her words exactly. But for propriety's sake, we keep that information to ourselves. I'm not ashamed of my work, but I have enough awareness to know that not everyone is so accepting, and plenty of people would be happy to make my life harder with that piece of information— especially where Jack is concerned.

After Madison leaves, I tiptoe down the hall and peek into the first room on the right. The shark night-light glows in blue and green against the walls and ceiling, and I have to creep over the scattered toys on the floor to reach his bed. He's sprawled face up on top of the covers in his blue-striped pj's, so I take a moment to be sentimental and stare at him.

Messy dark-brown curls fan out over his pillow. I reach down carefully and brush them out of his face before leaning in and pressing a kiss to his forehead. He's a deep sleeper like me, so he doesn't stir at all.

Then I take another moment to stare at him. As of today, he's officially seven.

His birthday has me reminiscing on the day he was born. Living in the guest room of Ronan's apartment in the city, I thought I had another couple of weeks before I'd have to make room for a baby. Ronan was out on business, and my water broke without warning as I was reading an internet article about the right and wrong ways to use a spanking bench. To this day, I can't even see one without remembering the pain that followed that moment.

I labored for hours completely alone, without a single person to hold my hand. By the time Ronan arrived at the hospital, Jack was sleeping peacefully in his bassinet.

A couple of days later, I brought home a seven-and-a-half-pound baby who changed my world forever. By the time he started crawling, we had the keys to this house, and I was running my blog full time.

On that day, I made a promise to myself that I would always put Jack first. It was just us, and it would always be just us. I would die before bringing home another man who could do to Jack what his father had done to me. No matter how charming or rich, I refuse to fall for that trick again.

Love is nothing more than a form of control.

And from here on out, I will be the only one in control.

Rule #2: Forbidden fruit always tastes the sweetest.

Clay

"Fuuuuuuck." I groan. "I'm gonna come."

Immediately, Jade pulls those beautiful lips from around my cock and gives me a playful, wide-eyed stare. "You're gonna get us caught," she whispers.

"I'll be good," I reply in a breathy mumble.

As her perfect mouth engulfs my cock again, I nearly break that promise. With my teeth clenched around the knuckles of my right hand, I keep it quiet as she sucks the life out of me through my dick.

Staying silent as pleasure radiates through every extremity of my body is damn near impossible. Especially when I open my eyes to find her swallowing with a mischievous grin on her face.

God, I love this woman.

Of course, I haven't told her that yet. That would be insane. Jade and I have only been seeing each other for a little over five months, and half of that was spent with me in a major post-breakup depression.

But she is amazing. Every single day, I see how easy it is to love her.

Then again, I thought that about someone else recently too, and look how that turned out for me.

Besides, Jade and I have a major hurdle to overcome.

"I'm going to miss sneaking around," she whispers as she rises to stand from under my desk. With her hands perched on either side of my chair, she leans toward me, and I reach for her mouth with mine for a kiss.

"We should really tell him," I reply as I tuck my shirt back into my pants and zip them up.

She pulls away. "Should we, though?"

I laugh, shaking my head. "The longer we keep it a secret, the more likely I'll end up dead when he does find out."

"I'll avenge you," she replies. Then her nose wrinkles up in that adorable way it always does.

Wrapping my hands around her waist, I hoist her onto my lap. "Baby, if you're really not ready, then I understand. You know I'll do anything you tell me."

"I do love that about you," she replies, finally pressing her lips to mine.

I'm caught on the fact that she said *love* when my watch buzzes on my wrist.

"His meeting is almost over. You better go."

She groans. "Fine."

"Make sure to look both ways before leaving."

"I will," she whispers. Once she's standing, she fixes her knee-length floral skirt and white tank top. Using my framed college diploma as a mirror, she brushes her chin-length brown hair and blunt bangs back into place with her fingers. Then she grabs her purse from on top of my desk and catches me gawking at her. "What?"

"You're just…perfect," I reply. Which is true, but it's not what I was thinking.

What I was thinking is that Jade isn't like any other woman I've dated. She's young, sweet, and funny as hell. She might as well be the polar opposite of the last woman I dated.

Maybe this is my way of protecting myself. Date a woman so different that I lessen the risk of fucking things up again.

But the weird thing is, as different as she and Eden are, my feelings for them are strangely similar.

With a quirky smile, Jade peels open my office door and looks both ways before slipping down the hall toward the exit. I'm lucky to have an office near the back door, so I can easily sneak her in and out undetected.

This is a good thing because a moment later, the boss's door opens at the opposite end. I hear Will Penner's footsteps, like ominous stomps nearing my door. Every time he makes that trek down the hall, my blood spikes with paranoia. But as he peeks his head in, he's wearing a smile, and I let out a sigh of relief.

"Hey, Bradley, you hungry?" he says, using my last name as he often does.

"Hell yeah. Where are we ordering from today?" I ask, swiveling back and forth in my office chair.

"I'll have Jade pick something up for us. How do you feel about sushi?"

"Sounds great," I reply.

My boss leans against the doorframe as he pulls out his phone and, I assume, composes a text to the girl who just snuck out of my office.

"Dragon roll?" he asks, and I nod in return.

"Sounds good."

I like my boss a lot. He's lenient enough to make the environment enjoyable but tough enough to make me a better analyst. I've been like a protégé to him in his financial management company for the past five years, and I'm hoping that sometime this year, I'll have a promotion to look forward to.

Will needs me as a partner in this firm if we're going to take it to the next level like he wants to. He's a great financial planner, but he's impulsive and, at times, messy. We balance each other out well, and if I get that promotion, we'll be unstoppable.

His eyes lift from his phone just as the door to the office opens, and my skin pales as a familiar sweet voice calls from the end of the hall.

"Hey, Daddy!" Jade says as she approaches Will.

"Hey, Cupcake. I was just texting you. How does sushi sound for lunch?"

She steps into the doorway and glances at me for only a second. With an awkward wave, she sends me a casual greeting. "Hi, Clay."

"Hi, Jade," I reply, turning my eyes back to my computer, afraid they'll give me away without warning.

Out of the corner of my eye, I see Jade kiss her father on his cheek. Remembering where those lips were five minutes ago makes me want to die of shame.

Jade and I never planned this. Ever since she graduated from college, she's just been around the office a lot. And since it's only Will, me, and an unreliable temp, Jade's been picking up the slack. After so many late nights and lunch runs, things just happened.

And now, here we are. I've been fucking my boss's twenty-three-year-old daughter—sometimes in the same exact building—for the past five months.

Jade immediately picked up on my sour mood after things *happened* at the club that I never really told her about. She swooped in and gave me the attention and comfort I craved. One thing just led to another from there.

"I'll go if Clay drives me there. I hate trying to park downtown," Jade says with a pout aimed in my direction.

"You don't mind, do you?" Will replies, not even looking up from his phone.

"No, sir."

Jade shoots me a wink as I stand from my office chair and shove my keys into my pocket. Just as I shut my office door, Will levels his stern gaze on me.

"Be careful with my little girl, Bradley."

Doing my best to look innocent and obedient, I nod at him with my brows pinched inward.

"Of course. I always am." I say it like I'm the best, most trustworthy employee he could hope for.

With that, I head toward the door, Jade following closely behind. My cock has this habit of getting excited at the mere thought of being alone with her, so it's already starting to tent up my pants before I even make it out of the building.

We manage to keep our hands off each other the entire time, even after getting in the car and driving out of the parking lot. We make it all the way down the road before I have to pull into the parking lot of a run-down strip mall. Out of the corner of my eye, I see her slipping her panties down her legs in a rush. The car is barely in park before she's in my lap, those velvety-soft legs of hers clenched at my sides, straddling me as she kisses my face with passion.

"I can't get enough of you," I mumble against her neck as she fumbles with the belt of my pants.

And it's true. I can't seem to ever quench my thirst for this girl. When this started, I thought maybe it was just a fling, running only on passion and the forbidden nature of it, but it's been over five months now, and I'm growing attached to more than just her body.

I used to think she was so innocent, but her sweet, virginal appearance is all a front. Jade might be the most sex-crazed woman I've been with. I find it alluring.

"I can't get enough of you either," she says with a gasp at the exact moment she lowers herself onto my cock, sliding me inside with ease.

I let out a groan, my fingers gripping her hips. "You're always so wet for me."

Her replies are nothing more than moans and gasps as she bounces on my lap with fervor.

How the fuck did I get so lucky? I'm not that great of a guy. This can't possibly be good karma coming my way. I certainly don't deserve to feel this fucking good so often, but this perfect little gem of a woman seems to think I'm deserving of no fewer than four orgasms a day.

I've gone through enough bad patches in my life to know that my good fortune should have run out a long time ago.

Jade is sweet and good, and most days, I swear my own mother can't stand the sight of me.

What the fuck is the catch?

"Yes!" she cries out only seconds before I come, groaning loud enough for anyone in that strip mall to hear us.

She slumps against my chest, trying to catch her breath. "See, these lunch runs won't be as fun once he knows."

"There won't be any lunch runs once he knows," I reply.

"You're probably right." She picks herself up, putting her face in my line of sight. My hand lifts to brush the stray bangs back over her forehead. Protruding her lower lip, she tries to blow her messy hair back into place, and it makes me laugh.

When I'm caught staring at her too long, she furrows her brow.

"What is it?" she asks.

"Nothing," I reply, leaning forward to kiss her on the lips.

I could probably tell Jade that she's too good for me. Too sweet. Too smart. Too perfect.

But I don't because I'm afraid if I tell her, then I'll lose her.

There was only one person who ever fully understood what I needed. One person who made me feel like I could improve. One person who made me feel good enough.

And that was all a fantasy in my head—a fantasy that ended.

Jade climbs off my lap, cleaning herself up with the tissues I keep in the glove compartment for this exact situation. Then she slips her panties back on while I stuff my cock back in my pants for the second time today.

"Oh, are we still going to the movies tonight?" she asks.

I turn toward her, suddenly remembering that I had bought

us tickets for the seven o'clock show. "Yeah, if you still want to. You'll be able to get away, right?"

"I'll just tell him I'm going with some friends."

"Perfect." Then I lean over and press my lips to hers again. When she smiles back at me, I look for some sign as to why this woman seems to like me so much. As if the answer is hidden in her expressions. But there's nothing. Just a smile and eyes full of innocence.

"We better get going or he'll start to suspect something," she replies.

"Of course." With that, I put the car into drive and head out of the lot and down the street toward the sushi restaurant.

Rule #3: Don't let your kids talk to strangers.

Eden

"LOOK AT THIS FUCKING MESS," HE SAYS, SPITTING SALIVA IN MY FACE AS *he yells.* "Clean this shit up."

My molars grind together. I want to argue that the only mess around here is the one he made. Empty beer cans litter the floor, and his dirty plate is left on the table because he needs me to do everything for him.

But if I argue with him, it will only escalate, and then it will get violent.

So I shut my mouth and march into the kitchen, grabbing his dirty plate on the way. Slamming it down in the sink, I shut my eyes and think about the thousand dollars I have stashed in the bottom of my underwear drawer. Once I get up to two thousand, I can get out of here. Away from his house. Away from him.

I used to think it would get better. He loved me once—he could do it again.

He used to be kind, but now I'm nothing but the scapegoat for everything that goes wrong in our lives. The bad days outnumber the good to the point where I can't remember the last time I felt the warmth of his smile.

Shoving the thought down, I turn on the faucet and start washing off the dirty plate in the sink.

Unexpectedly, I feel the harsh impact of his hand as it slams against the side of my head. Then he yanks violently on a fistful of my hair, sending me to the ground as I let out a scream.

"I've been at work all day, and I come home to a messy house. Now you want to slam dishes and throw a fit?" he yells. "You are such an ungrateful bitch."

As I curl up into a ball on the kitchen floor, crying into the dirty linoleum and listening to his footsteps as he stomps angrily away, I realize that it doesn't matter what I do anymore.

There are no more good days, and there may never be any ever again.

"Mama, wake up."

Jack's soft voice whispers against my ear as I feel him climb over me in my bed, nuzzling himself under the covers and using my arm as his pillow. His little pajama-clad body is warm as I scoop my arm around his waist and tug him closer, breathing in his familiar scent.

Daylight shines through the cracks between the curtains and the walls, so I reach for my phone and check the time. *Nine fifteen.*

I can hear cartoons playing on the TV hanging from my bedroom wall over the dresser. Jack watches an animated Spider-Man swing between buildings while I slowly wake up.

"Mama, do you know what today is?" he whispers.

"Saturday," I reply, feigning sleep.

"Mamaaaa," he whines. His tiny fingers try to pry my eyes open, and I laugh, quickly pinning them to his side.

"It's my birthday!" he shrieks.

My eyes pop open, and I stare at him in dramatic surprise. "Your birthday?"

"Yeah!" he replies excitedly.

I shrug dramatically. "Well, if you're seven now, then you can make your own breakfast."

He giggles. "No, I can't."

"Sure, you can. I'll take an omelet, too, while you're at it. Oh, and some pancakes."

He laughs again, tugging on my arm to try to get me up, but I crack a smile as I fake sleep.

My eyes open as I pin him underneath me and cover him in kisses and tickles until he's howling with laughter, fighting to get out of my reach.

Even as he leaps out of bed and sprints toward the kitchen, I follow him, but with a lot less energy. He launches himself onto the couch while I stumble toward the coffeepot.

While it brews, I watch him scrolling on his tablet, a smile stretching across my face. Inevitably, I do that thing I've been doing a lot lately. I imagine someone else standing in this kitchen with me. Or maybe sitting on the couch next to Jack.

I imagine his long brown hair with Saturday morning bedhead, sipping coffee with me while Jack plays quietly by our side. The image of Clay existing in my everyday life grates on my nerves. How on earth did I let him get under my skin in such a short amount of time? After so many clients, how did *this one* get to me?

I'm perfectly content living alone with Jack. He doesn't need a father or a family. *We* are a family, and I've never once felt wrong or bad about that. And I sure as hell don't feel bad about that now.

There is no need or room for a partner in my life. I provide for Jack. I can handle it all on my own.

But then…that damn image of Clay standing in my kitchen, flipping pancakes while I pour the coffee, ambushes me again. It's so irritating I want to throw my cup across the room.

No matter how alluring that thought is, it's not worth the risk. I have no reason to believe Clay would ever pose a threat to me or Jack, but I used to think the same thing about my ex.

And nothing is worth putting my son in danger.

———————

A few hours later, Jack is zooming down the road in front of our house on an electric scooter, and I'm staring daggers at Ronan Kade, who's watching Jack with a proud smile.

"Really?" I ask with my head tilted and a glare directed at him.

"What? He asked for a scooter," Ronan argues.

"So you got him an electric one? He's seven, Ronan."

"Be glad it wasn't an electric car," Daisy, Ronan's much younger wife, replies with a laugh, bouncing baby Julian in her arms.

"I wouldn't put it past him," I say, standing next to her and rubbing my thumb over the soft skin of the baby's cheek. I almost forgot how cute they are as babies. That phase seemed to fly by with Jack. Life was so hectic back then that I hardly had the opportunity to slow down and enjoy it.

But watching Julian's tiny little mouth around the green pacifier and that adorable little suction noise suddenly has me wishing I could go back in time and experience it all over again with Jack.

"You'll blink, and he'll be seven," I whisper as I lean down and kiss the top of Julian's head.

"That's what I'm afraid of," she replies, nuzzling him closer. "Have you thought about having another?"

My eyes widen, and I pull away. "God, no."

"Why not?" she asks. Sweet, innocent little Daisy.

Well, not *that* innocent.

"I'm thirty-five," I reply as if that's reason enough.

"So? Ronan is fifty-seven," she argues.

"Yeah, well, he didn't carry and birth anything. Besides, being pregnant would really cramp my style at the club."

The three of us laugh as Jack whips back around on his scooter. Every crack in the pavement or bump in the road has me tensing, even though he has kneepads and a helmet. I still imagine the worst. But he really is a natural, zipping around the turns and even managing a little jump off the curb.

My watch buzzes on my wrist, and I glance down to see the reminder I set.

"Hey, Jack, we have to get going soon if we're going to make the movie."

His scooter comes to a screeching halt as he stares at me with a curious expression on his freckled face. "What movie?"

"Oh, it's just *Galaxy Warriors 2*. You did want to see that, didn't you?"

His face lights up with surprise. "Really? I thought you said I couldn't see it because it's PG-13."

I shrug, fighting my smile. "Well, you're seven now. That's practically thirteen."

He jumps off the scooter, leaving it on the ground as he whips off his helmet and runs toward me, hugging me around my waist. "Thank you, Mama!"

"You're welcome, buddy," I reply, ruffling up his brown curls. "Now, go pick up your scooter and tell Ronan and Daisy thank you."

He does, sprinting back to pick it up and wheeling it into the garage while shouting a rushed *"Thank you."* Ronan is laughing to himself as Jack bolts into the house. I'm almost certain he's going inside to change into his *Galaxy Warriors* T-shirt.

"Well, I think he's having a good birthday," Ronan says. He's giving me that proud smile, and I have to look away before he makes me get emotional. I know what he's thinking. We've come a long way. Or, rather, *I've* come a long way from terrified, penniless, and pregnant to this. Jack is happy and safe, which means I'm pulling off the one thing I was afraid I couldn't do.

"Thank you both for coming. And for bringing the presents. It means so much to us."

I can't make eye contact with Ronan, but he pulls me in for

a hug anyway. Then I kiss Julian's head again, inhaling that sweet newborn baby smell before hugging Daisy and watching them climb into Ronan's car.

Jack bounces with excitement all the way to the movie theater. Once we arrive, his eyes light up when he sees the arcade of games on one side of the lobby.

"Mama, please," he begs, hanging off my arm. Normally, I'd say no or tell him to wait until after the movie, but it's his birthday, and he just seems so happy.

So I fish into my purse for a couple of dollar bills and put them into his eager hands. Before I let him run off, I hold his hands and give him a serious, wide-eyed look. He gazes up at me, still practically bouncing in place.

"Stay where I can see you. Don't talk to strangers. You have five minutes."

"Thanks, Mama!"

With that, he dashes off toward the bright lights and arcade sounds. I watch anxiously from the line at the concession stand as he puts a dollar into one machine, picking up the game's blaster, which is nearly bigger than he is. He's wearing an excited smile as he plays.

Once his turn runs out, he takes his second dollar and hops into a game pod. I can't see him anymore, but I keep my eyes on the machine, watching to make sure no one else goes in or out as he plays.

"I can help the next guest," someone calls, and I turn to find I'm up next. Quickly, I order a large popcorn and soda, glancing back at Jack's video game every couple of seconds.

I've taught Jack well about safety when we're out in public. He knows not to talk to anyone or go anywhere with someone he doesn't know. But I still can't seem to relax in public, even when I know he's safe. I hate that my mind still reels back to the possibility that someone would take him or hurt him.

There's no possibility of his biological father coming back

into our lives—thank God—but that fear still lives inside me, even without any rational reason why.

I grow more and more anxious with every second as the cashier takes his sweet time ringing up my order. I'm practically shoving my credit card at him when he tells me my total.

Glancing back at the arcade, I still can't see Jack, and I'm growing paranoid.

When the cashier hands me back my credit card, I shove it into my back pocket and scoop up the popcorn and soda, bolting toward the arcade. Every step toward the game pod feels harrowing. But when I hear his laughter only a few steps away, I breathe a sigh of relief.

"I'm beating you!" he shrieks with excitement.

"You wish," a man's voice replies. As I approach the machine, I first see Jack in the seat, his little hands wrapped around the steering wheel of the game. Then I lean in farther to see he's not alone. There's a man sitting next to him, but I can't see his face with the curtain in the way.

"Hey, Mama," Jack calls when he sees me standing next to him. "Can I have another dollar?"

"I got it," the man replies. When he leans forward to put another bill into the machine, I nearly drop the popcorn as I recognize him. The blood drains from my face as I pop back up and turn my body away from the machine, praying he didn't see me.

Why is *Clay* sitting in a video game machine with my son?

It's a coincidence.

Relax, Eden.

It's just a coincidence.

But still…these two worlds colliding make me want to run. He's a *client*, and he's with my *son*. I know I shouldn't feel ashamed about this, but for some reason, I do.

Behind me, they keep playing their game, and while I'm currently reeling with anxiety, Jack seems to be having the time of his life. His laughter is full, and I catch the way Clay laughs along with him, giving him directions and encouragement.

Something in my chest shudders at the sound.

"I got second place!" Jack shouts.

"Good job! I told you to take those turns slowly."

"Thanks," Jack replies, and I feel frozen with fear again. I need to try to get him out of here without Clay seeing my face.

"Come on, Jack," I say, keeping my voice an octave higher than normal.

"What movie are you going to see?" he asks Clay, ignoring my order.

"Jack," I bark.

"*Galaxy Warriors 2*," Clay replies, and I wince.

"Me too!"

"Well, then we should get going. I think it's going to start soon."

"Come on, Jack," I call again. My hands are too full to reach in there and pull him out, or I would.

As Jack hops out of the pod, I start walking, hoping he'll follow.

"Mama, wait," he calls, but I don't look back at him. Instead, I feel Jack gallop next to me. "He's going to see our movie too. Can he sit with us?"

"They're assigned seats," I reply.

Clay laughs from behind me. "I'll see you in there, Jack. I have to wait for my girlfriend anyway."

My feet stop, and I look. It's completely instinctual, as if my body reacts before my brain has a chance to process this information. But I can't help myself as I turn my head to look at where Clay's standing now.

I think a part of me wishes I was wrong when I thought I saw him in the driver's chair. Because Clay doesn't have a girlfriend. He *can't*. Only six months ago, he was mine.

But as my gaze lifts and finds him standing there, and our eyes meet, everything happens at once.

I realize, with disappointment, that it is him, with his slicked back brown hair and chiseled cheekbones. I'd know his face anywhere.

Then I feel the pain of knowing he has truly moved on.

And then he sees me.

It takes him more than a split second to recognize me, which I can understand. Instead of the leather and lingerie he is used to seeing me in, I'm wearing ripped jeans, black boots, and a worn T-shirt.

His face falls as recognition dawns. Then his eyes dart down to Jack and back to my face.

I watch his mouth form the shape of my name. "Eden?"

"You know my mom?" Jack says, wrapping an arm around my leg.

"Umm…" Clay and I stammer at the same time.

A beautiful young brunette bounces up to Clay's side. "Ready?" she asks him before following his gaze to Jack and me.

I'm too busy staring at her to react. This is his girlfriend. The girl he's moved on with.

She has a short bob haircut that stops just above her chin and blunt straight bangs framing an almond-shaped face with large blue eyes and full pink lips.

I swallow down the suffocating disappointment and jealousy as I glance down at Jack. "We're going to be late."

"Where are your seats at?" Jack asks, his attention still clinging to the couple.

Clay glances down at his phone. "Row Q. Seats nine and ten," he says, looking nervous and mildly uncomfortable.

"What row are we in, Mama?" Jack asks.

I wish I could pull him away. Go to a different movie in a different theater. Honestly, at this point, I'm considering a different city in a different state.

But I can't drag Jack away. And I can't ignore him or brush off his questions. It's not his fault he doesn't know who these people are or how much it pains me to stand here and look at them.

I glance down at my son. "Row P. Seats five and six."

"Aw, man," Jack whines. I smile down at him. I've always found it endearing how my little social butterfly can somehow make friends with complete strangers in the frame of five minutes. But I do find it somewhat unsettling how quickly he's latching on to a man who's shown him the bare amount of attention, especially after I told him not to speak to strangers. I'll have to have a serious talk with him later about that.

"Well, we'll see you in there," I mutter, not making eye contact with Clay or his date.

Positioning the popcorn under my arm, I take my son's hand and pull him toward the entrance to our theater.

The entire time, my mind is reeling. Just as we take our seats in row P, I glance up to see Clay as he enters, our eyes meeting for a split second.

Why him? I've never once run into anyone from the club in public. Of course, out of everyone, it had to be him.

Rule #4: If you ask the question, be ready for the answer.

Jade

I'm not an idiot. I can spot an awkward ex-girlfriend encounter from a mile away.

The way they kept glancing at each other throughout the movie—it was *obvious*.

Clay is strangely quiet on the entire drive to his place, so I decide to attack the awkwardness head-on.

"Who was that woman?" I ask, turning toward him.

"What woman?" he replies, making me roll my eyes.

"The beautiful one with the black hair and the little boy. There was clearly some tension between you two. You knew her name."

He spins his head in my direction. He clearly didn't think I heard that part, but I did.

"Babe, relax," I say, reaching across the center console to rub a hand up his leg. "I'm not the jealous type. I promise."

"Then why does it matter?" he asks, turning his attention back to the road.

I settle back into my seat and stare straight ahead. "Because you're clearly caught up on it. You've been weird ever since. I figure I have the right to know why a complete stranger is ruining my night with my boyfriend."

"Who says she's ruining our night? I'm not caught up on it."

My brow furrows. "Don't get defensive. I hate that."

He scoffs and looks back toward the road. "So what, you want me to tell you the dirty details?"

"Are there dirty details?"

"I thought you didn't get jealous," he responds, looking at me with a crooked grin.

"Are you kidding? Jealous?" I laugh. "I might be turned on."

With a shake of his head, he lets out an awkward chuckle as he pulls into the parking lot of his apartment building. After putting the car into park, he turns toward me, running his thumb along my jaw.

"You really want to ruin our night with talk about my ex?"

"So she is an ex," I exclaim. "I knew it."

Leaning back, he runs his hands through his hair. "Technically, no."

"What's that supposed to mean?"

His head flops in my direction. "It means it's complicated."

Then he reaches for the door handle and opens it without another word. Even after he climbs out, I'm stuck in some motionless trance. "Come on, babe," he calls.

Clay and I have been seeing each other for five months now, and everything with him has felt so right the entire time. But there is this part of him I can tell he's holding back from me. Not that I think a person has to reveal everything to the person they're seeing after only five months, but I'm not asking for deep, dark secrets here.

I just want him.

Not the fake front he puts up for everyone—the charming, clever, confident facade he assigns to himself when the true Clay wants to hide. I've known him long enough to know the difference.

My father calls me a bleeding heart. I think he means it in an endearing sort of way, but I sort of hate it. Because I *care*. And right now, I care about Clay.

For as long as he lets me, I will.

Reluctantly, I climb out of the car and face him. My heart seems to lurch right out of my chest every time I look at him. With his warm-brown hair and stunning green eyes, he's the most handsome man I've ever met, but that's not it. I see right through the mask and notice things no one else does, like the sadness in his eyes or the way he seems so desperate for my touch. I think he must have been deprived of human contact.

When he sees my despondent expression, his shoulders sag. He corners me against his car, running his hand over my arms and kissing my forehead.

"Do you wanna come up?" he asks softly.

I do. I always want to come up.

But when I get the feeling the person I've poured my heart out to isn't pouring their heart out to me…it makes me feel vulnerable. And a little silly.

His fingers touch the spot under my chin as he lifts my face to look at him. I'm staring into his emerald-green eyes, wishing he'd just be real with me.

"You're mad because I won't tell you about some woman at the movie theater?" He tries to laugh it off like I'm the ridiculous one, and it pisses me off. Clenching my teeth, I try to weasel myself out of his grasp.

"You don't get it," I mutter.

"You're right, Jade. I don't. Why do you want to know so much?"

I spin on him and stare at him incredulously. "Because I care about you, Clay. And it's not about the woman. It's about the fact that something has been bothering you since you saw her, but instead of opening up to me, you fake a smile and tell me *it's complicated*."

Turning away from me in frustration, he runs his hands

through his hair. As I watch him struggle with what to say, I want
to wrap my arms around him.

Being in a relationship is hard. I thought when this all started
that I could just love him and that would be enough, but it's not.
There's so much worry and frustration and emotions that get lost
in translation. On top of everything is this nagging fear that I'm
giving too much or not enough.

Is loving a person truly enough when existing together
requires so much more?

He still has his back to me, his fingers laced at the back of his
neck as he stares out at the traffic on the road passing us by.

"Forget it," I mumble as I turn toward my Jeep, parked just a
few spaces down.

He lets out a frustrated, strangled noise, looking as if he's
pulling out his hair. "Fuck it."

Then he mutters something in a surrendering tone. "She was
my Domme."

His voice is low but frantic, clearly uncomfortable with
saying…whatever he just said.

I pause and stare at him with my brow wrinkled in confusion.
"What?"

A loud, heavy sigh full of aggravation comes barreling out of
his mouth as he turns toward me. As his eyes meet mine, I realize
he's not giving me the fake Clay right now. He's being real.

I step toward him.

His fists are clenched, pain etched in his features. "I can't
believe I'm telling you this. But I don't want secrets with you."

My lips part in surprise. "Okay…" I whisper.

Releasing his fists, he steps away. We're alone in the dark
parking lot, cars moving on the busy street in front of us. It creates
a comforting white noise that's better than silence. It makes us feel
less alone.

"She's a Dominatrix. I paid her to be my Domme," he says,
looking at the ground as he speaks.

"What does that mean?"

Finally, looking up, he replies, "It means…we'd go into a room, and I would do whatever the fuck she told me to."

"Like sex?"

"No," he replies quickly while walking one way and then spinning back toward the other. "Yes. Sort of."

"What is sort of sex?" I reply.

He chuckles. "We *had* sex, but that's not what I paid her for."

My brows pinch inward even farther. "I'm so confused."

"Yeah, well, so was I," he replies, laughing to himself. He always seems to cover up his insecurities with humor, but I don't laugh with him.

"Why?" I ask, shaking my head. "Why would you pay her for that?"

Looking utterly defeated, he drops his hands by his sides and gives me a shrug. "I don't fucking know."

"Where did you meet her?"

Rubbing the back of his neck, he winces. "At a sex club."

My eyes widen as I stare at him in surprise. "A *sex* club? What is that?"

"Well…it's a place where people go to have sex."

"Obviously," I reply, rolling my eyes. Then my gaze settles on him, clearly looking distraught and flustered by having to admit all of this to me. "I'm just shocked that you were at a sex club."

This is what he was so concerned about? That I wouldn't understand his kinky past?

Or is it his present?

Rewinding the conversation in my head, I realize something.

"Was?" I ask. "She *was* your Domme? But she's not anymore? Is it because of me?"

There is something intimate in his eyes. Then he steps toward me, pressing me back against the car again. "No, baby. She stopped being my Domme before you came along."

"What happened?" I whisper.

He's struggling again, clearly keeping everything he wants to say locked behind a wall, afraid to let it all spill out. He softly mutters, "I just realized I wanted more."

My mouth forms an *O* shape. "More from her?"

He stares down at me with a softness in his eyes. "More from anyone."

This makes my heart ache for him.

"Remember six months ago when I was in a funk?"

I nod.

"That's why. I was paying a woman to give me the attention I wish someone had given me for free."

My hands wrap around his waist, and I pull him closer, burying my face in his neck. "I'm sorry, Clay."

He holds me close, running his hands over my back. Then he presses his lips to my hair.

"It's okay. She was just doing her job. That's all it was." He sounds so despondent, and it makes me wonder if there's more I don't know.

Neither of us says anything for a while. With my face against his chest, my mind is racing.

Am I the rebound for this other woman?

Was it really just a job to her?

Did she give him something I can't?

"Do you want to come up?" he asks again.

I want to—I really do. But my mind is a mess, and I don't want to have sex when I'm so in my head.

Pulling away, I gaze up at him with an apologetic expression. "Mind if I don't? I'm just ready to go home."

With a half smirk, he nods. Then he kisses my forehead again as he mumbles, "Of course, baby. Text me when you get home."

Pressing up on my tiptoes, I lean in and give him a kiss. His hand wraps around the back of my neck as he deepens the kiss, massaging his tongue against mine. My body starts to warm from the kiss, so I pull away before it gets too tempting to stay.

"'Night, Clay," I murmur, walking toward my car.

"'Night, Jade."

When I reach my Jeep, I stop and turn back toward him. He's watching me.

"For what it's worth," I say, "I'm glad it didn't work out. I like you better with me."

When I smile, he smiles.

"Me too," he replies.

After climbing in my Jeep, the entire drive home is spent thinking about how it took him a second too long to say that.

But maybe that's in my head.

I'm curled up on my bed with an episode of *The Bake-Off* playing in the background while I scroll through various websites on my phone. There's a knock on my door, and I look up to find my dad slowly peeking in.

"Hey, Cupcake," he says softly.

"Hey, Daddy."

"How was the movie?"

I shrug. "It was good."

"You went with Nettie?" he asks, referring to my best friend. My eyes cast down to my phone as my mouth twists into a knot at the corner of my lips.

It's bad enough that I'm twenty-three and still living at home, but it's even worse that I have to lie about whom I'm spending my nights with.

"Yep," I mumble without looking at him.

"Hmm," he replies with a nod. "Well, good night, Cupcake. Love you."

"Love you," I call back.

As he shuts the door, I stare blankly at where he just stood, lost in my thoughts.

How did it get like this?

This was never the future I had planned for myself. Five years ago, I went to college, and while I was gone, my mother decided marriage wasn't for her anymore, and she left. Now, she's gallivanting around Europe with her rich boyfriend, and my dad is left here alone. After I graduated, I probably could have done something else—like find a job that would afford me my own place, move somewhere new, and start my own life, but I couldn't leave him like that.

I remember the day I asked my dad if I could stay with him after college while I figured out what to do next. I'll never forget the way his eyes lit up.

I think I started hanging out with Clay out of boredom. I could have easily found a job with my education degree, but I was so focused on my dad. College just felt like a distant memory. Everyone I went to high school with was moving on with their lives, and I was slipping backward.

Clay was a step forward.

At first, it was just flirting. Something I never saw becoming real.

I always saw him as a total sleazeball and ladies' man, cocky and self-absorbed. He just seemed like the kind of guy who hit up clubs and was only interested in one-night stands. We never seemed compatible at all. I'm an education major with a good girl reputation—despite the fact that I am *not*.

Flirting was fun for a while, especially given the forbidden nature of our relationship.

But then something changed. He showed up at the office looking broken, like his armor had cracked, and I was getting my first glimpse at the man hiding inside. So I spent more time with him, desperate to see behind the curtain.

Then flirting turned into feelings.

And here we are.

Clay doesn't treat me like a kid. I feel safe with him, and it's like I'm in a relationship with my best friend.

But now I can only wonder if I truly know him at all. Why wouldn't he tell me about the sex club? He knows I'm no saint. I'm not scared of sex clubs.

Which is what led me to this particular search on my phone.

What is a Dominatrix?

With every website definition, article, blog post, and image that pops up, I grow more and more uneasy.

This is what he wants?

Or worse. This is what he *needs*.

But I can't give him this.

Dominatrix: a female-identifying professional who engages in a dominant role during sex or in a BDSM relationship with a submissive.

This doesn't make any sense. Clay has always been dominant with me. It's not like he ever asked me to take control. I mean... sometimes I'm on top, I guess. But I don't think that's what this means.

The deeper I get, the more aroused I get. The women on these sites are sexy and confident, and I'm not sure if I want to be them or be *with* them. What would it feel like to dominate someone like this? To feel that type of control and power?

I could do this. If he just opened up to me about it, then maybe we could.

Although I guess he did open up about it. But only after we saw...

Her.

My fingers freeze over my phone screen as I see a familiar face staring back at me. I only saw her for a few brief moments today, but it was enough to commit her face to memory. It's not like you can forget the most beautiful woman you've ever seen.

And now she's on my phone.

Madame Kink's West Coast Escapades.

And there she is. Right on the first page, covered in leather and looking, well...dominant.

Rule #5: Just say no to Emerson Grant.

Eden

I'm two steps out of the voyeur hall when I see him.

"Shit," I mutter as I watch club owner Emerson Grant stride toward me with a sense of confidence that I've lately found incredibly irritating. Normally, I welcome any and all conversations with my old friend, but since he started harassing me last month, I dread it.

"Don't run away," he says in a cool, cocky command.

"I don't have to listen to you," I reply with snark.

With my head up, I walk right past him toward the bar. Geo lifts his gaze from the sink where he's washing glasses and bites back a smile when he notices me blowing off the big guy himself.

I drop my clutch on the bar and settle myself on a stool. "Vodka martini, Geo."

"You got it," he replies. His eyes scan over my shoulder, where I know Emerson is following.

"Bourbon on the rocks," he says, knocking on the counter with his knuckles once.

"You're insufferable," I say, tilting my head to stare up at him.

He takes the seat next to me and smiles as if this is so entertaining to him. "At least tell me you've given it some thought."

"I don't have to, Emerson. I told you I'm not interested." As soon as the words come out of my mouth, my stomach twists with regret and anxiety. But I can't let that show. If he sees even the slightest chink in my armor, he'll tear my entire argument to shreds.

"I don't believe you," he replies.

Arrogant prick.

"I appreciate the offer. Really, I do. But I'm fine with my job as it is."

He turns toward me, leaning one elbow on the bar as Geo sets our drinks in front of us. "Look, I'm desperate. The only one I have left is Garrett, and it's only a matter of time before he and Mia start trying to have a family. I feel like I'm losing Hunter a little more every day. And Maggie's been gone for nearly two years now. Even Ronan has a new baby at home. You're the only one I would trust to bring on board."

I try not to meet his gaze. It's the pain of harboring secrets from the people I care about that makes eye contact a killer. So I stare straight down at my glass and try to hold it together.

Emerson doesn't know about Jack. Besides Ronan, no one does. I made that promise to myself years ago before I started working at Salacious and collaborating with the owners. They ran the dating app, and I had my kink blog. I never saw the relationship evolving to where it is now. It just became too late to confess that I had a child of my own at home that I never happened to mention over the years.

When the club opened, Emerson was so impressed with my knowledge and popularity that he offered me a private room at the club to use for my own clients and business. I've never worked *for* Salacious. I've only worked *at* Salacious, which has been great. It gives me a safe space to work and brings in an abundance of business for the club too.

Ronan tried to convince me so many times to come clean, but I don't think he understands what it's like to be Madame Kink *and* Eden St. Claire. There's an invisible wall between my two lives that I can't bring myself to cross. He and Daisy are the only people alive to have seen both.

Until two nights ago at the movie theater, that is.

"So people with kids can't own a sex club?" I ask with a curious smirk.

"Of course they can. But I don't want to stretch Garrett too thin. And Hunter has two babies at home. He wants to spend more time with them."

"I get the feeling you're trying to make room for me, even if there isn't any."

He scoots closer and draws my eyes up from my glass so I'm forced to stare at him. "You might be right. That's how much I want you on our team. You should be running this club with us, Eden, not working your ass off in these rooms every night. Plus, I know you have some ideas that you're dying to share with me."

I laugh, rolling my eyes.

"I can't buy out a portion of the business, Emerson. I don't have that kind of money, and I won't take it from Ronan."

"I know you won't," he replies as he leans back. "But I can hire you on as a club director. It would be a significant raise, Eden, which you *deserve*."

Forcing my gaze away from him, I swallow down the anxiety creeping its way up. Taking on a management role at the club would mean more work and more time away from Jack. But it would also mean more money for him too. At least now, I can create my own hours and work when he's sleeping.

Emerson rests a heavy hand on my back. My jaw tightens as I fight the urge to take the job, if only because there is a part of me that really, *really* wants it.

"Think about it," he mumbles softly.

Finally, I turn my eyes to meet his. In his expression, I read the concern he has for me. Emerson has invested in me for my entire career. He brought me into the club because he saw something in me, something people wanted. To him, I've always been a valuable asset to his company. He's never once treated me like an employee.

In another life or another world, I would take the job. But Emerson has no idea what I have on the line. I'm all out of *me* to give.

"I will," I reply earnestly.

With a lopsided smirk, he nods before taking his bourbon and walking away. For a while, I sit at the bar and let his offer play out in my head. What would I change around here if I had the chance? How would I feel being a part of their team? Like one of the owners. Since this place opened three years ago, I've invested in this club. I believe in the owners and their mission with this place, and I want to see it succeed.

Succeed it has. Even without me drawing in clients, this club gives our community something it had been missing. I had been to clubs before, but the vibe was never quite right for my tastes. I never felt half as safe as I do here—and safety has always been my top priority.

Like I told Charlotte on that first night, this club was never built for men alone. This was the only place I've ever been to that felt as liberating and as comfortable as it does. I've seen lives change here. And I want desperately to be a part of that, even more than I already am.

How do I tell Emerson there's not a single thing I would change, but I would be honored to protect it the way it is right now? I want Salacious Players' Club to be here forever.

It truly is my home away from home.

Lost in my thoughts for a few moments, I nearly jump out of my seat as my phone alarm vibrates in my clutch. I quickly pull it out and see the reminder set for my eleven o'clock appointment.

It's for a consultation with a new client—something I don't often do. Most of my services are a little more hands on, but occasionally, I'll get someone who wants to pay a nice chunk of change to talk to me for an hour.

All I know about my appointment tonight is that it's a young woman dating a new guy with some particular tastes, and she'd like ideas on how to please him.

Never a dull moment.

I take the next couple of minutes to finish off my martini. Then I say goodbye to Geo and head toward the hostess stand in the lobby at the front. I give her the name and information of my client so she can let her in and direct her to where I'll be waiting.

Then I head upstairs to my private room.

Maybe Emerson is right. Maybe I do need to start thinking about something more than working on the floor like this forever. Would I miss it? The adventure of meeting a new client every night. The power I feel when they submit. The sex. The pleasure.

I mean, there's nothing saying I couldn't still have some fun at Salacious, even if I were a club director.

Or is there?

I'd definitely miss it. I love my job.

I can still remember that day seven years ago when Ronan opened my eyes to what was out there waiting for me. I never in my life considered myself a dominant woman, but once I got a taste, I couldn't quit. I started my blog as a starry-eyed, naive young woman with an insatiable appetite for knowledge.

Just a couple of years in, I had over a million subscribers and was officially ready to do this professionally. There was never sex in the beginning. I couldn't believe how many people would pay me to be their Madame. To bark orders at them, make them my footstool for an hour at a time, have them licking my boots and taking lashes from my flogger.

My craving to learn was insatiable. Ronan and I toured a few different clubs. We even hosted a few sex parties of our own at his place.

I was good at being Madame Kink and couldn't get enough.

In a lot of ways, I think becoming a sex worker was the last great liberation from the life I used to live and the small-minded world I grew up in. I was finally free and in charge of my own life. There was no shame. No fear.

And then Salacious opened, and everything only got better. This club changed everything for me. Finally, I had a place where I felt safe. No one judges me here. We are truly free to be and do what we want.

My reputation quickly grew, and now, there's not a member of this club with more room invites than me.

So would I be stupid to take this job now?

There's a knock at the door, and it pulls me from my thoughts and memories. My heels click against the marble floors as I cross the room toward the door.

Before opening it, I push my shoulders back and fix my tight black dress. Then I twist the handle and plaster the Madame Kink expression on my face. After I open it, I stare at the young woman standing nervously in front of me.

Instantly, my expression falls.

"Hi," the girl stammers, looking back and forth down the narrow hallway.

I blink a couple of times to make sure my eyes aren't deceiving me. The lighting is sort of dim out here, so maybe I'm wrong. But I swear this is the exact same girl I saw with Clay just last weekend.

Chin-length brown hair and blunt bangs aren't exactly a forgettable or common hairstyle. Not to mention, she's still dressed like a kindergarten teacher in her knee-length skirt and tight white tank top. I'm actually a little surprised they even let her in like that.

"Come on in," I stutter, opening the door wider so she can enter. The chorus of group sex echoes behind her from the curtained-off VIP room. She glances back, clearly spooked by the sound before I close her in with me.

It's quiet in my room. There's only light, sultry house music playing in the speakers overhead, and with the soundproof walls, it's enough to mask what's going on just a few feet out the door.

As the girl turns around to face me, I realize I'm supposed to be the one to speak. But I can't stop staring at her face. That is definitely the one from the movie theater. Even without the hairstyle, I'd remember those freckled cheeks and her cute button nose.

She's the kind of girl who stops you in your tracks. She exudes the sort of beauty that makes you want to either *be* her or *kiss* her...or both. Stunning and perfect like a gemstone.

"Welcome..." I say with hesitation. "I'm Madame Kink—"

"Do you remember me?" she asks, eagerly cutting me off. Her fingers are twisted in front of her, and her legs are pressed together as if she's tense.

My mouth opens awkwardly. I don't know how to answer that question.

"I probably should have told you in our emails that we met the other day, but I sort of felt weird about that. Plus, I thought you might not meet with me if I told you."

I must look like a deer in headlights because she takes one look at my face and starts rambling again.

"I'm not here to, like, bombard you or anything. I'm not crazy, I promise. Although I feel a little crazy right now. I just...I looked up some stuff, and I found your blog."

"Are you here for a consultation?" I ask slowly, trying to make sense of everything.

"Yes!" she chirps with excitement. "And before you ask, yes, Clay told me that he and you...you know."

I blink again. The room is bathed in awkwardness. If the dark-red rug on the floor suddenly swallowed me whole, I wouldn't be mad about it.

When the girl opens her mouth to start rambling again, I hold out a hand. "Stop," I command her.

She closes her mouth before so much as a squeak can slip

out. For a moment, I keep my hand out and stare at her without a word. I need to get my bearings, but this ambush feels the same way you do after you've been spun around too much and the world is tilting. I need everything to stop moving around me so I can think.

I should tell her to leave. That's the first thing I realize. This is clearly a conflict of interest and asking far too much of me to give a kink consultation to an ex…client's new girlfriend.

I'm sorry, but you should leave.

Just say those words, Eden. Just say, I think you should leave.

Maybe it's the innocence in her eyes or how afraid she looks at this moment. It must have taken some serious guts to make this appointment and walk in here. If I turn her away, that would be humiliating. Something she might never get over.

It has nothing to do with how precious she looks standing there on my rug with her bottom lip pinched between her teeth. In the split second it takes me to stare at her lips, I imagine him kissing them.

I think you should leave.

"Why don't you have a seat?" I say instead.

Rule #6: Keep your walls up.

Eden

"So let me get this straight," I say with a wrinkle between my brows. I'm clutching an empty glass of red wine in my right hand while staring at a meek and sweet Jade on the couch across from me. "You found out your boyfriend used to pay me to be his Domme, and after doing some internet research, you decided to schedule a consultation with me? Does Clay know you're here?"

She clears her throat. The entire time she spoke, telling me all about her conversation with Clay and her little investigative research later that night, I couldn't get over just how innocent she seemed to be. And I don't mean innocent in a pure, angelic sort of way. Her innocence is like naivete mixed with confidence. She's not afraid to look me directly in the eye and say what's on her mind. And I like her for that.

"No," she replies, shaking her head. "And I don't plan on telling him. I just want to understand."

"Understand what?"

She leans forward. "Not once in the last five months has he

asked for me to be…" She waves at me as if I am the embodiment of some internalized desire.

"Dominant," I answer for her.

She nods. "Yes."

"I'm sorry to tell you this, but it's possible he never will." I force myself to swallow, shoving away those buried feelings for the man we're referring to.

"Why not? If he liked it with you…why wouldn't he like it with me?"

I let out a sigh. How do I explain this to her? What Clay and I had wasn't something that came naturally, at least not to him. Which means he'll likely *never* ask for it from her. To him, I was a safe place to explore, safe from the judgment of others who had already imposed a sense of toxic masculinity into his psyche. With me, he didn't have to feel embarrassed by how much he loved to submit.

Not to mention, plenty of people seek out professionals to fulfill needs their partners either can't or don't want to fulfill. There's nothing wrong with that, but I've never had to explain it to someone's girlfriend before.

I have no clue how much he told her about us, but from the way she's talking now, I assume he left out some very key details about our relationship.

When I think about it, Clay and I have that in common. His kinky life is like his alter ego, which means he's likely to keep his normal life vanilla.

When I don't respond, she jumps in, eager to fill the silence.

"What if he leaves me because of that? I have no idea how to be like you or give him what he wants, and I'll lose him because of it. How is that fair?"

Since when has life been fair?

"I suggest you talk to him," I reply. "There's no reason to believe he'd leave you just because—"

"Or you could teach me."

I freeze again. This girl has a way of being so blunt it knocks me off my axis. I'm not used to people just saying whatever is on their minds. Normally, people are too intimidated by me to be so forward—but not this girl.

"That's not one of my services," I reply.

Her shoulders slump. "Please. I'm desperate."

Looking up from my wineglass, I get a glimpse of her round, innocent eyes, and I have to look away. Quickly, I stand and take my glass to the wet bar in the corner.

"Listen. If you're really concerned about fulfilling your boyfriend's needs, you should talk to *him*. If he does express an interest in a Domme/sub dynamic, then the two of you can do that research together. And honestly, if he's willing to leave you because he can't come clean about his needs, you're better off without him."

I'm pouring myself another glass when I sense her standing up in my periphery. There's a part of me that just wishes she'd leave. It's awkward enough to have a conversation about a client with his girlfriend, but it's made even worse by the fact that Clay was…different.

I should really be vetting my clients better.

"But you know him better," she whispers as I set the wine bottle down.

I force myself to swallow.

I *do* know him better. I know the way he fights back. I know the handsome smirk he wears just as he's about to give in. I know the way he seems to look right through my facade and into my soul. I know the way he melts when it's all over. I know that the man he presents to the world is cocky and guarded, but the man beneath that charade is…beautiful.

Picking up my wineglass, I turn toward her. "I'm sorry, but I don't. Your boyfriend was a client, and I have to protect his privacy, so I'm afraid there's nothing I can do to help you."

Her pretty face turns angry, her eyebrows pinched inward and her mouth set in a straight line.

"I thought you'd be more eager to help me."

"Why—"

"Because I read your blog, and not just the kinky stuff. I went far enough back through your posts to see that you were once curious and naive like me. You know what it's like to be a woman who wants to learn without real guidance. You know what it's like to be terrified, afraid you'll be taken advantage of."

"Yes, but I never did it to please a *man*." My voice is so flat and cruel I almost don't recognize myself.

Hurt floods her features as she stares at me, but I don't let my remorse show.

Without another word, she scurries out of my room, letting the door slam as she practically runs down the narrow hallway toward the exit.

I'm left standing on the deep-red rug, feeling like the world's biggest bitch. I shouldn't have said that. Yes, she did come in here asking for help in pleasing her boyfriend, but I also know the pressure she must have felt to drive her to that point. I could have helped her more by making her see how unfair that is. I could have convinced her to do something *she* wanted.

Instead, I humiliated her.

———————

The meeting with Jade stays with me all night. Even with my next client, a woman who goes by the name Lola—although I suspect that's not her real name. She's been coming to me since the club opened, and I normally look forward to our sessions.

But I can't seem to get out of my own head. I replay the entire conversation with Jade the whole time. Even during her aftercare, when we're both curled up on the bed, her with salve covering the red flogger marks on her back and me feeding her grapes and water, I know she can tell I'm in a weird mood.

Her hand drifts up and down my thigh. She's positioned down by my legs as I recline against the headboard. These intimate moments with my regulars are some of my favorites. It means we've gotten somewhere together. We've crossed the threshold of comfort with each other to the point where they can touch me as if I'm not a stranger.

"Do you have another session after this?" she asks softly.

"No." My voice is emotionless, and I don't give any more explanation.

"I can stay…" Her hand drifts a little higher on my thigh, leaving a tingling sense of arousal in its wake.

It's tempting. Drowning my thoughts in sex sounds like exactly what I need.

I touch her fingers with mine, letting her drift them to the hem of my thong. She shifts onto all fours, climbing over me until our mouths are inches apart. She smells so good, like jasmine and rose. When the soft locks of her wavy blond hair touch my shoulder, I beg my mind to get on board with this.

Even as her lips touch mine, I fight the memory of the girl standing in my room only a couple of hours ago. But it's useless.

Sex with Lola would distract me, but I'm not sure I want it to.

I pull away and look anywhere but into her eyes. "Not tonight," I mutter coldly.

Lola leans back, kneeling on her heels between my legs. She's in nothing but a pair of lace panties, and the sight of her sun-kissed skin nearly has me wanting to change my mind.

She looks disappointed as she touches my leg a little softer now, rubbing a soft line from my ankle to my knee in a way that I know is meant to be comforting.

And it is.

"Call me anytime," she says sweetly with a tilt of her head.

Then she climbs off the bed, leaving me feeling like a bitch—again.

I almost never turn down sex. And I feel especially stupid knowing that fucking Lola's brains out would have certainly changed my sour and distressed mood.

But as she leans down, now fully dressed, to place a kiss on my cheek, I know there's no turning back now. I can't just say, *Oh, I changed my mind. It turns out I am in the mood.*

"Thanks, Madame," she whispers, pulling away.

I reach for her hand, letting her delicate touch seep into my pores like an IV.

"See you next month."

She winks at me before walking to the door. I don't normally end sessions like this. I like to walk my clients to the door. I'm never sulking on the bed while they see themselves out.

I let out a grunt of frustration after Lola is gone. Then I toss one of the throw pillows across the room as if that's going to help, which it doesn't.

If I could go back to that night one year ago when I let that good-looking, dark-haired man buy me a drink and make a little wager with me, I swear I would turn him down when I was given the chance.

He keeps glancing my way from across the bar, and it makes me laugh inwardly as I stare down at my empty glass. He looks like fresh blood, new to the club and likely new to the lifestyle. Just by looking at him, I can tell he's too cocky for his own good. He's so sure of himself that he tried to outbid the richest man in the club. Which clearly didn't work out for him tonight, hence the fact that he's still alone, even after I've returned from my date after the auction.

When I feel him approach, I clench my jaw.

"Can I buy you a drink?"

I don't look up. "No, thank you. I'm about to drive home."

"But it's only one o'clock."

Pulling my eyes away from my phone, I tilt my head and stare at him. He is very handsome but not as young as I first assumed. From this proximity, I can make out the subtle crevices of his face, lines worn in over time, something a fresh-faced baby in his early twenties wouldn't have.

For a moment, I get lost in the dark intensity of his almond-shaped eyes.

"It's been a long night," I murmur.

He pulls away just an inch before tightening the smirk on his face. Something in his expression falters as he softly mumbles, "Another time, then."

There's a moment's hesitation before he turns away. I should let him leave and call it a night, but I don't. Something in me has me calling after him.

"What's your name?"

He pauses and turns back toward me. "Clay Bradley. And yours?"

My eyes are glued to his face again, drawn like a magnet to the sharp cheekbones and the narrow bridge of his nose. I stare at him the way I sometimes stare at my son. As if my eyes can drink their fill.

"You're new here," I say without the inflection of a question, ignoring his request.

He nods. "I am. Is it that obvious?"

With a soft shrug, I smile. "I tend to know everyone around here."

"Are you a regular?"

"You could say that," I reply sarcastically.

Clay takes this as his opening to sit down, leaning on the bar to face me. "And what is it you like to do here?"

He's a good flirt. I'll give him that. I've sat here at this bar and been hit on by more guys than I can count, but Clay has a charm that's natural and undeniable. There's something strangely genuine in his charisma.

"I'm a Dominatrix," I reply, looking up from the bar. My response comes out more like a dare than an answer, but Clay doesn't even flinch at the word.

Instead, he smiles. "I can see that."

"I get a feeling I'm not quite your type," I reply, leaning in and *watching his lips pull into a smile he fights against. Licking his lips, he straightens his expression into a look of curiosity.*

"You think I wouldn't like to be with a Domme?"

A chuckle escapes my lips. "I didn't say you wouldn't like it. I said I'm not your type. There's a difference."

"So you think I would like it?" he replies. I notice he's a bit closer than he was before.

I erase the distance between us, whispering only a few inches from his face, "Oh, I know you would."

Technically...I don't know that. Not everyone is submissive, and I would never speak to someone like this professionally, but we're flirting. And he's pushing me.

The closeness of our mouths doesn't seem to affect him at all. "Prove it."

"That'll cost you," I say, finding his eyes with my own. We're mere inches apart as he smiles.

"That's not a problem."

"You'll have to do everything I tell you to," I add, still staring into his eyes.

"That's not a problem," he says again.

"And I'm not promising sex."

This time, the corner of his lip twitches before pulling into a lopsided smirk. Then he reaches up and brushes a lock of hair from my face with his featherlight touch. A flurry of chills runs up my spine.

Then he leans in and presses his lips to the side of my face before he whispers, "That's not a problem."

I swear I almost feel light-headed.

Quickly, I compose myself so he doesn't know how much he's getting to me as I pull away and give him a strictly-business expression.

"Five fifty for one hour."

His disarming gaze drifts down to my lips, almost as if he didn't even hear me tell him my rate.

"You never told me your name," he says, still staring at my mouth.

My lips part, and I reply with confidence, "Madame Kink."

There's not a moment of hesitation. With a shake of his head, he leans in again. "No, I mean your real *name."*

My real *name.*

I don't like to give my real name to strangers, but this man is staring into my eyes like he's looking right past Madame Kink. And I don't have a choice. Later, I'll wonder why I didn't tell him no or laugh it off. But I'll never fully understand why I make the most fatal mistake of all.

I let him see through the wall.

"Eden," I whisper.

Rule #7: Don't text your ex.

Clay

"STAND THERE," SHE SAYS IN A SOFT BUT AUTHORITATIVE COMMAND. SHE *enters the room, closing the door behind her. I watch as she walks to the back of the room, busying herself for a few minutes while leaving me waiting.*

Finally, after pouring a glass of water and pulling a dark-purple riding crop out of the cabinet in the back, she saunters toward me. Her expression is blank. And I can't explain why, but that grates on my nerves.

Give me a smile. A scowl. Anything.

"You sure are a pretty thing, aren't you?" she says in a sweet and sexy tone. Her eyes are visibly grading my appearance in a way that throws me off.

"Pretty?" I murmur.

"I bet you'd like to please me, wouldn't you?"

"I'd love to please you," I reply with a crooked grin.

She ignores my flirtatious line, keeping her expression flat as she says, "Your safe words are simple. They work like a traffic light. Green means go. Yellow means slow down or pause. Red means stop. Are we clear?"

"Yeah," I reply with a shrug.

"Madame. Yes, Madame."

A snicker slips through my lips. "Yes, Madame."

"Is something funny?" she replies seriously, stepping closer. This is not the same woman I just flirted with at the bar. As soon as we walked into this space, everything changed. I can't quite tell yet if I love it or hate it.

"No, Madame," I say, tugging my bottom lip between my teeth to keep from smiling.

"Then why are you laughing?" she asks, looking disappointed. "That's disrespectful. Are you being disrespectful?"

"No, Madame," I repeat, my smile fading.

Her eyes narrow as she scrutinizes me. "Should I punish you?"

Something flutters low in my groin at the idea of punishment. My eyes instantly track to the crop in her hand, and I imagine what it might feel like to have it slapped across my back. I could take it, but do I want to?

My dick doesn't seem to hate the idea. That's new.

"No, Madame," I reply, softer this time.

"On your knees." Her voice is both sweet and sultry as she presses the tip of the riding crop down on my shoulder. I fall slowly to the floor, my knees resting against the thick red rug.

From this angle, she's even more beautiful.

In a tight black dress that ends only inches from the very spot where I'd love to bury my face, she exudes sex and power. And I can't say I've ever been so into that before.

Most of the women I'm with are timid and acquiescent. They let me lead and are eager to please.

But there's something about this woman...

"You're a good little puppy, aren't you?" she asks, lifting her shiny black high-heeled shoe and pressing the toe against my chest. Without a word, I slink back to my heels, still staring up at her with a smirk on my face.

"I'll be your puppy," I reply snarkily.

"Tsk, tsk," she says, touching the crop to my lips. "The only words that should come out of your mouth, aside from your safe words, are yes *and* Madame. *Are we clear, pet?"*

I have to bite my lip to keep from smiling even more. "Yes, Madame."

A drizzling rain taps against the glass of my bedroom window as I lie awake, staring at the ceiling. I'm in my head again. And sometimes, my head is like a prison, and I'm locked behind the bars of memory and regret.

Sometimes it's work. Sometimes it's my mother. But lately, it's *her*.

Eden. My *Madame*.

I can't keep the two straight, as if they've blended in my consciousness like two sides of the same coin. Either way, she's stuck in my mind like a virus.

I turn in my bed, struggling to find a comfortable position as I beg my thoughts to quiet and allow myself some rest. I shut my eyes, letting the dark silence wash over me.

Did I push her too hard?

Did I do the right thing?

Was our connection one-sided?

Did she care about me at all?

Was I not good enough?

"Fuck." I groan, turning to the other side. To distract myself, I pick up my phone. An unanswered text to Jade still waits on the screen. She never ignores my messages, but when I asked her two hours ago if she wanted to come over, she read it and never responded.

Things between Jade and me have been off since we saw Eden at the movie theater. I never should have told her about the Domme thing. It's not important, so I don't know why I did. Is she freaked out that I went to a sex club? Or that I paid a woman for sex?

I think a part of me told her about the kink stuff in a panic because I didn't want to tell her what *really* went on with Eden. That I paid her to be my Domme for three months, and then I stopped paying, but I kept seeing her.

"You really are a sweet thing. You listen so well," she says, and I can tell by the smug look on her face that she means it like a playful jab. She thinks my pride will get in the way, but she's wrong. "Crawl to me, pet."

This is all a game. If I do what she wants, I'll be rewarded. How bad could it be?

I drop my hands to the floor and make my way slowly toward her. She's standing across the room now, staring at me as if grading my performance.

Am I good enough, Madame?

Is this to your liking?

I don't say any of that because that's against the rules. She said I could only utter two words: yes *and* Madame.

Well, that and red, yellow, *and* green *for the safe word system if I need to stop anything, which I won't. There's nothing this goddess of a woman could do to me that could make me say* red.

This feels ridiculous, though, crawling across the floor like a dog. But judging by the serious expression on her face, it's not ridiculous to her.

She can't actually like this stuff, can she? Is it just a job for her?

When I reach her feet, I look up as I wait for further instructions.

"Eyes on the floor, pet," she snaps, this time a little colder than before.

Feeling stung by her tone, I turn my gaze downward, staring at the black patent leather of her shoes.

"Here's the deal, pet. You do as I say, and I'll reward you. Maybe I'll wrap my lips around your cock. Maybe I'll let you bury your face between my legs. Either way, you get what you want by pleasing me."

Her riding crop touches my chin as she guides my face upward.

"And you want to please me, don't you?" Her voice is gentle and seductive.

"Yes, Madame," I stutter.

"You like pleasing people. And you like knowing exactly how. Don't you? Because then I'll tell you how good you are, and that's better than a blow job, isn't it?"

I mean...there's not much better than a blow job. So I sure as fuck don't think getting called a good boy is going to compete. But for her sake, I lie.

"Yes, Madame."

She releases my chin, and I stare downward again.

"Good. Now kiss them."

I glance up at her face. She must be joking.

"What? Why?" I reply.

She tilts her head. "Because I said so. Can you not obey simple orders?"

With a slight grimace, I stare back at the floor. Then she repeats the command.

"Kiss my shoes."

I don't move. What is the point of this?

When she leans down, pressing her mouth closer to my ear, I feel a wave of excitement from her proximity.

Then she whispers, "I want you to worship me, pet. It's so simple, but you can't do it, can you? And I thought you were such a good boy."

Fuck that.

Without another thought, I lower my body to the floor, pressing my lips to the top of her right shoe. Before she can even ask, I move to the left one, giving it a quick kiss before lifting back into a kneeling position.

I'm somewhere between irritated and aroused, too curious to stop now. My eyes stay on the floor when she touches my chin with her fingers.

As she lifts my face upward again, she smiles. "Now, that wasn't so bad, was it?"

Revisiting these old memories feels so foreign. I was a different person then. She changed me. She altered my brain chemistry until I was nearly unrecognizable to myself.

Then she broke me.

For the hundredth time since that night at the movies, I think about the boy she had with her—a new piece of the puzzle I've been trying to put together.

Her son.

Eden has a *son*.

Resentment burns at the thought. Never in the eight months we were seeing each other did she ever mention having a kid. That's how little I meant to her.

While I was secretly hoping for a life with her, she had an entire life she was actively keeping me out of.

Why?

I throw back the black silk sheets of my bed and sit up. Resting my elbows on my knees, I bury my hands in my hair. I can't keep living like this. I can't keep calling Jade over to distract me from the pain of the open wounds I have from another woman.

For a moment, I thought I was doing better. I was moving on. Then one quick encounter and it was like being catapulted right back in time to the very beginning—falling in love with her all over again.

Do I get rewarded now? *I wonder as I stare up at her. She's crossing the room toward the large chair in the middle. Turning around, she sits on it and rests her eyes back on me where I'm waiting on the floor.*

For a long time, we sit in silence and stare at each other.

"Come here," she says in an assertive command.

I crawl to her without hesitation. Stopping just at her feet, I feel the moment grow tense with anticipation. I want something more than crawling, kneeling, and kissing shoes.

"Are you ready for more, pet?" she asks, leaning forward.

"Yes, Madame."

"Then I want you to stand up for me."

I rise to my feet, keeping my eyes on her face. She has sharp cheek-bones and soft red lips I'm dying to press mine to. Every word she utters through those perfect lips is like a strike of lightning to my dick. I'd do just about anything to feel them wrapped around my cock, but even I know that's not going to happen—not like this.

I'm here to please her. The whole purpose of this is to be hers.

"Let me get a look at you. Take your clothes off." Leaning back in the large chair, she rests her elbow on the arm and stares at me while she waits.

For some reason, I hesitate. She's literally asking me to get naked for her, and something is stopping me.

When a moment passes without me moving, she asks, "If you're no longer comfortable with the boundaries we set, that's okay. Just say the word, and we'll stop."

"No, Madame," I whisper. My fingers move to my shirt, sliding each button through the hole before taking it off. I move to my belt, sliding it open and easing down the zipper of my pants. Shakily, I drop my pants. Then I remove my socks and shoes.

When her eyes drift down to my boxer briefs, I swallow. She wants me naked, exposed, and vulnerable.

I don't know why the idea of being naked in front of her feels so difficult. But I want to prove her wrong. I can do this.

In a quick swipe, I drag my boxer briefs down, and my cock springs free.

She stares at it as if studying it.

"Come closer," she says, and I step up to her so my cock is pointing right at her chest.

"You're perfect," she mumbles, looking up at me. "Why are you nervous?"

"I–I don't know."

Reaching out, she wraps her hand around my length, and I shudder.

"Is this all for me?" Her words nearly steal the breath from my chest as I gaze down at her.

"Yes, Madame," I reply, a bolt of electric arousal shooting down my spine.

She strokes, and I let out a muffled grunt, trying to maintain my composure. My breathing gets heavier as she touches my cock, lifting it to inspect my balls hanging heavily beneath. Then her finger rubs firmly in the place between my ass and sack, making me stumble where I stand. There's a playful smirk on her face as she brings her soft hands to my shaft again, stroking and rubbing to tease me without enough pressure to make me come.

"You really are perfect. I want to make you do so many things, pet. Would you like that?"

"Yes, Madame." My voice is strained as I try to focus on the pleasure of her touch.

"Would you like to come?"

A whimper escapes my lips, and it's humiliating.

"Yes, Madame," I reply.

Her movement speeds up, and I feel myself growing hotter with each stroke. With her other hand, she softly grips my balls, giving them a gentle squeeze. My abs contract, and my heart pounds harder. I'm dangerously close to coming all over that pretty black dress of hers.

I've gotten blow jobs and hand jobs, but I've never come like this—on command and under someone else's control. It's unsettling and strange, but I'm trying to embrace it.

As my balls tighten and my body seizes in anticipation of the climax, she tugs down on my sack and releases her hand. I let out a gasp and stare down at her in disbelief.

"Do not come," she commands in a cool, ruthless tone.

What the fuck?

She leans back and stares at me without pity. I'm out of breath and in shock as I wait for her to speak.

Then she whispers, "Good boy," and something inside me changes. "I like the way you obey me, pet."

And just like that, I want something far more than an orgasm.

Leaning forward again, she takes my length in her hand and begins stroking, this time faster and more motivated. I'm careening toward my climax. By the way she is stroking me, twisting and rubbing the head of my dick, I'm practically ambushed by my orgasm.

Before I know it, I'm releasing all over her cleavage and coming on a loud, strangled moan. It hits so fast that I can hardly enjoy it. I'd much rather draw it out and savor it.

Standing there breathless and panting, I stare down at my shaft still in her hand. The expression on her face is almost excited as her eyes focus on the head of my cock, still leaking with a drop of my cum.

When our gazes lock, it feels like the most intimate moment of my life. She leans forward with her tongue hanging out and licks the last drop. I audibly shudder at the sight.

After she releases me, she glances down at her dress.

"Look at the mess you made."

I'm stuck in silent postorgasm befuddlement. She looks even fucking hotter, covered in my cum. What the fuck am I supposed to do now?

With casual confidence, she leans back in her big chair and stares up at me as if I'm her servant and she's the queen.

"Well, aren't you going to clean this up?"

I look around the room, wondering what I'm supposed to use, and when my eyes cast downward to her face, I know.

Something makes me hesitate—shame or embarrassment. But then I remember it's just her and me. And she doesn't judge me here. She's literally telling me to do it.

From that moment, I realize how free I am in this room.

Slowly I drop to my knees and gaze up at the spots on her chest. Then I do something I've never done before. I draw my tongue along the surface of her chest, licking up the salty mess I left behind.

And it's not terrible. In fact, I almost like it, and I don't know if it's the taste, how dirty it is, or just the act of pleasing her.

When I look up into her eyes, she's wearing an expression resembling pride.

Then she winds her fingers in my hair and smiles. "Good boy."

And just like that, those two words become my undoing.

———————

For some reason, my memory keeps returning to that first night and how something inside me changed in that session. How *she* changed me, and I grow more and more frustrated.

This is all her fault. She made me dependent on her.

Her approval.

Her praise.

I became addicted to how she made me feel, and now I'm like a recovering addict, stuck in withdrawal.

I didn't ask for this. I wanted to get laid and have some fun, but she manipulated me into falling in love with her, and I'll never get my old self back now.

I'm not drunk, and I know very well this is a terrible idea, but I pick up my phone again and open the text messages, and this time, I find her contact.

The last message was six months ago, and it's another unanswered text from the night it all ended. The last thing I said to her:

Yes, Madame.

In a fit of frustration, I type up a new message.

I always trusted you, and I always obeyed. So now, tell me to stay gone, and I will.

I don't even read it back before hitting Send.

Rule #8: Never break your own rules.

Eden

WISPS OF SOFT HAIR BRUSH MY NOSE, ROUSING ME FROM MY SLEEP. I try to brush them away, only to find that someone is sleeping on my arm. I peel my eyes open to see Jack's messy curls only inches from my face. The light peering through the blinds is blue, meaning it's still early, and he has another hour before he needs to wake up for school.

Carefully, I drag my arm out from under his head and reach for my phone on the nightstand. Any other morning, I would roll over and go back to sleep until the alarm went off, but today, my head is swarming with reminders of last night.

Jade.

I was a royal bitch to Clay's new girlfriend. Although I have a right to be, don't I? It was way out of line for her to come to me in the first place.

Of course, she had no idea just how much Clay and I shared. She had no idea I was far more than his Domme. If she had known, last night might have gone differently.

The phone screen is too bright, blinding me in the dim room as I check the time.

But I don't see the time. All I see is a new text message—from Clay.

I bolt upright and stare at the notification. My first thought is that she must have told him that she came to see me, and I know the moment I swipe open the app, it's going to be a message from him about how heartless and cold I can be.

Fully knowing I should probably block him before reading it, I do the foolish thing and swipe open my phone and scan the message. The time stamp is from late last night.

I always trusted you, and I always obeyed. So now, tell me to stay gone, and I will.

Everything stops. For what feels like hours, I stare at the text in shock.

This is not what I expected. It has nothing to do with Jade.

What the fuck?

I haven't heard from Clay in six months, and suddenly, he's messaging me out of the blue. He has a girlfriend. Why the hell does he need me to tell him to stay gone?

I should immediately reply with those two words: *stay gone*.

I should.

But I need to think first. So I climb out of my bed and make a pot of coffee like a zombie. The entire time, I'm replaying every moment of our…relationship—if you can even call it that. I took things too far with him. I broke all of my own rules, and I let him be more than a client. Clay and I never once saw each other outside the club, except, of course, for that day last week.

Is that what brought this on? Seeing me again stirred up memories for him? It certainly did for me.

"Fuck!" I whisper-shout as I drop my coffee mug so hard onto the counter it breaks. As I stare at the mess, I wonder what the hell got me here. I'm Madame fucking Kink. I don't get attached to clients. I don't get lovestruck and hung up on men like Clay Bradley.

What is wrong with me?

Jack stumbles out of my bedroom as I'm cleaning up the mess from the broken mug. He's rubbing his eyes as he watches me dump the dustpan full of broken ceramic into the garbage can.

"What happened?" he mumbles.

"Nothing, buddy. Mama was just clumsy."

When I try to lift him into my arms like I always do first thing in the morning, I frown at the way he barely makes it off the floor. He's growing too fast, his life flashing by like a gust of wind I can't seem to catch.

So I kiss his head and pull out a chair at the table for him to sit on. He climbs on sleepily and stares ahead with an unfocused gaze as I turn on his morning cartoons.

While I pour his cereal and then my coffee, I glance back at my phone, waiting as if another message will pop up at any moment.

It doesn't. The rest of the morning is quiet everywhere except in my head. Even as I walk Jack to the bus stop down the street, he can tell I'm distracted. He's gabbing on and on about his baseball team and then something about the movie we saw over the weekend and then about some video game.

When I hear the words *arcade guy,* I pause.

"Wait, what arcade guy?" I ask.

He looks up at me with his cute little eyebrows pinched together. "The guy from the arcade. At the movie theater. He played the racing game with me."

I swallow, glancing away as we continue our stroll to the end of the street. "Oh, yeah. What about him?"

"How do you know him?" he asks.

"What do you mean? I don't know him," I reply defensively.

"Yes, you do. He said your name, Mama." Jack rolls his eyes

dramatically, one of those adorable little kid traits he picked up from an adult—likely me.

"Oh yeah."

"So how do you know him? Maybe you can call him and we can play games at the arcade again?"

"I don't think so, buddy. I don't know him that well."

I'm lying to my seven-year-old.

"Well, he knew you. He knew your name was Eden. He said it. So how do you know him?"

"From work, buddy. It's just…grown-up stuff."

The bus isn't here yet as we reach the corner, and I avoid making eye contact with the other moms waiting with their kids. I hide behind my sunglasses like I always do, refusing to look anyone in the eye because there's not a conversation in the world I want to have with these strangers. I feel the way they look at me—a single mom, usually looking sleep-deprived and wearing last night's makeup.

"What does *grown-up stuff* mean?" he asks loudly, and I grimace behind my sunglasses. "Does that mean he's your boyfriend or something?"

I feel the eyes of the other moms as I pull Jack away from the group and kneel down to talk to him in private.

"No, he's not my boyfriend. And you can't ask stuff like that out loud, buddy."

"Why not?"

"Because it's embarrassing," I reply with a quiet laugh.

"Oh, sorry."

"It's okay," I say with a smile, brushing his hair off his forehead and planting a kiss there. Before I stand up, he adds, "My friend London's mom has a boyfriend, and he takes him to baseball games."

My heart aches as I stare into his eyes. "I'll take you to a baseball game. I don't need a…boyfriend for that."

"I know," he replies softly. "But you don't play arcade games with me."

"Well, I will. Next time we go. I promise."

I have to swallow down the pins and needles building in my throat. As the bus pulls up, I give Jack another kiss on the forehead and pull him against me for a hug. When he finds his seat on the bus, he looks out the window and waves to me. His expression isn't as exuberant as it normally is.

The entire walk back to my house, I'm sulking.

Jack doesn't need a man in his life—that's just bullshit. He has me and Ronan and Daisy and his nanny, Madison. There is no void and no reason to believe a man could be any better a role model for him than I am.

I am his family.

Keeping him sheltered is worth it, knowing he can't be hurt the way his useless sperm donor of a father hurt me. I'll keep his circle even smaller if it means keeping him safe.

And he's sure as hell never going to see Clay again. He'll have to get over that.

———

When I return to the house, I stand at the kitchen island and stare at my phone. The unanswered message from Clay shines on the screen like a beacon.

I can't believe he reached out to me.

I can't believe he went behind his girlfriend's back to do it.

Jade might have been out of line last night, but she still seems like a nice person, and she doesn't deserve this.

I shouldn't respond.

But therein lies the problem. If I don't respond, then I'm essentially *not* telling Clay to stay gone. So I should respond with *stay gone.*

And yet the thought of responding with those two words feels like a blunt blade pressed against my chest. I *do* want him to stay gone, so why can't I type that?

Instead of responding, I walk away from my phone. Going

to the shower, I do my best to quiet my mind and think about anything else, but it's impossible. Every step of the process echoes his name and that damn text message that waits for me.

Not to mention, I'm still wearing a layer of grimy guilt from the encounter with Jade, and before this whole Clay situation, I had considered calling her to apologize.

How the fuck did I end up in the middle of their relationship without even trying?

The more I think about it, the more irritated I feel. I'm practically fuming as I blow-dry my hair, wash my face, and pull on my clothes for the day. I'm rehearsing everything I want to say to him—how this is crossing a line, how I never asked for this, how I was always doing my job, but he clearly overstepped when he made it personal.

Before I know it, I'm holding my phone in my hand, and instead of texting him back, I hit Call, and the phone starts ringing.

He picks up almost immediately.

"Eden." He sounds alarmed and serious.

Just the sound of his voice uttering my name washes away everything I had planned to say. The anger dissipates as I remember every tender moment we shared. It's a blaring reminder that while he started as a client and seeing him was my job, it quickly became something else. I grew an unhealthy addiction to Clay, putting aside everything in my life to have *more* of him.

"For fuck's sake, Eden. Say something," he says, sounding desperate.

"I don't know what to say." The words sound pathetic on my lips, but it's exactly how I feel.

"Fuck." He groans. "I never should have sent that text. I was having a rough night."

"You have a girlfriend now, Clay," I whisper as a reminder in case he forgot.

"Yes, I know, and I'm on my way to her house right now. She

won't answer my calls, and I'm worried sick about her, but for some fucking reason, I'm on the phone with *you*."

My eyes shut with a wince as I rest my forehead against the countertop. Is it because of me that she won't respond to him? Is she okay? She seemed upset last night when she went running out of the club. Fuck.

When I don't reply, he speaks again. "You really fucked me up. You know that?"

Still, I say nothing.

"I have a good thing here, Eden. I could move on and be happy, but you won't let me. It's like you live in my brain, and I can't function without you, and I don't know if it's because I want you to be my…"

His voice trails off on the word I know he struggles to voice— *Madame*. Clay was always so resistant to the labels. But he loved everything we did.

"Or?" I say quietly.

"Or if it's because I just want you."

Why does this conversation hurt so much? Why does everything with him have to feel so out of my control?

"I think it's the former," I reply, trying to maintain some composure. "I think you found security in the Domme/sub practices, and you need—"

"Oh bullshit, Eden!" he barks into the phone. "Why do you have to do that? Why do you have to make everything sound so cold and emotionless? Why can't you admit that what we had wasn't just part of your job? What we had was fucking amazing."

My throat stings as I stare ahead at a spot on the floor, my vision blurring. "It's not my fault, you know. It's not my fault I'm still on your mind."

"Then why can't I let you go?" he replies bitterly. Those words cut like a knife.

"You should go check on your girlfriend," I say, shutting down the argument.

"Yeah, I should," he replies with the sound of surrender in his voice.

When the line is quiet for a while, he adds, "Just say it."

My brow furrows. "Say what?"

"Tell me to stay gone, Eden. One last command that I promise to obey. I always was good at obeying, wasn't I?"

The stinging in my throat is excruciating now.

"Please say it, Eden. I'm fucking begging you to. I just need to hear you say it so I can move on."

When I blink, a tear slips over my cheek, taking me by surprise. I stand up in a rush and wipe it away.

"I have to go," I mutter. Before I can speak another word, I hit the red button, and the line goes dead.

"You came back," I say with appreciation when I open my door to find Clay standing just outside.

He booked his hour with me tonight, so it's no surprise to see him now, but seeing as how it's only been three days since that night, I was a little surprised to see the request.

"Yes, Madame," he replies obediently.

I can tell by how his molars grind that this is hard for him. Slipping into submission isn't something he's familiar with, at least not on the surface level. Deep down, I can tell he loves it.

"Come in. Take your clothes off. Just down to your boxers for now." Turning my back to him, I give him his orders as I cross the room toward the wet bar, where I pour two glasses of water and wait for him to do as I said.

"Yes, Madame," he mutters softly.

When I turn around, I'm pleasantly surprised to find him kneeling on the floor, staring at the rug.

As hard as I try to hold a flat expression, I can't fight the smirk that starts to grow. He really does love this.

"Have you had any water today?" I ask as I walk toward him.

His brow furrows as he gently lifts his head to look at me. "Um... yes, Madame."

"Here. Drink this," I say as I pass him the water. He takes it with confusion and gulps the whole thing down. "Whenever I see you at the club, you're drinking alcohol. If you're going to be mine, then I want you to stay hydrated. Understand?"

"Yours, Madame?"

I walk over and touch his chin, tipping his head back. "You want to be mine, don't you?"

His breath hitches as his piercing green gaze bores into mine. "Yes, Madame."

"Good. Then I expect you to take care of what's mine. Hydrate. Eat well. Exercise. Understood?"

On his next exhale, something calm and at ease washes over his expression. And in that moment, I start to truly understand Clay. He loves to know what is expected of him. He loves easy tasks explained to him, and he loves praise.

"Good boy," I reply, and judging by the way his eyes light up, I'm right.

I take his glass and walk away, setting them both on the counter.

"Last week was just a trial, but if you're going to come back, we need to discuss the rules and boundaries. When you are here with me, you will submit to me. I want you to do exactly as I tell you. Some of it will be sexual, and some of it won't. But as long as you come to me, you are mine. If you don't do as I say or you break one of my rules, I will punish you. But if you do as I say and please me, I will reward you."

Spinning back toward him, I pause at the sight. His long brown hair hangs over his forehead, and a hint of a smile tugs at his lips.

"Is that what you want, pet? Will you come back?"

His smile grows. "Yes, Madame."

Rule #9: Tell him what you want.

Jade

MY PHONE BUZZES ON THE NIGHTSTAND FOR THE TENTH TIME today, but I ignore it. Instead, I'm trying to focus on this *Gilmore Girls* episode, even though I've seen it a hundred times and I already know Rory will say or do something stupid.

Maybe watching a fictional character make poor choices is therapeutic in recovery from making my own poor choices.

I didn't sleep a wink last night, still reeling from the humiliation at that sex club. So much for being *bold* and doing things without regrets.

I have regrets, all right.

I never should have made that appointment. I never should have shown up at some classy sex club in the city. And I never should have asked that beautiful woman to teach me how to be a Domme just to please my boyfriend.

Now, even though Clay has no idea what I did, I still can't bring myself to face him. The shame is internal. I don't think I could look at him now without thinking about him and her together, knowing I'll never live up to her. And it was wrong of me to try.

I'm *nothing* like her. She's the embodiment of sex and power, flawless in every way. I'm a bumbling, naive people pleaser without a clue as to how to be sexy or confident.

The phone buzzes again, and guilt gnaws at my stomach. I hate for him to worry, so with my bottom lip pinched between my teeth, I pick up my phone.

Except when I see the number on the screen, I realize it's not Clay.

It's a local number, and while I normally decline those, today I'm curious.

So I hit the Answer button.

"Hello?" I say slowly.

A woman clears her throat. "Is this Jade?"

The voice is familiar. I sit up a little straighter in surprise. "Yes."

"This is Eden St. Claire. We met last night."

For some reason, I'm now *standing* on my bed. The hand not holding the phone is now buried in my messy hair, and my eyes are as round as the moon.

"Ummm..." I stammer. "Hi."

She lets out a breath. Hell, even her breathing sounds confident.

"I wanted to call and apologize for the way I treated you last night."

Somehow my eyes get even wider. I don't speak as she continues.

"It's never my intention to turn someone away from the lifestyle, and it was wrong of me to make you feel ashamed of something that is meant to be liberating and empowering. I was wrong. I'm sorry."

I'm still standing on my bed. Rory and Lorelai are chatting a little too eloquently in the background while I fumble for something to say that isn't, *um, okay.*

She speaks again to fill the silence on the line. "I think you should pursue whatever it is that interests you, but you need to do it for *you*."

"I want to. I promise it's for me."

"Good," she replies.

"Does that mean you'll teach me?" I blurt out.

"Uh, no, wait—"

"Not for him. I promise. I just…" My voice trails. Carefully, I climb off the bed and hit the Power button on my TV. Then I sit on the mattress and stare at the carpet as I compose my thoughts. "I'm a people pleaser. I feel like I do everything to make other people happy, and I just…don't want to be like that anymore."

"I'm not sure this—"

"I know what you're thinking," I reply before she can continue. "I should probably go to therapy, and I mean, I can do that too, but you could also be like…a role model for me, you know? Maybe if I just came into your club at night, you could teach me to be more dominant. Teach me how to talk to people without being such a pushover. Make me more like you."

I'm rambling, and I literally have to bite my lip to keep from going on and on.

Just as I expect her to shoot me down again and give me another quote-unquote *good* reason for why she can't do this, she says, "All right, fine."

My mouth is hanging open as blood rushes to my cheeks. "Wait, what? Seriously?"

"Just a couple nights a week, and I'll tell you everything I know. Think of it like a mentorship."

"Yes! Perfect!" I squeal. "I have money saved up, so I can totally pay you."

"That won't be necessary."

I'm practically beaming with excitement when I hear a car door slam outside. While Eden talks, saying something about protocol and nondisclosures, I rush to the window to see Clay walking up the driveway to my door.

"I have an opening at ten o'clock tonight. For one hour," she says, stealing my attention.

"Perfect. Thank you," I say in a rush.

She lets out a sigh at the same time the doorbell rings, and my dad's English bulldog, Chief, starts barking like crazy downstairs.

"You have company, so I'll let you go," she says. "But, Jade…"

"Yes?" I reply, swallowing my nerves.

"Let's keep this between us for now, okay?"

I worry my bottom lip between my teeth, knowing Clay is downstairs waiting and I have to go greet him and keep this secret from him when I'm already so pumped and excited.

"Yes, of course," I answer confidently.

"See you tonight," she says.

"See you tonight!"

The line goes dead, and it takes everything in me not to scream. Something about this feels like exactly what I need. This could get me out of my rut. This could break me out from this spell I've been under since I graduated. I need a fresh start and a hand to guide me.

It's not about Clay anymore, even if that's how this started. Gone is that knot of regret and anxiety I've been suffering since last night.

But more than anything, I'm smiling because I know I get to see her again, and just being in her presence feels like a gift.

I barrel down the stairs after Clay rings the doorbell for the third time. Chief is losing his mind, spinning in circles and panting so hard I'm afraid he's going to have a heart attack and drop dead right on the landing.

When I peel open the door, I'm still wearing the same smile I had upstairs after my call with Eden. Clay's brows pinch together as he stares at me in confusion.

"Where have you been? Why haven't you answered my calls?"

"I've been sleeping," I reply. He steps into the house, his eyes never leaving my face.

"You're not mad at me?" he asks.

I shrug. "No. Why would I be mad at you?"

His jaw clenches as he crowds me toward the wall. His hands slide over my waist, and he tugs me so close to him I have to arch my back to look up into his eyes.

"I don't know. Because of that incident the other night. And you won't respond to me."

My smile stretches wider. My, my. How the cocky ladies' man has changed since I first met him. Now he worries and pines and needs reassurance.

"You're so cute when you're worried," I say, pressing on the little line between his brows.

His brow furrows deeper. "I've had a really shitty day, and I didn't sleep well last night because I was worried about you. About *us*."

Suddenly, my smile fades when I sense the sincerity in his voice. I nestle my body against him, wrapping my arms around his neck. Without a smile or teasing tone, I say, "Clay, I'm sorry. I didn't mean to worry you. To be honest, I was in my head too, and I just needed a couple of days to think."

"But we're fine?"

My thumb strokes his jaw as I pull his face to mine. "We're better than fine. I promise."

Then I pull him down and press my lips to his. He seems to melt into our kiss, and I feel the stress cascading off him from our embrace alone. Now I feel really bad about brushing him off, but honestly, in my head, I thought I'd be the one worrying about us. Not him.

To know he's so invested in our relationship only makes me feel better.

"My dad's at the office," I mumble against his lips. "Which means I'm home all alone."

He growls against my mouth. Then his hands slide down my hips to my thighs. He scoops me off the floor, and I wrap my legs around his waist. He's carrying me up the stairs to my room while I continue kissing him.

When we reach my bedroom, he tosses me on the bed. But instead of climbing on top of me, he stops and looks around. "So this is your bedroom?"

Reaching up, I grab his tie and yank him down on top of me. His eyes widen in surprise at my boldness.

"So eager," he says with a laugh.

"I missed you," I reply, pulling him in for a kiss, but he resists.

"Did you? Then tell me what you want."

Oh great. I suck at dirty talk. As his lips brush my neck, I close my eyes and try to imagine what *she'd* say.

"Come on," he whispers, dragging his hand up my thigh until he reaches the hem of my loose-fitting shorts.

Then I say the first thing that comes to mind.

"Be a good boy and lie down so I can ride your face until I come." My voice is raspy and deeper than normal as I mumble the words against his ear.

He immediately freezes, his hand stopping on my thigh, and I swear I can feel his dick twitch against my leg. Then he lifts up and stares into my eyes.

"Jesus Christ, Jade. That was so fucking hot." In a rush, he kisses me as he tears my shorts down my legs, pulling my underwear with them. He works off his tie and unbuttons his shirt before slipping it off and flipping onto his back next to me.

I let out a giggle as he wraps his arms around me and tugs me on top of him. My hips grind against his torso as he kisses me, letting out a growl when he smacks my ass.

"I want to go back to work with the taste of your pussy on my lips," he mumbles, and a wave of heat travels down my spine straight to my core.

Now that's some good dirty talk.

Letting out a whimper, I move up his body until my knees are on either side of his head. He grabs my thighs and buries his face between them.

I clutch one hand on the headboard as he licks and sucks, the warmth and pleasure coursing through my body.

"Yes," I cry out. My hips keep up their grinding motion, and I quiet my mind, focusing on nothing but his tongue, eagerly lapping at my clit.

It turns me on to see how much this turns him on.

He moans as he devours me, my body getting tighter and tighter with the approaching climax.

"Don't stop," I whisper.

When I close my eyes, I think about something sexy to get me there. The sounds of his ravenous moans and my heavy breathing are the backdrop for whatever I can conjure in my head to get me off.

Then suddenly, I'm picturing *her*. Which is unexpected.

Madame in black leather, long black hair, and breasts spilling from the top of her bra. I can practically hear her voice, sultry and commanding. She's talking me through it. Telling me how good I'm doing. Telling me how hot I look. Telling me how dirty I am.

Then, in my mind, she tells me to come.

And I do.

Letting out a loud gasping moan, I shudder as my body contorts, spine curling and muscles tensing. Pleasure radiates through every extremity, pulsing behind my eyes, wave after wave after wave.

I slump against the headboard as Clay continues peppering soft kisses against my thighs, licking up the arousal and making me tremble from the scruff of his beard against my sensitive flesh.

After catching my breath, I collapse onto the bed beside him.

"Fuck, that was hot," he mumbles, pulling me into his arms so my head is resting in the crook of his shoulder. His fingers find my chin and tilt it up until I'm looking at him. For a long time, we stare into each other's eyes before he speaks, the tender affection in his words cutting right to my heart.

"You make me so happy, Jade. I hope you know that."

The corner of my mouth lifts in a gentle smile. "You make me happy too."

He buries his hand in my hair at the nape of my neck and pulls me in for another kiss. "I'm serious," he says as he pulls away.

I wrap my arms around his chest with a smile. "You didn't even get to come."

He laughs. "I don't need to. Making you come is more than enough for me."

I giggle against his bare skin as we lie there, and I think about Madame again. It's weird how much she's infiltrated my mind already. And it's weird how much I want her to.

Rule #10: Unlearn everything you thought you knew.

Eden

"A MENTOR?" MIA ASKS WHILE APPLYING FALSE LASHES TO HER right eye.

"Yeah, don't ask me why I agreed to this," I reply, fixing my lipstick in the mirror next to her.

"Do you know this girl?" she asks, blinking and checking herself in her reflection.

I snap the lid back on my lipstick, hesitating before I answer her. I haven't told my friends at the club much about anything, not even about Clay and his very frequent visits to my room nearly every night last year.

"Not really," I reply. "It's complicated."

She sits up straight and looks at me skeptically. We're sitting in the club's dressing room, each of us getting ready for the night. Mia has a solo performance in the voyeur hall tonight, as she does nearly every Friday night. She will undoubtedly draw a crowd because that's just what she does. No one can command an audience like Mia.

"This wouldn't happen to have anything to do with Clay Bradley, would it?"

I freeze, one hand in my makeup bag. "No. Why would it?" I ask nonchalantly.

"Because things with you were almost never complicated— until he came along."

I swallow, forcing my face to stay even. "He was just a client, but he's stopped coming."

A soft hand touches my arm, and I turn to stare into Mia's round blue eyes. "You don't have to lie to me, you know? If you want privacy, I get it. But I'm observant enough to know he was more than a client."

My teeth clench as I nod. "It doesn't matter, though. It's over now."

"I'm sorry," she whispers.

"It's fine. I'm fine."

Her mouth presses into a thin line. "Well, if you ever want to talk, I'm here. For anything. Seriously."

"Thank you, Mia."

It's an excruciating three seconds that we stare at each other before she finally turns away. I don't know why I suck so badly at female friendships. Maybe because I was never really allowed to have them when I was married. And then, after that, I became too guarded.

"Well, I think it's amazing that you're offering to mentor this girl. If I wanted anyone to teach me the Domme/sub lifestyle, it would be you."

She zips up her makeup bag and stands from her bench seat. Walking to a storage locker, she slips her bag in before closing it.

"I honestly have no clue what I can teach this girl."

She turns toward me, wearing an expression of surprise. "Are you kidding me? You're Madame fucking Kink. She's literally learning from the best."

I roll my eyes with a laugh.

"Just think about it this way," she adds. "Teach her everything you wanted to know when you were learning. The rest will come naturally because you're not a pretentious bitch."

I laugh again, turning in my seat to look at her.

That's when I notice her lingerie. She's in a royal-blue one-piece that accentuates her hourglass shape and makes her full hips and thick thighs look sexy as hell.

"Damn, Mia," I say, raking my eyes over her body. "You look fucking hot. They're going to go nuts."

She blushes and gives me a sweet smile. "Thanks. Garrett picked it out."

"He still sends you secret gifts, then?"

"No. *Player428* does," she replies, smiling to herself.

"Who is Garrett."

She laughs. "Yes. But you know...we're married now. We have to keep that spark going for the rest of our lives."

"I don't think you're going to have that problem, babe. That man is crazy about you."

Looking contemplative, she nods. "Thanks. I'm crazy about him too."

After she finishes her hair, I wish her luck on her show, and she waves goodbye on her way out of the dressing room. While I'm sitting there alone for a moment, I think about what Mia has with Garrett and what Charlotte has with Emerson, Isabel with Hunter and Drake, and Maggie with Beau. It's hard not to feel a hint of resentment toward them.

I never wanted what they have.

I had my chance at love fifteen years ago. I picked the wrong guy, jumped headfirst into marriage, and paid the price. One very bad man ruined the entire idea of love for me.

But now...I feel differently when Mia talks to me about her and Garrett. I used to be so uninterested; there was never even a shred of jealousy.

So what's changed?

Why now do I feel like I'm passing up on something amazing by choosing to live alone?

I have Jack. My life is fulfilling. The idea that I need a partner is so…ridiculous.

My phone buzzes with the reminder that it's almost ten. After some quick finishing touches on my makeup, I put my things away and head out of the dressing room. I stop by the front desk to give the hostess my guests' names for the night, and then I head to my room.

Jade arrives ten minutes early, knocking on my door with five quick taps. When I open it to greet her, she's practically bouncing in place, beaming from ear to ear.

"Hi," she chirps excitedly.

"Come in," I reply.

"Thank you so much for doing this," she says as she steps into the room. I close the door behind her, waiting to offer her a drink, but she continues to ramble. "I know you're really busy and your time is valuable, but honestly, it's not like there's anyone else I can learn this from. I heard you were the best, and I trust that you're the best. And I promise this has nothing to do with Clay—"

With a wince at the mention of his name, I hold up my hand, and she stops.

"Sorry. I ramble when I'm nervous," she says meekly.

"I've noticed. Would you like something to drink? Maybe a glass of wine to settle your nerves?"

"Yes, please."

She follows me to the wet bar and watches as I uncork the bottle and pour two glasses. "Do all the rooms have a bar like this?" she asks.

"No," I reply, handing her her glass. "Just mine and Ronan's."

"Oh."

I watch with interest as she presses the glass to her lips, taking a sip of the dark Merlot. I can't help but wonder if this girl is really Clay's type. She's so cute, naive, and oddly wholesome. I have a feeling she's the kind of wholesome that's secretly harboring an inner freak. But is this the kind of girl Clay really wants? He needs someone to see past his insecurities. Someone unafraid to cut the bullshit and say it like it is. He needs brutal honesty, not an innocent people pleaser.

But she is cute. I have to give her that. There's a part of me that's dying to see just how dirty she can get. It wouldn't be the first time I've suspected I have a corruption kink.

That's not what we're here to do, Eden. Get your head straight.

Not that I know exactly what it is we're here to do. I'm still not a hundred-percent sure why I agreed to this in the first place.

Looking curious, she glances around the room as she clutches her wineglass to her chest. "So you…tie people up in here?"

"Sometimes."

Her eyes widen in my direction. "What else…do you do to them?"

Something about her questions makes me laugh. I make my way to the sofa, inviting her to sit next to me. "Why don't we back up a bit and start at the beginning?"

She perches on the edge of the seat and takes another sip of her wine. "Yes, good plan."

"Tell me everything you do know," I say as I take a sip.

I let her ramble for a few minutes. Mostly to grasp a better understanding of how much she understands but also because…I like to watch her talk. She's so animated and enthusiastic. Jade doesn't seem like the kind of woman who embarrasses easily, and I find that endearing but also…sexy.

There's so much a person could do with a woman like Jade. She's curious and eager, without fear or shame or judgment. As much as she wants to be dominant, I have a feeling she'd also be a beautiful submissive.

When she stops babbling, I hold out a hand to interrupt. "It sounds like you've done your research. You understand the *what*, but do you understand the *why*?"

Her brows pinch inward as she shakes her head. "No."

I lean back in my chair. "Dominance is about so much more than control. It's about connection and trust. It's about pleasure and knowing what you want. Does the idea of having control of someone else turn you on?"

She seems to think about this for a moment before she bites her bottom lip and smiles. "Yes. But not always."

"That's okay," I reply.

As I lean back in my seat, I stare at Jade and try to decide what the hell I'm going to teach this girl. I could start from the very beginning of my blogging days and walk her through every single step I learned, but for some reason, that doesn't feel right for her. It's not that she wants to learn how to be dominant in the bedroom. It's that she wants to be more dominant in her life.

"Actually…" An idea hits me, and I stand up. She follows suit, jumping up and staring at me expectantly. "Let's go for a little walk through the club," I say.

It's hard to describe the expression that passes over her face—half excitement, half fear. And once again, it makes me chuckle a bit to myself.

"Okay," she says eagerly, placing her wineglass on the glass coffee table. I do the same and lead her to the door.

As we reach the hallway, I walk, glancing back at her as she follows. "The first thing you need to do is completely unlearn everything you know about sexuality and shame. You grew up in a world that conditioned you to believe that men are more sex-driven than women and that any woman who enjoys and values sex is a whore, slut, et cetera. So our first lesson is going to show you what an empowered, sexual woman looks like."

Rule #11: Be confident.

Jade

MY HEART IS GOING A MILE A MINUTE AS I FOLLOW EDEN THROUGH the dim hallway on the club's second level. As we make our way toward the same set of stairs I had walked up to get here, I pick up on the sounds of sex to my left, just beyond the thick black curtain.

We pass through the VIP bar upstairs and then down the grand staircase. Throughout the entire walk, Eden talks, and I scurry behind her to hear everything.

"The first step in understanding dominance is harnessing the confidence to demand what you want and knowing it's your right to take it. Yes, it sounds selfish. It's supposed to be."

"Okay," I stammer as I catch up.

The farther we get through the club, the harder it becomes to listen to what she's saying. We enter the main room on the first floor. There is a bar on the left, surrounded by patrons, and a small stage on the right. It's empty at the moment, but there are more people gathered around high-top bar tables scattered through the space. Loud music with a heavy beat plays over the speakers throughout the entirety of the club.

We don't stop in the main room, though. She leads me all the way through to a curtained hallway on the other side.

With a quick nod to the bouncer standing next to the entrance, she passes through as he opens it for her. I'm quick to follow, shooting him a nervous smile.

Then we're bathed in darkness. I stay close to Eden, who weaves her way carefully through the dark space. There are people scattered throughout, but the lit-up windows on either side steal my attention. There are rooms on display, but they are currently empty.

I don't really need people in there to figure out what the spectators would be watching. There are beds and sex swings and ropes hanging on the walls.

"People just watch…" I mumble. I never finish my question because a moment later, we're standing among a crowd gathered around one particular window.

Then I'm struck speechless.

Inside the room, with dim blue lights painting the space in a soft ocean-like hue, stands a beautiful curvy blond. She's dancing in a slow, sexy sway, caressing her own body with her hands before digging them into her long hair. She's wearing a royal-blue lingerie set, but her full breasts are exposed, and when her hands come down, she caresses each one, squeezing and pinching as her face expresses both pleasure and pain.

Immediately, I feel the warmth of arousal percolating in my belly. There's just something about the way she's moving and how people are watching her with rapt attention. My eyes cascade over the audience, noticing the way the women, in particular, are watching her, biting their lips and squeezing their thighs together.

There are a few men back here too, but they're all with partners, except for one who is leaning against the back wall, watching her with a playful smirk on his face.

My eyes catch on a couple near the other side of the window. The man is clearly grinding against the woman's backside, and his other hand is buried down the front of her black leather pants.

Suddenly I feel someone behind me, a breath against my ear. "There is no shame in expressing yourself sexually here. Which means women pleasure themselves without judgment."

"Here? Just out in the open?" I whisper with a gasp. A few heads turn and glare at me, so I quickly shut my mouth.

The woman in the room stops dancing and moves toward the other side, pulling something out and carrying it over to the plush bed in the middle. Her movements are fluid and mesmerizing, like a performer.

After climbing onto the low platform bed, she lies on her back and fans her blond waves out around her. Then, with her legs facing the window, she lets her knees fall open, exposing herself to the crowd and revealing that the lingerie is open and crotchless.

I feel myself tensing, but Eden is directly behind me, pressing her body against mine in a way that feels comforting.

Then the woman in the room shows us what is in her hand—a sleek pink dildo.

My jaw drops.

She's not going to—

My heart rate picks up, and the arousal between my legs turns into a blazing inferno as the girl in the room runs the vibrating pink wand over her clit. Her back arches and she lets out a groan loud enough to be heard over the music and through the glass.

She teases herself with it for a while and, in a sense, teases us too. I glance around the crowd again and notice that nearly everyone is either touching themselves or touching their partners. There is a sense of privacy from the lack of light in the hallway, but even in the dark, it's easy to tell what that movement looks like.

Then I glance back through the window just as she slides the toy inside her, letting out another carnal noise of pleasure.

I can hardly move or tear my eyes away either.

We're all just standing around watching this woman masturbate like it's completely normal.

Then I feel Eden's breath on my cheek again. "If you're going to be a people pleaser, then the first person you need to please is yourself."

"I can't," I whisper.

Her warm hand rests softly on my waist. Her breasts are pressed to my back so I can feel the movement of her chest with each breath. The arousal pooling in my belly travels all the way up my spine.

I find myself leaning into Eden's tall frame as we watch the girl on the bed work the toy faster and harder, her cries getting louder along with each movement.

My head grows dizzy from watching her and feeling Eden so close.

"You can please yourself if you want to." Her voice is so quiet next to my ear that it's like she's inside my head.

"I can't," I reply.

I feel every breath and pound of my heart like my body is louder than it normally is.

"Why not?"

My head shakes slowly in response. "I don't know."

"Don't you want to?" she asks. "Don't you have an aching need between your legs right now?"

It's suddenly hard to breathe. Slowly, I nod.

"Does she look embarrassed?" she asks, nodding toward the girl who looks ready to come at any moment.

"No."

"Because she takes what she wants and is not ashamed of it. It's what she *deserves*. Before you can ask for what you want in the bedroom, you have to learn how to put yourself first."

Just then, the girl behind the window seizes in a screaming orgasm. There are soft moans and sighs in the crowd around me, and I feel so tied to this moment and this space that I can hardly move. It's like an out-of-body experience.

A moment later, the light in the room goes dark, and the people around us start moving away from the window, but I'm glued to my place. I keep replaying Eden's words in my head about taking what I want and learning to please myself before others.

I can do that. Just today, I expressed what I wanted with Clay, but it was hard for me, wasn't it? I was nervous that I was asking too much by wanting him to go down on me and make me come without receiving anything in return. But how much have I offered to do that for him? Do I really put him first more than myself?

Eden pulls away from me, and I immediately miss the warmth of her body.

"It's only the first day, but eventually, I want you to be comfortable with this. Then maybe you can get in one of these rooms to see what it's like." She says it so nonchalantly that I stare in shock at her as she walks toward the exit.

"Me? In there?"

"Eventually," she replies confidently.

"Do you go in there?" I ask as we reach the main room, heading toward the bar.

She responds with a sexy sort of chuckle. "Yes. All the time. I find it empowering."

As we reach the bar, she mouths something to the bartender, a cute tan-skinned man with soft curls and piercing eyes. A moment later, he delivers two glasses of ice water, and she hands one to me.

I don't realize how parched I am until the cool liquid hits my lips, and then I'm suddenly guzzling it down.

"Have you ever masturbated in front of someone before?"

I choke on the water currently going down my throat, and it goes down the wrong pipe, making me cough into my glass. She laughs again, this time handing me a napkin to clean up the water all over my face.

"You'll get used to that," she replies with a smile. "So have you?"

"Not like that," I reply, nodding toward the hallway we just walked out of.

"No. Not like that. But with a partner. Maybe while they do it too?"

"Um…no," I say, thinking back to the people I've been with. Although I don't have to think that hard. I'm pretty sure I'd remember something like that.

"Okay, that's your homework then. Tell your partner that's what you'd like to do. It will give them a chance to see how you pleasure yourself and also make you feel more comfortable with expressing yourself sexually."

"You mean with Clay?" I reply as she takes a sip of the water in her glass. I can't help but notice the way her eyes unfocus and her jaw clenches at the mention of his name.

"Yes, of course." Her voice is even and cool. "You didn't tell him about coming to see me, did you?"

I shake my head. "No." Then I chew on my lip as I stare at her skeptically. "Do you mind me asking why?"

She swallows and straightens her spine. "Because he was a client of mine, and this is a conflict of interest."

"But what if I brought him in with me? You could teach me while he and I are together—"

"No," she snaps. Then she takes a deep breath and forces herself to give me a calm expression. "This isn't about Clay, remember? I'm not teaching you how to be a Domme for him. I'm teaching you to be more dominant."

"Oh, yeah," I reply, relaxing my shoulders. "I won't tell him if you don't want me to."

Then, as we stand in silence for a moment, I feel the question creeping up that I've been dying to ask her. He told me he stopped coming. But I need to hear it from her too.

This is the woman Clay had feelings for, and while she didn't feel the same for him, I still have a gnawing sense of jealousy burrowed deep in my bones.

"You're not still…" I mumble. When her fierce eyes land on my face, I straighten my shoulders.

Be confident.
Ask for what you want.

"You're not still seeing him, are you? As a Domme, I mean."

Her brow folds inward, and her eyes narrow. "No. Although that information is technically private, I can tell you I haven't seen him in a few months."

I could ask more, and I'm dying to, but if I press her for more information, she might shut me out. My goal here is to learn to be more like her; then Clay may feel for me the way he did for her.

This might be about me more than him, but with every passing day, I realize I want him to be a permanent part of me. Which means I'm doing this for *us*.

Rule #12: Don't teach your ex-boyfriend's current girlfriend how to tie you up.

Eden

"HAVE YOU EVER TIED ANYONE UP LIKE THAT?" JADE WHISPERS A bit too loudly from the back of the instruction room.

I nod, keeping my eyes on Silla at the front of the room. She's currently demonstrating various knots, and I want Jade to pay attention to this, but she can hardly keep still, let alone pick up on the skills Silla is teaching.

Jade is holding the ropes in her hands, her brow furrowed as she glances at her hands and back up to Silla, comparing her square knot to the instructor's.

"I might have to stick to handcuffs," Jade says, and I stifle a silent laugh as I reach out to help her.

"This rope should go through that loop."

"Oh, shit," Jade curses before tossing the mess of rope on the table.

"Practice these knots," Silla says to the class. "I'll come around to assist where it's needed."

Jade is growing flustered as she undoes the knots she made and tries again.

"Don't get frustrated," I say softly as I turn to her. "You're the one in control, remember?"

"Yeah, well, I'm not very good at this."

"Here," I say, holding out my wrists together. "Try a simple knot, like Silla showed you on me. Doing it on another person might be easier."

Jade takes a deep breath and protrudes her lower lip to blow her bangs out of her eyes. They need a trim, but I'll admit—it's pretty cute when she does that.

Now that I've spent a few days with Jade, I can see why Clay likes her so much. She's confident but not cocky. Cute but also sexy. Smart yet curious and naive. She's a walking, talking paradox, and I don't think I would ever get bored unraveling all of her personality's complicated bits.

All this to say, I like her.

More than I expected and far more than I should.

In fact, I've started looking forward to our little lessons. Tonight is only her fourth session, but I am not supposed to be enjoying them so much.

I'll admit, that first night I threw her into the deep end. I figured if she couldn't handle public masturbation in the voyeur room, she wasn't cut out for this, and she likely wouldn't bother returning.

I was wrong.

The second and third time she came, I scaled our lessons back a bit. I might have even made them boring on purpose. Spending an hour each night explaining the rules, boundaries, and safety protocols of the business. Not once did she seem to lose interest or appear bored.

If anything, it had the opposite effect.

I wasn't actively trying to make her quit, but I wasn't making our lessons appealing enough to stay, either.

And it wasn't until tonight, when I found myself looking forward to our lesson, that I realized maybe I didn't want her to quit at all.

While Jade winds the nylon rope around my wrist, deep in concentration, I study her face and all the expressions she makes. I bite my bottom lip to keep from smiling as she masters the first knot.

"I did it," she says with excitement.

"Good job," I reply. "Now try the second one."

"Do you prefer ropes or cuffs?" she asks while she works.

"It depends. Rope bondage requires patience from both the rigger and the bunny. Not everyone enjoys that."

"Do you?" she asks, glancing up at me.

"Sometimes. Rope bondage allows for control over your submissive. Rather than just binding their wrists or ankles, they surrender control over their entire body."

She shudders as if the thought makes her cringe. "I don't think I would like that."

"All forms of bondage take a great deal of trust," I say. "The more of their body they surrender to you, the more they trust you. Having that level of power over someone else is…"

"An honor," she says, finishing my sentence. When she lifts her gaze to my face, our eyes meet. They linger for a moment, and suddenly, I imagine Jade in that role, giving herself and her body to me. Then I picture the opposite—giving myself to her. And that's not something I think about very often.

I never give up control.

But the idea of yielding control of my body to her…is oddly enticing. She's so headstrong and eager. We could have some fun.

"Very good," Silla says as she passes our table, commending Jade on her work.

We break eye contact at that moment as Jade softly mumbles, "Thank you."

"Keep practicing," Silla says to her as she drifts to the next table.

My cheeks grow hot as I stare down at my wrists, where Jade is still practicing her knots. She works in silence, and it's deafening.

I know she must feel it, too, because I've noticed Jade is never not talking. She can't stand the quiet.

But I don't know what to say now to fill the lapse in our conversation. My mind is reeling from this sudden realization.

I like Jade too much.

It would be very, *very* stupid of me to develop feelings for my ex's new girlfriend.

But I don't think there's much I can do about it at this point.

"Jack, you need more sunscreen," I call to him as he jumps off the monkey bars and comes running toward where I'm sitting on the bench.

"Yes, Mama," he says as he stops in front of me. His cheeks are bloodred from exertion as he picks up his water bottle and guzzles it down. I put a dollop of sunscreen on my fingers before rubbing it over his cheeks and forehead.

My son might look like me, but he inherited my ex's pale complexion and burns easily in the sun. I let him get a bad sunburn once when I took him to the beach as a toddler, and he cried so much it broke my heart. Now I've become obsessed with sunscreen, and at this point, he's used to it.

"Can we go to the movies tonight?" he asks, and I give him a confused look.

"We're at the park right now, and you want to go to the movies tonight?"

"Yeah, maybe the arcade guy will be there."

My heart sinks. "No, buddy. We can't go to the movies, and I doubt the *arcade guy* will be there anyway," I say, shoving the sunscreen into my bag. "We're not stalkers," I add in a low mutter.

"What's a stalker?" he asks, and it makes me laugh.

"Forget I said that, please."

"Can you call him?" he asks in a desperate whine.

"No, buddy. I can't call him." I wish he would drop the whole

Clay thing, but he's literally been bringing him up almost daily for two weeks. He met him once and for literally five minutes.

Once he realized Clay and I knew each other *from work*, he became obsessed with seeing him again.

"Well, can we just go to the movies and maybe—"

"Jack, drop it!" I snap.

He freezes, staring at me in surprise. As his expression morphs into sadness, I feel the hot sting of guilt.

"I'm sorry, buddy. I just…"

"It's okay," he replies. He turns away to go back to the playground, and I reach for him, hoping for a hug to let him feel how sorry I am, but he brushes my hand away.

I watch him playing from the bench while tears well in my eyes, hidden behind my sunglasses.

My son is lonely.

The thought echoes in my mind like a spell, hurting more and more each time it runs through it.

What if I'm not enough?

Am I a monster? He wants a friend, and I keep denying him that.

So what if I brought Clay around for Jack? He would do it if I asked.

He knows Jack exists already as it is, so why bother trying to hide him?

God, am I actually considering this?

I could enforce strict boundaries. We could meet Clay in a public place, and I would be there the entire time to watch him. It's not like I'm letting Clay back into my life romantically. But he is one of the few men I know I can trust.

Jack is playing in the sand alone, and it breaks my heart to watch him.

I pull my phone out and find the text message thread with Clay. *This is crazy*, I think to myself.

Against my better judgment, I type up the simple question

and hit Send before I can change my mind. When the text message says *Sent,* I throw my phone back in my purse and try to pretend I didn't just do that.

A moment later, Jack sprints over. "I'm hungry," he complains.

"Let's go home and have lunch then," I reply, standing up and taking his little hand in mine. As we walk back toward the house, I glance down at him, and he smiles affectionately up at me.

"How about this?" I ask. "We'll go to the arcade tonight for pizza and games. If your friend happens to be there, cool. If not, I'll play the games with you. Okay?"

His walk turns into a bounce as he grins excitedly up at me. "Really?"

"Yes."

His arms latch around my waist as he hugs me so tightly I feel the tears threaten to sting again. "You're the best mama in the whole world."

Leaning down, I brush his curls back and kiss his forehead. Then I take his hand in mine as we continue our walk.

Deep down, I hope Clay shows up tonight, for Jack's sake.

Deep down, I hope he doesn't, for mine.

Rule #13: Don't waste a second chance.

Clay

"SHOW ME HOW YOU TOUCH YOURSELF."

My skin buzzes with excitement and anticipation. Standing in front of her, naked and hard, my fingers ache for her skin, but she's telling me to touch myself.

"Yes, Madame," I reply, although what I want to say is, Please let me touch you.

Her pleasure is all I care about anymore. Pleasing her. Making her proud. Hearing her praise. For weeks now, it's been all I want. It's like she's rewired my brain.

Morning, noon, and night, Eden is on my mind.

And not once in the three weeks that I've been seeing her have we had sex. I haven't even had the privilege of coming—not since that first time. Not at the club. And not at home. She gave me strict instructions to keep my hands off my own dick, and I obeyed.

I'm not sure why. It's not like she'd know. Maybe it's because I love a challenge. Or because whatever this is, it is starting to mean something to me. I don't want to break the rules because the rules are important.

I get the feeling she's training me. She's dangling my own orgasm in front of me like a carrot on a string. Every time I come into the room, my satisfaction belongs to her. I show her all the obedience she wants. And now I'll gladly devote my life to making her come on the hour every hour if that's what she wants.

So her telling me to touch myself is monumental.

My breath is held in my chest as I wrap my hand around my hard length. On the upstroke, I squeeze the head of my cock, and my eyes start to roll into the back of my head. But I keep them open and watch her as she stares at my hand, moving up and down my shaft. It's like she's studying me, memorizing the way I move and what makes me shudder.

Then she says the words that make my knees weak: "Make yourself come."

The three-word command freezes my movement. When she notices my hesitation, her gaze flicks up to my face. She furrows her brow as she waits for me to obey.

"Yes, Madame," I say as my hand starts moving again.

My mind is a mess of questions and thoughts as I stroke. What is the point of this? Am I being rewarded? For what? Should I put her pleasure first? But no, I'm supposed to submit and obey without question every time—unless I need to say yellow or red.

With a wince, I try to focus on my dick and work to make myself come. She's right here. I don't have to imagine her. So what is my problem?

After a few minutes of quickly stroking my cock, I start to panic. What if I can't do it? What if I let her down?

"Pet, look at me."

I slow my stroking and lift my gaze to her face. Her expression isn't hard or disappointed, but with her lips parted and her eyes dilated, she looks almost...aroused. Does getting myself off...turn her on?

"Keep going," she says, a little softer.

Then, as I start moving my fist, I watch as she glides her own hand down the front of her body, over her breasts, and down to her thin black panties.

Sitting in the red-velvet chair only a few feet away from me, she slips the fabric aside and plunges her middle finger deep inside her wet pussy.

A sound escapes my lips at the sight—something like a grunt and a whimper. I pick up speed, and my cock grows even harder as I watch her. She pulls her finger out and uses the moisture to stroke her clit. Arching her back, she pleases herself right along with me.

Our eyes meet again, and I nearly come.

Suddenly, it's like we are connected. I am hers, wholly and unconditionally. The look on her face tells me so.

And when I come, it's not from watching her fuck herself or play with her clit. It's from the look on her face that says she's proud of me. That I'm doing good. That I deserve this.

Sitting at my desk in my office, I'm ignoring my emails and my to-do list to reread the text message I received this morning.

Are you free at seven tonight?

It's Saturday afternoon, and I haven't responded yet. I came into the office to busy my mind, even though it's not technically an office day, but it's not working. I can't stop thinking about it.

It's the kind of text I expect from Jade or my mother or my boss—not from Eden St. Claire. Not anymore.

Is she trying to lure me back to the club? Does she want to see me again for sex?

What the fuck am I supposed to say? She knows I'm with Jade. I can't betray her. I just can't.

But this is Eden.

I feel like I'm being pulled underwater, down to the pitch-black abyss.

I love Jade. I want to give her everything, and I meant what I said last week. She makes me so fucking happy.

And yet here I am typing my response.

Yes.

The whooshing sound of the text message guts me. It makes me sick, and I slam my phone face down on the desk as I fight the urge to throw up into the small trash can next to my desk.

What the fuck is wrong with me? Am I seriously considering this? What if she wants to have sex with me? What if she wants to be my Domme again? Do I even have what it takes to say no?

Fuck no.

The sound of feet running down the hallway has me picking up my head. Jade bursts through the door with a smile.

"We have this whole place to ourselves," she says with a beaming smile.

It's impossible not to grin in return. There isn't a lick of makeup on her face, just a spattering of freckles and a slight blush on her cheeks. And if I ever caught her putting anything on those perfect round eyes, I'd throw whatever she used in the trash. Jade is perfect and immediately distracts me from whatever is waiting for me in my text messages.

"Then get that sexy ass in here," I reply, pushing my chair away from the desk.

Will is out of town for the weekend, visiting a client who lives upstate, so it's literally just Jade and me in the entire office.

Jade drops her purse on the chair by the door and sprints over to me, jumping into my lap and kissing me hard on the lips. She's in a short dress with straps tied on her shoulders. It's light blue with white daisies, and I feel like a sick fuck for how much I want to screw her in it. With her spotless white sneakers on too...for some fucking reason.

"Let's fuck in every room of the building," I mumble against her lips.

She giggles as she wraps her arms around my neck. "Actually...I have another idea."

My brows rise as I pull back and stare at her. "I love your ideas."

She laughs again, biting her bottom lip. My cock is already hard behind my zipper as she fidgets on my lap. With my thumb, I pull her bottom lip from between her teeth and pinch it between mine. She yelps a little as I bite down; then I quickly release and lick the teeth marks I left.

"What's your idea, baby?"

She fidgets some more. Then she hides her face in my neck. "God, I don't know if I can say it."

With a laugh, I stroke her short brown hair. "You didn't have a problem last time. Plus, whatever it is, I promise I'm going to be down. Unless the idea is not to have sex at all."

She sits upright and lets out a deep breath. "Okay, I can do this."

I smile, stroking her chin. "Tell me."

She looks directly into my eyes. "I want you to watch me... while I watch you."

My smile fades, and I blink at her.

"Oh, God. You hate it," she cries, noticing my less-than-enthusiastic reaction.

"No, it's fine. It sounds...hot as fuck, baby."

"Then why did you look like I just suggested we paint each other's fingernails?"

I open my mouth to reply, but nothing comes out. How can I tell her that I reacted that way because just a few moments ago, I remembered that very same scenario with Eden? That until that day with her, masturbating with someone was something I would have dreaded. That mutual masturbation requires a level of intimacy and vulnerability I only had with one other person.

"I just...was hoping I could touch you," I say, running my hands up her thighs.

"I know," she replies, "but I heard somewhere that if we watch each other touch ourselves, we'll know better how the other person does it. So we can please each other. We don't have to, though."

"Yes, we do. You're right. It is so hot. In fact…" I lift her from my lap and place her on her feet. Then I use my arm to sweep away all the papers and files on my desk. They fall to the floor in a mess I'll have to clean up later. I place my hands under Jade's arms and lift her onto the desk in front of me. "I want to watch you masturbate right on my desk so every day I can picture it while I work."

I drop into my office chair and lean back, unbuttoning and unzipping my pants as I stare at her. Jade is biting her bottom lip with a mischievous smile.

"Touch yourself, baby. Let me see you."

"Well, now I'm nervous," she replies, looking to the side.

I roll the chair so I'm sitting between her legs. Then I clench my jaw, remembering that night with someone else. I reach into my unbuttoned pants and pull out my cock.

Jade's eyes dilate at the sight, and she watches as I stroke myself.

It's like déjà vu. After a few minutes of watching me, she reaches down under her dress, sliding her panties to the side and showing me as she touches herself.

But something is different this time. It has nothing to do with this being a different person and everything to do with this dynamic between us. Jade needs my encouragement and my support. She needs *me*. I'm not doing this to impress her or please her. I'm doing this because I want to be the person she trusts. The person to take care of her.

I was Eden's.

Jade is mine.

I'm stroking faster now, sliding my thumb through the precum leaking from the tip. And I can't take my eyes away from the way she touches herself. Her middle finger strums fiercely on her clit, pressing down so hard her nail has turned white.

"Lie down, baby. Let me see you."

She reclines across the surface of my desk, letting her hair hang over the edge as she spreads her legs for me. I release my cock long enough to tug her panties down her legs.

Her fingers return to her cunt, and her thighs clench around her hand. Standing up, I continue stroking myself as she watches. I find myself smiling down at her, admiring just how beautiful and brave this woman is.

And for some reason, she wants to be mine.

"Does that feel good?" I ask, my voice strained.

"Mm-hmm," she replies with her lips pressed together.

"God, you're so perfect," I say, shoving down that evil voice that likes to pop up in moments like these, reminding me that Jade is *too* perfect for me.

"So are you," she replies sweetly. "I love watching you do that."

"Let me see you come on my desk, baby. My dirty, filthy girl. Show me how fucking nasty you can be."

Talking her through it does the trick. Her mouth hangs open, and a desperate-sounding moan escapes her lips. I watch her pussy as she comes, pulsing under her finger, slick with her arousal.

My balls tighten, and the head of my dick swells moments before I press the tip to her belly, shooting my cum all over her.

"Fuck, Jade." I groan as I finish. "I love it when you visit me at work."

She laughs as she drops her hands to her sides and catches her breath. After I've zipped myself back up, I rush into the bathroom and come back with a wet paper towel. I use it to clean her up before putting her panties back on and lifting her up to place a kiss on her mouth.

"Let's go get some lunch, and then afterward, we can do your idea," she says sweetly.

"Sounds like a plan," I reply as I kiss her again.

She excuses herself to the bathroom, and I drop back into my office chair. When I hear a buzzing from the floor, I reach down and brush some papers away to find my phone waiting for me.

I'm pierced with anxiety as I read: *New Message from Eden*
Swallowing my shame, I swipe it open.

I'm taking Jack to the arcade on 5th Street tonight. He's been asking to see you. You should come.

It takes my slow brain a while to comprehend who Jack is.
Her son.
Eden is texting me about her son.
I literally thought she wanted to see me, and I was ready to do what? Fuck her if that's what she wanted.
No. I wouldn't have done that. Would I?
I'm not that guy. Or am I?
"Ready?" a sweet voice chirps from the doorway.
I wipe the grim expression off my face and smile up at her. "Ready, my nasty girl."
She smiles, blushing as she reaches a hand out toward me. I take it and press my lips to her knuckles.
"The sooner we eat, the sooner we can get back here and dirty up every room in this place."
I drape my arm over her shoulders and press my lips to her head. "Then let's hurry."
As we make our way out to the car, I think about that text and the control that woman has over me. I may have thought about doing something, but I didn't.
This means I have a chance to do things right by Jade, and it's a chance I don't plan on wasting.

———

"Do you understand why I made you do that?" she asks as we're both sitting on her couch during the aftercare portion of tonight's session. She makes me do this every time. In the last fifteen minutes or so,

we have to unwind together, and she forces me to eat something and drink water. It makes me feel like a child, and I hate it.

I do love how much she touches me during this part, though. Stroking my back or holding my hand. I crave it more than sex.

"No, Madame," I reply, lying back so my head is in her lap.

She runs her fingers through my hair. "Don't you think you deserved it?"

I hesitate for a moment. "No. I didn't do anything."

"You obeyed me. You've done as I told you to for weeks. Does it make you uncomfortable for me to watch you rewarding yourself?"

"Yes," I reply.

"You're not kind enough to yourself, pet. I notice the way you don't like to receive rewards. You think you don't deserve them or that you're not good enough. I can tell. But you're mine, aren't you?"

I have to force myself to swallow. Her words ring with truth, but it's the kind of truth we keep hidden and don't talk about. The ugly, embarrassing truth.

"Yes, Madame," I say, forcing my voice not to crack.

"That's not how I want you to treat what's mine. You should pleasure what's mine. You should value what's mine. Never think or talk bad about what's mine. Understand?"

My molars grind as I stare at a spot on the wall. My eyes close because I'm starting to feel their sting.

Carefully, I reply, "Yes, Madame."

Rule #14: Never let your guard down.

Eden

"CAN I HAVE ANOTHER DOLLAR, MAMA?" JACK SPRINTS UP TO where I sit on the bench at the edge of the arcade.

"Of course, buddy," I reply, digging into my pocket for another dollar. He takes the bill and bolts over to the token machine.

My eyes scan the entrance again. It's ten minutes past seven, and I'm starting to think he's not coming. He never replied after I told him where I wanted to meet.

This is so wrong of me, using a client to entertain my kid—especially considering that sub was also someone I cared for so much. Maybe even loved.

I know the power I still have over Clay, and I know this is crazy, but I would do anything for my son. I trust Clay. He won't hurt my son, and Jack deserves to have as many people in his life as he wants. It's my job to keep him safe. So this is my only option.

I'm doing my good deed with Jade, so I shouldn't feel so bad. Of course, Clay doesn't know that part, and he never will, but I can rest easy knowing I'm helping their relationship.

"Mama, look who's here!" Jack shrieks from the basketball machine.

My head snaps up, and my gaze connects with Clay as he crosses the room toward where Jack and I are. His expression is solemn as he stares at me. Then he looks at my son, and his face lights up with a smile. He waves to him as Jack sprints to meet him halfway.

"Hey, remember me?" Jack says with excitement, hanging on Clay's arm.

With a laugh, he replies, "Duh. Of course I remember you. I've been asking your mom all week if we could meet at the arcade." He nods toward me, and I shoot him a tight smile as I mouth the words *thank you.*

"Can we go play, Mama?" Jack says, looking at me.

"Of course, buddy." I reach into my pocket to pull out more money, but Clay waves at me to stop. "I got it." Then he pulls a twenty out of his wallet and hands it to Jack, who runs off to the token machine.

Clay pauses near me for a moment. Our eyes meet in a heated, tense glance as I cross my arms in front of myself.

"Thanks for doing this," I whisper.

With a cold expression, he says, "I'm not doing it for you." I glance toward my son again and swallow down my guilt. "He's a cool kid. Only wish I knew about him sooner."

I shift my gaze back to his face. "Clay—"

"Come on, guy!" Jack calls from the blaster game.

Clay laughs as he leaves me to follow Jack. "My name is Clay," he tells Jack as he picks up the other orange blaster.

For the next hour and a half, those two don't stop. They bounce from machine to machine as I watch. The entire time, Clay never looks burdened or bothered by the seven-year-old. In fact, he laughs right along with him, and it makes me feel very strange inside.

The only other man I've seen with my son is Ronan. And

while he loves Jack, the chemistry between them is different. Ronan treats him like the nephew he never had. He spoils him and protects him but never really *plays* with him.

Watching Jack with Clay, I start to feel less and less guilty about orchestrating this. They're clearly both having a good time.

After they're done playing video games, Jack runs over to show me his collection of tickets, pulling them out of his pockets in tiny folded bundles.

"Let's go get you a prize then," Clay says, knocking him playfully on the shoulder.

"I'm hungry," Jack complains, rubbing his stomach. "Can we get pizza?"

"Yeah, we'll get something to eat, but I'm sure Clay has to get going," I say without looking him in the eye.

"Pizza sounds great," Clay replies, and I glance up to meet his gaze for a moment.

"You really don't have to—"

"Why don't you order some food and I'll take him to redeem his tickets?"

I glance over to the prize center, clear on the opposite side of the large room where the food counter is. Anxiety crawls up my spine at the idea of being unable to see Jack.

Then Clay touches my arm. "I'll watch him. He'll be fine," he says as if reading my mind.

"Stay by Clay," I tell my son as I stand up.

He's barely even listening as he gathers up his tickets and nods at the man standing next to him. "Let's go!"

I shoot Clay one more expression of gratitude before heading in the opposite direction.

A few minutes later, I return to the table with a soda cup for Jack and a pitcher of beer for Clay and me. The two of them are sorting through the candy Jack won, and when I catch him trying to hide the already-emptied wrappers, I glare at Clay.

"Normally, we eat dinner before we have candy."

"Oops," Clay replies with a mouthful of chocolate, which makes Jack giggle like crazy.

While Jack fills his soda cup at the drink station, I pour two glasses of beer for Clay and me.

"Thanks," he mutters as he takes one.

"So…" I say to fill the awkward silence. "How have you been?"

When he lifts his gaze to my face, I can tell it is the wrong thing to ask. "Better," he mumbles in a low, angry tone.

I glance down at my beer and let the shame wash over me. *Better* implies there was a time when he was bad.

"Well, I hope you understand why I couldn't tell you about him."

"And yet here I am," he mutters over the rim of his glass.

"If you want me to apologize for putting my son first, I won't."

"I never asked to be first," he replies spitefully.

"You have no idea what we've been through, Clay," I reply angrily.

"You're right. I don't. Because you wouldn't tell me, Eden." He bites out my name like an insult.

"I was the one who tried—"

"I got Dr Pepper!" Jack chirps as he sets down his soda and climbs onto the bench beside me. I quickly close my mouth and pray that he didn't overhear anything.

"Good choice," Clay says with a smile, putting his fist out for Jack to bump it.

A moment later, one of the employees brings our pizza and some plates. The three of us dig in, and the two of them spend the entire meal chatting. Jack tells Clay about school, and then he gets him on the topic of *Galaxy Warriors*, and Jack doesn't stop. I must admit Clay does a great job showing enthusiasm throughout the entire conversation. He never treats Jack like a kid but talks to him like an equal, and I love that.

Before the pizza is gone, I already know this isn't going to be a onetime thing. Jack is already getting attached to the idea of Clay, a grown man who shows him attention and interest in the things he cares about. Where else does my son get that aside from me? Ronan is too busy with his own family, and even before, he wasn't really the video game, *Galaxy Warriors* type of guy. Even though I know he'd be whatever Jack wanted him to be.

"You're on a baseball team?" Clay asks.

Jack nods with his lips around the straw of his soda. "Yep! I play first base."

"No way!" Clay replies enthusiastically. "I used to play first base!"

"Really?"

"Yes."

"Do you want to come to my game? Mama, when is my next game?" Jack asks, tugging on my shirt.

"Clay's probably busy, buddy," I reply.

"I'm not busy," he argues, winking at Jack.

With a sigh, I glare at the man across from me. "His game is next Saturday at one."

"Saturday at one. Got it."

"At the Little League field by the harbor," I add reluctantly.

"I'll be there."

"Yes," Jack says, bouncing in his seat.

I can't help but crack a smile when I see his excitement. But I'll admit…there's a part that hurts. The part that knows I can't keep my child to myself forever. I've been a constant in Jack's life since he was born, but someday, I won't be his number one. And while it'll probably be a long time before that happens, it still hurts to think about it.

I'm Madame. And I'm Mama. Who am I without those two things?

After the pizza is gone, Clay cleans up the table while Jack collects his winnings, shoving the candy into his pocket. Then the three of us make our way to the exit. Clay walks us to our car, Jack gabbing the entire way.

"This was fun," Clay says as we pause in front of my car.

"Can we do this again?" Jack asks excitedly.

"I'd love that," Clay responds. Then they both look at me, and I can't help but smile and shrug.

"Sure, I guess."

Then Jack wraps his arms around Clay, who hugs him back, lifting him off the ground as he does. After their embrace, Jack climbs into the back of the car, leaving Clay and me alone.

"He's a great kid," Clay says.

I nod. "Yeah, he is."

"Thanks for letting me hang out with him," he adds, and that warm feeling in my chest returns.

"I just want what's best for my son," I reply, looking up and finding his eyes with my own. The intensity burns between us, so many memories and tender moments returning in the blink of an eye. My feelings for him never truly left, and I realize I have to be very careful about spending time with him or I could fuck everything up and fall in love all over again.

"I know you do, Eden," he says carefully as he backs away. On a second thought, he turns back toward me. "I'm with Jade now. I won't betray her trust. Not even for you."

It feels like a knife in my chest as I swallow down the bitterness building there. Jade has Clay and Clay has Jade. I'm supposed to respect that. I'm supposed to be happy for them.

But how can I pretend this doesn't hurt?

"I know, Clay. I'm proud of you for that," I say, staring down at the ground.

He pauses for a moment, and the air between us grows uncomfortable. Neither of us can say anything. I can't blame him for what happened. Not now.

So I break the silence first. "See you next Saturday, Clay."

"See you next Saturday," he replies weakly.

My gaze lifts, and I watch as he walks away, getting into his sleek red car. Then I climb into my car and glance into the rearview mirror to find Jack resting his head, eyes closed against the seat belt.

During the drive back to the house, I think about Clay. In my mind, I try to reconcile the version I know now, the exuberant man unafraid to show his playful side, and the man I knew before, the reluctant submissive who swallowed his pride to find himself. There are layers upon layers with this man, and once upon a time, I had the privilege of peeling back each one. I was there the night he cried. I was there the night he opened old wounds and bled his feelings to me. I was there every single step of the way.

———————

"You love this aftercare shit, don't you?" he asks with a smug grin as I tip up the water bottle, insisting he drinks.

"It's not about whether I love it. It's an integral part of the process," I reply.

We're sitting on the bed. His back is to the headboard with his legs splayed out before him. I can't take my eyes off his face, watching how he locks up his emotions behind a cynical laugh or sarcastic joke.

"I let you treat me like a footstool, and then I got to wear your thighs like earmuffs. I don't understand why I need water after that." He laughs again, taking a swig.

As soon as each of our sessions ends, Clay crawls back behind the facade, forced to silence the vulnerable part of himself that we work every night to unleash.

"Everyone needs water to survive, Clay. I'm just taking care of what's mine. Remember?"

When his eyes meet mine, there's a warm familiarity there. He's comfortable with me after only one month. "And I thought there would be more whips and paddles," he says.

"We'll get to that eventually," I reply, reclining beside him on the bed. "You haven't required punishment...yet."

"You assume I'm coming back," he says, which makes me laugh because it's turned into a running joke. I say, 'See you next time,'

and he says, 'If I ever come back.' Which he inevitably does every night.

"You're coming back," I mumble. "You're far more interested in this lifestyle than you want to admit."

A deep, sexy chuckle reverberates through his chest. "Lifestyle?"

"Call it what you want, Clay, but when something becomes a part of who you are and infiltrates every aspect of your life, even when you aren't actively participating, it's a lifestyle. And there's nothing wrong with that."

I tip back his water bottle again, and he shakes his head with a smile as he drinks. After he swallows, he turns toward me.

"So what about you?" he asks, and I lift my head to stare in confusion.

"What about me?"

"How did you get started with this lifestyle?" he asks innocently as if he doesn't see how invasive that is.

Our eyes meet momentarily, and I feel something I've never felt with a client. It's intimate and disarming.

Maybe that's why I suddenly feel comfortable divulging such personal information.

"Umm…" I stammer, sitting up. "I got out of a bad relationship and needed to feel empowered and regain some control. It helped me discover a part of myself I had kept hidden my entire life."

"Wow," he whispers, those stunning green eyes still focused on my face. "How long ago was that?"

"Six years," I whisper.

"Did it help?"

"Immensely," I reply, staring into his eyes again.

———

Looking back, I realize that was the first time my guard was down between us. He had asked something no one else had. It was the first time someone truly cared. It's like there was a weak spot in the armor I had built around myself, and Clay easily found it.

Rule #15: Life is not black and white.

Jade

"I THOUGHT IT WAS GOING TO BE EMBARRASSING, BUT IT WASN'T AT ALL. I mean…it's not like I've never had an orgasm during sex with someone else, but masturbating like that with another person was so…I don't know…liberating!"

I'm rambling again, but instead of seeming annoyed, Eden actually looks a little amused. We're sitting across from each other at one of the high-top bar tables downstairs at the club. We've been chatting for nearly an hour, and I'm not sure if this is part of her teaching plan or just two friends having a drink and talking about sex.

She's slowly running the pad of her finger over the rim of her martini glass while I go on and on about what Clay and I did in his office yesterday. She's wearing a lopsided smirk as she gazes down at the drink in front of her.

"So you understand why I encouraged you to do that?" she asks in a flat tone.

"Sort of. So I'd prioritize my own pleasure, right? And stop feeling so ashamed of taking what I want."

She nods with a small smile. "If only I could teach every woman that much."

"You should," I reply, taking a sip of my vodka and cranberry juice. "You should write a book! Or be president."

That makes her laugh a bit more; it might be the biggest smile I've seen her express. For the first time, I notice the gentle laugh lines around her mouth and how pretty she is when she grins in a way that shows her pearly-white teeth. The front two have a sliver of a gap, and I realize now that it must be something she's tried to hide, although I don't know why. Eden is stunning as it is, but a happy Eden is out-of-this-world gorgeous.

When she catches me staring, I quickly avert my gaze, turning my attention downward.

"So…what's next?" I ask without looking back up.

I wait as she drags in a breath and lets it out slowly. "To be honest, I don't know. It's not like I had planned for this."

She's leaning on the table, and when I finally pull my gaze up to her face, she's staring at me. She seems less tense today than normal, and it makes me wonder what her life outside this club is like. I don't want to pry, but I sort of want to know everything about her. I want to crawl inside her mind and know her like no one else does.

Even being at this table alone with her feels like an honor not everyone is afforded.

"What do you like about being a Domme?" I ask, folding my arms on the table.

She tilts her head to the side and deliberates before answering. "To be honest, I used to be like you—a people pleaser. I didn't know how to take what I wanted, which landed me in a mess of trouble. So, after I clawed my way out, I decided I didn't want to live like that anymore. I wanted to be a better version of myself."

"Wow," I mutter. Then she leans forward and looks into my eyes.

"There's nothing wrong with being submissive or selfless, but you have to know your own boundaries before you can expect anyone else to respect them."

I lean toward her, mirroring her position so we're only inches apart, hovering over our drinks. "What if you don't know what you want? Or who you are? Or what your boundaries are? What if…you love someone and you want to give them everything they need?"

Her brow furrows, and her lips pinch together tightly. Then her face softens in the blink of an eye as if she suddenly understands me.

"Have you ever loved someone like that?" I ask with desperation.

To my surprise, she nods. "Yes, I did and I do." Then her hand lands softly on mine. "But what you want and who you are matters, Jade. No amount of love for someone else can change that."

When our eyes meet, the moment between us is charged and burns with intensity. My hand under hers is suddenly buzzing, and I slowly pull it away.

After we've both sat up properly, we each take a drink and let the moment pass.

"Have you met any couples with mismatched kinks before?" I ask after I've taken my sip.

"Oh, tons," she replies. "My best friend and his wife, actually. She loves impact play, and he doesn't like bringing her pain, no matter how much she wants him to."

"So what do they do?" I ask.

This makes her smile. "They bring in reinforcements."

By the wicked smirk she's wearing, I assume *she* is the reinforcement. Just the thought of Eden joining a married couple in the bedroom has my stomach stirring with excitement. Does she only do the impact play stuff, or does she have sex with them too?

A couple more of these vodka cranberry drinks, and I might be ready to ask those exact questions.

"The important thing is communication," she says more seriously. "Always."

"But what difference does it make? If you want different things, how is communicating going to help?" I ask.

She shrugs. "Because we all want the same thing—to feel safe, satisfied, and seen. We just take different roads to get there. If my friend's wife loves pain and wants it, then is he really hurting her, or is he just giving her exactly what she wants? If a submissive's only desire is to please their Dom, then who is really in control if the sub is getting exactly what they want? These are all just dynamics that exist here in this club and out in the real world. We're all after the same thing, but sometimes we have to get a little creative with how we work with those around us to get it."

I'm nodding along, but the crease between my brows deepens as she talks. It all feels so overwhelming and confusing.

Just as I open my mouth to ask another question, her phone vibrates, and she sneaks a peek at it.

"I have another client in fifteen minutes," she mumbles softly. My stomach does a strange little flip-flop at that.

"Oh, of course," I reply nonchalantly.

She must notice my apprehension when she gazes up at me because her expression softens. "For homework tonight, I want you to really think about what *you* want. And take the quiz on the app I sent you."

Without a word, I nod. She sent me a link to the Salacious kink quiz last week, but I just haven't gotten around to taking it yet. Or maybe I'm dreading it and don't really want to. Something about having to decide what I want feels daunting and uncomfortable.

"I will," I reply softly.

Then she stands, and I feel the weird stomach somersault thing again. She gestures to the drinks on the table. "Take your time. You have full access to the club while you're here as my guest, so don't feel like you have to rush out."

"Okay, thanks," I mutter.

She almost looks reluctant as she starts to leave me. And I can't help but wonder if she's feeling the same twisting feeling in her stomach that I do. It's not that I'm afraid to be in the club without her, but spending the last couple of weeks with Eden hasn't so much given me confidence as it's made me feel codependent on her.

I feel better when she's around. I love every second we're together, and I genuinely look forward to it every other moment of my day.

"I'll be fine," I lie with a fake smile, straightening my spine and curling my hair behind my ear.

"Take that quiz," she says again, and I give her a grinning nod.

Then I watch her walk away.

A moment later, the bartender comes by and offers me another drink. I'm only allowed two, so this will be the last one. Hoping it will ease some of the tension in my gut, I nod.

"Yes, please."

"You got it," he replies, tapping the table and walking away.

By the time he returns with another vodka cranberry on ice, I've downloaded the kink app. I take a long, cold sip before opening the quiz. The first questions are easy.

Age—twenty-three.

Sexual orientation—straight, I guess.

Gender—female.

Then it gets into the more private stuff, and for the most part, it starts out easy. They're all things I know for certain about myself that don't feel too hard to answer.

Then the app literally says: *You are good at making decisions. Agree or disagree.*

"Well, that's just rude," I mumble to myself.

Disagree.

I'm terrible at making decisions. They're easy if the decision is decided for me by someone else…but that's not really a decision, is it?

Do you see sex as a way to please your partner or yourself?

I swipe the app closed. These questions are just hitting a little too close to home.

This quiz will never truly understand me. How can a bunch of questions grasp who I am as a person?

It's like what Eden said—if pleasing my partner pleases me, then we're both getting what we want, right?

But that's not entirely true. I'm always satisfied in bed with Clay. Just the last few times we had sex, I told him what I wanted, and we both ended up with orgasms. And yet here I am…trying to learn how to be better for him.

With an audible huff, I pull out my phone again and go back to the quiz. There are no right answers here. Just be honest.

Both.

Do you like to be dominated in the bedroom? Sometimes.

Would you be open to multiple partners in the bedroom? Maybe.

How do you feel about being watched by others while masturbating or having sex? Neutral.

Okay, I suck at this.

All of my answers feel so boring and indecisive. Am I broken? So I like the idea of being in control and also the idea of being controlled. Doesn't everyone? I suck at making decisions, but I love the idea of knowing exactly what my partner needs and giving that to them. Where is that question?

Life is not black and white, and we don't all fit into neat little prescribed boxes.

If you could not fulfill your partner's desires, would you be open to allowing them to seek that fulfillment with another partner?

My thumb hovers over the options as I read that question once, then twice, then three times. This is what Eden was talking about with her friend, wasn't it? Something about this question makes me feel both relieved and terrified. It seems like such a simple solution—to allow someone else to satisfy my partner if I couldn't.

Then I think about Clay. If I can't be what he needs, how would I feel about him getting that somewhere else? Like with Eden.

The thought burns. Not because he wouldn't be faithful to me, but because...then they would have something without me. I'm not normally so territorial with my partners, but it seems everything is different with Clay.

By the time I reach the end, I've lost complete faith in myself and this quiz. While the results generate, I suck down what's left of my drink.

When the results page says the word *Switch*, I first assume that means I'm supposed to switch answers or life choices. But then I click on the link provided and read up on what these results mean.

Switches prefer to change roles in the bedroom depending on their mood, partner(s), or situation. They enjoy both dominant and submissive roles and often pair well with other switches.

"Well, great," I huff. Even my sex life is unable to make a decision.

Rule #16: You can't run from yourself.

Jade

After finishing the quiz, I pocket my phone and rise from the high-top table. I take my empty glass to the bar and wave at the bartender as I set it down.

The results of my quiz and the conversation with Eden are haunting me as I stand there, deciding my next move. I could go home, maybe call Clay or stop by his place. I haven't seen him today, and I'm starting to feel guilty about that. Something about not telling him about my meetings with Eden feels like lying.

But there's also something holding me here at this club. Eden did say I have full access, and if my homework is to decide what I really like, then there's no harm in taking a look around, maybe down that hallway where we went the other day.

Giving myself a little mental pep talk, I turn from the bar and head toward the voyeur hall instead of the door. To my surprise, no one stops me, gawks at me, or makes me feel weird about this. Even the bouncer pulls aside the curtain for me, ushering me inside.

The hallway is oddly quiet compared to the main room, and

immediately upon entering, I hear the muffled sounds of sex and pleasure. Unlike the last time I was in here, there is more than one room lit up and on display. In fact, every room is active tonight.

To my right, a man is spanking another man over his lap. His ass is marked red as he howls with each slap. I find myself watching them for a few moments, putting myself in each of their shoes. If I'm truly a switch, then I'd enjoy both of those roles, right?

I picture myself as the man in the chair, rubbing the raw, cherry-red flesh of someone's ass before inflicting more pain just to hear them scream. I don't consider myself much of a masochist, but the idea of inflicting pain and holding that control does arouse me in a unique and exciting way. I feel the warmth pooling between my legs as proof.

Then I picture myself as the man in his lap. By the way he's rutting, he's clearly getting off on the scene. The idea of being in trouble and punished is oddly arousing too, and I never realized that before.

After a few moments, I drift away from the men in the first room and slowly pass the second, which is less exciting. A man and a woman are on the bed, and she is riding him with her back turned toward the window.

When I turn around to see the next room, my feet freeze on the floor. I stare in shock as I take in the sight. It's a woman tied like a starfish to a large black platform bed. There's a man sitting in a chair near the corner, half naked and watching as the woman on the bed is practically tortured—with pain or pleasure, I can't tell.

It's the person doing the torturing who has my mouth dry as sandpaper and my heart thumping rapidly in my chest—Eden.

Or, rather, this is truly Madame Kink. She's in black leather, her long black hair pulled into a tight ponytail at the back of her head. She's leaning over the woman strapped to the bed, teasing her with a vibrator between her bare legs. The woman is writhing and crying out as she seems to be getting closer to her climax. Just as she's about to peak, Eden pulls the toy away and squeezes the woman's nipple hard in her fingers.

I watch as Eden leans closer to her, petting her body with her soft hands as her mouth forms the words *good girl*.

My stomach turns, and the arousal I felt a moment ago feels more like sick regret. I have no idea why I'm reacting this way. I've always wanted to watch Eden work, but now…it feels wrong. It feels like…a betrayal, like being cheated on.

Which is stupid. This is her job. It has nothing to do with me. Of course she has other clients. I mean…I asked her to teach me her ways. I never truly hired her to do this. Why would I?

It's not like I can be jealous for not getting something I didn't ask for.

Duh, Jade.

And yet watching her give this woman such precise care and focused attention makes me so…irritable. What is wrong with me?

I definitely need to leave. I need to go straight to Clay's house and be with him because that's where I belong, not standing here watching this woman I barely know edge a complete stranger in a sex club.

If only I could tear my eyes away.

The longer I watch, two things happen.

I get more upset.

And I get more aroused.

I didn't even know you could be both at the same time, but here I am.

My thighs are clenched together so tightly it's creating intense pressure on my clit, and I just keep remembering what she said when she brought me in here the first time.

If you're going to be a people pleaser, then the first person you need to please is yourself.

While Eden continues to torment the woman on the platform, every muscle in my body tightens. She places nipple clamps on her breasts, drags a feather down her body, and drips candle wax along her chest.

My hands are clasped tightly in front of me. Ever so slightly, I slide my fingers between my thighs, squeezing them there to create even more pressure. The thick denim seam of my jeans rubs against my clit, and I grow closer and closer to my climax.

The air grows thick, and it's hard to breathe. I can practically hear my own pulse in my ears. And my body is on fire. It might be the most aroused I've ever felt, even more than watching the blond woman the first day.

Eden is so captivating in her actions. She's like an artist at work, and although the attention she gives this other woman drives me crazy, it's also endearing in a way. Eden cares for her work, which means she cares for every single person who comes to see her. Something about that makes my heart swell. Especially when I momentarily close my eyes, picturing myself on the platform.

Never in my life have I fantasized about being tied up by a woman and brought to the brink of ecstasy over and over, but all of a sudden, it seems to be doing the trick. Especially when the woman holding the power is *her*.

"Please," the woman on the platform cries out, louder this time, and my eyes pop open. Eden smiles wickedly down at her as she says something I can't hear.

"Yellow," the woman calls out.

With a patient nod, Eden sets the vibrator down and strokes the woman's hair. Then she says something to the man in the chair, and with his bottom lip pinched between his teeth, he rises and crosses the room toward them. He's shirtless, with sculpted pecs and ridged abs. Something about watching him bend down and kiss the woman on the lips makes me miss Clay.

I assume she is his girlfriend or wife. He whispers to her, and Eden stands off to the side to watch. Is this what she does for other couples? Like what she said she does for her friend and his wife? Like some hired tool used to spice up their love life?

Why does that annoy me?

It's clearly her choice and her job, but the thought of Eden being used like a pawn for other people's relationships has me fuming and wanting to burst into that room and drag her out.

Who's spicing up *her* relationships? Who's whispering encouraging words in *her* ear? Who's checking up on *her*? Why does she settle for this?

Before I know it, I'm standing in front of the glass, only inches away, far closer than anyone else. And I freeze, the blood draining from my face, when Eden looks up and locks eyes with me.

Can she see me?

I just assumed this glass was like a mirror on one side and a window on the other. But judging by the way she's gazing wide-eyed directly at me, I think I was wrong.

Still sickly aroused and filled with shame, I spin on my heel and practically run out of the voyeur hall. I feel as if I've been caught with my hand in the cookie jar as I dash out to my Jeep, starting it in a rush with trembling fingers. Without much thought at all, I pull onto the main road and completely miss the turn toward my house.

But maybe I did that on purpose. Because soon enough, I'm parked in front of Clay's building.

Sliding the Jeep into park, I sit there and stare straight ahead. Nothing seems to make any sense right now. My heart is confused, but only slightly less confused than my body.

First, I got off thinking about Eden while I was having sex with Clay.

Then I literally started masturbating while watching her pleasure another woman.

What on earth is going on with me? What is my obsession with this woman? That feels like a stupid question. She is walking sex and beauty. Her confidence and perfection are otherworldly. Who wouldn't be attracted to her?

But am *I* attracted to her?

All signs at the moment point to yes.

Does that make me bisexual?

I mean…sure, I kissed a few girls in college, but only when I was drunk. And I occasionally watch a little girl-on-girl porn if the mood strikes, but again…who hasn't?

Okay, fine.

Now that I frame it all that way, it feels pretty obvious. Maybe I am. That's fine.

A bi awakening with Madame Kink surely isn't cause to panic.

However…realizing that I'm secretly seeing a person I'm also wildly attracted to and hiding that from my boyfriend *is* cause to panic. Surely, I can keep things between Eden and me professional and platonic even if the thoughts in my head are less than innocent by far.

But am I cheating? Not in the literal sense, obviously. But part of me still feels guilt, and where there's guilt, there's blame.

When my phone buzzes in my lap, I nearly scream. Fumbling and almost dropping it, I gasp when I see her name on the screen. With shaking hands, I swipe to answer the call.

"Hello?" I stammer.

"Jade," she says calmly. "Are you okay? You ran off and had me concerned."

Don't ramble, Jade. Be cool.

Rubbing my fingers around my forehead, I let out a deep breath.

"Yes…uh…no. I don't know. I just… Something really bothered me about that. Seeing you with them. And I know what you're going to say—it's your job, and I get that. But why do you just let them use you like that? You're so much better than an accessory in other people's relationships. Why…do you always focus on everyone else and not yourself?"

The moment the words leave my mouth, I hear them.

She doesn't respond right away, probably to be sure I'm done with my rambling rant.

"Is this about me…or you?" she asks softly.

"I don't know," I reply, a quiver in my voice. "I just…" My voice trails.

"Listen, Jade. I wish you had stuck around and watched the whole thing. Maybe you'd see that I am happy with my job and I do like helping people. I'm not an accessory. I'm a professional, and I do my job with pride."

"So why am I so upset?" I murmur into the phone.

She doesn't respond for a moment. The line is quiet for too long, which might be why I blurt out something so ridiculous I'm immediately regretful.

"Help us."

"What?" she replies with confusion.

"Help Clay and me. Clearly, you know what he wants better than I do, and I trust you. So if you want to help other couples, then help *us*."

"Jade, I can't do that."

"Why not?" I press, although, deep down, I think I know.

"Because Clay was my client already and—"

"That's exactly why you should," I reply.

"A moment ago, you didn't want me to be an accessory in other people's relationships, and now you're asking me to be one in yours?"

"Yes, and you said this is your job, and you love it, so help *me*."

"Is this really about your relationship with Clay?" she snaps in return, and my brow furrows.

"What is that supposed to mean?"

"If you're so concerned about your relationship with Clay, why are you spending so much time with *me*?"

My lips close, and I fall silent, fighting the tears that are building behind my eyes. I force myself to swallow and take deep breaths through my nose.

"I should go," I mutter into the phone.

"Jade…"

"And you're right. I should stop seeing you."

"Jade," she snaps in desperation.

Before she can say anything else, I hit the red End Call button and drop my phone in my lap. My head hangs back against the seat as my fists clench at my sides.

It hurts, probably more than it should. It hurts to fight with her, be scorned by her, and be mad at her. For reasons I don't understand, she's the last person on earth I want to be mad at.

And I realize she's right. I'm not mad that she helps other couples. I'm seething with jealousy because the only couple I want her to help…is Clay and me.

She says she won't help us because he's a past client, but maybe if *he* asked her.

But how on earth am I going to get him to do that without revealing that I've been seeing her in secret this whole time?

I can't really stop seeing her. I spoke too harshly. I didn't mean it.

I need to see her again, but this time, I want to do it as a couple.

And if she won't do it for me, then maybe she'll do it for him.

Rule #17: Communication is key.

Clay

SHE'S LETTING HIM TOUCH HER. AND JUDGING BY THE SMUG LOOK ON *his face, he thinks that he owns her. Or that he's entitled to some part of her that's private. Some part that belongs to me.*

And she makes him believe it.

Is that how she is with me? Does she make me believe I'm special to her? Do I mean nothing?

I'm more than her client. Our sessions are more than the physical stuff. We haven't even had sex yet, and I've been telling myself it's a sign that what we have means more.

But watching her walk out of her room with some strange man's hand on her back, I feel the gut punch of jealousy. I've known this whole time what she does and who she is, but to see it with my own eyes hits harder than I expected it to.

I watch from the bar, a cold glass gripped tightly between my fingers.

Six weeks. I've been coming here for her *for six weeks now, nearly every other night. I might as well hand her my credit card and the keys to my Audi with how much I've spent just needing to see her. The need to be around her has become almost unbearable.*

I feel like I'm going insane. Every single moment that I'm not with her, I feel myself slipping further and further away from this version of myself that I can actually stand. With her, I can be exactly who I want to be.

I should stop.

It's borderline insanity at this point. Constantly thinking about her, hearing her voice in my head when I'm not with her, stroking my cock every night to some fantasy of her. That is if she lets me. What the fuck has gotten into me?

And it's not just about the dynamic and what we do in that room. It's really become so much more.

I watch from the bar as the man by her side says his goodbyes to her, pressing his lips to her cheek before slipping out of her reach and down the stairs toward the exit. When she spins around for her room, her eyes land on my face.

I watch her expression obsessively, waiting to decipher what it all means. And the only thing I can ascertain from the look on her face now is affection.

The way her mouth turns upward and her eyes crinkle with a smile. When she looks at me, she looks almost happy to see me.

I'm a fool if I believe it.

I quickly down the rest of the vodka in my glass as she approaches.

"You're early," she says as she leans her arms on the bar and gazes into my eyes.

"I didn't know you had a client right before me." My voice is cold and flat. I hate the way I sound—jealous and petty. This isn't me. I'm not this guy.

But with her, everything is out of my control.

"Stop it," she says in a clipped, authoritative manner, as if she's already giving me orders.

"Stop what?" I ask without meeting her gaze. "I'm just having a drink, making an observation."

"Follow me," she says in the same tone. Without even looking at me, she turns on her heel and heads toward her room on the other

side, past the hallway. Part of me actually considers not following her. I've never been obstinate or rebellious with her, at least not since I fully committed. But now, the idea of making my own decisions feels enticing.

I do follow her, of course. Because…I don't know. I'm weak or stupid or head over heels for a woman I can never have. And maybe I'm a masochist who loves to torture himself. It doesn't matter.

When we reach her room, she closes it behind me, and I find myself gazing around the space, looking for signs that he was here before me. There are none.

"Sit," she barks, pointing at the bed. The way she refuses to look at me and snaps her commands without emotion tells me she's angry with me.

I hate that.

So I sit and watch her with my teeth clenched.

"You're clearly feeling insecure today," she says, standing between my open knees and staring down at me. "Do you need me to remind you how good you are?"

My teeth grind even more. I don't want the formalities today. The charade. The performance.

I tear my gaze away, staring straight ahead at the black fabric of her tight dress. "No, Madame."

Her fingers press under my chin, directing my face upward. Before my eyes meet hers, I jerk my face from her touch. My heartbeat becomes rapid, and my breathing is labored.

"Yellow," I mumble as I feel my temper rise.

She immediately backs away, and I hear the hitch in her breath. I just used the safe word, and we haven't even done anything.

"Talk to me," she says softly. "Tell me what you're feeling."

"I'm feeling…" I grit my teeth. "Like none of this is real. Like it's all a bunch of bullshit."

"It's not bullshit," she replies as my eyes flick upward to hers.

"Then what is it?" I ask desperately. When she doesn't answer, I get more irritated. "Fuck this."

I burst up from my seat on the bed and cross the room. "I'm just a client, right? This is your job. I pay you to be here, don't I? So why does the sight of you with someone else drive me insane?"

"Clay..." she says in a pleading tone.

"It's all gone to my head, Eden. I can't do this anymore. I can't stand the thought of feeling something for you if you don't feel it for me."

When I turn back toward her, she's there, and it takes me by surprise. Unexpectedly, she places her hands on either side of my face and stares intensely into my eyes.

Suddenly, it feels as if we're in uncharted territory together.

"Is this okay—"

"Yes," I snap. "I didn't mean to use a safe word. You can touch me."

"But you did use a safe word."

"That was stupid of me," I reply, staring at the floor.

"No, it wasn't. I always want you to use your safe words when you need to. I'm proud of you for saying that."

My head lifts, and I gaze at her. Why do I have to react this way to her? This strange warmth in my chest from the way she said she was proud of me. I hate myself for how much I need that.

"How are you feeling now?" she asks.

"Green," I say, my tone like a surrender.

Slowly, she pulls me to the bed again and climbs onto my lap, straddling my hips on either side. My hands glide up her bare legs and around her lower back. As she settles her weight on my thighs, I feel the air leave my lungs. Her fingers slide over my jaw and around to the nape of my neck.

Being this close to her, I get lost in the intensity of her eyes. I want to crawl inside and wrap myself in the comfort of her body. It's like being drawn to my own death by a siren in the sea.

"I do feel it too, Clay," she says again, this time in a soft whisper.

"Am I just another client to you?"

She hesitates, staring frantically back and forth between my eyes. "I told you. You're mine."

"Who else is yours?" I ask.

Her silent response is a knife to my heart. I don't want to hear what I know is the truth. Right now, I want to pretend the truth doesn't exist.

"It doesn't matter who else is mine," she says firmly. "When you're in this room, there's nothing else that matters. You are mine. You are perfect. You are everything to me. And I don't want to hear another word of insecurity from your mouth."

Before she can say another word or back away from my embrace, I close the distance, capturing her soft lips with mine.

It's our first kiss.

And it changes everything.

Our mouths open together, our tongues colliding as we both devour each other in a ravenous kiss.

Her body melts into mine as it grows more and more passionate, as if we've broken through this dam and we're both being dragged under the surface together.

"Yes, Mother," I drawl into the phone. My feet pound against the treadmill as she carries on, talking about someone I don't even know from her country club. As if I care.

It's late. Past ten, but my mother seems to believe I should be available to her at all hours. Burning calories on the treadmill is the only thing that seems to keep me from going crazy when she calls.

I hear the slur in her voice, and if I could, I'd hang up on her right now.

"And Trina has two grandkids already, and she's only two years older than me."

"Uh-huh," I reply flatly. Of course, she brings up grandkids again.

The more and more she goes on, the more I look for an out or a chance to say, *Okay, Mom. It's past ten o'clock at night. I should go.*

But that chance never comes. So on and on she goes.

Not once does she ask about my work or my life. Or acknowledge me at all.

I don't know why I answer the phone when she calls.

Sweat pours down my spine as I pick up speed on my jog, imagining for a moment I could run away from this conversation. Not only do I have this talk with my mother in my head, but I also can't get the memory of tonight with Eden and Jack out, seeing her as a mother.

There was something comfortable and inviting about being there with both of them. Not only is Jack an amazing kid, but Eden is a wonderful mother. And being there with them felt… right and wrong at the same time.

What does any of this mean?

Just when it feels like I'll never get off the phone with my mother, there's an abrupt pounding coming from the other side of my apartment. I quickly hit Stop on my treadmill.

Someone is banging on my door.

"Mom, I gotta go," I say, interrupting her.

She gives me an offended-sounding huff, but I hang up before she can say anything else.

Grabbing the towel from the treadmill, I drape it around my shoulders as I jog to the living room.

"Clay, it's me." Jade's voice sounds frantic through the door, and I don't hesitate to tear it open. She's standing on the mat outside my door, looking frazzled and upset, like she's been crying.

She rushes into my arms, and I wrap them around her, racking my brain for what might have happened to have her like this.

Did Will find out about us? Would he really make her cry over this?

Is this my fault?

"Baby, what's wrong?" I ask. The idea of Jade being so distressed bothers me more than I expect it to.

"Nothing," she murmurs into my neck. "I just needed to see you. I missed you."

Pulling away from my embrace, she grabs my face and kisses me hungrily.

Normally, I'd be all for it. But something is not right. So I pull away and stare into her eyes. They're bloodshot and puffy.

"Jade, what happened?" I ask, closing the door behind her and pulling her into my apartment.

"I said nothing happened. I just…missed you, and I needed to see you. I'm tired of having to tiptoe around to be together. Why don't we just come clean? We should tell my dad."

My brow furrows as I stare into her eyes, looking for a sign that she's being honest.

"This is about your dad? Did something happen?"

Tearing herself out of my arms, she lets out a huff as she crosses the living room toward my room. "Nothing *happened!*" she shouts.

I can't stand this. Trying to understand what someone else needs when they so explicitly try to hide it from me is exactly why I hate relationships. This cryptic, emotionally charged roller coaster is exhausting, and it has me feeling irritable.

When she notices my demeanor change from patient and worried to frustrated and irritated, she changes her argument.

"Okay, fine. This is about…her," she says, the single word slipping through her lips like a bomb. Because I know exactly who *her* is.

My face falls as my mind reels. Did Jade find out about me seeing her tonight? Not that anything inappropriate happened. Unless you consider acting like a weird pseudo–family unit with an ex-Domme and her kid a form of cheating.

"What about her?" I ask carefully.

Jade runs her hands through her hair. It's normally neatly styled and straight, but tonight, it's a mess. Her bangs are strewn about her forehead.

"I just keep thinking that she's who you want. She's who you need."

My brows pinch inward even farther. Fuck, I never should have told her that. What the hell was I thinking?

"Jade, stop."

Instead, in typical Jade fashion, she keeps spiraling. "I keep imagining you two together, and it's not about the sex, although that bothers me too. All I can think is that I'm *nothing* like her. And I never will be. So am I really enough for you?"

Tears brim in her eyes as I softly mutter, "Jesus Christ."

Then I yank her into my arms and kiss her wet cheeks. Grabbing her face in my hands, I hold her where I can see her, staring into her eyes.

"Stop it. I'm sorry I told you about that. I'm sorry you think I have some ex that you need to live up to. Baby, it was never meant to be anything more than what it was."

"Do you still have feelings for her?" she mumbles, and my heart breaks.

"I never had feelings for her, Jade. I was just a client," I lie.

That is supposed to make her feel better, but instead...she almost looks disappointed, her face contorting in anguish as she buries her face in my neck.

I rub her back, hoping that it is enough to convince her.

She wraps her arms around my waist, holding me tight, and it feels nice. It makes me realize something disheartening—I can't see Eden again. I can't keep doing this to myself or to Jade. It might have been one innocent encounter, but I know in my heart that I was ready for it to be more, and nothing good could possibly come from that.

"I took a quiz," Jade says as she pulls away from my embrace.

"Huh?" I ask, brushing her tear-soaked hair out of her face.

"I found it online. It's like a...kink quiz."

Uh-oh.

"Why did you take that?" I ask the first of many questions I have.

"Because I just wanted to see what it would say," she replies without looking me in the eye.

"And?"

"And…it said I'm a switch? Although I don't know what that even means."

It's like having déjà vu. Eden made me take a quiz like that almost a year ago. I remember the results being as confirming as they were surprising. As if they unlocked secrets I was keeping about myself.

Because my first result was *submissive*.

And my second…was *switch*.

"It means you enjoy being both dominant and—"

"Okay, okay, I get it," she says, cutting me off.

I stroke my hands over her arms. "You're overthinking this. It's okay, Jade. *We* are okay. We're better than okay."

"But…" She stares up at me with hope and innocence in her eyes. "It means I can be what you need. I just need…to learn."

My eyes close on a sigh. "No, Jade."

"Why not?" she pleads.

"Because I've closed the door on that life. I don't want to go back. Yes, it was fun, but what you and I have is better."

She looks down, her chest still moving with her heavy breaths. And I get the sense that she's hiding something from me. Or not saying everything she truly wants to say.

"It's what you want, isn't it?" I ask.

Without looking at me, she shrugs. "Maybe I do. I don't know."

This is the moment when I really want to kiss her lips, quiet this conversation, and carry her to my bed. This is a tempting road I'm not ready to walk down.

Because what if she really wants me to take her to Salacious? What if she tries to be what Eden was and it all turns to shit?

"What if," she mumbles softly, "we had someone to teach me? What if…we didn't have to do it alone?"

I know immediately that she's talking about Eden.

And from that moment, I know…there's no going back.

Rule #18: Never trust a good girl.

Eden

I DON'T KISS CLIENTS.

Random people in the voyeur hall or a date who wins me at the auction, sure.

But not clients. Not like this.

My control is slipping, and that's not good.

But it feels so good.

He feels so good.

His body in my arms. The passion of his kiss.

What is wrong with me?

Before I know it, we're on the bed, and his mouth is leaving marks all over my neck and chest. He wants to claim me, and I'm letting him. In some strange way, I want him to.

My hands reach for the buttons of his shirt, and I tear open each one, hungry for a touch of his skin. I need to feel him. Soon, his shirt is off, and then he's slipping my dress over my shoulders.

"God, I need you," he mutters before taking my mouth in a bruising kiss.

"Yes," I say with a gasp. "I need you too."

Fuck, what am I doing?

I do need him. I'm just realizing how badly I've wanted this and for how long. He's always been different, hasn't he? Something about him has set him apart from the rest. And this hunger is real.

I don't have to understand it to see what's right in front of me.

I want Clay in a way I've never wanted any other client. I'm crossing a professional line and breaking rules, but I don't care.

As he tears down my panties, I let out another moaning gasp. Moisture pools between my legs, and I can't remember the last time I was this turned on. Instantly, his tongue is there, eagerly lapping up the moisture and devouring me as if I belong to him. And not the other way around.

My fingers lace through his hair as I muffle my own cries. Right now, I could scream.

"Fuck me," I say, reaching for him.

Standing up, he rips down the zipper of his pants, and I help him work them down his thighs. His cock stands proudly, a drop of precum waiting at the tip. My tongue darts out as I fold myself forward to suck that single drop from the head of his dick.

He moans loudly, the sound like a shock of arousal to my core. So I pull him down to the bed and climb on top of him. I slather his length with saliva as I ravenously work my mouth up and down his shaft.

Then I move my mouth to his lips and kiss him as he lines himself up with my cunt, pushing my hips down until I'm impaled on him. My cries are desperate, raspy sounds of pleasure and need.

"Fuck yes," I say against his lips.

"Fuck me," he replies.

My hips start grinding in a quick motion. There is no starting slow at this moment. We're too fevered and needy for some relief.

It's wrong of me to fuck him without a condom. Even knowing everyone is regularly tested and I take my pill without fail, this is just how out of control I feel with him. But I have no regrets or fears. I trust him.

But more importantly, I need him.

My fingers are digging into his chest as he takes my hands in his.

I love the way his hands feel clasped in mine. How many men and women have I been with and never before felt these incessant butterflies with the smallest of touches?

As he flips us around so that he's on top, our hands stay clutched together. It brings us closer, and it's a good deal more intimate. Never mind the fact that he's fucking me. It's the way our fingers are intertwined that makes my heart speed up.

His gaze barrels down on me as he pounds between my legs even faster. The passion is palpable. Like a storm we can't escape.

Not that I'd want to.

"I'm not coming until you do," he says through his heavy breathing.

"Fuck me harder." My voice shakes as I cry out.

I can't take my eyes off him. I'm enamored by him. Possibly even obsessed. And I have no idea why. It's as if he was made for me. Perfect in every way, no matter how hard I search for a flaw. I love the way he moves. The sounds he makes. The expression on his face. All of it is so genuine, so real.

Our eyes meet, and I'm immediately swept away down a river of pleasure. My body seizes, and my legs tighten around his hips. The sensation courses through every inch of my body as I cling to him as if I can bring him with me.

Seeing me come makes him come.

His movements slow to an intense pounding as he groans out his release, and I feel his cock shudder inside me.

Our foreheads touch as we gasp the same air. Once we're both spent, he relaxes himself over my body, pressing his lips to mine.

What has gotten into me? What is it about this one that seems to infiltrate every aspect of my life?

My personal rules are being broken, not to mention I've turned down clients for him. If only he knew that man he saw me talking to before was a man I had to refer to another Domme.

Every time I tell myself I need to stop this with Clay, I look into

*his eyes, feel the way he looks right through the facade I've built and
into my soul, and know I'm fucked.*

"Boo." A sweet, familiar voice pops up in my left ear, tearing me
away from the memory I've been replaying in my mind like a
movie reel.

Charlotte smiles at me as she takes the empty stool at the table
where I'm sitting.

"Oh, hey," I mumble.

"Am I bothering you?" she asks with concern.

"No," I reply with a shake of my head. "I was just thinking."

"A penny for your thoughts…"

Charlotte, or *Charlie*, and I have been friends for three years
now, but like every relationship I've cultivated here at the club, it's
remained impersonal, mostly due to the fact that I keep it that way.
As far as everyone here is concerned, I have no life outside the club.
I only exist within this space as Madame Kink, and that's it.

In Charlie's case, it's not for lack of trying.

"Oh…just thinking about work stuff," I answer nonchalantly.
It's not a complete lie. Jade and Clay and the mess I've gotten
myself into with them are still technically considered work. Jade
is my mentee, and Clay is an ex-client.

"Anything I can help with?" she asks.

With a tight-lipped smile, I shake my head. "Not really.
Thanks, though."

Then she leans toward me. "This wouldn't happen to have
anything to do with that new little protégé I've been seeing you
with, would it?"

I have to force my face not to give me away as my heart rate
picks up speed. How obvious have my actions been that everyone
suddenly notices my every move around here? Mia noticed how
much I was with Clay, and now Charlie has noticed me with Jade.
What is wrong with me?

"I don't have a protégé," I lie confidently.

Charlotte rolls her eyes. "Come on, Eden. I've seen the way that girl follows you around. If she's not your protégé, then she obviously wants to be."

"She's just a client." *More lies.*

"Whatever you say," she replies. It's quiet for only a moment before she speaks again. "You know…on the opening night of this club, when Emerson brought me here, I felt so out of place. Salacious might as well have been another planet with how foreign it was to me. But on that night, I met you. And it was *you* who made me believe that this club was built for me as much as anyone else. *You* were the one to make me feel welcome. You make everyone feel welcome."

My gaze lifts from my hands to her face. I remember that night very well. I had been on board with the owners before the club even opened. I put in so much of my own input and ideas, hoping they would listen. At one point, I felt in over my head, too.

"I guess I'm just saying…you inspire people, even if you don't mean to."

My eyes narrow as I stare at her. Suddenly, I can't help but feel as if I'm being played. Charlotte has a motive, and I'm willing to bet it has to do with that job her husband has been pressuring me to take.

"Did your husband put you up to this?"

She bites her bottom lip and rests her chin in her hands, giving me an innocent expression—a *fake* innocent expression.

"No…" she replies, batting her lashes. "But my Dom did."

At that, I roll my eyes. "I knew it. He sent you here to talk me into taking the job, I assume."

She shrugs. "Maybe."

"Traitor," I jab.

After another laugh, she straightens her posture and gives me a sincere look. "Seriously, though. Emerson didn't have to tell me to talk to you. I would have anyway."

I lift my gaze to her face again and place my folded hands on the tabletop. "Well, then go ahead, I guess."

She doesn't miss a beat. "You should have been running this place all along." She says it so matter-of-factly as if she's not backhandedly insulting her husband at the same time. But I don't let the compliment sink in. Because it doesn't matter.

"I'm going to tell Emerson you said that," I reply sarcastically.

"Go ahead. He agrees with me."

"Who says I even want to?" I ask, rerouting to a different defense.

"You do," she argues.

"How so?"

"You're here almost every night. You come to every event. You know every single member, and you raise hell every time something goes even the slightest bit wrong. There's hardly a decision made around here without *your* input. You're practically already running this place, Eden. Emerson is just offering you proper compensation and recognition for the job you're *already* doing."

My lips press together tightly as I look away.

"Emerson Grant always has to be the hero, doesn't he?" I mutter loud enough for her to hear.

She giggles at that but doesn't respond. I'm right, of course.

"And I don't know *every* member," I add.

"Will you please just take the job?" she begs. "He's already created the position. We met with the accountant this morning, and everything is in place."

My eyes widen as I stare at her in shock. "He did?"

"Yes, but it's only for you. He won't hire anyone else."

"You're manipulating me into taking this job. You realize that, right?"

"So that's a yes?" she asks with a beaming smile.

"It's a *maybe*."

"Good enough for me."

"I hope your Dom is proud," I reply.

Again, she bats her eyes at me. "I'm nothing if not a good girl."

I scoff at that, shoving her on the shoulder. "What would happen if you didn't do exactly what Daddy Emerson says all the time? Maybe a little punishment would do you good. If he's not up for the task, I'd be happy to do it."

With a smile, she leans in, popping a kiss on my cheek before whispering, "Never." I laugh as she bounces away.

I can't really take that job. I love their persistence and how much they clearly value me here, but I can't possibly be away from Jack more than I already am. It's not their fault that they don't know how much I have at stake.

I'm so lost in my thoughts that I nearly jump out of my seat when Charlotte returns, her excitable voice in my ear. "Oh, by the way, you have a friend at the bar downstairs."

My spine straightens, and I turn toward her with wide eyes. Before I can ask who it is, she's rushing away again. From the second-level VIP bar, I can't see the bar downstairs, so I don't know if this *friend* is male or female—Clay or Jade.

I haven't spoken to either of them in days. I've been working on my apology to Jade for the way we ended our last session and what I said to her on the phone, but I can't seem to bring myself to make the call.

I never intended for her to see me with that couple in the voyeur hall, but it never should have mattered. Jade and I are not intimate. There is no relationship between us, so why would I care if she did? It's just the way she spoke to me on the phone that dug its way under my skin.

I'm *not* ashamed of what I do with couples here at the club. And I *don't* feel like an accessory in other people's relationships. Everything I've done here has been *my* choice.

And I haven't spoken to Clay either. That night with him and Jack was good—too good. But I'm embarrassed for ever asking him to come. It was a weak moment and broke one of my cardinal rules. And I *don't* break my rules.

At least, I didn't…until they came along.

"Fuck," I mutter to myself, rubbing my forehead and mentally preparing myself to face one of them.

How the fuck did I get so entangled in this couple's relationship?

And how the hell do I get myself out of it?

Rising from my stool, I make my way down the stairs toward the main level. With my fingers gliding softly along the banister, I let my eyes cascade over the crowd tonight, trying not to look too eager or desperate.

When they land on a muted blue suit and long brown locks, my breath hitches in my chest. I watch his hand lift the glass with his usual gin and tonic toward his lips, and I'm shaken by his presence as if it's the first time I've seen him in six months. Even though it's not.

I just saw Clay last weekend.

But sex club Clay and real-life Clay are two different people, and seeing him here is like having the air punched out of my lungs.

My heels click against the floor as I make my way toward him. I'm rushing like someone might beat me to him. The mere thought of someone else taking him into a room makes my stomach clench and my blood boil.

As if he can sense my approach, he turns toward me, our eyes meeting just before I touch his arm.

"What are you doing here?" I ask, sounding far too possessive for my own comfort.

"Relax. I'm just here to talk to you," he answers with a harsh bite in his tone.

I lean in closer until our faces are only inches apart. "There is absolutely no talk of *him* here, understand?"

He knows instantly that I'm talking about Jack. There is no

mention of my son at the club. His gaze burns with intensity as he subtly nods in agreement.

Turning on my heel, I start toward the stairs again, expecting him to follow. When I don't feel him behind me, I stop and glance back.

He hasn't moved from his spot at the bar-top table.

"I can't be in a room alone with you," he mumbles quietly as I return to where he's standing. "I have a girlfriend now."

I force myself to swallow as I stare into his eyes, suddenly realizing that he has no idea how many times I've had his girlfriend in a room alone with me in the past few weeks.

I also realize just how little he trusts himself with me, and that thought makes me ache with both regret and hope.

"Fine. We'll talk here," I reply, taking the stool across from him. "What is this about?"

I seem annoyed, and I don't mean to. But I *am* annoyed. Maybe not annoyed with him, but with the whole situation. I'm annoyed that I feel so much with this one man, this one *client*. I'm annoyed that I'm entangled in his relationship and that he's become a part of my son's life, even in the smallest way. More than anything, I wish I could go back to that night one year ago and never strike up a conversation with a certain young, cocky suit at the bar.

No, I don't.

He clears his throat and shifts in his spot, tugging on the collar of his shirt. "You owe me," he says with conviction.

I flinch, my brow furrowing as I stare at him in confusion. "Excuse me?"

Leaning in, he wraps his hand around my arm before catching himself and letting go. "You ruined me, Eden. You've made it impossible to move on, and I asked you to tell me to stay gone, and you wouldn't. So then you gave me hope, and that was unfair."

"Clay, I'm not responsible for—"

"And after all of that, I *helped* you," he says. He's staring point-blank into my eyes, and my argument slips from my lips. "So now you owe me."

Everything is so simple to him, like everything has a value that can be traded and paid for. It doesn't work like that.

"What do you want?" I ask softly, both hesitant and excited to hear what he has in mind.

His lips close, and he eases backward. As his eyes cast downward, he speaks as if hesitant to admit something. And when the words finally leave his lips, I realize why. Because his favor isn't a favor at all—it's insanity.

With a rasp in his voice, just above a whisper, he mumbles, "My girlfriend wants to watch us."

Rule #19: Be honest with your Domme—even when it hurts.

Clay

SHE'S STARING AT ME LIKE I JUST SUGGESTED SOMETHING UNFATH-omable.

Because I did.

And I know how it sounds. I had the same reaction when Jade asked me. And I'm pretty sure even *she* thought it was crazy, but let's be real. This is one of those things none of us can deny.

Eden ruined me. Jade loves me. And I'm clearly so fucked that I need this to make it work.

Because I'm out of ideas.

"I'm sorry…what?" Eden stammers, leaning forward. Her fingers, with their matte-black nails, are clutched so tightly around her forearm she's leaving marks.

"I don't mean…watch us have sex," I say begrudgingly. Even the mention of sex with Eden dredges up old hurtful memories. "I just mean…she wants to watch the way we were together. Before the sex."

The tight grip on her arm softens, and she leans back a little. "She wants me to demonstrate my dominance over you for educational purposes."

I hate when she talks like that. She makes it all sound so impersonal and formal, but it was never like that at all, at least not for me.

"Sure, whatever," I mumble.

She glances around the room hesitantly. "Is she here?"

"No," I answer quickly. "And I'd really rather not bring her here."

Her brow pinches inward as she stares across the table at me. "You sound ashamed of this place," she says. "She would be safe here, you know."

"I'm not ashamed of this place," I reply. "I just don't want her coming here."

"She's an adult, Clay. That's really not up to you."

"It has nothing to do with shame," I reply through gritted teeth.

"Then what is it?"

"Forget about it," I argue.

"This is where I work, Clay. You can't just—"

"I don't want her here because this was *our* place, okay?" I say, finally meeting her gaze with my own. That shuts her up. "But I guess if there is no more *us* and she's about to watch us together, then it really doesn't matter anymore, does it?"

She scoffs. "I never agreed to this."

As we stare at each other for a moment, it all feels so intense I have to look away. What happened to us? There was a point in the last year when I felt closer to her than I ever felt to anyone in my life. Now, it just feels…broken.

"Please," I say under my breath.

"You can't really be serious, Clay," she replies harshly.

When I glance up, I see softness in her eyes.

"Is the thought of being with me again so bad?" I ask, not bothering to hide the pain.

"You know that's not it," she says, leaning close enough for me to smell her perfume.

Being with her like this is nothing like being with her outside the club or even in bed when it was just the two of us. Right now, she's Madame Kink. Her face is caked with makeup. Her hair is immaculately straight and neat. There isn't a strand out of place.

But I like the real person. The woman with eyes so green and intense she's even more beautiful without the full lashes and thick eyeliner. I like the woman who lets her hair fall naturally to the sides, small little flyaway wisps framing her face like a halo.

"Then what is it?" I ask, leaning even closer. We're playing with fire. Fuck, this whole idea is more than playing with fire. It's walking directly into an inferno and expecting to come out of it alive.

"I think you know," she whispers.

"I don't think I do, so why don't you spell it out for me?"

I'm toying with her, I know. But the version of me that used to make things easy for her is gone. I want to hear her say exactly what I *know* she's afraid to say. I want her to admit that being with me again would be too *good*, not bad.

"I just don't think you and I working together like that is a good idea anymore."

She never could be honest. That was always the problem with her. She's a liar. Or rather…the persona she puts forth is a lie. And for someone who always preached about honesty, that's infuriating. The truth of who Eden really is has always been a well-kept secret. And she'd rather lie to everyone in her life than be real for even one second.

"One time, Eden. Give Jade this *one* time, and I'll be gone. Whether you tell me to or not, I won't come back. I won't bother you, and I won't ask you for ridiculous favors anymore."

"Do you really think you can do that after we share another time together?"

"I've done it before," I reply. I hope she sees the hurt on my face. If I could make myself bleed for her, I would. Not that it would make a difference. She'd still walk away.

"Besides," I add. "I'll have Jade, so hopefully, I won't miss you as much."

I wish I could say the pain in the subtleties of her expression feels good to see, but it doesn't. No matter how much anguish she's caused me, I can't seem to find joy in bringing her the same. I hate this. I hate hurting each other, but it feels inevitable. Our love had to go somewhere when the fire went out. It just turned into anger.

"One time," she mutters coldly, her vivid green eyes on my face. "I'll teach her whatever she wants to know, and then we have to be done."

"Thank you," I say, adjusting my tie. This suit is constricting, and I want nothing more than to tear it off and feel the cool air on my neck. She has me feeling hot and irritated. The sooner I get this over with, the sooner I can leave.

"I'm free next weekend," she says, but I quickly shake my head.

"I can't wait that long."

"Fine. Tomorrow night at eleven."

I force myself to swallow. "Where?"

"Here," she replies. "I need to know your limits and expectations. You still have those forms?"

"I still have them," I say. "And the limits are the same as before."

"But you said no sex," she replies, causing my eyes to snap back up to her face. I did say there would be no sex, but we both know I didn't say that on my forms when I first started seeing her. I was *very* open to sex then.

So what about now?

Jade wouldn't want to see that.

"Let me talk to her first," I say, and Eden gives a tense nod. For someone who always exudes so much confidence, she looks very unsettled tonight.

"And I'll send the payment the same as before," I add, which has her wincing.

"No payment. Not for this."

So it's personal, then. I don't say that out loud, but we're both thinking it. And I'm not sure how that makes me feel. I sort of expected her to treat it like a job.

"Tomorrow at eleven, then." As I step away from the high-top table, I feel her eyes on me. But I don't feel safe looking into them just yet. Especially as I add, "Oh, but I'll see you in the morning first."

She pauses and stares at me with a questioning look. "Morning?"

"For the baseball game," I reply, knowing full well that I'm bringing up something I shouldn't. Her jaw tightens, and her chin lifts in defiance.

"That won't be necessary."

"He invited me," I say. "And I don't think either of us wants to let him down."

She can't argue with that, so without another word, she lets out a heavy sigh and turns her back to me. As I watch her walk away, I try to force myself to be mad at her. I even try to hate her. But it's useless. It's probably about time I accept my fate. I may never stop loving her.

———————

"Too tight?" she whispers in my ear from behind.

My arms are bound behind my back with a thick rope that makes my skin itch and my fingers pulse with pressure. But I don't complain. I'm here with her. How could I be uncomfortable?

Instead, I shake my head. "No, Madame."

"I'm going to have you bending over, and the ropes may tighten, so I need you to tell me if you feel any pain or numbness."

"Yes, Madame."

"Good boy," she replies, licking a line across my cheek that makes my dick twitch where it hangs between my thighs. "Now kneel."

I do as she says while she continues binding the rope across my torso in intricate knots. Every little touch of her fingers on my skin takes me to a place where I feel calm and at peace. The more she tightens the rope, the further I fall into my euphoria.

It's never been so easy with another person before. And sometimes I worry that I'm being lazy with her. I'm used to being the one in charge, the protector, the leader, the dominant. But with her, I do what she tells me to and eat up her praise. She's so easy to please that I can't get enough.

And then, if I'm really good, she rewards me with little nuggets of intimacy that feel more special than an orgasm or some words of affirmation. She lets me in. Now being in her life is the only reward I'm interested in.

I just want her.

She works in silence as she continues to tie me up, folding me until I'm bent over and bound. Soon I can't move anything. I'm not sure of the point of this, except that it might be a test of discipline—a test I'll pass. My fingers are numb now, and my shoulder is aching, but I can take it.

"You look beautiful like this," she says, softly running her fingers down my curled spine. I don't respond, but then again, I've never been called beautiful before. It feels foreign and strange.

Coming from her, I love it.

As her fingers reach the base of my spine, where I know I'm exposed in this position, I clench up. My eyes pop open, and my heart beats faster. I know I say I'm down for her to do whatever she wants to me, but some things are still too new for me.

"I'd love to fuck you like this," she says, teasing her touch around my lower back and over the soft globes of my ass.

I force a laugh. "Fuck me?" I'm breaking the yes-Madame-no-Madame rule right now, but she doesn't seem to mind.

"Only if that's something you'd be interested in trying."

"Is that what you want?" I ask, and her touch stops.

"Yes, I would."

"Why?" I ask with genuine curiosity. What the hell is in it for her?

"You fuck me all the time. Any act of penetration requires a certain level of trust. You trust me, don't you?"

"Yes, of course."

"Good. Not to mention, I get off on the idea of making you feel good. And I think you would feel really, really good."

My cock twitches again. I try to imagine it, feeling her take control like that, fucking me like the roles are reversed, but I still can't quite picture it.

"Well, if you're fucking me, then who's fucking you?" I ask. My voice is low and level. With my face pressed against the top of my knees, I have to relax into the binds instead of fighting against them.

"That's the point, pet," she whispers in my ear. "I think about fucking you all the time. I think you'd be such a good boy for me, and I think you'd come so hard you'd beg me to do it again."

I let out a groan as my cock hardens to the point of pain. There isn't much room for it, but the more I shift, the more friction it gets. "Yes, please, Madame," I say with a moan.

"You want me to fuck you, pet?" she asks in a sultry, teasing tone.

I smile against my thigh. "Yes, Madame."

"Then say it."

"I want you to fuck me, Madame," I say with a gentle rasp in my voice.

She lets out a sweet little laugh. Then I feel her lips against my back. Her fingers rake through my hair and down my spine. Her touch is loving, and it distracts me from the now sharp pain shooting up my arm.

"You're so perfect," she says, this time with more sincerity than the dirty talk. When she says things like this to me, I believe it. "So perfect and all mine."

"I'm yours," I reply. This is the easy part. If people in my real life knew what I was doing here every night, they'd think I was crazy, but I stopped caring about that. Why would I care when everything here feels so fucking good?

The moment is tender and quiet for a while. It feels like fifteen minutes go by until I feel her jerking on the ropes tied around my right arm. The pain intensifies, and I realize my entire arm has gone numb. "Your hand is turning blue. Does it hurt?"

"I'm fine," *I reply calmly.*

"Answer the question, Clay. Does this hand hurt?"

"I can take it, Madame."

"Dammit, Clay," *she snaps in a frantic, angry tone.*

The calm moment is gone, and now she's quickly pulling and untying the knots around my legs and torso until she finally loosens the ones cascading up my arms. The minute she does, it's like needles pulsing their way down from my shoulder to my fingers. I immediately wince in pain.

"I told you to tell me if it hurts," *she barks. She's kneeling in front of me now, rubbing my hand, even though it aches the way it does when your limb is waking up and every touch is like a stabbing pain.* "Do you have feeling in your fingers?"

"Yes..." *I stammer, trying to wiggle them. The tingling is intense and throbbing, but I try to hide it.*

"You could suffer serious nerve damage, Clay. You have to tell me when it hurts like that."

"I'm fine, Eden."

Her head snaps up, and she glares into my eyes with animosity. "Why do you do that?" *she asks.*

"Do what?"

"Try to be tough for me. Put yourself through pain just because you think it pleases me? I don't want to hurt you, Clay. I never want to really hurt you, and I need to trust that you'll be honest with me so that I never do. Do you understand? It's not about you being tough and manly for me. We can't do this if I can't trust you. We have to be honest with each other."

She's clearly upset, her eyes wide and filled with fear. Shaking off the rope, I wrap my arms around her and pull her against me.

"I'm sorry," *I whisper into her neck.* "I'm okay. I promise. I'll tell you next time. You can trust me."

"*This is all built on trust, Clay. If we don't have that, we don't have anything.*"

Pulling away, I take her by the shoulders and stare into her eyes. "*You can trust me.*"

After she slowly calms down, I notice the way she catches herself. I think she took herself by surprise with her panicked reaction. I guess it's good to know I'm not the only one thrown off by this relationship of ours.

"*I just don't want to hurt you,*" she says carefully, inspecting my hands again.

Leaning forward, I press my forehead to hers. "*You could never hurt me.*"

Rule #20: Let them in.

Eden

JACK IS STANDING AT THE PLATE, LOOKING FAR TOO SMALL, AS THE coach slowly lobs a baseball toward him. With his tiny hands clutched tightly around the bat, he swings so hard it nearly knocks him off his feet. The ball lands in the dirt behind him, hitting the fence with a soft crash.

"That's okay, bud!" Clay cheers from beside me. "Choke up on the bat a little."

Jack turns toward us, his helmet too big for his head as it falls over his eyes. After adjusting it, he smiles at Clay and moves his little grip higher up on the bat.

"That's it. Good job. Now keep your eye on the ball."

Jack nods obediently to Clay and then smiles at me. I give him an encouraging expression before he turns back toward the plate with renewed confidence.

On the next pitch, he swings and makes a resounding impact with the ball, sending it flying toward the coach, who quickly dodges with a high jump before it can knock him on the shins. Every parent in the stands around us starts to cheer, and it takes

Jack a few moments before he realizes he's supposed to start running.

"Go, buddy!" I scream as I bounce on my feet, clapping with a wide grin.

He takes off in a sprint toward first base and lands on the white square with a proud hop. When he turns toward us, he's pumping his fists in the air. Clay and I are still cheering as if he just won the whole game with that one play.

"Nice hit, Jack!" Clay cheers.

I risk a glance in Clay's direction, feeling the sting of attraction when I see the wide, handsome smile on his face. It's not the same man who came to the club last night. Today, he's in a tight black T-shirt, dark-gray joggers, and crisp white sneakers. His hair is hidden in a ball cap, and while I've always considered myself a lover of expensive suits, this casual look on him has me feeling surprisingly feral.

His appearance isn't the only difference from last night. When he showed up this morning, he greeted me with a smile—a stark contrast from the scowl or pure avoidance I received at the club the night before.

We haven't spoken a word about what our plan is for tonight, and we won't. Not here. He knows that much. For now, I'd like to pretend I didn't agree to this plan and that there's nothing happening tonight.

"He's doing great," Clay says as we sit down at the end of the inning. Jack was able to score a run for his team when the girl who batted after him hit the ball clear into the outfield.

"He really likes playing," I reply warmly.

"It shows."

We don't look at each other as we talk, but it's easy like this. It's like nothing happened at all.

"Did you play…when you were a kid?" I ask, daring to request something personal.

He clears his throat. "Yeah. All the way up to college. Then I tore my ACL, and it was all over."

Delicately, I glance up at him. Our eyes meet for only a second before we quickly look away.

"I'm sorry," I mumble. "About your knee."

He shrugs. "It's okay. I wasn't going pro or anything. I just liked to play."

How did I never know how long he played baseball? While I feel like we shared so much about ourselves before, I'm starting to wonder how real any of it was.

"Thank you for coming," I mumble quietly.

"Anytime. He's a good kid."

I nod as I smile at Jack, watching him laughing with the other kids in the dugout.

It's only quiet for a few moments before Clay asks the question that steals the smile right off my face.

"Where's his father, Eden?"

I feel frozen as I stare straight ahead.

"He's out of the picture," I reply in a whisper.

"Does he know about Jack?"

I turn my head toward him, meeting his curious gaze with a cold glare. This topic is off-limits. Doesn't he know that?

Instead of backing down, he leans closer so none of the other parents around us can hear. "I'm part of his life now, Eden. Can't you see I care about him? Does that entitle me to anything?"

"No," I reply sternly. "It doesn't." Feeling suddenly caged in, I jump up from my seat on the bleachers and walk down to the grass and around the back toward the side of the field. Clay is right behind me the entire way.

"That's right. It's always on *your* terms, isn't it?" he replies, sounding annoyed and wearing a sarcastic smirk.

"When it comes to my son, it is," I snap in return.

"Because you love him, right?"

My brow furrows. "Of course."

"That's why you protect him."

"What are you getting at?" I ask, spinning toward him and waiting for him to make a point.

Then he leans even closer so he's practically whispering in my ear. "I'm just trying to understand why you push me away all the time, Eden. Because all I want is to protect and take care of you too. The fact that Jack's father isn't here when I am—"

"He's dead. His father is dead."

His lips part as he stares at me in surprise, his face only inches from mine. "I had no idea…"

"It doesn't matter," I reply. "He wouldn't have been here even if he were alive."

"Does Jack know?"

Before I can muster a response, there's a cheer coming from the field, and I turn to see that the game has ended. Jack is running toward us with a beaming smile.

Clay shakes off his serious expression and turns to my son with excitement.

"You came!" Jack squeals as he barrels into Clay's arms, and Clay hoists him off the ground with a laugh.

"Of course I came. You asked me to."

"Did you see my hit?" Jack asks.

"Dude, that line drive was sick," Clay replies, which makes Jack laugh.

It's the first time I'm not the first person Jack runs to after a game. It doesn't hurt as much as I expected it to. Instead, I relish the smile on his face and how comfortable he is with Clay.

After he gives Clay a high five, he turns toward me and hugs my legs the way he often does. I ruffle his hair affectionately.

"You hungry?" I ask.

"Yeah, can we get cheeseburgers? Clay, you want cheeseburgers?"

My eyes snap up to Clay's, and he looks momentarily taken aback. "Well…I have plans to meet up with Jade."

"Is Jade your girlfriend?" Jack asks.

I can't tear my gaze away as Clay nods. "Yeah, she is."

"Does she like cheeseburgers?"

"Umm…" Clay looks at me, and I realize he's waiting for my approval. I could easily shake my head and stop this whole thing. But the thought of seeing Jade in an environment outside the club is appealing to me, and given the opportunity to mend what I broke between us, I can't turn it down.

So I give him a quick nod.

He turns toward Jack with a smile. "Dude, she fucking loves cheeseburgers."

This makes Jack laugh and slap his hand over his mouth. I level a tilted glare at Clay as he grins contritely.

"Sorry."

Then the three of us walk together toward the parking lot, and I know this is probably a very bad idea. One more person to get my son attached to is dangerous, but I'm too anxious to see her to care.

An hour later, we're standing in the parking lot of a burger place in town. Jade climbs out of her red Jeep and approaches us with a warm smile.

It's only awkward for a second as Clay introduces us like we don't know each other. Jade stares at me timidly as I reach my hand out to shake hers.

"Nice to meet you," I say.

We haven't spoken since she hung up on me the other night for saying the awful things I said.

She doesn't look like she's still mad at me, though. In fact, she almost looks oddly excited. In her typical Jade demeanor, she chews on her lip and stares at me for guidance. I glance down at my outstretched hand before she gets the hint and plays along.

"Nice to meet you," she replies before shaking it. In a daring move, I shoot her a quick wink, which makes her smirk to herself.

That's a good sign she's no longer angry at me. Until I get a chance to talk to her alone, I won't know for sure, but it's enough for now.

"And this is Jack," Clay adds proudly. I don't miss the way he holds a hand on my son's shoulder as if he's *his*. The thought sends a warm wave of affection through my chest, and it's so foreign I wish I could bottle it and hold on to it forever.

Jade immediately kneels so she's on his level. "Hey, Jack," she says. "I like your baseball uniform."

"Thanks, I got a hit today."

"Shut up," she replies, feigning shock. "Did anyone get that on camera?" She looks up at me and Clay, but we both shake our heads. Then she turns back toward my son. "Next time, I'll come, and I'll make sure to record all of your hits."

Jack giggles. "Thanks."

The four of us find a table inside Jack's favorite burger place. Then Clay goes up to the counter by himself to order our lunch, and Jack quickly trails along as if he can't stand to be away from Clay for one second.

There's nothing wrong with him having a friend, I think to myself. It doesn't need to be anything more than that.

When Jade and I are left alone at our table, I don't waste a second. "Jade, I'm sorry," I mumble quietly.

"Don't," she replies, stopping me. "It doesn't matter."

"Yes, it does. It was incredibly unprofessional of me, and I apologize."

She turns toward the boys in the line on the other side of the restaurant. Then she turns back toward me. "Thank you."

Only allowing for one second of awkward silence, she immediately starts in with her rambling. "This is weird, though, right? I feel a little bad that he had to introduce us like we don't already know each other. I mean, what's going to happen tonight? We still have to act like we barely know each other. It feels wrong, but at the same time, it's not like we did anything inappropriate."

When I hold up my hand to stop her rambling, she doesn't.

"Thank you for agreeing to tonight, by the way. I know I should have come to you, but I thought you were mad at me, and I figured if he asked, you might be more inclined to say yes."

"Jade, stop," I say, stifling a laugh. "We don't need to talk about that here. In fact, when we're not at the club, we don't talk about club stuff."

"Oh," she replies, sitting back in her chair. "Then what should we talk about?"

I bite my lower lip to keep from smiling. Before I can even respond, she starts in again.

"You look different, you know, outside the club. Better, if you ask me," she says.

I feel a blush rise to my cheeks, which is abnormal for me. "Thank you, I think."

We both laugh a little. "You look good, too," I say, although she looks exactly the same as she does when she comes into the club. She's in a steel-blue one-piece jumper with a thin bralette underneath. It's both adorable and sexy at the same time in an effortless way that only Jade can manage. As I let my eyes cascade over her petite shoulders and down to her nimble fingers, I try to act as casual as possible.

My only female friends are the women at the club, and our friendship is hardly conventional. I'm not an idiot, so I understand why it's suddenly so hard for me to act normal around Jade. I just can't let *her* know that. It doesn't matter how much I want Jade. She's Clay's, and that's not going to change. So I avert my eyes and let her ramble on without saying a word myself.

When Clay and Jack return a few minutes later, they have their hands full with milkshakes, fries, and a tray of burgers. As they sit down, the four of us dig in, enjoying easy conversation and effortless laughter. I know it should worry me how easily I'm breaking more of my rules for them, but for some reason, it doesn't.

Rule #21: Always do the paperwork.

Jade

I'd be lying if I said I wasn't nervous. Of course I am. Who wouldn't be?

I'm about to watch the man I love with another woman. And I asked for this.

"Jade, you have to be really specific about what you want."

"Ugh," I groan as I flop back on his bed, letting my head hit the pillow. The form he gave me to fill out falls to the side. "This is too hard."

"Then maybe we should cancel," he replies softly.

My eyes widen. "What? No!"

He pulls my arm until I'm sitting up again. Then he places the form back in my lap. "Then fill it out."

I tap the pen on the paper as I chew my inner lip. After lunch with Eden and Jack, Clay and I came back to his apartment because he said we needed to talk about tonight. He seems tense, and I understand why. But he agreed to this with very little hesitation. In fact, I expected more of a fight when I brought it up.

Then he texted me this morning to let me know we'd be

having lunch with Eden and her son. He told me he had been invited to her son's baseball game.

Did I find it a little strange that he's suddenly building a relationship with his ex-Domme's seven-year-old son? Yes.

Did I ignore the red flags because I was excited to see her again? Yes, like an idiot.

Do I have any room to talk since I've been seeing her in private for weeks? Nope.

If he were going to cheat on me with her, he wouldn't have invited me to join them or let me watch them together tonight.

Which brings me back to our current dilemma—what am I comfortable with them doing tonight?

The whole reason we're doing this is so I can see exactly what she does for Clay so I can learn to do the same. There's nothing weird or wrong about that. If anything, it sounds completely healthy and normal.

But if I asked them to fuck in front of me...

That's *not* normal, right?

I mean, why would I even ask them to do that?

"Earth to Jade..."

I'm staring down at the form, completely lost in my head, when he touches the spot under my chin and lifts it until our eyes meet. My bottom lip is rolled between my teeth as he notices my apprehension.

"Do you want to cancel?" he asks.

"If you ask me that one more time..." I reply.

"Well, you seem nervous. I want to make sure this won't affect *us* in a bad way."

"It won't," I reply, tilting my head to the side. "It's going to help us."

"Would it be easier if you just tell me what you want us to do instead of having to fill out that form?" he asks. His eyes are soft and kind. His brows are lifted as he leans forward to press a kiss to my lips.

I screw up my face as I think about his question. "Honestly, no. I just need to think this through."

"How about this?" Without warning, he yanks my legs until I'm reclined, my back against the headboard. Then he stretches out on his stomach in front of me. "I'll kiss my way up your body for every question you answer."

Then he presses his lips to my ankle, and I can't fight the ear-to-ear smile on my face.

"That would be very distracting and not helpful to my thought process at all." Still, I can't help the giggle that escapes my lips as he teases his way up to my calf.

"Are you sure?"

Doing my best to play along, I stare down at the form. It's a questionnaire that she apparently gives to couples who come in to see her. Clay said it's best if I fill it out first and then we talk about it. This means I now have to decide exactly how much I'm comfortable watching my boyfriend do with another woman.

Most of the questions are easy. Ranked from *Desired* to *Off-Limits,* there's a list of activities I have to decide whether I would like to see Clay and Eden do.

Domination—Desired.

Impact play—Desired.

Restraint—Desired.

Nudity…blank.

Humiliation…blank.

Degradation…oh, Desired. Is that bad?

Praise…Desired.

Penetration, which is a somewhat impersonal way of saying sex… blank.

Oral sex…blank.

"I don't see you ranking…" Clay teases, hovering his lips over my inner thigh.

"Okay, okay, I'm on it," I say with a whine as I quickly circle *Desired* on more than one of these items. When he sees me circle another, he presses a kiss right in the center of my panties. Warmth cascades down my spine as I bite my lip excitedly.

Just as he hooks his fingers under the elastic to pull them down, his phone rings. We both glance at the phone on the nightstand at the same time. Part of me worries it's Eden calling to cancel on us tonight.

Instead, his mother's name appears on the screen.

I can't help but notice the way the light in Clay's eyes diminishes the moment he sees it too. With a heavy sigh, he lifts himself off the bed.

"You keep working on that. I'll be right back."

"Okay," I mumble quietly as he picks up his phone and walks out of the room.

"Hi, Mom," he mutters from the hallway. His voice carries until he's in the living room, and I can no longer make out what he's saying.

Clay doesn't talk about his family much. He mentioned that his parents both grew up wealthy and so did he. He dismissed the idea of me ever meeting either of them. And it's obvious when he speaks about them that he's not too keen on them either. He's an only child and doesn't hold a strong relationship with his parents. That much is obvious.

He raises his voice in the living room, and although I can't tell what he's talking about, I pause with my pen over the paper to listen.

He sounds distraught, and I don't like the sound.

Should I ask him to open up? Or is that being too needy? If he wants to talk about them, he'll tell me, right?

Instead of worrying about the call with his mom, I focus on the form instead. And I realize that what Clay really needs right now is honesty and openness.

Looking down at the list again, I softly mutter to myself, "Fuck it."

Then I circle every single *Desired* left on the page.

I'm not going to be embarrassed or ashamed. This is what I want, and I'm not sorry. I can't explain why I want to see Eden and Clay together intimately. Maybe it's because I'm just as attracted to her as I am to him. That's fine…I guess. And maybe it's a testament to the trust I have in Clay. He wouldn't leave me for her. He cares about me. We're happy.

So what am I so afraid of?

A moment later, he walks into the room looking flustered. He tosses his phone down on the nightstand again and walks to the bathroom. Then he shuts the door, and he *never* does that.

Climbing off the bed, I walk across the room and gently rap on the door.

"Clay," I softly call.

"Yeah," he mutters.

It's not exactly a *come in*, but it's not a *fuck off*, either. So I twist the handle and stare through the crack at him. He has his hands pressed to the counter and his head hanging forward.

There are moments when I can tell people want to talk and moments when they really don't. It reminds me of the months after my mom left and I'd find my dad sitting at the kitchen table alone, staring straight ahead, looking as if the world lay heavy on his shoulders. If I pressed him to talk, he'd shut down. He would tell me he was fine and leave the room. So I quickly learned not to ask. Instead, I'd make him a cup of coffee or bake his favorite pistachio cookies. We wouldn't utter a word as I moved around him in the kitchen. But it was peaceful, and I think it was what he needed.

So I don't press Clay for information about his mother or answers as to why she causes him so much distress. I just walk into the bathroom and wrap my arms around his waist.

When he lets me, I maneuver myself to the space between his body and the bathroom counter, and I stand there, letting him rest his head on my shoulder. Soon, it's his arms around me and his breath against my neck.

Clay isn't like any guy I've ever dated before. Things with him are simple but never easy. He wears his heart on his sleeve, but only on his terms. There are secrets there too, but I know the more I push for them, the less likely I am to get them.

"Did you fill out that form?" he murmurs into my neck.

"Yes," I reply. Thinking about the form and everything I circled has my stomach turning with anxiety. Immediately I want to run out there and undo everything I just did. Will he think I'm depraved or perverted? Watching him have sex with someone else was never part of the plan, but if I was supposed to fill out the form honestly, that's what I did.

It doesn't mean they have to actually do it.

Slowly he pulls away from our embrace. Then without meeting my eyes, he clears his throat and turns toward the door. I follow, chewing my lip, as we reach his bedroom, where he picks up the form from the mattress.

I watch nervously as he reads, his brows growing more and more pinched together as he goes down the list.

Then his expression relaxes from confusion as he swallows and glances my way. "This is what you want?" he asks.

I shrug. "You told me to be honest. I just…tried to be honest."

"You know all of this isn't happening tonight," he says, pointing to the paper.

"I know."

"But watching me with another woman…would turn you on?"

I feel my insides start to warm up with embarrassment. Why is this stuff so hard to talk about?

"Not any woman," I reply, which I thought would ease his nerves. Instead, his eyes widen even more as he glances down at the list and back up at me.

He rubs his brow before tossing the paper down on the mattress. It feels like a torturous hour before he finally lifts his gaze back to my face.

"You kinky little minx," he mumbles. Completely by surprise, he wraps his arms around my thighs and lifts me from the floor before tossing me onto the bed and covering my body with his.

His mouth lands against mine with a crash, and he kisses me until I feel like I can't breathe.

"You drive me absolutely wild, Jade. Do you know that?"

"Yes," I say with a gasp. He drags my skirt up and grinds himself between my legs.

Then he lifts up and stares down at me affectionately. "And you're the only one I want to fuck."

That might be the opposite of what I just asked for, but it manages to warm my heart regardless.

"Then fuck me," I reply breathlessly.

So he does, right on top of the stupid list.

Rule #22: Don't second-guess yourself.

Jade

Eleven o'clock rolls around slowly. It feels like waiting for Christmas morning.

Clay and I arrive at the club and check in at the front before going through the crowd toward the stairs leading to Eden's room. I feel bad about lying, but I have to pretend that I'm here for the first time. So I follow behind him, keeping my hand linked in his as he guides me.

When we reach Eden's door, he gently raps on the surface. A moment later, she opens it, and just like that, the three of us are together again—under *very* different circumstances.

"Come in," she says in greeting.

Clay walks in first, and I trail behind, keeping close to him. Unlike most other times I've come to the club, I actually dressed for tonight. I'm in a pair of tight black leggings and a black lace bralette. It's nothing compared to what Eden normally wears, but I feel sexy and powerful in it, and that makes all the difference.

"Do you have the paperwork filled out?" she asks, turning toward us expectantly. Clay hands her the paper we worked on this afternoon. My mouth goes dry as her eyes scan the list. Then her gaze lifts slowly to our faces, no doubt noticing how *Desired* is marked for a lot of sex acts she might not have expected.

"You filled this out together?" she asks.

"Yes," he replies.

Looking contemplative, she takes the paper and walks across the room, placing it on the counter by the bar. With her back to us, she says, "Tonight is meant as a demonstration. You both realize that, right?"

So no sex. That's what she's saying, right?

"Yes," we both reply at the same time.

When she turns back toward us, she's wearing such an impersonal expression on her face I find it unsettling. It's as if she doesn't know us. Didn't have lunch with us. As if we're strangers.

I *hate* it.

"Jade, sit in that chair. For tonight, you are the voyeur, but at times, I may ask you to participate. Are you comfortable with that?"

I nod, willing her to meet my gaze one time so I know it's still *us*.

"Then sit."

When she doesn't look at me, I walk toward the chair and take my place, a feeling of anxiety creeping its way up my spine.

Then she looks at Clay. Really *looks* at him, and I'm assaulted by jealousy.

"You remember the safe words?"

"Yes, Madame," he replies confidently. His expression is unreadable, but I do notice a tic in his jaw, and judging by how quiet he's been, he's nervous.

"Tell me."

"*Green* means *go*. *Yellow* means *slow down*. *Red* means *stop*."

"Very good," she replies, taking a step back. "And you want to please me tonight, don't you?"

My mouth goes dry when I hear the change in her tone. It's dry and authoritative but also sexy and gentle.

"Yes, Madame," he replies.

"Then you know what to do," she says with confidence.

The air in the room changes. Suddenly, it's like I no longer exist. Clay immediately starts undressing, slipping each button through the hole of his long-sleeve shirt. Once it's off, he folds it messily and drops it on the velvet stool by the door. I watch as he slides down his pants and kicks off each shoe.

There's something captivating about watching him undress for her, knowing that he's done this probably a hundred times before. The familiarity between them now is obvious, even being clear across the room from each other. They've done this dance before.

Looking back at Eden, I notice she's slipped off her black silk robe and is now wearing a black harness-style outfit, criss-crossed at her chest and exposing her cleavage. The bottom half of the lingerie is just a thong with a garter that clips to thigh-high stockings.

It's so different from the woman we had lunch with, in her casual T-shirt, joggers, and baseball cap. That was Eden—this is Madame Kink.

My mouth falls open, and I gape at her like a fish.

Never in my life have I seen someone with more confidence, including the woman who masturbated in front of an audience like it was just another day at work.

Eden is more than a sexy body and beautiful face. She's a force. She's like the sun, and we are all orbiting around her, basking in her glow. We are just grateful to be in her presence.

What I wouldn't give to press my body to hers, feel her breasts against mine. I imagine myself running my tongue up her neck and across her cleavage. I wonder what sounds she makes when she comes or how her tongue would feel with mine.

I suddenly find myself crossing my legs, unable to take my eyes off her as she stares at him. I've never felt this way about a woman before. It feels so right.

Out of the corner of my eye, I see Clay standing in nothing but his tight black silk boxer briefs.

Eden reaches for something hanging from the wall behind her. It's a long black flexible rod with a tiny rectangle flap of leather at the end. It takes me a moment to remember the name—riding crop.

When she barks her first order, I jump in my seat.

"On your knees."

My eyes dance over to where Clay is slowly lowering himself to the floor.

"Eyes on the floor," she adds. Her commands are so clear and confident.

Clay stares at the deep-red rug as he waits for his next instructions.

"Come here." She snaps her fingers at her side. Her tone is a little softer this time.

He moves to all fours, staring down as he crosses the room in an obedient crawl. When he reaches her feet, he doesn't look up or move. He just waits.

"You listen so well," she says in soft praise. "As a reward, you can worship me. You know what to do," she says, nudging one black stiletto shoe closer to him. "Kiss them."

As if he's done this a hundred times before, Clay lowers himself until his lips are pressed to the shiny black surface of her shoe.

As I sit in the chair, watching them, I'm mesmerized. There's something powerful and intimate between them. Clay is so naturally submissive to her, and it doesn't look like weakness. It looks like control, loyalty, and dedication. It's like he lives only for her, to obey her and please her.

Eden reaches down and grabs a fistful of his long brown hair and pulls him upward as she places her mouth near his ear. I stop breathing entirely as I watch.

"You see, Jade," she says to me, and I perk up at the sound of my name. "Clay likes to come into these sessions feeling like the filthy, dirty dog he is. He loves it when I call him that, don't you?"

His voice is rough, and his neck is strained as he replies, "Yes, Madame."

"He wants to prove to me that he can be good. Don't you, pet?"

"Yes, Madame," he repeats.

"Sometimes that means letting me use him like a fuck toy, and sometimes it means being my footstool. But tonight, you're going to prove yourself to me by showing me how you can take the pain. How does that sound, pet?"

"That sounds good, Madame."

I'm hunched forward, my elbows on my knees as I chew on my nail, unable to take my eyes off of them. How are they so good at this? He's not struggling or looking uncomfortable at all. If anything, he looks more like himself than I've ever seen.

"Then get on the cross," she says, and I sit upright, confused as to what this means.

My eyes are wide as Clay stands from the floor and walks obediently to the large wooden *X* fastened to the wall. He faces it and spreads his arms out wide to meet the harnesses positioned on either side. His feet do the same.

"Jade, fasten that side," Eden says to me in a cold, authoritative command.

I quickly stand from my seat and take his right arm. I stare at his face as I slip the leather buckle around his wrist. He won't look away from the wall, no matter how much I wish he'd look at me.

After his arms and ankles are both bound, I move toward my seat again.

"Stay," she says to me, and I pause just a few feet to her right. With my arms by my sides, I try not to let my nerves show.

Eden cascades her hands down Clay's back, softly massaging the muscles that are stretched and defined. "Give me a color," she says to him.

"Green," he replies without hesitation.

"Good boy. Deep breath."

I watch his back, already glistening with sweat, as he drags in a lungful of air, the cords of muscles expanding with the movement. It's unexpectedly beautiful to see him displayed like this.

"Just three rounds of five tonight, but we'll use the flogger."

"Yes, Madame."

"I want you to count, and don't forget to thank me."

He gives her his reply of obedience once again before she takes a step back. Before she rears her hand back to make the first hit, her eyes meet mine. We stare at each other for a moment before her mouth twitches at the corner, and I sense a small delicate smile. I find myself wanting to smile in return.

But before I can, her expression turns flat and serious again. Then she lets the flogger fly, connecting with the flesh of Clay's back with an audible *thwap*. He moans before saying, "One. Thank you, Madame."

Without giving him any time to recover, she sends it flying again.

"Two. Thank you, Madame."

With every hit, some softer or harder than others, he says the same thing.

"Three. Thank you, Madame."

All the way up to five, when she sets the flogger down on the counter and walks up to his back, stroking her hand over the reddening skin.

"You're doing so well," she murmurs softly as her fingers glide over his sweat-soaked skin.

"Thank you, Madame," he replies.

"Do you think you need more? To prove how good you are."

"Yes, Madame."

"Then give me a color," she says, moving to his side and looking into his eyes. There's about a foot between his body and the cross, and his head is hanging forward, pressed sideways to the surface.

"Green, Madame," he croaks.

She strokes his head, her nails against his scalp, as she brushes his hair back in the slicked way he normally wears it. I can't help but feel the intimacy radiating from them, giving me that third wheel feeling that settles in the back of my throat like unshed tears.

It's becoming increasingly clear that these two have something with each other I will never have. No matter how much I learn tonight or how well I play this role for him in the future, I'll never be *her*.

Will I be enough?

These thoughts plague me during the next two rounds with the flogger. I can hardly focus on the hits or take mental note of everything she says and does because I'm distracted by the notion that while I can pretend to be Madame Kink in the bedroom, I'll never be Eden.

And that might be what he truly wants, after all.

By the time he gets to the end of the third set, he's taking long meditative breaths.

"See how strong he is?" she asks, stroking his head again. "Not such a filthy little man anymore, are you?"

"No, Madame," he replies with a rasp in his voice.

"You're such a good pet, aren't you? Always pleasing your Madame. Making me so proud."

Spoken by anyone else, these words would feel silly and awkward, but spoken by her...they're genuine. She really does make him feel *good*, and I can tell by the change in his demeanor. He does seem stronger and more confident.

As her eyes cascade down his body, letting him slowly recover from the punishment, I notice the way they settle on his boxer briefs.

"You love making me proud, don't you, pet?" she asks, a slightly teasing tone in her question.

"Yes, Madame," he groans.

"I can see that. Jade, come here."

When I hear her utter my name, I quickly step forward so we're standing on either side of Clay's body.

Her eyes have a twinkle of mischief in them as she stares down again. "Go ahead. Feel how much he loves it."

When I glance down, looking between Clay's body and the wooden cross, I see her hand outstretched for me. So I slowly put my hand in hers and she brings it to his body, pressing my palm against the rigid length of his cock, taking up the front of his underwear.

He lets out a desperate moan when both our hands gently wrap around his erection. My breath hitches as I slide my fingers around him, hers settled above mine so we're both holding his dick at the same time. When I feel her squeeze, I do the same.

He moans again, pitching his hips forward to seek out the pressure from our hands.

As I lift my gaze from his groin to his face, I'm overcome with so much arousal I have to squeeze my thighs together for an ounce of relief.

Then my eyes find hers.

We're staring at each other behind his back while our hands are wrapped around his cock.

And I know at this very moment that I want more. I want more of *this*, whatever it is. More time watching them or being with them or anything. It suddenly feels like the possibilities are endless—like we could do anything.

I wonder if she feels it too.

"Do you think he's been good enough?" she asks, squeezing him again.

"Good enough for what?" I ask, my voice sounding like a squeak compared to hers.

"Good enough to come."

My mouth goes dry, and Clay lets out a strangled grunt as he presses his forehead to the wall.

"Yes," I reply before licking my lips. I feel like the answer to just about any question right now would be yes.

Do I think he deserves to come? Yes.

Do I think *I* deserve to come? Yes.

Do I think we should all just get naked and make each other come all night? Yes, yes, yes.

"And how would you like to make him come?" she asks, looking at me again with that evil twinkle in her eye.

"Umm…" I stammer, suddenly feeling as if I have stage fright.

Immediately, she cuts me off. "You need to be confident and assured. You know what you want, so if you're going to be dominant, don't stammer or second-guess. Just say what you want."

Say what I want? Okay then.

Pushing my shoulders back, *still holding his dick*, I look Eden right in the eye as I say exactly what I want.

"I want to watch *you* make him come."

It wasn't what she expected me to say. Judging by the sudden look of surprise on her face, it wasn't what she expected at all.

But judging by the way she's squeezing his dick again, this time with a small stroke, I'm willing to bet she doesn't hate the decision either.

Rule #23: Sometimes, you have to earn the right to come.

Clay

JADE'S WORDS HAVE THE BLOOD DRAINING FROM MY FACE. IT'S BAD enough they each have a hand wrapped around my aching cock, but now she's asking to watch as Eden finishes me off.

This is bad.

This is very fucking bad.

It's my fault that Jade has no clue what she's asking. To her, Eden is just a Dominatrix, and I'm one of her ex-clients. She wants to watch the performance. She has no clue that she's throwing me into the fires of heartbreak again.

Will Eden even do it?

I lift my head from the wall and wait for Eden to look at me. When she does, it feels like being punched in the stomach and having the wind knocked out of me. It's one thing to see her in any other situation and pretend that we're just two random people who weren't in love just a few months ago.

But now, it feels as if we're falling backward, slipping into our old selves that it took me months to let go of.

Who am I kidding? I never really let go.

Eden pulls her hand from my shaft, and Jade does the same, leaving me feeling cold and aching.

"Give me a color," she whispers, and I close my eyes, forcing myself to swallow.

Green. Fucking *green.* I couldn't be any more green than I am right now.

But I don't want to come across as too eager, so I open my mouth and let out a raspy, "Green."

I hear her intake of breath. She's not even touching me yet, and I can feel her fingers on my skin.

From the moment she told me to kneel, I tried to block my heart from getting too attached. It brought back too many memories, but I can't go back down that road. I'm just doing this for Jade. It means nothing.

But now I'm catapulting myself headfirst into what I know is going to hurt later. For one touch from her, I'd do far more.

"Unclasp him," she says to Jade, and they both work quickly to unfasten me from the cross. The muscles in my shoulders and hips ache as I'm finally able to move them again. Having to hold myself in that position for even fifteen minutes is brutal, but luckily, I had the pain of the flogger to distract me.

"Get on the bed, lying face up." I take one step toward the bed before she stops me, her hand on my arm, and then she adds, "Naked."

My cock twitches at that word.

I quickly tear my boxer briefs down and throw them onto the pile on the stool by the door. Then I climb onto the bed, raising my hands above my head because I already know she'll want me restrained.

She always loved to have me restrained.

The click of her heels against the floor sends another rush of blood to my cock. I'm not going to last long.

Just as I expected, she lifts each of my wrists to the Velcro cuffs situated at each corner of the bed. She'll leave my legs untethered because she loves to see me writhe.

We've been down this road before.

Oh, the things she's done to me in this position. Some of them familiar, but some of them very, *very* new.

And I loved them all.

Once my hands are bound, I feel her weight on the bed. I look up to find her climbing over me. She straddles my chest and sits down, resting her weight on my hard cock pressed against my lower belly.

I can't help the pained-sounding groan that climbs up my chest.

Staring up at her, our eyes meet, and everything hits us both at the same time. It's like we're suddenly transported to the past. It's as if the last six months never happened. Her weight is on my body. Her ass is warm against my aching dick. Her nails are digging into my chest.

I'm so fucked.

My hips lift, grinding against her when she seems to snap out of it. With one hand, she turns my head, forcing me to face Jade.

"Eyes on her the entire time. That's your woman. That's your Domme. Understand?"

My response gets caught in my throat. Because I don't understand.

Eden is my Domme.

My gaze connects with Jade, and it stings in my chest to feel the intensity of her eyes on mine.

Jade is mine too.

I've never been so confused in all my life. My heart and body both ache in ways I can't comprehend for two separate women.

"Do not take your eyes off her, understand, pet? This isn't for you. It's for her."

I swallow. "Yes, Madame."

"And you won't come until she tells you to. I make you come. She *lets* you come."

"Yes, Madame," I croak again.

"You're only getting this because you earned it. You took the pain so well, and I'm proud of you. She's proud of you too."

With a tight smile, Jade nods. She looks ready to fall out of her chair. She's leaning so far forward it's as if she's about to lunge out of her seat and join me on the bed. Her thighs are pressed together, and her bottom lip is pinched between her teeth. I know this means she's turned on.

I find myself smiling at her—my sweet, dirty girl.

Lost in the eye contact between Jade and me, I almost don't register when Eden lifts from my lap and shifts herself downward. It's not until I feel her warm tongue circling the head of my cock that I'm torn from her gaze.

My eyes close as I throw my head back, letting out a garbled string of curse words. Eden doesn't tease me. She takes me all the way into the back of her mouth without hesitation.

My toes curl, and every muscle in my body strains as she works me over quickly, getting me as close to the edge as she can as a form of torture.

She's so good at this. How could I forget?

"Fuck, fuck, fuck," I stutter, working hard to keep from unloading into the back of her throat without permission.

Again and again, she drags me to the edge and immediately pulls back, keeping me from going over. It's excruciating. Her mouth is skilled and perfect. Every pull, lick, and nibble is exactly what it takes to get me right where she wants me. It's like she knows my cock better than I do. Within minutes, I'm sweating and panting and lingering somewhere between pleasure and pain.

When I open my eyes, I stare at my girlfriend with a look of desperation.

Just let me come. Say the word. Please, baby, don't torture me like this.

But when I really take in her expression, I realize that she's not focused on my torment. She's watching Eden.

Fuck.

With her pupils dilated and her lips parted to accommodate her heavy breathing, it's clear Jade is actually enjoying this. She is turned on by watching another woman go down on me, but not just any woman.

When she brought it up at the apartment, I don't know why, but I didn't quite buy it. I thought she was simply flirting with the idea, but she doesn't seem to be flirting with it now.

By the look of things, there's a good chance Jade will come before I do.

And seeing how aroused she is doesn't exactly help my don't-come situation.

I let out another anguish-filled groan, my back arching off the bed and my wrists pulling so hard on the restraints I'm sure I'm going to break the bed.

Eden pops her mouth off my cock, sending shivers down my spine as I gasp for air.

When she looks at Jade, there's a look of astonishment on her face. "You really want to torture him, don't you? I don't think your pet is going to last much longer."

"I'm not ready for it to be over," she says with a mischievous grin.

The expression on Eden's face looks downright evil. "Well, if you want to torture him some more, then get over here and help me."

Oh fuck.

Fuck, fuck, fuck.

Before I met Eden, I never thought getting a blow job could be torture. I would have loved the idea of having two women taking turns with their mouths swallowing me down, and don't get me wrong, I love this. But the need to come is agonizing.

The only thing worse is breaking the rules and feeling her disappointment. So I have to obey the rules, which say I can't come until Jade tells me I can.

And I'm not exactly sure how she's going to manage that while her mouth is stuffed with my cock.

She rises from the chair, looking excited as she crosses the room and climbs onto the bed near my legs. I stare up from my reclined position to see her meeting Eden's gaze again, something warm and familiar passing between them.

"Don't go easy on him," Eden says just before Jade turns toward me and lifts my cock from where it's lying against my stomach. Our eyes meet again just as she lowers her sweet little mouth around my throbbing shaft.

Immediately, I want to come. It's right there at the edge, ready to spill over, but I have to use every muscle in my body to hold it back. My forehead and the back of my neck are beading with sweat, and I have to focus on every breath, careful not to lose control.

When Jade does that little twist with her hand, sucking hard on the head of my dick, I nearly lose it. My stomach is starting to cramp, and my balls are drawn up so tight I'm afraid I'll never see them again.

"Please, please, please," I beg.

As if she knows exactly what to do, Jade reaches between my legs, wraps her soft little hand around my sack, and pulls it away from my body. It feels so good and bad at the same time.

I just want to feel relief.

"Please, Madame. Just let me come. I was so good."

"He was good," Jade says in response.

"He's always good," Eden adds, and I stare into her green eyes.

My heart is pounding in my chest, and not just because of the torture these two are putting me through. When she says stuff like that, I can't help but hope. Surely this won't be the only time we do this. It's *too* good.

Jade likes it. Eden seems to be enjoying herself too.

God knows I like it, even when I'm so fucking miserable I could cry.

"I think we should let him," Jade replies, and I throw my head back again.

"Please, please, please. I just need to come."

"Go ahead. Finish him off, but make him come on his chest. Let him feel how filthy he is," Eden says in a merciless tone.

I look up in time to see Jade smiling with her lips close to the head. Even though Eden told her to make me come, I know better. Jade has to give me permission.

"You can come now, pet," Jade whispers sweetly.

Just hearing her call me the name Eden gave me a year ago sends a thrill of pain and excitement down my spine. I love hearing her say it, but I'm afraid of what it means. Does this mean she's truly taking Eden's role? Am I no longer Eden's pet? Am I no longer hers at all?

I keep my eyes on Jade as she slides my cock against the surface of her tongue, swallowing when I reach the back of her throat.

Then I watch as Eden strokes Jade's head, almost guiding her movement as she bobs up and down. There's a crooked smirk on her face, and at the exact moment our eyes meet, I lose it.

Jade quickly pops her mouth off as the warm, messy cum shoots all over my abs and chest. I'm too assaulted by pleasure to care. The buzz from the orgasm is harsh and almost too intense to enjoy. But I get lost in it regardless, letting my eyes close as a deep groan emits from my body. It never seems to end as I continue to cover my chest with cum.

Jade strokes me relentlessly through my climax, and when I finally melt into the mattress, she stops, sweeping the head of my cock with her thumb to clean up the last drop.

I open my eyes in time to find her hovering over me. She licks her thumb before softly mumbling, "So good."

I let out a whimper. If I could manage to come again, I would.

Closing my eyes, I doze off for a moment as they both climb off the bed. My eyes are closed when I feel something warm and soft against my chest, slowly cleaning up the mess I made. Another set of hands releases my restraints. I can't tell who it is; at this point, I don't care. They both feel so good.

A few minutes later, the bed dips again.

"How are you feeling?"

I open my eyes to find Eden sitting next to me. She's wearing the same black robe she had on when we showed up.

"Good," I reply sleepily.

"Can you sit up for me?"

I find myself smiling. It really is like old times. She was always a lover of aftercare, and honestly, so was I. Not at first. At first, I hated feeling so spent and helpless. The idea of hydration and important conversations were never what I wanted after the best sex of my life. But before long, it became my favorite part because it meant attention from her.

Begrudgingly, I sit up, placing my back against the pillows stacked against the headboard.

"You know the drill," she says, handing me a green bottle. My brow furrows as I stare down at it. I wonder if she bought this for me or if she keeps them in her fridge now.

"Normally, I encourage my clients to eat something and replenish their sugar and energy, but this one," she says, talking about me to Jade, "was stubborn. He refused to eat, but the best I could do was give him these."

I'm holding the store-bought green smoothie in my hand, reminiscing on the arguments we used to have after we were done playing and she'd pressure me to eat, but I hated the idea of needing a snack after sex. So we compromised with these.

Hiding my smile, I unscrew the lid. While I sip down the smoothie, I watch the two of them. For the most part, we're quiet. They're both watching me like I'm a patient in the hospital, and oddly enough, I like it.

I could get used to this, and that's dangerous. Just when I felt as if things were starting to settle down after our breakup, we disrupted the peace. Now I have no clue what the future holds. I just know I'm staring at two women I love, knowing full well that even if we can have our fun, there's no way I'll be able to keep them both.

Rule #24: Just because you can carry it all doesn't mean it's not heavy.

Eden

I'VE CANCELED ALL OF MY APPOINTMENTS FOR TONIGHT. I NEVER do that. But I have two very good reasons for it.

For one thing, I just feel off. How can I be Madame Kink when I've broken every single rule I've ever set for myself? It's like the signal is scrambled and I no longer know *how* to be Madame Kink.

I blame myself.

And him.

But mostly her.

If Jade had never come into my room at the club that night, I wouldn't have gone back down a road I swore I'd never go down again. If she hadn't somehow gained control last night, getting me to do something I said I'd never do again, I wouldn't be lying here reliving every second.

I wouldn't be missing him.

The other very important reason for canceling tonight is that Jack is running a mean fever that won't quit. When I came home last night, Madison informed me that his temperature was creeping up when she put him to bed but she was able to give him some medicine to bring it down.

But the moment he woke up this morning, he was burning up again.

Now he's sleeping next to me with flushed cheeks and breathing in that quick way that makes me so uncomfortable. I can't leave his side for a moment. I skim through some parenting search results on my phone, worrying myself over a mild fever.

When they don't give me the reassurance I want, I text Ronan.

Should I take him to the doctor?
What's his temperature?
100.7
Just give him some ibuprofen.
Do you have some in the house? I can have it delivered.
I have it.
I'll give it to him.
Is everything else okay?

I chew on my lip, staring at his question. Ronan has barely been at the club since baby Julian was born. To be honest, I miss him. Even with everyone else there, it doesn't feel the same without him.

Part of me wants to open up about the situation with Clay and Jade. I never shared things with him, even when I knew I could. At the time, Ronan and Daisy were getting married and expecting a baby. I wouldn't bother him with drama at work with a client.

Everything is fine.
Have you given thought to Emerson's offer?
Oh no. Not you too.
I'll be the last one to pressure you into something you don't want.

But you'd be great at it.
And you deserve more.
Are you done?
Yes.
I told him I'd think about it, and I am.
Good.
Let us know if you need anything for Jack.
Give him some medicine, and he'll be fine.
Thank you.

Jack is starting to stir next to me, so I press my hand to his forehead. It's hot to the touch.

When he peels his eyes open, he squints up at me as he asks, "Do I have a fever?"

"Yes," I reply, combing his hair back with my fingers.

"Do I have to take more medicine?" He screws his face up in disgust.

"I'm afraid so."

With a whine, he covers his face with his hands and rolls under the covers to hide. "I don't wanna!"

Great. This won't be easy.

"Sorry, buddy," I reply as I stand up from the bed and walk out to the cabinet where I keep the medicine. I measure out the appropriate amount for him and snatch a Popsicle out of the freezer on my way back to the bedroom.

When I return, he's staring up at me with a disgruntled expression and flushed-red cheeks.

"Here's the deal. If you take your medicine, you'll get this." I produce the purple Popsicle from behind my back, and his eyes instantly light up.

Immediately, he tries to bargain with me. "Just a little medicine, though."

With a stern look, I quickly shake my head. "Nope. You have to drink it all."

This goes on for far too long. Our negotiation turns into an all-out battle, and I feel myself losing control minute by minute. I'm trying hard to stand my ground as he begs, whines, and barters for any deal that would mean he doesn't have to drink *all* the medicine.

Madame Kink doesn't have to put up with this shit.

"All the medicine or no Popsicle, Jack!" I say firmly when he tries to cry his way out of it. He's kicking his feet dramatically, and I feel like I'm losing the battle. I hate having to yell, and I immediately regret it.

My phone is ringing on the counter in the kitchen, and it only adds to my irritation.

"Fine!" he shouts, letting big pitiful tears roll down his cheeks.

I swoop in, afraid he'll change his mind. I quickly hand him the medicine and watch him gulp it down. Then he looks up at me with an angry scowl as if *I'm* the bad guy.

Unwrapping the Popsicle, I hand it to him with an impatient huff. So what if I'm bribing him and spoiling him? He took the medicine, didn't he?

It's like I'm arguing with a silent critic in my head that tries to remind me I'm the worst mom on the planet.

Immediately, he looks content, so I flip on the TV and turn it to his favorite cartoons. Then I kiss his head and leave him in my bedroom, where he's likely to get melted Popsicle juice all over my sheets. Honestly, at this point, I'm too tired to care.

After tossing the wrapper in the trash, I perch my elbow on the counter and rest my face in my hands. It's hard on days like this not to feel like a constant failure. Everything that goes wrong in Jack's life might as well be my fault. Every illness, every tantrum, every misbehavior, it's all on me. And it will always be on me.

It's better than if we had stayed.

That's the only viable argument I have. During the worst of my day-to-day struggles, I'm constantly reminded that being a single mother is far better than raising my son with that monster.

My ex-husband never hesitated to lay his fists on me, berate me for every mistake, and call me the worst names in the book until I felt like the lowest form of dirt on the earth. I can't stand to imagine what he would have done to Jack.

It's not even nine in the morning, and already my mind feels bombarded. There are too many things happening at once—Jack's fever, Ronan's texts about the job, the pressures of being a single parent, and, oh yeah, giving Clay a blow job last night at his new girlfriend's request.

I'm a mess.

And Emerson wants me to run that club? I can hardly handle my life as it is. Madame Kink might appear like she has her shit together, but Eden is drowning.

Lifting my head up from where I'm slumped against the counter, I shuffle my way to the coffee maker. I'm going to need more caffeine for this existential crisis.

By the time I get a full pot loaded and ready to go, my phone is ringing on the counter again. I snatch it up and stare at the name on the screen, but it takes a moment too long to register who is calling me.

Clay Bradley.

Why is Clay calling me?

I let my thumb hover over the phone screen for a moment, contemplating whether I'm going to answer this. I know I shouldn't, but I find myself hitting the Answer button regardless.

Who am I kidding? I was never really contemplating it.

"Hello?" I say.

"Hi," he replies immediately. It sounds as if he's in the car, white noise buzzing in the background.

"Can I help you?" I ask, my tone dripping with curiosity.

"I'm checking on you." He says it so astutely, and I know he's serious, but I laugh anyway.

"What's so funny?" he asks, sounding offended.

"*You're* checking on *me*? Why?"

"Well, last night was heavy, and I'm afraid it got out of hand. I just want to see how you're handling it."

Okay, now I feel bad about laughing because that's sort of sweet.

"I'm handling it by moving on with my life."

Ouch, Madame.

I know that response must have stung because he's not saying anything.

I squeeze my eyes closed and rest my face in my open hand. "I didn't mean for that to sound so harsh. I'm sorry. I just meant…I was doing my job, Clay."

"Okay," he mutters in response. Fuck, he sounds bitter.

"Clay, I'm sorry, but—"

"Don't bother, Eden. It's clear nothing has changed. I'm a client. Last night was just a job. I get it. I'm sorry I called."

The petty anger in his voice makes me want to scream. I keep doing this. I keep hurting him and then hating the sound of his pain. What the fuck is wrong with me?

It's for the best. Hurt him so he leaves and moves on with Jade.

But I can't leave it like that. I just can't. Because, as it turns out, hurting people you care about isn't so easy.

"I'm sorry, Clay. I didn't mean to sound so cold. It's just… been a stressful morning already. Jack is sick, and I haven't even had my coffee—"

"Jack is sick?" he asks, interrupting me. The resentful tone in his voice is replaced with frantic concern.

"Yeah, it's just a fever," I reply nonchalantly as I move toward the coffeepot, pulling a cup from the cupboard.

"Did you take him to the doctor? What are his symptoms?"

My brow furrows as I pull the phone away from my ear and stare at the screen in confusion. All of a sudden, I'm the one playing the calm role.

"He doesn't need to go to the doctor every time he gets a little fever. And he has no other symptoms, so it's probably just his body fighting off a virus. Kids get sick all the time, Clay."

"Well, how is he feeling? Does he need anything? Do *you* need anything?"

"In about six hours, I'll have to give him another dose of medicine, and I'm all out of Popsicles."

"You need Popsicles? For a fever?" he asks, sounding confused. It's laughable how little Clay knows about kids.

I'm chuckling as I pinch the phone between my shoulder and ear, pulling the coffee creamer from the fridge. "No. The Popsicles are what I bribe him with to get him to take his medicine. But I think they're losing their luster because it *barely* worked this morning."

As I pour coffee into my cup, talking so casually about Jack, I briefly realize how I've never really spoken to anyone about parenting like this. Well, no one except Ronan.

Why, all of a sudden, does it feel so natural talking to Clay about this?

"Let me talk to him," he says flatly.

"What? No," I snap.

"Do you want him to take his medicine or not?"

I let out a sigh. "Fine. Give it a shot if you want."

Without another word, I carry the phone into my bedroom and hand it to Jack. His Popsicle is gone, but he's still sucking on the stick. His lips and chin are stained purple, as is a small spot on my sheets.

When he looks up at me, his face contorts into an expression of confusion.

"Someone wants to talk to you," I say.

Slowly he reaches out his little hand and takes the phone. One second he's holding it up to his ear, looking lost, and the next, his face lights up.

"Clay!"

It's too much to watch. My chest starts to sting with emotion as I watch them talk to each other on the phone, so I turn around and walk back out to my waiting coffee. Wrapping my hands around the warm mug, I let the heat calm my racing mind.

Jack is getting too close to him. That's my fault, isn't it? And the longer I let it happen, the worse it's going to be in the end. But I can't seem to stop. Why?

What's one more thing to throw on my pile of worries?

I'm slumped over on the counter, hovering over my cup of coffee, when Jack's little feet run across the living room toward where I'm standing.

He quickly hands me my phone with a smile. When I take it, I notice the call has ended, so I set it down on the counter. Then I reach out and feel Jack's forehead, which is thankfully cool and a bit clammy.

"What did Clay want?" I ask, expecting Jack to tell me how he will take his next dose of medicine without giving me a hard time because Clay somehow convinced him to.

Instead, he grins up at me as he replies, "He's coming over."

My face falls as I watch my son bounce back to my bedroom.

I'm standing in my mismatched pajamas without an ounce of makeup on my face. "Wait…what?"

Rule #25: When your Madame tells you to stay, you stay.

Clay

> You don't know my address.

I SMILE DOWN AT HER TEXT MESSAGE. IT'S TRUE THAT I DON'T know her address, but I also know that she's going to give it to me.

I'm not trying to manipulate my way into Eden's life, but it's becoming more and more obvious to me just how weak the wall she's kept up is getting. It's like I planted a seed six months ago that is finally growing. Deep down…she finally wants what I asked for back then.

But now…it's too late.

> *Yes, but you're going to give it to me.*
> No, I'm not.
> *I'm stopping by the grocery store now.*
> *What type of Popsicles should I get?*
> Clay.
> *I'll just get an assortment.*
> *What about medicine?*

Stop.

Let me help.

No strings.

Please.

My phone goes silent for a few minutes. I'm sitting in the parking lot of the local market, waiting for her reply. I don't know why I'm suddenly so eager to help her, but I am. Maybe because this was the version of Eden I wanted months ago. And it really does have nothing to do with sex—something even I'm surprised by.

The old me didn't give a shit about kids. And to be honest, this is the only one I do give a shit about. Maybe it's because he's her kid or because he seems to really like me for some reason. But this sudden, unexplainable need to be there for him is like nothing I've felt before.

For the first time in my life, I have someone else to care about other than myself.

1024 E. Barclay Dr.

My mouth stretches into a wide grin as I stare down at the address on my phone. Without responding, I quickly jump out of the car and walk into the store.

The basket is already full under my arm before I even reach the Popsicles in the frozen section. I grab every snack that looks like something a kid would like. Then I pick up four different brands of children's fever reducer, just in case.

I'm loading up three heavy bags into my car when I feel my phone buzzing in my back pocket. After slamming the trunk, I pull it out and feel the heavy weight of shame when I see Jade's name on the screen.

Why do I feel bad? I'm just taking some groceries to her house, to my *ex-girlfriend's* house. Who Jade thinks is just my ex-Domme and has no idea how much really happened between Eden and me.

Fuck.

"Hello?" I say as I answer the call.

"Hey," she replies in a chipper tone.

"How's the day with your dad going?" I ask as I slide into the driver's seat of my car.

"Good. It's a beautiful day for a boat ride. Too bad you couldn't come."

"I know, baby. But you're the one who wanted to wait to tell him, remember?"

She lets out a huff. "Yes. I know. I do love sneaking around, but I'd also like to just be together out in the open too. Then he'd invite you on the boat and over for barbecues. It would be fun."

"Yeah…it would. Hey, where is he anyway? You didn't throw him overboard just to call me, did you?"

She chuckles into the phone. "No. We haven't left yet. I'm grabbing food, and he's getting the boat ready."

"Be careful," I say.

"I will," she replies. I start the car, putting it into reverse as the Bluetooth picks up the call so I don't have to hold my phone. "What are you doing today?" she asks, and I pause.

I don't want to lie to Jade. I *can't* lie to her. At least not any more than I already have. Things have been so good, and I actually *don't* feel like the piece of shit I used to feel like. Besides, I'm not cheating on her. And I don't plan on cheating on her. So what am I so afraid of?

I clear my throat as I continue pulling out of the parking spot. "Jack is sick."

"Oh no," she replies without hesitation.

"I'm taking some groceries over to them. I just want to help out."

There's a beat of silence on the line, and I find myself wincing as I wait for her to respond.

Jade might be a saint, but I just admitted that I'm going over to the house of the woman who had my cock down her throat less than twenty-four hours ago. No one in their right mind would be okay with that.

"That's nice of you," she murmurs.

"You're not…mad?"

More hesitation.

"A little jealous," she replies with a forced laugh. "But not mad."

When I don't respond, she continues.

"I trust you, Clay. And I trust her. Besides, last night was the hottest night of my life. So if you do cheat on me, at least record it and let me watch."

A loud laugh bursts through my lips. "What is wrong with you?"

"Honestly…I don't know." She's laughing too. The sound is warm and soothing, washing away the cold feeling of regret and shame.

At times like this, Jade really does feel like the best friend I've ever had. That's how our relationship started, anyway. She made me laugh, and for the first few years that I knew her—when she was far too young for me—I wasn't actively trying to fuck her. It gave me a sense of freedom just to be myself with her. That might make me an asshole, but at least I can recognize it now.

Because now she is all of those things, and I'm not dumb enough to throw that away.

"Last night was really hot," she adds.

"It was," I reply, my cock twitching in my pants at the memory of them both taking turns wrapping their lips around my shaft.

"I know she said it was a onetime thing…" She lets her voice trail, and I know without even asking what she is implying.

"But…" I reply, encouraging her to finish that thought.

"Don't tell me you don't want to do that again," she says with accusation.

Of course I want to do that again. Fuck, I'd like to do that every day of my life if I could, but Jade is reckless. She doesn't seem to be giving any thought to what this could result in if we're not careful.

"If Eden said it wouldn't happen again, then it won't happen again."

"Then talk to her," she says eagerly.

"I'm just taking her groceries, Jade. Her son will be there."

Jade lets out a sigh. "I know. I just...can't stop thinking about it. You and her together, and then her watching you and me..."

"Driving with a hard-on isn't pleasant, babe."

She lets out a giggle while I have to adjust myself in my loose gray sweats.

"Okay, I'll stop. Sorry," she replies.

She sounds as if she's walking, and neither of us says anything for a while as I drive. Directions to Eden's house are playing on the screen in my car, and a feeling of restless excitement settles itself deep in my bones.

I'm driving to Eden's house. My girlfriend is encouraging me to talk her into another night together. I should be cautious, but I'm too fucking needy and excited. For what...I don't even fucking know.

"You know...it's not only because it was hot," she adds because my sweet Jade can't handle a moment of silence.

"Then what is it? Why do you want to do it again?"

"I don't know. The chemistry between you two was amazing. It was just...special."

And I get it. It's the most sense she's made all day. Because I don't understand it either. I just know that I need to feel it again.

Eden's house is so suburban. Not that I thought she lived in some kinky lair in the city's underbelly, but I did not expect this. She has a perfectly manicured front lawn, a deep-red front door, and flowers growing in the flower bed in front of the porch.

I check the address three times to make sure I'm in the right place.

I pull the car into the driveway and text her that I'm here. I'm praying that she'll at least let me in, but part of me is ready for her to take the groceries and slam the door in my face.

I *am* invading her privacy. She has a fortress of well-constructed boundaries that are meant to keep others out of her private life, but I seem to be bulldozing my way right over all of them.

When she opens the front door for me, I'm struck speechless by the sight. With the heavy bags cutting off circulation to both of my arms, I'm staring at a version of Eden St. Claire that might be my new favorite. It's even better than casual movie-theater Eden.

Her long black hair is pulled into a loose, messy braid cascading over one shoulder. She's wearing a dark-red hoodie and a pair of tight black leggings. Her eyes look so much brighter than normal, now a vivid green hue without those heavy lashes casting a shadow over them. Her full lips are not covered in color, and even with the dark circles under her eyes, she looks so stunning I can't look away.

"Can I come in?" I ask.

She stares at me cautiously before letting out a heavy breath and stepping aside. As I walk into her house, I immediately notice how cozy and homey it is. It's nothing like the home I grew up in. My childhood was spent in various penthouse suites across multiple cities, and there was never anything cozy about them. They were designed for taste and show, not comfort or living.

When I spot the kitchen down the hall and to the left, I carry the bags there and place them on the counter.

"You said you were getting Popsicles," she says with her arms crossed, staring at the massive pile.

"Yeah, well…I figured while I was there, I might as well pick up a few more things."

She picks up the boxes of medicine as I busy myself with

emptying the bags. I notice her blinking down at them as she softly mumbles, "You didn't have to do this."

"I know I didn't," I reply.

She lifts her gaze, and I spot the moisture in her eyes. She looks so tired and beaten down that I'm suddenly acting on impulse. Before I know it, I'm gathering her into my arms, holding her in a warm embrace with her cheek resting against my chest.

We don't say a word as I rub my hand in circles around her upper back. It takes her a few moments before she gives in and wraps her arms around my waist, letting me just hug her. I get the feeling she needs it.

"Thank you," she whispers.

It occurs to me at this moment that for months I assumed Eden was letting people into her life but excluding me and me alone. It fueled my jealousy. But from what I know about her now, I realize that Eden doesn't let *anyone* into her life. And she never accepts help.

My heart aches with the realization of how lonely she must be.

"Clay!" Jack's small voice is scratchier than normal as he shouts in excitement from across the house.

Eden and I pull apart in a rush as I turn to find him sprinting toward me.

"Hey, buddy!" I reply as he launches himself into my arms. "I heard you're not feeling well."

"My head hurts," he says with a sad grimace.

"I brought some medicine for that," I reply, turning to grab the tablets the pharmacist suggested.

"What else did you bring me?" He eyes the groceries on the counter behind me.

I snatch the bag of Flamin' Hot Cheetos and hold them up with a smile.

"Mom never lets me have these," he replies excitedly.

"Well, if your mom says it's okay, you can have a few, but *only* if you take your medicine." I set him down on the floor and hold the bag out of his reach.

"I will. I promise!"

Jack and I both look at Eden at the same time, waiting for her approval. "Mom?" I plead, holding back a laugh.

"Please," Jack begs with his hands clasped together.

With a smirk, she relents. "One small bowl, and you *have* to take your medicine at three."

Jack cheers, bouncing on his feet in excitement. As she prepares his snack, he grabs my hand.

"You're staying, right? We can watch a movie, and I can show you my room."

Very carefully, I glance up at Eden. Our eyes meet in a loaded gaze. I can see her fighting the same battle I am—wanting something we know we shouldn't want.

Finally, she nods. "Stay."

And I know instantly why she phrased it that way. Not "you can stay" or "you should stay." But she said it as an order. Because she knows there's not an order from her I won't obey.

———————

I march through the club, already loosening my tie as I bang my fist on the door of Eden's room. My palms are itching with need. It's been a very long four days since I've been here.

She opens her door, and her expression falls as soon as she sees my face. Or, rather, my state.

My hair is disheveled, not in its usual slicked back style. My eyes are swollen from crying, and there are heavy bags hanging beneath them.

"Clay," she says, reaching for me.

"Can we skip the formalities today?" I ask as I storm into the room and tear off my jacket and tie.

"Is everything okay?" She's hovering near me, but instead of kissing me and tearing off her clothes like she should be, she's touching my shoulder and trying to make eye contact with me.

"It's fine. I just missed you," I say frantically as I wrap an arm

around her waist and haul her body to mine, kissing her lips like it's the first gulp of fresh air I've breathed in days.

When I reach for the clasp of her bra, she pulls away. "Slow down. Let's talk."

"I don't want to talk," I snap. "I want to fuck."

"What happened on your trip? Are you sure you're okay?" she asks. Her brows are folded inward, and her mouth is set in a frown. She's concerned for me.

I should love that. The attention and consideration I receive from Eden should right all the wrongs I'm currently feeling, but they don't. They just feel wrong.

I don't get attention. No one cares about me. I'm not worth any of it.

My hands are shaking, and I feel as if I'm watching myself from outside my own body. I see how out of control I'm behaving. I see what's wrong with this scenario, but I can't seem to fix it. I can't seem to feel any differently than I do now.

"Nothing fucking happened on my trip, okay? Nothing. We spent four days on my parents' fucking yacht, and nothing happened. I'm sorry I'm in a bad mood, but I missed you, and you're not acting happy to see me."

Her expression falls, and she steps backward.

"Don't do that," she mutters.

"Do what?"

"Don't blame me for your fucking issues when I asked you to open up and tell me what's wrong. If you want to be like that, then you can leave."

I take two angry steps toward the door. I place my fingers on the handle and pause just long enough to see what will happen if I leave. I'll get in my car and drive home, where I'll sulk, complain, and feel sorry for myself. Then I'll wake up tomorrow and move on with my life; nothing will change.

Instead of opening the door, I place my head against the surface and take a deep, shuddering breath.

After a moment, I feel her hands sliding down my spine until her warm hand applies gentle pressure to my lower back.

"Please stay. Talk to me."

"Tell me to, and I will," I say.

"I don't want to tell you to, Clay. Not this time. You have to want it."

"What right do I have to complain about anything? A rich boy like me. I've never wanted for anything in my entire life, so what the fuck am I so sad for?"

"That's not true," she replies softly. "I know you must want something."

I pull my head away from the wall and turn to face her. "Four days, Eden. For four days, she wouldn't even look at me. My father barely spoke to me. I'm their son. And they spent the entire weekend keeping me around their rich friends without treating me like a real person."

She's gently stroking my back, staring into my eyes, and I feel like I'm devouring her eye contact like I need it to live.

"Come on," she whispers, taking my hand and pulling me to the bed. Without speaking, she strips off my shirt and then my pants. Then she unclasps her bra and slides off her underwear so both of us are naked when she pulls back the covers on the bed, drawing me under them with her.

Then she drapes her body over mine and stares down at me. "I'm always happy to see you, Clay," she says as she strokes my face. I force myself to swallow as she gazes into my eyes with affection. "And you can always talk to me, no matter how you feel."

My hands can't seem to get their fill of her body, softly stroking over her hips and back. It's not a sexual thing, either. I'm touching her because I meant what I said—I missed her so much.

She takes my jaw in her hands and holds my face still as she stares at me. "If your parents don't give you the attention you deserve, that is their problem. Understand?"

"Yes, Madame," I mumble.

"I see you, Clay. I see how perfect and kind and wonderful you are, even if they can't."

My breath comes in a quiver. "Yes, Madame."

"You are mine, and from now on, I don't want you seeing them alone. Do you understand me?"

I force myself to swallow the painful emotion brewing in my chest. "Yes, Madame."

Then she leans down and presses her lips to mine. As my lips part, her tongue slides into my mouth, gently caressing mine. She hums into the kiss, and my cock twitches with desire.

"I missed you," she murmurs against my lips.

"I missed you too," I reply, tightening my grip around her waist.

"Then show me how much. And never leave me again."

Flipping her onto her back, I wedge myself between her legs, grinding my hardening cock against her as I groan into the crevice between her neck and shoulder.

"Yes, Madame."

Rule #26: Even good boys break the rules sometimes.

Eden

I WAKE UP TO THE SOUND OF DISHES IN THE SINK, AND MY EYES pop open. Quickly, I grab my phone from the nightstand and look at the time, 4:15 p.m.

Shit. Jack's medicine.

Clay insisted I lie down and take a nap when he and Jack put on a movie after lunch. I tried to fight him on it because I don't normally take naps. It's not often I can get my mind quiet long enough to drift off in the middle of the day, but I must have needed it today because I was out for over three hours.

I jump up from my bed and rush out to the living room. Jack is curled up on the couch under his Spider-Man blanket, fast asleep.

Clay is standing in my kitchen, filling the coffeepot with water.

"He needs his medicine," I say, rushing over to check on Jack.

"I already gave it to him," Clay replies, stopping me in my tracks.

"How much did you give him?" I ask, sounding panicked.

"Exactly how much the dosage chart on the box told me to," he replies calmly. "Relax, Eden. He's fine."

When he says that, it's not condescending. It's encouraging.

"I'm sorry," I say with a sigh, walking into the kitchen. I stand next to him as he loads the coffee maker. There is something so soothing about watching him try to find his way around my kitchen. "No one has ever given Jack medicine but me and his babysitter. It's hard to get used to."

He lets out a soft chuckle. Then he pauses what he's doing and glances up at me. "My mother never gave me medicine. Not once."

My brow furrows. "Really?"

He shakes his head. "I had nannies growing up. Mean ones."

Even though he smiles, I don't. Clay has shared enough with me about his childhood that I know he hides a lot of his pain behind laughter and avoidance.

Maybe that's why I do what I do. I can give people the healing and release they want without having to reveal too much.

"You're a really good mom, Eden." His voice is soft and warm, and that compliment hits me harder than I expect it to.

"I don't feel like one," I reply.

He scoffs, closing the lid on the coffee maker. "Seriously? Out of all the times you scolded me for talking bad about myself, listen to you."

My throat starts to feel tight. "You have no idea how hard it is, Clay."

"I know I don't. Because you never gave me a chance…"

"Yes, I did," I reply softly.

"Did you, though? By then, it was too late, wasn't it?"

"It's never too late," I reply, giving him a pleading expression.

"Maybe. But I wish things had happened differently. I wish I knew you then the way I know you now."

"You know it was never because I didn't care about you," I reply, but that only makes him spin toward me.

"No, I don't. I don't know that. I had no idea it wasn't because you didn't care about me. I felt like *nothing* to you."

He's standing so close the proximity makes it hard to breathe.

"You were *everything* to me," I reply in a hushed shout.

"Then why?" he asks, those emerald-green eyes boring into mine. What is it about his face that brings me so much comfort? How do those sharp cheekbones and full lips seem to always make me break all my rules?

When he gestures around my house, I take a deep breath to ready myself for the same fight all over again. "When were you going to tell me about all of this?" he asks.

"I couldn't…I couldn't risk ending up like I did before."

His brows fold together as he waits for me to elaborate. But I can't.

Instead, I walk away from him as if I can escape this conversation. But there aren't many places for me to go. Jack is asleep in the living room, so my feet carry me to my bedroom.

Naturally, Clay follows.

Big mistake.

"Eden, please. Talk to me," he begs, sounding defeated.

When I spin around to find him standing in my room, closing the door so we're shut in together, I feel a sense of worry building in my chest. This is bad.

I back myself into a corner, leaning against the dresser and staring at him with my arms crossed.

"What did you mean by ending up like you did before?" he asks. "You mean with Jack's father?"

"Yes," I reply.

"Did he hurt you?" He takes another step closer. "Did he hurt Jack?" His voice takes on a dark and menacing inflection when he asks that.

"I left before Jack was born," I reply without meeting his gaze. "If it wasn't for Jack, I might have never left."

I take a deep breath and hold my head in my hands. Why is

this so hard to talk about? I know I have nothing to be ashamed of, and still…it's so hard. "And yes…he did hurt me," I add.

"Fuck, Eden." He runs his hands through his hair. It's not gelled back like it normally is, so it falls to each side, framing his face. "Why didn't you tell me?"

I look down, unable to meet his gaze. "I don't know if you picked up on this yet, Clay," I say with sarcasm, "but I don't really share personal details about my life with people."

"I noticed." He takes another step closer. I can feel my heart beating faster. We're alone in a bedroom, and he looks far too good for this to end well. I need to tell him to leave now, and I know well enough that if I gave him that order, he'd obey. "But I thought I was different."

I glance up at him. The sincerity on his face steals the air from my lungs.

"You were different," I whisper. "You *are* different."

"Don't tell me that now," he replies, looking pained. "Now that I can't have you."

"You do have me." My voice is so low now it's almost silent. And with each word we utter and each step he takes toward me, the room grows more and more charged. It's like slowly building pressure that will eventually explode. And neither of us is doing anything to stop it.

"Say that again," he whispers. He's standing so close now our feet are touching. I uncross my arms and hold tightly to the edge of the dresser behind me. I have to crane my neck to see his face at this distance.

"You have me, Clay. You'll always have me."

He inches closer.

"But I also have *her*," he replies, and my stomach drops at the reminder. In my mind, I see her face. Those sweet blue eyes and that innocent smile. It tugs on my heart to think about her, something painful and yet lovely.

He leans his face down toward me, and I feel myself pulling

back as if it's my only defense, which it's not. I know full well that if I told him to leave, he would. But I don't.

With his lips near my ear, he says the words that make my knees practically buckle beneath me.

"She wants to have you too, you know. I saw it in her eyes last night. She wants you the same way I do."

My breath hitches as I let those words sink in.

"You felt it too, didn't you?" he mutters against my cheek. "How good we could be together."

"Did you tell her you were coming over? Or are you keeping me a secret?" I ask, pulling back far enough that I can't feel his breath against my face anymore.

He peers into my eyes. "I told her."

"And what did she say?" I ask.

"She said she was jealous," he replies with a smirk.

"Of me?" I ask, feeling the guilt sink in.

His smirk stretches wider. I let out a gasp as his hand winds its way under the back of my hoodie, drifting his fingers along the skin of my waist. He leans in again, whispering into my ear as he replies, "Of me."

My mouth goes dry as his words sink in.

"I don't believe you," I argue, peering up at him. "You're just saying that."

He shakes his head slowly. "No, Eden. She asked me to talk to you about the three of us being together again."

"I said it would be a onetime thing," I mumble weakly. Even I don't buy my own argument.

Ignoring my reply, he leans in again, his lips hovering over the skin of my neck. I feel my resolve crumbling with every whisper of breath against my flesh. "If you tell me to drop it, I will. I'll do whatever you say."

"I know you will," I reply, digging my fingers into his hair. My nails scratch his scalp as I hold him just an inch from my skin.

"You should tell me to leave." He's struggling to keep his lips off me, and honestly, so am I.

"I don't want to," I reply breathlessly.

"Then tell me to kiss you."

"I shouldn't."

"Then tell me you'll see us again. Both of us." He drags his hovering lips up my neck and along my jawline.

Our mouths are separated only by a soft breath as I reply, "Okay. Yes. I'll see you both again."

His intense gaze burns as I stare back at him. His other hand reaches up and slides along my jaw and into my hair, holding my head as if he's going to kiss me.

As he leans in, I panic. "Don't," I bark, just as our lips are about to touch.

Like a good boy, he stops.

For a while, he holds the position, just staring at me as if he's waiting for me to change my mind.

One second.

Two seconds.

Three seconds.

"Fuck it," he mutters. Then his mouth crashes against mine as he devours my lips in a blazing kiss.

I could push him away. I could tell him to stop.

I don't.

I hold a hand in his hair and pull him closer, tangling my tongue with his and biting on his lower lip every chance I get.

I never forgot how good his kisses were. I've relived them every single day since our relationship ended. The way his mouth makes me forget everything in the outside world.

His body presses firmly against mine, and I let out a groan at the way his hardening cock grinds against my hips. We are lost in an inferno of passion, grabbing, biting, and touching one another.

With a tight grip around my thighs, he hoists me onto my

dresser and grinds himself between my legs, humming into my mouth like he's possessed.

"God, I missed you," he murmurs, and part of me starts to panic because it feels like I'm losing control. We are not getting back together. I did not agree to this.

But I can't stop it, and I don't want to. Because the truth is I missed him too. I missed the comfort of his touch and how, without reason, the intimacy between us reached further than something sexual. It was almost spiritual.

"I missed you too," I whimper.

To my surprise, it's he who ends the kiss first. Breathlessly, he pulls away, and we gasp for air at once.

Our hands don't leave each other's bodies while our foreheads rest together. After a moment, I slide off the dresser to stand with my body flush against his.

"Are you going to tell her about that?" I ask in a panting whisper.

"Yes," he answers without hesitation. "I have to."

I nod, swallowing the uncertainty.

Will she hate me for having a moment with her boyfriend? Or will she really be jealous that they were his lips and not hers?

"Will you please tell me to leave now so I don't do something that will be much harder to explain?" he begs playfully.

I smile as I push on his chest. "Get out of here."

When he steps backward, looking disheveled with flushed cheeks and swollen lips, it's hard not to pull him right back to me and indulge in the magic of his mouth again.

"Tomorrow night?" he asks.

"Maybe. It depends on how Jack is feeling. I'll text you."

His lips are pressed together tightly as he backs up toward the door. "Oh, and Eden?"

I raise my chin in expectation.

"I don't want to do it at the club again. I want you to come to my place."

My smile fades, and I freeze in place. He takes a step back toward me. "Don't start panicking. It'll be fine. It'll just be…us."

Finally, I nod. "Okay."

He smiles as he backs up again. "Tell Jack I said goodbye. And let me know if you need anything else."

I nod again as he opens my bedroom door. I can barely move as I hear him cross my house and leave through my front door.

I'm not sure what just happened or what I just agreed to. But it seems that's a common theme lately. Where he and Jade are concerned, I'm always blissfully and hopelessly lost.

Rule #27: Don't bring up your forbidden boyfriend with your dad.

Jade

"Grab me a Coke from the cooler, Cupcake," my dad calls from his seat behind the wheel of the boat.

I'm sitting in the passenger seat on the opposite side, my feet crossed on top of the cooler as I stare out at the harbor in the distance. The sun is starting to set as we make our way back to dry land.

Pulling my feet down and popping the lid, I grab two cold red cans and slam the cooler shut.

My dad and I have been boating together since I was in middle school. My mother wasn't much of a fan, so more often than not, it was just him and me. I'd like to think that someday it won't be just me. Maybe I'll be able to bring along someone I love. Then one day, I can pass this tradition down to my kids.

"You have to stop calling me that," I say, passing one to him. "I'm twenty-three, Dad."

He pouts at me, looking offended. "You'll always be my cupcake."

Rolling my eyes and fighting a giggle, I cross my legs over the cooler again. It's warm for early spring, but I'm still wearing a light hoodie to keep the cool ocean wind off my skin.

"Even when you're old and married, I'm still going to call you Cupcake."

"What about if I'm young and married?" I reply, cracking open my drink. The very mention of marriage makes me think of Clay. I've gotten to the point now in our relationship where I'm constantly looking for an opportunity to come clean with my dad. Sooner or later, we have to tell him.

And no, I'm not thinking about marriage with Clay yet. We've only been secretly seeing each other for a few months, but deep down, I'm committed to making it last. I *want* to love Clay forever. We just have some hurdles to overcome first.

Hurdles like…a sexy Dominatrix and exhilarating threesome encounters that have me fidgeting in my seat every time they cross my mind.

"Don't get married young," my dad replies with bitterness in his tone.

Inwardly, I wince. Okay, so maybe marriage is a bad topic with my dad, seeing as how my mother decided twenty-five years was long enough and decided to split two years ago. Just when they were ready to have their lives back without me around, she basically told him she didn't want to be alone with him for the rest of her life.

It breaks my heart to think of what that did to him.

But my dad and I have always been comfortable talking about everything, far more than my mom and me. So even though I should, I don't drop it.

"Not all young marriages are bad," I reply, squinting up at him.

"I know that," he replies grumpily from his captain's seat. "But I don't want to see you settle. Go see the world before you make that commitment."

Biting my lip, I keep pressing him. For what? I don't know.

Validation, I guess. Like I'm priming him for the big talk.

Surprise, Dad. I'm already in love, and it's with your protégé and, hopefully someday, business partner. Please don't kill him.

"Yeah…but I don't want to see the world alone. I want to experience all the great things in life with someone I really, really like by my side."

"Yes…but you won't know for sure someone is right for you until you discover yourself first."

The thing about my dad is that he's just as stubborn as me, if not more so. So when we get into these little *discussions,* they tend to be never-ending.

"But what if I meet someone when I'm young? I'm supposed to just push them away until I'm thirty?"

His head spins in my direction. "Why? Did you meet someone?"

Oh, shoot.

I quickly look away, keeping my eyes forward while I feel his gaze practically drilling into the side of my face.

"No," I mutter. "I have no social life. I'm either with you or Nettie or at your office, making lunch runs with Clay."

See? There's my in. I just bring up his name casually to carefully plant a few seeds—just to make sure they don't explode.

I glance up at him to see his reaction.

He doesn't really respond. He just…huffs. Which is weird.

"What was that for?"

"Nothing. It's just… It's guys like Clay I worry about."

Something queasy and uncomfortable blossoms low in my belly. His words are like acid.

"What's wrong with Clay?" I mumble, afraid of what answer I might receive.

"Nothing. I love Clay. He's a great guy. You know I'm training him to make him partner eventually, but he's a charmer, Cupcake. It's honestly what makes him good at his job too. He can sell anything with a smile, but everything he does has a motive."

No. This is not Clay at all.

It's just the version of Clay he projects. But my dad wouldn't know that, and I certainly *shouldn't* know that, so I can't defend him, and it's painful to keep quiet.

In my silence, my dad continues.

"All I'm trying to say is guys like Clay will dazzle you into some situation that you'll end up regretting further down the road."

Again, I don't speak, and at this point, it's noticeable. But I couldn't possibly voice a word past this lump building in my throat.

Clay hasn't *dazzled* me into anything. I wish I could say that. It's actually been me doing the pushing and the convincing and the charming.

When I still don't respond, he turns toward me. "Everything okay, Cupcake? Clay hasn't…tried anything with you, has he?"

Remember those seeds I planted by bringing up Clay in the first place? Well, they are currently exploding. And it's a big, stupid mess.

I can't lie to my dad. And I don't want to.

"Clay has been nothing but nice to me. I promise." I force a smile as I squint up at him from under my baseball cap.

In the back of my mind, I remember that Clay is currently with Eden. And what's strange is that deep in my gut, I'm not as angry about that as I probably should be.

Why am I not jealous?

Am I being…*dazzled*?

No. If anything, Clay has been seeking out a connection with me that I don't think he's getting from people like my dad or his family. It's the same thing he's been pursuing with Eden. And I still don't quite know what that is, but I'm getting there. The more I see him with Eden, the more I understand.

When I glance up at my dad, noticing that he's still wearing a frown, I hop out of my seat and put my arm around his broad shoulders. Then I lean against his side, and we stare out at the water together, both perfectly content to embrace the tender moment.

I feel a little guilty for pushing a subject that obviously stung him a little.

"Thanks for a great day, Daddy," I whisper, squeezing him a little tighter.

I know deep down my dad is just afraid of losing me. I'm all he has left. And on top of that, he's afraid to see me make the same mistakes he did.

I have a feeling that in this scenario, my dad might be relating a little more to Clay than me, and he's afraid that Clay will do to me what he did to my mother. He thinks he charmed her into a long relationship and it was never perfect. They had their issues for years, and we could both see my mother's restlessness, but neither of us was willing to face it.

Okay, maybe I'm carrying guilt for that too.

And maybe she stayed when I was a kid because she knew that if she left, I would stay. I was always my dad's, first and foremost.

But that's the thing, isn't it? Love and family life are complicated. They are never perfect, and problems are truly unavoidable. Guilt, fear, and resentment are just shadows—inevitable dark spots behind where love, trust, and happiness shine.

My dad is just trying to protect me. I love him for that, but I also know that the thing he's trying to protect me from is already happening. I'm already falling in love, charmed and dazzled beyond hope. And there's nothing any of us can do about it.

"How's Jack?" I ask, lying on my bed later that night with my phone pressed against my ear.

"Better. It was just a fever," he replies. He's on his treadmill. I can tell by the way he's panting while he talks and the pounding of his feet in the background.

"And how is she?" I ask innocently.

"She's good," he replies casually, but I can tell there's more to it. When I don't say anything for a moment, I hear the beep of his treadmill as he stops running and breathes into the phone. "Jade, I have to tell you something."

I force myself to swallow as my skin erupts in goose bumps. This feels bad, and I'm nervous for what he's about to say. The worst-case scenario is him telling me they're madly in love and he's leaving me for her.

"I kissed her."

Those three words hang on the telephone line while I let them sink in. I try to digest them to form some kind of reaction, but I must be broken. Because I feel...almost nothing. That can't be normal.

"Did you at least record it like I asked?" I reply sarcastically, but he doesn't laugh.

With a huff, he says, "Jade, I'm serious."

I sit up in my bed. "I'm serious too, Clay. I think you're expecting me to be mad about that, but I'm not. I probably should be. You're my boyfriend, and you kissed another woman. Maybe if it wasn't for the chemistry we shared last night, it would be different."

"God, this is so weird." He groans.

"No, it's not," I reply. "Because I trust you. You didn't sleep with her, did you?"

"No," he says on an exhale.

"Did you ask her if she wanted to be with us both again?" I ask, worried that my hopes are about to be dashed.

"Yes," he replies, dragging out the word.

"And?"

"Tomorrow night. My place," he says, and my jaw drops.

"Your place?" I reply. "That feels different."

"It is." There's a hint of worry in his voice.

"I mean, did you discuss what we would do? Is she going

to demonstrate again, or is this…just sex?" I ask, biting my nail again.

"What do you want, babe?" he gently asks.

"I thought it was pretty obvious what I want," I reply, trying to dodge the words I'm not ready to say.

"I need to hear you say it, Jade."

Dammit.

Taking a deep breath, I squeeze my eyes shut as I just come out with it. "I want more than a demonstration. I don't want to just watch this time. I want to really be with her, both of us. I mean…if that's what she wants. Do you think…that's what she wants?"

On the other end of the line, he lets out a breathy laugh. "Well, when I told her today how much you wanted her, she seemed pretty interested."

My jaw falls open again. "You told her that?" I shriek.

He laughs a little harder. "Yes, I did. And judging by her reaction, I think she wants the same things you want."

It feels impossible. A woman like her wanting someone like me?

But what are we talking about? Just sex? Or something more?

I can't help but recall my conversation today with my dad, wondering if I'm jumping into this too fast. He's in my head now, making me worry about everything.

Should I be more jealous of Clay and Eden? If their relationship was just about her being his Domme, then I have nothing to worry about. Unless there really was more.

And how do my feelings for her fit into this equation?

"Tomorrow night, Jade," Clay adds. "Are you sure this is what you want?"

I take a deep breath and answer as honestly as I can. "Yes. This is what I want."

Rule #28: Don't be afraid to try something new.

Eden

"Relax. I've got you."

"Fuck." *He groans as I thrust again. It's a good* fuck, *which means I was right. He does love this.*

With both of us kneeling on the bed, me behind him, I love how his body leans into mine as I hold his cock. With a tight grip, I stroke to the rhythm of my thrusts. I can feel every tremble. Every spasm and shudder.

Reaching behind, he grabs my hip as the toy grazes his prostate, making him groan again. This time, his cock leaks precum onto my fingers.

"I told you you'd like it," *I mutter in his ear.*

"Fuck, don't stop." *He groans.* "Harder."

With my hand on the back of his neck, I shove him onto all fours and grab his hips, driving the strap-on farther inside him.

"You want to come, don't you?" *I ask in a teasing tone.*

"Yes, Madame."

"Then ask nicely," *I say on a thrust.*

"Please…can I come?" *he begs breathlessly.*

"*Good boy,*" I reply, petting his back. "*You can come now.*"

"*I'm coming,*" he cries with a strangled moan.

He quickly reaches down and strokes his own cock as he comes, making a mess on the bed as I pound into him relentlessly. A sense of pride washes over me at the sight.

I did that.

"*Holy fucking shit,*" he mumbles as he collapses onto the bed.

I carefully pull out and slip off the harness, dropping it onto the floor. Then I crawl into bed behind him, stroking his back.

"*Why did I go so long without trying that?*" he asks, and I laugh as he pulls me into his arms.

"*I don't know, but I'm so glad you finally let me,*" I reply. "*Because I love watching you come like that.*"

He rolls onto his back and pulls me onto his body so I'm straddling his hips. My hair is fanned over my face, and he gathers a handful, using it to pull my face down to his for a kiss. I'm smiling against his mouth as he says, "*It's always good to try new things.*"

"*What would you like to try next?*" I ask with a smile as I lean on his chest and stare into his eyes.

He makes a face like he's thinking hard. "*Hmm...I don't know. There's gotta be more, right?*"

I press a finger to the divot in his chin. "*Oh, there's so much more.*"

Digging his hand into my hair, he drags my lips to his. "*Teach me everything, Madame.*"

"*Anything for you, pet,*" I reply with a smile.

"*Right now, I'd like to try to see how long I can hold my breath.*"

When I give him a perplexed expression, he grabs me by the hips and hauls me all the way up until my thighs are around his ears. I let out a loud laugh as my hands latch on to the headboard.

"*Now sit,*" he says, grabbing my legs and pulling me downward.

My laugh quickly turns to moans as he sucks ravenously on my clit. I relax into the sensation, and I let him take control. I'm not worried about roles or right and wrong at this point.

When I'm with him, I stop thinking. I focus only on how it feels. Because everything with him feels so good.

———————

What am I doing?

I'm standing outside Clay's apartment building, ready to walk inside and break all the rules.

If I do this, who will I be? Eden or Madame Kink?

It's like I'm reliving the same dream over and over and I can't seem to wake up.

I'm a Dominatrix. I fulfill the role of Domme for money. I don't form intimate, personal relationships. I'm a fucking businesswoman.

I don't stand outside shaking nervously because I know that if I go in there, everything will change.

I don't do that.

I'm the walking, talking embodiment of confidence. I am the woman in the mirror who stared back at me seven and a half years ago. Not the one trembling and on the run.

But here I am. Fucking trembling.

All I have to do is text Clay and Jade and tell them that this is crossing a professional boundary and I think it's best we go our separate ways. Then I can just drive to Salacious, find a willing partner, and go back to the way things were before. Everyone loves me there. I don't need to seek out attention or validation from these two people. I don't need anything from them.

But if I go in there and stare into their eyes again, then there is no going back.

Because I know how this will go. The three of us will get entangled in something erotically blissful and intimately euphoric. And we won't be able to stop.

The next thing I know, I'll be canceling clients again and stepping further and further away from my role at the club. I'll be hooked on them the same way I was hooked on him just a few months ago.

They will ease into my personal space, becoming a fixture in my son's life. And then what?

They'll grow tired of me and move on to live their own romantic bliss, leaving Jack and me in the dust.

Or I'll split them up until they're both fighting for me and I've broken both of their hearts.

Either way, this will end badly.

So I should definitely walk away.

But I don't.

I stride across the parking lot toward the door to his building, barely able to suck in a full breath as I reach for the buzzer outside. As my finger presses the white button labeled *Bradley*, I notice the shaking of my hand.

Get yourself together, Eden.

This is the first time I've been to his home, which is already a lot more than what we had before. It's only one second before the door buzzes, and I open it. My heels click on each step as I approach the elevator, clutching my purse to my side.

Once I've completely given over to the decision to do this, that sense of excitement starts to creep in. With each floor I climb in the elevator, my anxiety is slowly replaced by anticipation.

I don't even know what tonight will bring. I've almost forgotten why we started doing this.

What started as a demonstration turned into an invitation.

When the elevator doors open, the two of them are already waiting in the hallway. The door to Clay's apartment is open, and they're just hovering together, staring at me with stifled grins and elation in their eyes.

"You came," Jade says first, reaching out a hand toward me.

I glance up at Clay. "I said I would." I slide my fingers into hers, and she holds me tightly as if she's afraid I'll float away on a breeze.

"Come in," he says, holding the door open for Jade and me to pass through together.

The moment I step into the room, I feel the sense of control slide onto my shoulders like a sharp suit. I force myself to assume the Madame Kink role.

But then Jade smiles at me again, clutching my fingers, and I realize I'm in Clay's *home*, not at the club, and that sharp suit of dominance slides away. Now I just feel naked and vulnerable.

"Would you like a drink?" he asks casually.

"Yes," I reply with control, setting my purse down on the table by the door and following him through the foyer into the kitchen on the right.

Jade stays by my side, and I find her presence comforting. Glancing at her, I realize she's wearing makeup tonight, which she normally doesn't. It's nothing more than a little mascara and glittery eye shadow, but it makes her already stunning eyes pop.

"We need to discuss boundaries and expectations—" I start, grasping at any sense of normalcy, but Clay holds up his hand with a pleading expression.

"Can we just…have a glass of wine together first?"

I swallow down my discomfort. "Yes," I reply.

"I know you're uncomfortable," he says, twisting the cork in the bottle.

"I'm not," I argue, straightening my spine.

"It's fine, Eden. I can just tell."

"I'm not uncomfortable." My voice takes on an urgent tone.

"Then what is it?" Jade asks. "You seem stiff."

My hand is still intertwined with hers, but my eyes are on him. "You think because I want to get down to the protocol quickly that I'm stiff or uncomfortable, but I'm not."

There's an argument already brewing in his expression. "You just walked in the door, and you're already *working*."

"Don't argue," Jade pleads sweetly.

"I was *not*," I say to him, feeling heated and frustrated.

"I really thought that if we did this outside the club, you'd be different," he replies, yanking the cork from the bottle with a sense of anger.

The tight string of anxiety in me snaps, and I let the words fly from my mouth.

"I was just excited, okay?"

The room grows silent. They're both staring at me.

Jade is the first to speak, naturally.

"Well, we're all excited," she says as if to make me feel better and less alone.

Clay stays quiet. He's gazing into my eyes, his strong brow line folded inward to create a gentle crease between them. Neither of us looks away for a long moment.

"I've never done anything like this before," I whisper, holding his gaze.

"Really?" Jade says in astonishment.

I shake my head. "No, I mean...I've never come to someone's apartment like this. I've never been with a couple and felt like *this*."

"Like what?" she asks.

"I don't know," I reply. It's too early to admit something so delicate. That I don't feel like an outsider with them. I'm not an addition to the relationship. I'm *part* of the relationship and after only one time together. Well, one time and a couple of weeks of bouncing back and forth between them.

"It just feels different," I say, covering up what I really want to say.

She squeezes my fingers and clutches me closer to her side. "Because it *is* different."

When my eyes meet hers, I remember what Clay told me yesterday. That Jade is just as interested in me as he is. Most of the couples I'm with make me feel like a novelty to the women. They like to experiment or watch me with their men. They never seek me out the way Jade does. It's like they wouldn't still want me if the men weren't around.

But Jade does.

"Are you going to pour that wine or what?" I ask, breaking the tension in the room.

Jade lets out a sweet chuckle as Clay spins toward the rack holding the wineglasses and pulls three down. He sets them on the table, and he's biting back a smirk as he fills each one.

When he hands me mine, I pull my hand from Jade's grip and take far too big of a gulp. It's never a good idea to drink before going into a scene, but I have to remind myself that that's not really what's happening. I don't think I'm here to be Madame Kink.

"Why am I here?" I ask, feeling bold as I set down my glass.

They look at each other frantically before looking at me.

Before they can speak, I clarify my question. "I know you don't want to get into the protocol and all that yet, but I need to know. What are we doing?"

"Is *for fun* the wrong answer?" Jade replies before chewing her lip. She's leaning against the island in a simple black cotton dress. It's not revealing in the slightest with its boat neckline and exposed shoulders. But she still looks stunning in it.

"No," I reply before taking another big drink of my wine. "Fun is good."

I set down my empty glass, waiting for Clay to refill it.

"We just want you to be *you*." Clay's words strike me as familiar. While he pours, I remember the last night he was in my room at the club and those words were uttered—*I just want you.*

But why? Why me? If I'm not Madame Kink, then what's the allure? Then I'm just a woman. A lonely single mother watching her own life flash by her, too afraid of finding love because of what it's already done to her.

"Tonight, I—*we* thought we could skip the formalities," Clay says, glancing back and forth between Jade and me. "But if you're more comfortable setting boundaries…"

"No," I interject. No more boundaries. No more scenes. No more protocols.

No more Madame Kink.

"You're right," I add. "Tonight should just be about us."

Rule #29: There's a first time for everything.

Eden

WE TAKE THE WINE BOTTLE INTO THE LIVING ROOM, AND WE
each find a seat. Clay ends up in a chair by himself, and Jade is
next to me—*very* close to me.

Turning toward her, I read the eagerness in her expression.
She's biting her lip as she gazes at my mouth. If I had to guess, I'd
say she's excited to get things started.

It's only been a week since Jade and I have been alone. But
things are different now. We're both finally acknowledging the
desire that we hid before.

Before…she was off-limits. But now…she looks like she's one
second away from jumping into my lap.

"Have you ever been with a woman before?" I ask casually. I
want to know what I'm getting into with her. Is she curious, or is
that lust on her face real?

She shakes her head. "I kissed a few friends in college when I
was drunk, but that was it."

"And…now you want to experiment?" I force myself to

swallow, hoping that I'm not about to feel like just some random person she wants to *try* on.

Emphatically, she shakes her head. "No. I want you, Eden. I'm not experimenting. I *know*."

God, she is so bold.

My heart rate picks up speed in my chest, and I have to remind myself to breathe. She wants *me*.

Me. Not Madame Kink.

"Can I kiss you?" I ask, letting my gaze fall to her lips, pouty and pink and waiting for me.

She doesn't respond. She launches.

There is nothing *experimental* about it.

Her hands grasp either side of my face as she lunges toward me, pressing her lips to mine. And in pure, sweet, fumbling Jade fashion, she nearly knocks me off the sofa.

Sucking my bottom lip between her teeth, I moan as she licks her way into my mouth. It's as if she's been dying to do this for a long time. When she bites down, I actually whimper, and it takes me by surprise.

Barely coming up for air, she holds me tightly as her mouth devours my lips and tongue. My body is on fire with need and excitement. And it doesn't occur to me until this moment just how long I've wanted her too, especially like this.

In my mind, I'm remembering every single one of our stolen moments that led to this.

The night she showed up to my room.

The way she trembled in the voyeur room as we watched Mia.

The look on her face when I caught her watching me work.

They never compared to this.

I think I like dominant Jade.

"God, I want you so bad," I mumble into her mouth.

Then she's in my lap, legs straddling my hips, and I stop trying to take control. I fall into a sweet submission as she grinds against me, moving her mouth from my lips to my neck.

This night really went from zero to a hundred quickly.

My hands weave around her waist, exploring the slender shape of her body from her hips to her shoulders. The closer she edges toward me, the more her dress slides up, and I find myself inching my fingers beneath the fabric to squeeze her petite and perfect ass.

She's in a thong, and I groan into her mouth as I wrap my hand around the waistline of her panties and tug them down. Because of her position, they don't go far, but the idea of having her naked on my lap sends a bolt of lightning to my core.

Distantly, I remember that Clay is still in the room, watching from the chair. And while I want nothing more than to lay Jade on this sofa and have my way with every single inch of her, I need him to be involved. I need his touch as much as I need hers.

We must realize it at the same time because Jade and I come up for air simultaneously. We're both gasping as we stare into each other's eyes.

"You feel so good in my arms," she says before a grin stretches across her face.

Something flutters warmly inside me.

"So do you," I reply, digging my fingers into her hair and pulling her down for one more quick kiss.

As we pull away, we turn at the same time to see Clay reclined in his armchair. He looks relaxed as he casually watches us. One leg is propped on the other, and his head is resting on his propped arm.

"You two are so fucking beautiful," he murmurs.

"Care to join us?" Jade says cheekily.

As he stands, exposing an obvious erection straining against his pants, he smiles. "Baby, I wouldn't miss it for the world."

Then he walks toward us, and I'm expecting him to join us on the couch. Instead, he pulls Jade off of my lap and throws her over his shoulder with ease. She lets out an excited yelp, her sweet little ass exposed with red marks from where I was just gripping her too tightly.

"Why don't we take this to the bedroom?" he says with a wink. Then he puts out a hand for me.

"Don't even think about throwing me over your shoulder," I say as he pulls me to my feet.

With a laugh, he shakes his head. "You lead then."

My hand is still in his. But I don't move for the hallway just yet. Instead, I lean in and kiss him.

Any trace of anxiety or trepidation is gone. His kiss is familiar and warm.

As we pull away, I take his hand and walk toward the hall, where I assume his room is.

"On the right," he says, and I guide him there.

Immediately I notice how the room smells like him. His cologne. His scent. His essence.

It's comforting and arousing. I want to bury my face in his pillows and stake my claim on everything that belongs to him.

When I step toward the bed, he follows me and tosses Jade down on the mattress. She's staring up at me through hooded lashes as she bites her lip.

"You're wearing too much," I say as my hands slide up her thighs.

"So are you," she replies, quickly shucking off her dress. "Help her out, babe."

"Gladly." Clay growls as he steps behind me.

As I tug down Jade's panties, Clay's lips hungrily suck on my neck, and I can feel the moisture pooling between my legs. He tugs off my black silk blouse in one motion, and his hands wind around my waist while his mouth doesn't stop its ravenous exploration.

As soon as Jade's panties hit the floor, her legs spread for me, and I have to take a moment to compose myself at the sight. She's naked, open, and ready for me. I love how unashamed she is.

My hands slide eagerly up the inside of her thighs, and when I reach the top, her head falls backward in anticipation.

"God, Jade. Look at how perfect you are," I say with a hum as I lean over her.

Behind me, Clay is working down my tight black pants, and the moment he has them down my thighs, his teeth find the tender flesh of my ass. I let out a yelp from his bite, shoving my hips back against him.

When he stands up, his cock grinds between my cheeks. He's so hard it must be painful.

"You're both perfect," he whispers in my ear.

His compliment hits me deep in my chest, and I hum with pleasure as I reach behind me and stroke his long hair.

But I can't take another minute without touching her. I feel like I might explode.

"You don't mind if I eat your girlfriend's pussy, do you?" I whisper quietly with a wicked smile.

He wraps a hand around the back of my neck, and I let out another whimper. Then he drags my face closer, pressing his lips to my ear. "She could be your girlfriend too, you know?"

My body grows instantly hot with anxiety when he says those words. I can't have a girlfriend, not really. Or a boyfriend. Or anything.

He must notice my panic because he quickly distracts me.

"Look at how much she wants you," he says, purring in my ear.

Then, before I can respond, he shoves me forward, bending me at the hips until my head is between his girlfriend's legs.

I stare up at her through hooded lashes and spot an expression of excitement. So I don't keep her waiting, I quiet every doubt in my head and drag my tongue across her warm, wet cunt.

She shudders underneath me as my lips close around her clit, humming deeply while I suck.

That only makes her shudder more.

It's exquisite to feel her reactions against my tongue. I couldn't stop if I tried.

I lick her again, this time plunging my tongue deep inside, and she moans even louder when I do.

"Holy shit," she cries out with a gasp.

Dragging my tongue across her folds, I flick it hungrily against her clit, and she loses control again.

"Please don't stop," she squeals.

I feel her tensing already, so I pull away with a smile. "Not so fast, my sweet girl."

Lifting up to her elbows, she gazes down at me, looking flustered. She reaches for my face and pulls me in for a kiss before I've even had a chance to wipe it. I love the way she groans against my lips.

When I feel fingers spreading me from behind, I yelp into Jade's mouth. Then I feel Clay's warm tongue doing to me what I just did to Jade.

He's ravenous as he buries his face in my cunt from behind. His tongue strokes my clit, and I reach back to lace my fingers through his hair and pull him closer.

Jade is panting beneath me, and I turn to her with a smirk. Pressing my lips to hers, I say, "Tell me what you want."

Our eyes meet, and I know she remembers our lessons at the club when I encouraged her to be more vocal about what she wants. Now I'm putting her to the test.

"I want you," she replies sweetly.

"Oh yeah? And where would you like me?" I aim a sultry smile in her direction as I wait for her to give me her filthy instructions.

"Between my legs," she whispers before reaching up to bite my bottom lip between her teeth.

"That's my girl," I reply after she releases me. At that very moment, Clay plunges two fingers inside me, and I let out a sexy, crying grunt. He pulses his digits with force, and I know he'll have me coming in no time. And I'd like to come while my face is buried between Jade's legs.

"I want to feel how much you want it, Jade," I say as I kiss her. "Show me how much you want me to lick your pussy."

She doesn't hesitate. My girl learns so well.

Her fingers slide into my hair, and she forces my face down to where she wants it, slamming my mouth against her soaking cunt. Perfect.

This time my goal isn't passive pleasure. I suck her clit to make her come, and she starts writhing immediately. Mimicking what Clay is doing, I slide a finger inside her, hooking it upward to make her toes curl.

She's so tight and tense I can feel the walls of her pussy clenching around me. I know it's going to be so good when she finally comes, and I can't wait to hear the sounds she makes.

Her grasp on my scalp tightens, but the sting of it only draws me closer to my own orgasm. Clay is rough with me now because he knows how much I love it. His fingers fuck me harder and harder until my body is pulsing with pleasure.

I groan so loud against Jade's sensitive center it brings her coursing to her own climax. My suction gets even stronger as I come.

Her body goes rigid as she's thrown into pleasure so intense she's practically screaming. She is shaking and trembling, and I can feel it coming even before she does.

Just as I pull my mouth from her throbbing center, I'm met with her wet, pulsing arousal soaking my hand and landing against my chest.

"Oh my God!" she squeals while her body continues to convulse out of her control.

"Holy shit," Clay murmurs behind me.

I'm still coming down from my own climax, but I swear watching Jade squirt, much to her surprise, might send me into another torrent of sexual pleasure.

Her face is contorted in shock, her mouth hanging open, and her cheeks so red they look sunburned.

"What was that?" she cries out, staring down at the mess she's left all over my breasts.

I chuckle as I pull my fingers from her cunt and stare down at how wet they are.

"I take it you've never squirted before."

"I didn't even know I could do that," she shrieks with a gasp. Then she slams her hands over her face and turns on the mattress as if she's trying to get away from me.

"What's wrong?" I ask with a smile.

"I'm so embarrassed!" she squeals.

"Oh, baby," Clay croons as he slides up next to her on the bed. He must have taken his clothes off at some point because he's fully naked now. "That was the hottest fucking thing I've ever seen. It's nothing to be embarrassed about."

He pulls her close, but she still won't face him. So I climb onto the bed on her other side, sandwiching her between us. Then I peel her hands away from her face and kiss her lips with great tenderness. It has her melting in my arms.

Together, Clay and I stroke her softly, taking turns kissing her face, her neck, and her ears. Before long, she's no longer embarrassed but gobbling up every bit of our attention.

Rule #30: Always let your Madame come first.

Clay

I don't believe in karma. Because if karma existed, then there's no way I'd be lying here with these two incredible people who both seem to set my life, my body, and my soul on fire.

What did I do to deserve this? Is this the universe's way of repaying me for the shitty parents I was dealt? Or is this all just one big setup, only for them both to be taken away from me in the end?

I don't know if I'd survive another heartbreak.

This is only the second time we've had Eden with us in bed, and I already know it won't be easy letting her go. She fits right in as if she was always meant to be here.

Although, currently, it's Jade in the middle, still mortified by the way she squirted all over Eden. Which was, as I said, the hottest fucking thing I've ever seen.

I certainly couldn't make Jade do that, but now that I know she can, you can fucking bet I'm going to try.

As my hand slides up her hip, it brushes against Eden's, who's currently sucking on my girlfriend's earlobe and making her mewl like a kitten.

Oh yeah, she's never fucking leaving. She's stuck with us now.

When our fingers brush, I interlock them, holding on to her as I trail my tongue up the back of Jade's neck. I hear Eden whimper, so I move my mouth to her lips, kissing her hard as we hover over Jade.

We are a tangled mess of lips, limbs, and skin, melting into one body of pleasure. It's all so fucking perfect. They can both feel it, too, right? It can't be just me.

"I want to watch you two." Jade's small voice stops us both, and we freeze before pulling away and staring down at her.

"You want to watch us what, baby?" I ask, leaning down to give her a quick kiss.

"I want to watch you do it," she replies as if it's so obvious.

"What about you?" Eden asks.

"I just *squirted*," she says, adding emphasis to that word that makes the three of us laugh. "I'm fine," she adds. "Besides, watching you two is enough for me. I just want to see it."

"Are you sure? You won't get jealous?" I ask.

She stares at Eden as she shakes her head. "No. I won't. You're both sexy as fuck and both turn me on, so watching you together would be twice as hot."

With that, she sits up and climbs over Eden, putting her in the middle. My cock twitches at her proximity. Sliding my fingers down her thigh, I suddenly remember how it felt to touch her, to believe for one second that she was mine.

"All right then, *Mistress*," Eden says with a wicked smirk aimed at Jade. "What should we do?"

Fuck, that was hot.

My cock seems to love the idea of a dominant Jade, although it's not something I expected from her. Eden clearly seems to see something I don't. These two have a bond I didn't see coming, and judging by the way Eden just called her *Mistress*, I get the sneaking suspicion that these two have more going on than I realized.

Jade bites her bottom lip as she grins at Eden. Then she

reaches forward and grasps Eden by the throat, pulling her closer and licking a line across her lips. When she slides her tongue into Eden's mouth, a bead of precum drops from the head of my dick.

Holy fucking shit.

This is a side of Jade I swear I've never seen before. It's like she flipped a switch, taking on this sexy-as-fuck persona that's still adorable and quirky while also powerful and provocative.

I'm watching with my mouth hanging open, and I wouldn't be surprised if drool slipped out at this point. My hand is lazily stroking my length as I stare in aroused astonishment.

Jade pulls away from the kiss and stares through hooded eyes at Eden.

"Ride his cock," Jade mutters against her lips. I expect Eden to hesitate, but she doesn't.

"Yes, Mistress," she replies with a wink.

As Eden slings her legs over my hips, her eyes meet mine, and I can't fight the smile that softly pulls at the corners of my mouth.

It's as if I'm experiencing our relationship all over again, but this time, it's different. There's something *more* here, and maybe it's having Jade with us, or maybe it's because I've grown closer to Eden on a personal level in the past couple of weeks that being in bed with her just feels more real.

She rubs her already moist cunt against my shaft with her hands planted against my chest.

"Kiss him," Jade says in a sultry command.

Without hesitation, I lift up, and at the same time, Eden leans down. We meet in the middle with an explosive kiss. I grab the back of her neck, pulling her closer as our tongues tangle together in soft friction. I moan into her mouth as she continues to grind against me.

"I need to be inside you," I mumble against her lips.

"Wait," Jade says. She inches closer, sitting on her knees, as she pulls Eden's mouth to hers.

"I want to feel it go in."

Fuck me.

Jade's hand wraps around my cock as Eden lifts herself up. Then Jade guides me to Eden's waiting cunt. They stare into each other's eyes, lips parted and pupils dilated as Eden lowers her hips, sliding me home. Jade's fingers are there the whole time, feeling everything.

It feels like I'm fucking both of them.

It also feels like I could come already. The sensation is overwhelming.

"Fuuuuuuck." I groan as Eden seats herself all the way down on my throbbing cock. Jade moves her fingers to Eden's clit, and they're still staring at each other.

The connection between them is so fucking sexy and beautiful at the same time. But I don't feel like a third wheel at all. Both of them have a hand on me, and it's like we're all connected and moving as one, and I've never felt anything like it in my life.

Eden immediately starts grinding on my cock. I'm mesmerized by the motion of her hips, rolling and twisting in perfect rhythm as she suffocates my dick with her wet heat.

Yeah…I'm not going to last long at all.

After a few minutes of that, I feel like I'm going to lose it.

"Fuck, stop," I bark, grabbing Eden's hips to keep her still. They both stare down at me as I take slow, heavy breaths to keep from blowing my load too soon.

Eden has turned Jade into a squirter and me into a two-pump chump. We'll call that *the Eden effect.*

"I'm not ready to come yet," I mutter as the feeling subsides. "Just go slow."

Eden's nails dig into my pecs as she starts moving again, this time with more controlled, easy movements. Then she leans down and presses her lips to my ear, speaking in a low whisper. "Be a good little pet and let your Madame come first."

"That's not helping," I reply through gritted teeth. Hearing her even utter the word *pet* again triggers something inside me that makes it very hard to keep my dick from exploding.

She chuckles softly before rising back up. As she starts grinding again, I feel Jade's fingers brushing my cock as she rubs Eden's clit in tight circular motions.

The faster she moves, the faster Eden grinds, and I have to focus all my energy on riding out the blissful sensation without slipping off the edge. I stare up into Eden's eyes, watching the pleasure take over as she chases her own climax.

"Fuck," I say breathlessly as I watch her get closer and closer to her own orgasm. "Come on my cock, Eden."

Jade's fingers move faster, her lips trailing along Eden's shoulder and up her neck until she's nibbling on her ear. Eden whimpers, and I can tell by the pained expression on her face that she's about to come.

"Come on, baby. You're almost there. Use me. Just like that," I say.

Her hips are grinding so hard now in a quick, rolling rhythm. She's fucking herself so hard on my cock that I lose control and slam headfirst into pleasure. Grabbing tightly to her hips, I thrust upward with a roar as I come, filling her up. Her pussy tightens around my dick, and her fingernails dig deeper into my flesh.

"I'm—I'm…coming," she screams.

"Oh my God, yes," Jade says with a hum as she strokes Eden through her orgasm.

The room echoes with the sounds of sex as we all moan and cry in unison. It's so dirty and heavenly at the same time. I wish this moment could last forever.

Eden falls forward, draping her body over mine as she breathes heavily into the crook of my neck. Jade lies down next to me, and I turn my head to find her lips, kissing her fiercely as she nuzzles closer.

After a few moments of catching our breaths, Eden lifts herself from my cock, and we all stare down together to watch my cum drip down the inside of her thighs.

"Why is that so damn hot?" Jade asks innocently.

"Because it means I've claimed her," I reply, looking up into Eden's eyes with a lopsided smirk and a wink. I'm reminded of the moment yesterday in her room when she told me I still had her. That I'll always have her. And I don't know if she grasped how much hope that gave me.

Eden doesn't exactly smile in return, but there's a twitch at the corner of her mouth.

"She's ours now," Jade adds, her grin stretching all the way across her face as she wraps her arms around my torso.

I pull Eden to my opposite side, and she rests her head on my shoulder so the three of us are cuddled together. Jade's fingers linked with mine.

This could work.

It's the one thought in my head that rings true at this moment. Doubt and anxiety battle for dominance, but that is the single thought that screams the loudest.

This could really fucking work.

If Eden would let it. And that, I know, is going to be the hard part.

Rule #31: If you're falling in love with your boyfriend's ex-Domme, it's best to let him know.

Jade

"Hey, Cupcake, will you take this file to Clay? Just have him sign where it's tabbed."

"Of course, Daddy," I reply from the doorway of his office. He has his phone pinched between his ear and shoulder, which looks really uncomfortable, but he refuses to listen to me and get a Bluetooth receiver.

Crossing the room, I take the file from his hand, and he shoots me a smile before I spin away and head to the door.

To save some money for the company, he decided not to replace their last temp, so I just help them out instead. It keeps me busy anyway since I don't have much to do as it is.

It's only slightly awkward that every morning I show up at the office after a night of letting his coworker defile me. And on this particular morning, it's after a night when his coworker and his coworker's ex-Domme simultaneously defiled me.

Oh, poor me.

Last night was one of the best nights of my life. One to be remembered forever. And not only because it was hot and sexy and so, so, so dirty. It was also…strangely romantic. It's one thing to be so connected to another person but to be so connected to *two* other people is out of this world.

I wish we could have both stayed over at Clay's. Even more than the sex, I would have loved to sleep between them, feeling their bodies next to mine all night, waking up the next day to start the day together. But Eden had to relieve her nanny, and I didn't want my dad to wake up without me in the house. So after we cuddled and laughed in bed for another couple of hours, we left.

Then I went home and relived the whole thing with my magic wand. I even tried to make myself *squirt* again, but I had no luck. Apparently, only Eden knows that magic trick.

Clay's office door is closed, so I quietly peel it open and smile at him from the doorway. He's on a Zoom call with a client, and he's talking about stocks and yields and bonds, but I'm not really trying to catch anything he's saying. Instead, I ease myself into the room and walk to his desk behind his computer, where he is staring as he talks.

He keeps a stone-cold serious expression on his face, but I can see a little twitch in the corner of his mouth. Then I use one hand to tug down the front of my blouse, exposing my left breast and resting it on top of his computer screen.

"I think our best course of action for this account would be something less risky to ensure long-term growth and stability," he says as he leans forward and pinches my nipple between his fingers.

I open my mouth in a silent scream, and he keeps his expression cool and professional.

On and on, he talks, only glancing at my tits every few seconds without much of a reaction.

I even try lifting my skirt and resting my ass against his desk. But he still doesn't flinch.

Finally, he says goodbye to his clients and clicks off his computer. Then he glances at the open door before shooting me a wicked grin.

"You dirty little tease," he says quietly. Then he gestures to me to come closer, and I lean over his desk to press my lips to his.

"My daddy said you need to sign this," I say, dropping the folder on his desk.

"Did your *daddy* also tell you to give me a boner during my meeting with the Zimmermans?"

"No, that was just a treat from me."

He leans back in his chair with a smile. At times like this, I wish I could kiss him more and be more public with our relationship. It would be nice not to have to hide our kisses in silence.

"So...Eden texted me," I say carefully.

He looks up from the folder. "Yeah?"

"She wants to take me shopping."

His brows pinch together. "Shopping? That doesn't sound like her."

"For my Domme clothes. She said I need to find my style."

That makes his brows lift. "Can I come?"

Giving him a lopsided smirk, I shake my head. "No boys allowed. Besides, I'm excited to spend time together, just us."

He looks pleased with that, giving me an approving nod. Then his expression turns serious. "How are you feeling?" he asks quietly.

I know immediately that he's referring to last night.

"I'm feeling great. On top of the world. Better than ever. You?"

He contemplates for a moment. Then his crooked smile grows. "Yeah, I'm feeling pretty good too."

"How do you think *she* feels?" I ask, my eyes glancing toward the door to make sure no one can hear us. My dad has a heavy walk, so we'll know if he's coming. Besides, I can still hear him talking on the phone in the distance.

Clay's smile fades. "I've never been able to decipher her feelings well."

"But she seemed happy, Clay. She seemed really happy."

"You really like her, don't you?" he says, looking pleased.

"Duh," I reply with a groan.

Laughing, I hear him rise from his desk and walk toward me. "Baby, come here."

He holds my hands in his, his eyes carefully watching the door. "I think she really likes you too."

My heart swells at the idea, but I don't say anything because this is all so weird. Clay is my boyfriend. Eden is his ex. I just admitted that I'm developing feelings for her.

What are we even doing?

He wraps his arms around my body and pulls me to his chest. "I just want to protect you," he murmurs with his lips against my head.

"Protect me from what?" I ask.

"Getting too attached."

Then he pulls away and stares down at me. "As much as I love the idea of making last night something real, I can't let myself get too excited. This is just a job to Eden. Just getting her to come to my apartment last night was a miracle."

"Last night was not just a job to her," I argue.

"Yes, but what are you suggesting? Tell me right now what it is you want."

I don't hesitate. "I don't want her to see anyone else. I want her with *us*. She belongs to *us*."

"After a couple of nights, you feel this way?" He looks confused, and I let out a sigh of frustration. I can't tell Clay just how long I've been seeing Eden or how much she's taught me already. To him, she and I have barely met.

But to me...I feel like I'm already falling in love.

"Yes," I reply impatiently. "After just a couple of nights, I feel very strongly that you care about her, and I care about her, and she cares about us, so why the hell shouldn't we at least try?"

He goes silent for a moment as he stares at me in contemplation. It almost seems like he wants to come clean about something, but he bites his tongue instead. "I don't know if Eden does relationships, baby."

My forehead creases as I stare up at him in confusion. "Why not?"

He shrugs. "Because of Jack, I assume."

"But we've already gotten to know him," I reply. "Do you think there's something else?"

His gaze grows solemn, and now I can really tell there's something he's not sharing or maybe something he knows that I don't.

"That's her story to tell," he replies.

My face turns into a pout. "I don't believe her walls are impenetrable. I just think she struggles to let others in, but she's learning to trust us. She'll let us in."

He holds me by the arms and pulls away as he stares at me with a dire expression. "Do you realize what you're suggesting, Jade? Are you serious about this? Bringing her into our relationship? For good? Not just sex."

My answer comes flying out of my mouth without any consideration. "Yes!"

He wears a playful smile as he rubs my arms. "Please think about this. It's serious, baby. Not something to rush into."

"I don't think we're rushing into it," I reply. "We're all so good together. It just feels right. I can't explain it."

"So, on top of telling your dad that you're dating me, you're going to come clean about dating her too?"

I shrug. "Two birds, one stone."

"He's going to have a heart attack," Clay replies with a laugh.

I take his hands in mine and stand my ground. "Clay, I'm serious. I don't want to lose her."

He leans in and kisses my forehead. "Then we'll need to take it slow."

At that, I frown. Slow is the last thing I want.

But just as I ready myself to argue, we hear the heavy steps of my father down the hall. In a rush, Clay jumps to his desk, pulling out the file to finish signing. After a quick scribble on the indicated line, he tosses it back to me, and I spin toward the door just in time to hand it to my dad in the hallway.

I can't help but notice the way his gaze flicks back and forth between Clay's office and me as I present the file to him. "Hey, Daddy," I chirp with a smile. "I was just bringing this back to you."

"What took so long?" he asks.

I clear my throat, anxiety crawling up my spine.

But before I can answer, Clay shows up in the doorway. "Sorry, Will. I was stuck in a meeting with Mr. and Mrs. Zimmerman."

My dad nods knowingly before a hearty chuckle. "Ah, that makes sense."

"Are you guys hungry? Clay and I could go grab lunch?" I ask, bouncing on my feet.

My dad furrows his brow. "We'll have it delivered today. Sandwiches sound good."

As he turns away from us, I glance up at Clay, who looks pale and worried as he watches my father leave. If that is an indication, I'd say my dad suspects something.

And after that conversation with him on the boat the other day, he more than likely suspects Clay of *charming* me. I hate that my father thinks that. Clay has never done anything bad to me, regardless of what he might have done in the past.

Which means I need to set my father straight.

But is right now the best time? Clay and I are seriously talking about adding a third person to our relationship. Do we need the stress of my father's wrath on top of that? If things blow up with my dad and, God forbid, Clay loses his job, will it ruin everything with Eden?

Or will it ruin everything altogether?

Rule #32: There is no such thing as little moments.

Eden

I'M A TERRIBLE DOMME.

I didn't used to be. I used to pride myself on being the best and doing everything by the book. But this man has me messing up left and right. It's like I'm fighting with this inner voice that wants something different.

Maybe I'm tired. Maybe I'm taking on too much.

Or seeing him too much.

He comes every night now. Every. Night. And it's still not enough. I don't charge him anymore and haven't slept with anyone else in months. I still have my clients and keep up the job, but the intimacy belongs to one person now.

He's sleeping next to me, chest down on the mattress with his arms folded under his head. He looks like a god like this. So perfect with his olive skin, sculpted muscles, and flawless hair.

But it's not about his looks. It never was. I used to despise good-looking men like Clay. Men who knew they were so attractive, they used it to wield power. And maybe he tried until he felt what it was like to submit.

Now he's mine.

A feather in the palm of my hand. Delicate and fragile and soft.

I want to keep it.

Emotion builds in my throat as I force my eyes away from where he's resting peacefully. This can't be happening to me. Not once in the many years I've been doing this have I ever felt compelled to get so attached to the person I'm with.

Why now?

Why him?

He's just a guy—a cocky, sweet, submissive, sexy, charming guy. I've worked with a hundred just like him.

It doesn't make any sense. There is no discernible reason why my heart seems to flutter into my throat every time I look at him. Or why he just seems so perfect when I know he's not.

All rational thought has seemingly gone out the window. Everything I think I should be doing, I can't bring myself to do.

Cut him off.

Let him go.

Walk away.

Can't, can't, can't.

Like right now, I should crawl out of this bed and put some distance between us. Instead, I settle myself flat against the bed, flush to his side, as I run my fingers through his hair, brushing the long brown strands out of his face.

He stirs from my touch, and I bite back a grin as he wakes up.

With a groan and a stretch, he stares at me. "How long was I out?" he asks with a rasp in his voice.

"About an hour," I reply softly.

"Getting pegged really takes it out of you, doesn't it?"

I chuckle, watching his cheeks turn red as he blushes.

"It's an intense experience, being your first time and all."

"Yeah…intense," he replies.

I watch his features for any sign that he might freak out. Some straight men seem to have such a stigma about their asses, like there's something so sacred about them that being touched or penetrated changes them in some chemical and cosmic way.

Unless you count the mind-melting orgasms I've witnessed them having, it doesn't.

It's just an ass.

Pegging was never really about that, anyway. For us, it was about submission. Trust. Connection. And the liberation of no longer fearing something you once feared.

And out of all the men I've experienced this with, it's no surprise that Clay was by far my favorite. He was adorably nervous, trembling the first time I grazed his prostate while prepping him. His eyes stayed so set on mine the whole time. It was as if my gaze provided him the comfort he needed—like I was what he needed.

"How are you feeling?" I ask for the hundredth time tonight.

His brow furrows slightly as he rolls onto his side, pulling me into his arms. He's deep in contemplation, but I don't rush his response. I let my cheek settle against his forearm and savor the way it feels to relax with him, switching roles so I no longer have to be the dominant one.

"I feel good," he whispers. His hand strokes my arm, and my leg drapes over his. We're comfortable and quiet. Then he speaks again. "I've never felt so close to anyone before, Eden. I'll be honest...it freaks me out a little bit."

My heart pounds harder with each word because I feel it too, but I'm so afraid to let him see just how much. I slant my head toward him. "Why?"

He turns. "Do you have any idea what it's like to be so vulnerable with another person? Have you ever experienced it from this perspective?"

My head drops back to his arm. "Yes, of course."

"Well, did you feel like you were falling in love with the person you were with?"

There's a wounded tone to his voice that makes my chest ache. My head lifts up as I stare back at him.

Love?

No, no, no.

"No. Clay…"

He puts a hand up. "Please don't say anything. I know how fucking stupid I sound, but that's just how I feel, Eden. I experience emotions with you that I don't know how to put into words. Sometimes I feel like I barely know you and you know every intimate detail about me. But no matter what, I just keep coming back."

His gaze finds mine, and I cling to it like I'm suddenly the one finding comfort there. I've never felt so in tune with anyone before, as if I could just stare into his eyes forever, my twin flame staring back.

"I'm addicted to you," he whispers.

My heart is ripped from my chest, and I feel like if this conversation goes any further, it will go somewhere we can't come back from.

I can't start a romantic relationship with a client. I just can't.

"You don't sound stupid," I whisper, brushing my thumb against his cheek. "I'm sorry if this feels one-sided, but my personal life isn't—"

"I know, I know," he says, interrupting me. "It's okay. I understand. If these little moments are all I can have of you, then that's what I'll take."

It's not good enough for me. Something is still gnawing at my insides even as he tries to relax into our cuddled position.

"They're not little moments," I reply with my face now on his shoulder. My hands wrap around his midsection, my fingers tracing the ridges of muscle along his torso like they're trying to memorize every detail. "These are very big moments, Clay, for both of us."

His lips press against the side of my head. "I can live with that."

"Sold! To the man in the back for two thousand dollars!"

I watch from the bar as the girl with pigtail braids and a schoolgirl uniform bounces off the stage and walks to the back of the club to meet the man who just won a date with her for the next hour. There's obvious chemistry between them as she drops onto his lap, and they smile at each other with excitement.

I love auction nights at the club—or at least, I used to.

The thrill of the game, the promise of something new, the show of wealth and power.

Every week, I'd get on that auction block and watch as the people in the crowd spent thousands just for an hour with me. I'd be lying if I said that didn't fuel my need for validation. I'm only human. Of course I loved the attention.

But more than that, I loved getting to know someone new. I loved learning about their different desires and kinks. Then I *really* loved fulfilling those, watching the way it would change them, like a secret code only I knew.

Afterward, I'd send them on their merry way to fulfill those needs with someone else, armed with a new piece of information about themselves that would make their lives more enjoyable and stimulating.

I miss that.

I haven't been on the auction block in nearly a year. It was the night Daisy bid a million dollars on her now husband and I watched my best friend find his forever person.

Clay was there that night. And while things between us were still so new, there was a moment that hit me when this sudden craving for love and my newfound infatuation with him collided like a hurricane.

Falling in love with him after that night was not an accident. Maybe it was fate. I don't know.

I just know that for the first time in my life, I opened myself up to something new.

And now look at me. My life is in disarray. I'm being sucked into a relationship, and I can't seem to find the argument anymore for why I should walk away. Something about the other night erased all sensible rationale from my brain.

"Why aren't you up there?" a familiar deep voice says from behind me.

I turn to find Ronan smiling at me as he takes a seat on a barstool.

"I don't do these anymore," I reply. "You know that."

He nods before waving at Geo, who acknowledges him as he starts making his usual drink.

"Yes, I do know that. I wish I knew *why*."

"That's confidential," I reply with a smirk. "What are you doing here? And where's Daisy?"

"She's performing at the bar tonight, and I figured I might find you here, so I left a little early," he says as his drink is presented on the bar in front of him.

"Well, it's good to see you," I say, holding up my glass. He clinks his to mine, and we both take a drink.

"It's always good to see you," he replies. "Jack is feeling better then?" He says this quietly so no one around us can hear. Once I decided to make the existence of my son a secret for good, he respected that. He may never understand what it's like to live two different lives, but as a man, he never really had to make that choice.

Once people know I'm a mom, it threatens my image as a Dominatrix. I don't make the rules. That's just how it is. I think it's just as unfair as everyone else does.

Not to mention it's Jack's safety that motivates nearly every choice I make.

"He's fine. It was just a twenty-four-hour thing."

"Good," he replies, dropping the subject. "And how are *you*?"

My eyes cascade down to the drink on the table as I contemplate how to answer that question.

When I don't answer for a moment, he doubles down on his interrogation. "You know…you don't need to keep everything a secret, especially your happiness. It's not going to combust the moment you share it with someone else."

"How do you know?" I ask with a teasing glare in his direction. "Happiness is just a trick to make us make stupid decisions."

He laughs. "And what stupid decision have you made lately?" He bumps my shoulder, and I suddenly feel so desperate to talk to him about it. Or *anyone*, really.

"I started seeing *him* again," I say, knowing that Ronan will know exactly who *him* is even if he doesn't know the specifics. Everyone picked up on the change in my behavior last year. You don't go from openly having sex in the voyeur hall with a different person nearly every night to exclusively seeing *one* person every night without people noticing.

"Ahh…*him*," Ronan replies.

"And his girlfriend," I add.

Ronan nearly chokes on his whiskey.

"Of course you are," he replies with a playful tone as he wipes his face. "Is it serious?"

"I don't know. I think it's starting to be."

He heaves a big sigh, and it sounds like he's preparing himself to make an argument he's been wanting to make for years. Which I'm sure is the case. Ronan has been gently nudging me to be more open to relationships and my feelings, but I always wrote it off because that's just the guy he is. He has always worn his heart on his sleeve, his arms constantly open for whoever needed them to be.

I'm much the opposite.

"Go ahead," I mutter. "Say it."

"All I'm thinking is that if *you* say it's serious, then it must be. And if this guy and his girlfriend have you skipping auction night again, then it must be because you want to."

"None of it makes any sense," I argue. Turning toward him, I keep my voice down as I suddenly feel myself spilling everything. Ronan has always had this effect on me, maybe because he's safe and he always has been. But the moment I start voicing everything in my head is the moment it becomes real.

"I just wish I understood *why* these two have such an effect on me. I've been with tons of people over the last seven years, people I expected to be more compatible with. But then, all of a sudden, a cocky rich boy and a naive girl as sweet as sugar have me changing my entire life. Why? I wish I understood."

Ronan takes a moment to digest everything I just expressed, but then he finally lets his face stretch into a smile, and a laugh spills out. He places a hand on my knee, wearing a proud expression as he says, "Eden, what do you think love is? If it made sense, it would be like taxes or the weather. But it doesn't. That's why there are songs and art and literature—because we're all just trying to make sense of something that never, ever makes sense."

To my surprise, tears spring up behind my eyes, and I have to look away.

His hand rests affectionately on my back as I finish my glass of wine.

"If I had to guess, not that I'm trying to make sense of it, but…"

I turn toward him, waiting to hear his thoughts.

"It sounds to me like you and Clay have a lot more in common than you think."

My eyes widen at the sound of his name, and I find myself glancing around to make sure no one else heard it.

"How so?" I ask.

"You're both hiding the most vulnerable parts of yourselves. He pretends to be cocky when we both know he's just as lonely as the rest of us."

He's so right it hurts. The tears sting as I blink them away.

"And as for the girl…I don't know her, but naive and sweet reminds me of someone I used to know."

"I was never sweet," I snap, turning toward him with a look of anger.

That only makes him smile. "Keep telling yourself that."

When Geo sets my second glass of wine in front of me, I give him a warm look and mutter a quiet "Thank you."

After he walks away, I think about what Ronan is saying. And maybe it's true. Maybe I'm connecting to Jade and Clay because I see bits of myself in them. Or maybe I'm falling for them because we share more than similar traits. There are a shared experience and relatability with both of them that go beyond anything I've ever felt before.

Or maybe, as Ronan said, it doesn't make sense, and it never will. Maybe my feelings for them defy logic or reason, but that doesn't make those feelings any less genuine.

"I blame you," I softly mumble over my glass.

"Me? What did I do?" Ronan asks.

"None of this would have happened if you had let Clay win Daisy in that auction."

That makes his warm smile turn into an intense scowl in the blink of an eye, which makes me laugh. I do blame him, but not for that. I blame him because it was seeing him find love with Daisy that caused the slightest of cracks in my armor. It was just enough to let in the idea of love.

From there, the dam burst, and the waters came flooding through.

"I don't want to be in a relationship," I mutter as I turn to face him. "I just want to keep being Madame Kink until I'm as old as you."

"Hey now," he replies. With his mostly gray hair and fine lines, I do enjoy teasing him about his age, although he never acts it anymore. At fifty-seven, he's got a new bride and a new baby and still hits the club like a twenty-one-year-old.

"And who said you can't keep being Madame Kink?" he replies. "Plenty of sex workers are in committed relationships."

"Are people still going to want me?" I ask, hating the way my insecurities sound.

Ronan scoffs. "Eden, people will always want you as long as you keep being you. It's not about your age or your dating status or your homelife. You have this thought in your head that Eden and Madame Kink are two different people, but they're not. Eden is just as sexy and as confident as her Salacious alter ego. Being a mother or in a relationship is not going to change that.

"If anything," he adds, leaning forward, "I think it's time you let Eden work at the club too."

"What is that supposed to mean?" I ask with a tilt of my head.

"It means you could put those management skills I know you must have to good use and take the job Emerson is offering you."

I scoff. "What management skills?"

"The skills required to raise a kid on your own, manage your home, work a full-time job, run a blog."

"Psh," I reply.

"Fine. Don't listen to me. I'm just saying…you have what it takes, and taking that job might solve some of your problems if you no longer want to be a Dominatrix."

I do still want that.

But I want that job too.

I'm staring out across the bar, my mind spinning with so many thoughts and questions. After a few minutes, I feel Ronan drape an arm around my shoulder. I find myself leaning into his comforting embrace.

"Everything is going to be okay," he mumbles against my head. The words instantly settle over me like a calming rain. He always has this way of making me believe it, and he's never been wrong before.

Rule #33: When you feel sexy, you are sexy.

Jade

"I FEEL STUPID," I MUMBLE FROM THE DRESSING ROOM.

"You're not stupid," Eden replies with an exasperated sigh. "Let me see it."

When I slide open the curtain, I try to hide my nerves as her eyes rake over my body.

I'm covered in black leather. There's a tight black-and-red corset cinched around my waist and doing nothing for my nonexistent cleavage. Below that, I have on a pair of tight black leather pants that make my curveless hips feel underwhelming.

"See?" I say, dropping my arms in frustration.

She stands from the velvet couch and walks toward me. "Well…it's hot and definitely not stupid."

"But?" I reply.

"It's not you."

Our eyes meet, and I feel something flutter in my chest at the contact.

We're currently out shopping, just the two of us, to find my *Mistress* look. She called me after our night at Clay's, explaining that *finding her look* was something she did when she started out as a Domme. It was a big part of her feeling sexy and empowered in the dominant role.

"Well, not everyone needs to wear leather to feel sexy," she replies. "Want to keep looking?"

"Yes, please."

"Need help taking that off?" she asks.

I nod, biting my lip.

She shuts herself into the stall with me and closes the curtain so we're both standing in the small space. I put my back to her, the mirror in front of me, as she starts to loosen the ribbon straps at the back.

Being alone with Eden now is different—or at least for me it is. Now that we've had sex, I no longer feel like I'm a girl with a crush. She wants me.

Can I kiss you?

That one line from her the other night sent me into outer space. And I've been thinking about it ever since.

If I had any sort of self-control, I would have let her kiss me in that moment. But no. I had to jump on her like a horny teenager. I don't know what came over me. I just wanted her in a way I've never wanted anyone before.

"Should we tell him?" I ask, thinking about the fact that we're keeping our little lessons a secret.

"Do you want to?" she replies without meeting my gaze.

"I don't know. Is it bad that I like having something special, all our own?"

She stares with an unfocused gaze as she says, "No. It's not hurting anyone."

I'm relieved. It's not that I want to lie to Clay, but I already feel like a bit of an outsider, considering he and Eden have somewhat of a shared past, even if it wasn't romantic. Now, she and I have... somewhat of a past.

"What if I don't find my Domme style?" I whine. "Can I

seriously keep trying to do this in my stupid skirts and crop tops?"

She loosens my corset enough that it slides off my chest. "Yes," she answers plainly. "It's your choice. Your style. Make it yours and wear whatever makes you feel sexy. If you feel it, it will show. And your sub will feel it."

When she glances up, her eyes meet mine in the mirror. As I let the corset fall away, my breasts are exposed, and the air in the small dressing room grows thick.

My breasts are nowhere near voluptuous. Measly A cups, something that never bothered me much until I started standing next to her, with her fuller, sexier breasts.

"Stand up straight," she says. Her fingers trace my lower back as my shoulders rise. We stand in silence as her gaze rakes over my body, naked from the waist up. Then her featherlight touch moves from my back up to my shoulder and down the length of my right arm.

"You are so exquisite," she whispers. "When you look in the mirror, do you see how beautiful you are?"

So far, my eyes have been only on her, so I move them until I'm staring at the smaller, paler, meeker of the two women in the reflection.

"Yes," I say, notching my chin up a little higher.

"Good," she replies with a soft smile.

Her hand drifts downward from my shoulder, dusting the surface of my breast and then my stomach.

"I used to struggle with the woman in the mirror," she says. "It was like she projected lies. She was beautiful and bold and sexy—all the things I was not."

My eyes widen as I gape at her. Is she serious right now?

"The woman in the mirror was me, but my mind refused to see that."

"Why?" I ask in astonishment. Eden is the most beautiful woman I've ever seen. How could she possibly not see that?

Her eyes grow sad as she stares unfocused at something in the mirror. "If you're told enough how worthless, stupid, and hideous you are, you start to believe it."

"Who would tell you that?" I whisper, clutching her hand in mine.

"First, my father. Then my husband."

My blood turns to ice as I gaze at her in the mirror. "Your husband? What kind of husband would do that?"

"A bad one," she replies plainly. "He also did a lot of other terrible things I don't want to talk about right now. But let's just say some scars last longer than others."

When her eyes lift to mine, the intimacy and familiarity there make my heart swell. Squeezing her hand a little tighter, I think about what Clay said yesterday about Eden having secrets and stories we don't know yet.

"Thank you for sharing that with me," I say carefully.

Her reaction is hesitant as her eyes dart away, and she takes a deep breath. "I haven't told anyone that."

Turning away from the mirror, I face Eden. My hands are unsure as I slowly place them on the sides of her face. "I'm going to try really hard not to ramble right now, but I'm glad you told me. I feel honored that you share anything with me because…I like you. A lot. And not as a friend or, I guess…not *just* as a friend. And I know this all seems so crazy—well, maybe not to you, but it seems crazy to me, but it's crazy in a *good* way."

A gentle smirk tugs on the corner of her mouth as her gaze slides down to my lips.

But my lips don't stop moving as I ramble through the awkwardness of knowing what comes next.

"And it's crazy that I like seeing you with Clay, right? Because I think I love Clay, which is also crazy because it's only been a few months. But I want you at the same time. Is that weird to say?"

"Jade," she says, touching my cheek.

"What?"

"You're rambling," she replies, leaning toward me.

"Sorry—" I mumble just before her lips brush mine.

The kiss is soft—a lot softer than the one I pummeled her with a couple of nights ago. Her fingers are gently holding my jaw as her tongue slips between my lips and caresses mine. I melt into her arms as a throaty moan reverberates through me.

Eden is just a little taller than me, so I have to reach upward on my toes. Our kiss grows hungrier and more passionate but never flies out of control. My heart is pounding rapidly in my chest, and something warm pools low in my belly.

I feel so *safe* with her. And not just in a literal sense. She makes me feel like I can say what's on my mind or express what I want and she won't laugh at me or turn me away. She arouses so much more than my body, and I crave things with her I can't even define.

With two steps, she backs me against the mirror and runs her hand down the length of my body, starting at my neck, over my shoulder, and then across the side of my bare torso. Easing a hand under my ass on one side, she drags up my left leg and presses herself even closer.

I let out another moan, and I feel her smiling against my lips.

"I'm going to get us kicked out of here," I whisper as her kisses drift down from my mouth to my jaw.

"No, *I* am."

When her lips reach my neck, she sucks and bites, and my knees start to grow weak. If she does that again, I'm not going to be able to hold it in, and we will definitely get kicked out of here.

Just as her hand drifts to the waistline of my leather pants, I clutch tightly to the back of her neck because my legs are not going to be able to hold me up if she puts her hands down there. Her fingers tease the sensitive skin just under the button at the front.

"Can I unbutton these?" she whispers. My mouth goes dry, and I reply with a sound that is somewhere between "mm-hmm" and a moan.

Her fingers ease the button open on my pants, and I cling to her desperately as her hand slides down my torso and her fingers brush my clit.

God, why does her touch feel so good? Better than anyone's. It's like magic.

"Let's see how quiet you can be," she replies softly as her hand slides deeper, and I feel her finger glide through the moisture pooling at my entrance.

I let out a yelp when she presses her finger inside me, and she quickly muffles my cries with her lips against mine.

She's thrusting her finger at a slow and torturous pace, and I feel like my entire body is being dismantled by need and pleasure. She is my undoing. I am completely done for, for the rest of my life.

"Reach into my back pocket," she mutters against my lips. "Pull out my phone and record this for your boyfriend."

My hands are shaking as I do as she says, tugging her phone out of her back pocket. By the time I get the camera app open and focused on us, she's thrusting hard, and I'm soaring toward my climax.

I have to bite my lip and squeeze my eyes shut, clutching desperately to her as she makes my body orgasm so hard I see stars.

I'm doing a shitty job recording this, but when I finally open my eyes, Eden is staring at the phone screen as if she's watching herself get me off.

"Holy shit," I whisper as my head falls back against the mirror.

Just then, someone from outside the curtain loudly clears their throat.

Eden slowly pulls her hand from my pants and stares into my wide eyes. We wait in awkward silence until we hear their footfalls retreating. Then we both break into quiet laughter together.

"We should get out of here," I say in a low whisper.

"Fine, but we're going to another shop," she replies. "You're getting something today. Something you feel sexy in."

"Well, I think we have to buy these pants now," I reply, and she laughs again before placing a kiss on my mouth.

"Okay, you get dressed while I send this video to Clay."

I cover my breasts with my arm as she opens the curtain and slips out. After I take off the leather pants and replace them with my black cotton skirt from home, I feel as if I'm swaying on my feet, dizzy and drunk on nothing else but her.

––––––––––

At the next lingerie-slash-sex-toy shop, Eden leads me through the aisles. I'm too busy gazing around the room like a kid at the zoo to do any real shopping.

"I have some ideas of what might work. I'm going to pick you out some things, and I want you to try them on," she says without looking at me.

"Okay," I say as I move through the store toward the dressing rooms in the back. Before I get there, I stop in awe at the wall of punishment toys—paddles, whips, floggers. My fingers cascade over the leather.

It's a few minutes before Eden approaches with her arms full of clothing.

"Is this what you used on Clay?" I ask, touching the black flogger.

"Yes," she replies.

"Does he really like this stuff?" I ask.

"When he needs it," she replies plainly.

"Needs it?" I ask, looking at her with curiosity.

"It wasn't often," she replies, shifting the clothes to the other arm. "Clay was always very obedient, but everyone fails from time to time."

"What did he do to deserve this?" I ask.

"One time, he came without permission. And then another time, he spoke rudely to my friend."

"So you…beat him?"

She looks at me as if offended. "It was consensual. I knew his boundaries, and he knew his safe words."

Just then one of the workers comes up to Eden and puts out her hands for the clothing. "I can put those in a dressing room for you if you're still shopping."

"Thank you," Eden replies as she hands over the stack. "They're for her."

The worker looks at me and then at Eden, curiosity on her face. She might think I'm her sub, which makes me feel warm and excited.

She looks back at Eden as she says, "They'll be in room four for her when she's ready."

Eden nods, and the woman walks away.

When we're alone, Eden pulls me closer. "The thing you have to understand about Clay is that he loves to obey and please. He grew up without a lot of attention or praise, so he thrives in an environment where he knows exactly what is expected of him so he can be rewarded.

"Being punished is like getting to right his wrongs. He would slip up, and I would punish him, which to him was just as good as praise. It was still attention, and it would make all of his mistakes practically disappear," she says before looking at me. "Does that make sense?"

I nod, thinking back to that night when he and I got into an argument about Eden. He was so afraid to confess what was really going on with them, and it makes so much sense now. He just wanted to do or say whatever would make me happy with him, so my asking more about his ex-Domme probably threw him off.

"It makes a lot of sense," I reply with a nod.

"You can punish me if you want."

My eyes grow wide as I stare at her in shock. "Me? Punish you? For what?"

"Whatever you want. Or nothing at all. Would you like to feel what it's like to punish someone?"

It's suddenly hard to breathe. I force myself to swallow, and it's on the tip of my tongue to say no, but I don't.

I *am* curious. So without overthinking it, I nod.

"Yes, I would."

"Good," Eden replies with a smile. "Text your boyfriend and tell him you're coming to the club with me tonight."

Doing as she says, I pull out my phone and type out a message to Clay.

I'm going to the club with Eden tonight.
She's going to let me punish her.
Or teach me how, I guess.
I don't know, but I'm excited.

When I'm done, I go to the dressing room where my clothes are waiting. The selection that is hanging up is different than before. I don't know how I didn't notice before, but none of them are black.

There's a dark-green corset, a bright-pink skirt, a royal-blue dress, a bright-yellow bra and panty set, and a deep-purple lingerie skirt and shirt combo with sequins and gems so it sparkles.

"Am I in the right dressing room?" I ask, staring at each item.

From the other side of the curtain, Eden chuckles. "I figured we should try something different. You like them?"

I bite my bottom lip, inspecting the purple outfit first. "I do like them."

"Good. Try them on."

Just as I'm pulling the purple skirt up my legs, my phone pings from my purse. I pick it up and see a message from Clay.

Punish her?
Can I watch?

"Clay wants to know if he can watch," I say as I grab the purple top, ready to pull it on.

"Hmm... Tell him no. I want you focused on me without him there to distract you."

I type it out.

She said no.
You'll distract me.
Sorry.

I toss my phone down and inspect myself in the mirror. I feel a smile pulling at my cheeks. I really love this color, and I don't look so plain and scrawny in it.

When I pull open the curtain, Eden is typing something on her phone. When she looks up, her mouth hangs open.

"Fuck yes," she mumbles.

"Do you like it?" I ask with a cheesy grin.

"Do *you* like it?" she replies.

"Yes...but is it the right look? I feel sexy, but this isn't how you dress. Or any of the Dominatrices in the porn I've watched."

Her head tilts as her eyes widen. "Okay, we're coming back to that. But for now, I just want you to remember that this is about how *you* feel, and if you feel dominant in it, then you'll be comfortable acting dominant."

I place my hand on my hip and wipe the smile from my face. "Get on your knees and crawl to me."

Eden bites back her smile as she places her phone on the small table. "Yes, Mistress."

Then she slowly drops to her knees and slinks toward me in a sexy crawl. When she reaches my feet, I stroke her head. Leaning down, I kiss her on the forehead.

"Good girl."

Just then the employee who helped us before rounds the corner and sees Eden on her knees in front of me.

"Can—can I help you ladies f-find anything else?" she stammers.

Eden giggles.

I stand upright and press my shoulders back. "No. We're fine."

Then I look back down at Eden. "Back to your seat then."

She rises to her feet and walks back to her chair, and I shoot her a wink before I disappear back into the stall to try on the next outfit.

"He's texting me now," Eden calls from outside the curtain.

"Uh-oh," I reply. "What's he saying?"

"He's not happy with me taking you for myself tonight," she says, but I can hear the wicked smile on her face.

"You know…we need a group chat," I say as I try on the green corset and stockings. The bottoms are just panties and a garter belt, so I feel very exposed, but it's still really hot.

Plus, it is green, and my name *is* Jade.

I pull open the curtain to find her looking pleased as she watches me emerge in a new outfit.

"Yes. We're getting that."

I bite my lip in excitement, but maybe she notices my hesitation. I can't afford all of these. Not without breaking into my daddy's emergency fund, which this hardly qualifies for.

Eden stands up with an empathetic expression. "These are my treat. I'm buying them all for you, and you're going to take them without arguing. Understood?"

As she steps up toe to toe with me, I swallow down the warmth building in my chest.

"Yes, Madame," I whisper.

Then she leans forward and presses her lips to mine. "Good girl," she murmurs.

After our quick kiss, she pulls away, and I see her phone light up.

"Should I be worried about what you two are talking about?" I ask.

Her grin grows more mischievous as she turns away and returns to her chair. She continues typing as she speaks. "He said he'll be fine now that he has this video to watch over and over."

I let out a chuckle as I stare at my reflection in the mirror. I do feel like a Domme in this outfit, even if I don't look like one. The way I just commanded Eden felt good.

Something about this outfit reminds me of the beautiful blond woman in the voyeur hall that night. And while I stare at myself a moment longer, I realize I might be ready for something I've been thinking about a lot lately.

It might be crazy, or it might be amazing.

Rule #34: Show her whom she belongs to.

Eden

Are you stealing my girlfriend?

Of course not. I'm just keeping her from you for one night.

At least let me watch.

I want her to focus without distraction.

Well, what am I supposed to do?

Be a good boy and wait at the club until we're done.

Yes, Madame.

PART OF ME DOES FEEL BAD BECAUSE I KNOW HOW INSECURE CLAY can be, but I meant what I said. Jade needs a night to practice in a safe space.

But I'd be lying if I said I wasn't also looking forward to a night alone with her for less practical reasons.

As we pull up to her house so I can drop her off after our day of shopping, I notice a car in the driveway and a man climbing out.

"Oh shit. My dad is home."

"Is that a problem?" I ask, noticing Jade grow instantly tense.

"Don't say anything about Clay," she mutters quickly.

"Why?" I ask as I stop on the curb.

Her dad waves casually at us, and I feel bad just dropping her off and leaving, so I open my driver's side door.

"Oh God," Jade mutters quietly as she climbs out at the same time.

"Hey, Cupcake," he says to Jade, and I smile at the cute nickname.

"Hi," I say politely from the driver's side.

Her father looks to be in his forties. He's a large burly man with a grayish-black beard and thick eyebrows. I immediately notice the way his eyes track back to me and stay there.

"Who's your friend?" he asks.

Jade winces as I round the front of the car and walk toward him. "I'm Eden. A friend of Jade's."

He puts out his hand, so I do the same, letting his large grip engulf mine in a tight shake.

"Will Penner," he replies. "Nice to meet you."

"Nice to meet you."

Jade looks so uncomfortable it makes me smile. Is she that nervous about me meeting her parents? It's not like she has to come out of the closet right here on the driveway.

"What have you girls been up to?" he asks, shoving his hands into his pockets.

"We were just doing a little shopping," I reply, gesturing to the discreet black bag Jade is holding.

"Nice," he says with a pleased smile. "You'll have to show me inside, Cupcake."

Jade groans. "Okay, well, thank you, Eden." She waves to me as if to get rid of me, and I send her a confused expression.

"How did you two meet?" Will asks.

"Dad, Eden really has to get going. Her son is going to get off the bus soon," Jade says, cutting him off.

"A mutual friend," I say, shooting him a polite grin.

His eyes linger on me a moment longer, and Jade starts tugging on his arm.

With a laugh, he looks back at me. "Well, goodbye, Eden. It was nice to meet you."

"Nice to meet you," I repeat as I head back to my car. "I'll see you later, Jade," I call up to her before she disappears into her house.

———————

I don't get to the club until after eleven. After putting Jack to bed, I had a million things to do before Madison came over, including showering and getting ready.

I've been anxious about tonight since I dropped Jade off. I don't normally enjoy going into a submissive role, but for her, I will—*gladly*.

Jade is unconventional. The entire time I thought I was mentoring her to be more assertive and independent, I finally realized that she was all of those things all along. She does it in her own way. It's like…sweet dominance. She holds her own, demands what she wants, and isn't afraid to put herself first, all while looking like a bubblegum princess.

It's hot as fuck.

I'm sitting at the bar, making another napkin list, when I look up to find Geo smiling at me.

"Red wine?" he asks since I don't order the same thing every night. It all depends on my clients and my plans. Sometimes I'll drink, and sometimes I won't.

"Not tonight," I reply. "Just a club soda with lime. Thanks, Geo."

"Of course," he says as he fixes my drink.

While he's filling the glass, his eyes stay on me. "There's a change in the air."

"A change?" I ask, not really liking the sound of that. I hate when things change.

"Yeah. First, Maggie left. Now Emerson works from his home office. It's only a matter of time before someone else steps in, right?"

I rest my arms on the bar and glare up at him through my lashes. "Did Emerson put you up to this?"

With a laugh, he furrows his brow. "No. Put me up to what?"

I calm my expression. He really doesn't know. "He…offered me a job," I say carefully.

That makes Geo's glossy full lips pull into a wide smile. "Of course he did. Who else would he ask?"

"I don't know if I'm going to take it," I reply.

Solemnly, he nods, leaning against the counter behind him. "They'll need to bring someone in eventually."

I swallow the nervous way that makes me feel, but he's right. Charlotte said they created the position with me in mind, but let's be realistic. If it's not me, it'll be someone else. And then I'll be stuck with a stranger managing this place.

"Maybe *you* should take the job," I say to drive the attention away from me.

Geo lets out a soft chuckle. "Not me. I'm out of here by the end of the year."

My head snaps up as I stare at him in shock. "What? Where are you going?"

Geo has been the lead bartender at Salacious since it opened. This place won't be the same without him, and my heart aches to think of him leaving.

He shrugs. "I've lived here my whole life. I'm ready for something new. Emerson said he'd help me find a new job at another club wherever I decide to go. Maybe Nashville or New Orleans."

I reach out a hand and place it on his. Geo has really grown into his own over the past three years. I've watched him blossom from the man who used to try to blend in to the beautiful person he is now, born to stand out.

"I'm going to miss you," I say, my eyes growing moist.

"I'll come back to visit," he replies. "When you're the owner."

I roll my eyes with a smile and pull my hand away. "Nice try."

"No one knows this place like you do, Eden. Owner or not, Salacious has always belonged to you."

He turns away and starts preparing someone else's drink, and I let those words settle. Could I really see someone else take over this place? Even if Emerson, Garrett, and Hunter remain the owners, they're going to need more help here, and I don't know if I could watch someone else take the role made for me. What if this new person changes it? What if I dislike it so much that I have to leave?

What will I do then?

Lost in my contemplation, I almost don't notice when Mia approaches and leans her elbows on the bar next to me.

"Nice work with that pixie girl."

I glance up from my napkin list and stare at her with a furrowed brow. "What?"

She turns her body toward me as she smiles. "That cute little set of bangs that's been following you around. She's killing it."

Jade? Killing it at what?

Mia must sense my confusion because she laughs. "She's in the voyeur hall right now. I think she's gunning after my job."

"In the voyeur hall?"

None of this makes any sense. I left Jade at her house hours ago, and I'm supposed to be meeting her here in thirty minutes. Mia must be confused.

"Yeah. She's in the cutest little purple outfit, drawing a crowd. You should go watch."

My cheeks start to grow hot as I drop my napkin on the bar. "She's in a *room*?"

I don't even hear Mia's response as I leap off the barstool, practically running toward the voyeur hall.

The moment I slip through the heavy black curtain, I see the small crowd of people gathered around the third window on the right. I stomp down the hall, hoping to God Mia was just confused and it's not *my* Jade in there with someone else.

She wouldn't.

And she and Clay wouldn't go in there without letting me know, would they?

When I reach the third window, I screech to a halt when I see her familiar bob haircut and purple sequined outfit we just bought today. To my relief, she's in there alone.

My jaw drops when I see her nervously smiling at the people on my side of the glass. She's shaking her ass and smiling over her shoulder.

I must be hallucinating.

I *wish* I were hallucinating.

What *the fuck* is she doing?

I'm standing there in shock, dissecting my own reaction to this. I've encouraged countless women to go into the voyeur rooms. Hell, I've even taken a few in there myself. But this feels different for some reason. I'm not excited or turned on by the sight. I'm furious.

Because this is Jade.

My Jade.

My blood is boiling as I push my way through the crowd, moving toward the door of the room she's in. It's a discreet black door, and I use my key card to unlock it, noticing the way my hands are shaking as I move.

As the door opens, she jumps and stares at me in shock.

"Eden?"

Without a word, I grab her by the wrist and tug her toward the exit. "What the fuck are you doing?" I say, seething with anger.

To my surprise, she snatches her hand away. With her chin held high, she looks me right in the eyes as she boldly says, "No."

I feel my heart pound faster. Stepping into the room, I let the door slam behind me.

"You're not my Domme," she says, but it's not like she's mad at me. I know we're not fighting. She's just stating a fact. I am *not* her Domme.

Of course, my rational brain is not processing any of this.

And I feel completely out of control of myself at the moment, let alone capable of controlling anyone else.

It feels like an out-of-body experience. This primal, deep need to do…something. I don't quite know if that something is to yell at her, hurt her, keep her, protect her, or fuck her.

Or all of the above, perhaps.

Regardless, I snap.

Before I can register what I'm doing, my hand is around her throat, and I'm shoving her against the empty wall. My face is close to hers, and her eyes are wide with either terror or surprise.

"You're right. I'm not your Domme, but you are *mine*, and I don't appreciate you flaunting what's *mine* for everyone to see."

Her surprise morphs into an expression I can only describe as adorable mischief. It's a wide smile with her bottom lip pinched between her teeth as she gazes up at me through hooded eyes.

Then I feel her hips pressing forward, grinding them against mine, and I use my free hand to shove her back against the wall.

Without arguing with me, she raises her arms and breaks my hold of her neck. Then she pushes me backward until I hit the bed, and she uses her palms against my chest to drive me to the mattress. Our arms struggle, fighting for control. When she gets a hold of my wrists, she forces them above my head and climbs on top of me.

With a wicked laugh, she leans down until her face is just an inch above mine.

"That's where you're wrong, *Madame*," she says, using my title in a mocking tone that makes my molars grind. I let out a frustrated grunt. "You're all mine," she says with a smile.

Maybe it's the struggle, or maybe it's how delicious she looks from down here, but I feel the effects of arousal building between my legs.

She presses her lips to mine, forcing her tongue into my mouth. I'm trying to ignore the fact that I'm frustrated and angry with her. She whimpers into my mouth, grinding herself against my hips and making me crazy.

I'm on fire.

Using my strength and size over her, I manage to get her to the bed facedown. She lets out a scream as I climb on top of her, using my knee on her back to hold her in place. She struggles to get away, but as soon as I lift the hem of her tiny purple skirt to reveal nothing more than a simple lace thong, her body stills, and her fight dies.

"You want to give them a show? Then let's give them a fucking show," I say with a raspy growl.

She's panting into the mattress, her ass on display to the whole crowd on the other side of the window.

My right hand pets her ass cheek softly, squeezing and kneading it in my fingers as that fire inside me only grows hotter. Then I raise my hand and land a hard slap on her tender white flesh.

She jolts and lets out a delicate whine.

"Let them see what a naughty little girl you are," I say, my voice still laced with anger as I spank her hard on the opposite cheek. Her cry is a little louder this time.

But she's not fighting me anymore.

"Were you going to show them your pussy?" I ask, slapping her ass again.

Her whimpers turn to moans.

"Without *my* permission," I add on the next one.

"Yes," she cries out when I do it again. Her ass is turning a beautiful shade of red, and I can't keep my hands off of it, squeezing and pinching her sore cheek.

I lean down until my face is near her ear. She's sweating and panting and writhing on the mattress. "Why don't we give them a real show, then?" I ask in a sultry tone. "Let them see how needy you are. Let them watch me fuck you until you beg me for mercy."

She groans into the mattress.

Lifting up, I stare down at her perfect little ass. Then I tug on the string of her thong, pulling it to the side to reveal her moist cunt.

My body is like an inferno, and I need her so bad I can't take another minute. So I run my middle finger through her folds, teasing her entrance and smiling at the audience on the other side of the glass.

"Look at how perfect my girl is," I say, although they can't hear me. "I'm showing you off like my perfect little gemstone."

Then I plunge my finger inside her, and she perks her ass up to meet my hand as she moans, face down on the bed.

Making her feel good only makes me crazier. Lifting her ass a little higher and moving behind her, I rub myself against her hip as I fuck her faster and harder. I add a second finger, and she gets louder. She mewls and whimpers, her fingers clenching the sheets tight in her fists.

"You want more?" I ask.

"Yes, Madame," she hums.

Pulling my fingers from her pussy, I lick the length of them before leaning down and closing my teeth around her ass cheek.

She screams, jumping up from her position. Grabbing my shoulders, she flips me until I'm on my back, and she kisses me hard, groaning into my mouth. After she pulls away, I force my fingers in her mouth, and she sucks them greedily.

"That's my girl," I say with a taunting smile.

"I'm not your girl," she argues in return, her expression mirroring mine.

Then she crawls down my body and digs her fingers under the hem of my leather pants. In a rush, she jerks them down, not stopping until I'm naked from the waist down. Sitting up, I tear off my blouse. Then I stare down at her as she lowers herself between my legs.

Shit—has she ever done this before?

Is she nervous?

Biting her bottom lip, she stares at me with hunger in her eyes. Then she dives forward, latching her mouth around my clit and licking and sucking so hard, I nearly scream.

"Oh fuck," I cry out, falling onto my back and digging my fingers into my hair.

If she is nervous or doesn't know what to do, it surely doesn't fucking show.

Her tongue is flicking my clit, alternating between sucking and lapping, and in my already aroused state, it's enough to have me losing control.

Leaning upward, I stare at her. "Oh God, Jade. Look at you."

I grab the back of her head, grinding myself against her mouth.

"You like that, don't you?" I say, feeling like half Madame, half Eden at this moment.

"I want to feel you come on my tongue," she murmurs against my throbbing cunt.

"Keep doing that, and I will."

I hold a hand against her head, loving the sounds of her moans vibrating against me.

"Oh fuck," I cry out as my legs start to shake. "Jade…you're going to make me—"

She keeps her assault on my clit, slipping a finger inside me as every nerve ending in my body explodes in pleasure. Legs shaking and spine arching, I ride out my orgasm, holding her head between my legs.

It crashes against me, wave after wave.

When I can finally breathe again, I open my eyes and lift my head to stare down at Jade, who looks pretty pleased with herself. Reaching down, I grab her by the back of the neck and haul her to me to crash my mouth against hers.

The kiss is ravenous and heated, and we're still fighting for dominance to get her clothes off. When she's finally naked, I shove her down on the bed and climb off to cross the room to where the toys are stored on shelves against the wall.

Grabbing the smallest, thinnest vibrator I can find, I carry it back to her.

Smiling as I climb on top of her, I twist it on. "Time to prove just how *mine* you are."

Rule #35: When Madame Kink has you pinned, don't fight it.

Jade

THE SLIGHTEST TOUCH AGAINST MY CLIT WITH THAT VIBRATOR IS too much. I let out a scream as Eden places her hand over my mouth.

"Keep it down. We wouldn't want your boyfriend to know what I'm doing to you back here."

I smile against the palm of her hand as she touches the vibe to my skin again. Nearly everyone at the club is probably watching us through that window, but the idea of sneaking around and keeping this secret makes me hot.

How is every moment with Eden so intense and hot and perfect? Is it her? Is it *us*?

I don't know if she knows just how much she turns me on but also how much she pushes me. I would have *never* been so bold before I met her.

Okay…that might not be entirely true. I do let Clay fuck me with my dad down the hall sometimes.

But it's like by being with Eden, I've met my match. She lets me fight her and push her around, and she does the same back to me, and it's so *fucking* hot.

She's sitting on my upper legs, teasing me with the vibrator. She pulls it away just as I feel my orgasm starting to build. I let out a strangled cry against her hand.

Then she moves her legs, straddling my right leg and hoisting the left one up to make room as she lowers herself over me. I'm confused for a moment until I feel the warmth of her pussy against mine. My body shakes with a desperate sound, this time softer and higher pitched. It feels like heaven.

Forcefully, she snatches my wrists in one hand, so I'm helpless against her as she grinds harder and harder. She looks into my eyes as she crushes herself against me, our clits rubbing together to create intense, beautiful friction. As we stare at each other, she pulls her other hand from my mouth and leans down, pressing her lips to mine. I have to swallow down the emotion rising in my throat.

I want to grab the back of her neck and kiss her deeper, needing *more*. But I can't move. I'm at her mercy, a slave to her command. My thighs tremble around her as she keeps up the roll of her hips. We're a sexy tangle of legs and arms until it feels like we're one.

Pulling back, she looks deep into my eyes once more before rising up and reaching for something on the mattress. I almost forgot the vibrator was here. Until I feel it pressed between us, the sensation so intense it makes me scream again.

She holds it there to tease me before taking it away, so it feels like I'm free-falling, hovering somewhere between pleasure and pain.

"Tell me you're mine, and I'll let you come," she says, still slowly grinding against me.

I struggle against her hold, desperate to get the vibrator in my hands, but she's stronger than me.

"Fuck," I cry out. I'm desperate. My entire body is buzzing, and I just need a little relief. I grit my teeth and look into her eyes.

"Fine," I mutter. "I'm yours."

She smiles. "Are you ever going to show off what's mine without my permission again?"

My molars grind, and I desperately want to argue with her. I *can* be submissive. Right now, I desperately want to make her mine. But I can't do that if I want to come.

"No."

She tilts her head. "No…"

I fight to hold back my smile. "No, Madame," I say obstinately.

"Good girl," she replies, and I know she does it just to drive me wild. Mad or horny…I'm not sure which.

Placing the vibrator where our bodies meet, she drives me straight to the edge again. Only this time, she doesn't pull away, and I fly over the cliff, throwing my head back as I come undone.

Judging by the shudder in her legs and the groan from her lips, she's right there with me. We are clutched so tightly together my muscles grow sore, and it becomes hard to breathe.

After my climax crests, she releases my arms, and they fall to my sides. Then she collapses on top of me.

"Holy shit," I mutter, feeling my heartbeat pulsing in my skull.

"Yeah," she replies, pressing her face to my neck. When she lifts up, our eyes meet again.

I wonder if she feels it too. I hope it's not just me, but I truly feel like I get to see a part of Eden no one else gets. Well, no one but Clay.

We have become her safe space. We will always protect her and keep her, but does she know that? Does she even know how important she is to us?

Our eyes meet in a burning gaze, and it just feels like the right time. Here's my opening.

Isn't she the one who taught me to be open and bold about what I want?

"Eden, I—"

Her eyes fill with panic in one split second. "We should go," she says, quickly cutting me off.

I feel blindsided, my mouth hanging open in surprise.

I don't know if it's because she didn't know what I was about to say...or because she did.

Judging by the way she climbs off the bed without a word and starts putting on her clothes without looking at me, I assume it's because she did.

Is Eden still running away from her feelings? From love and commitment? Is being in a relationship really that scary? I don't understand and maybe I'm still fired up from our little sex brawl a few moments ago, but I'm tired of letting her just sweep things under the rug.

I climb off the bed and grab her arm, spinning her toward me. "Can you look me in the eye, please? I have something to say."

Her brow furrows as she stares at me in confusion. Then she walks to the wall and hits a button that turns the window wall opaque so the people—who I forgot existed until this moment—can no longer see us.

Then she turns toward me with confidence. "I'm looking at you."

But her tone is all wrong. She's defensive already, and I haven't even said anything.

Suddenly, I'm fumbling for the right words because, to be honest, I don't quite know what I was about to say a moment ago. I just wanted her to know how I feel, but how do I feel?

Am I in love with her? Is that too much? Too soon?

Or do I just want her to know that I really like her?

I want her in our relationship. No, that's not right. It wouldn't be my and Clay's relationship anymore. It's *our* relationship, as in all three of us.

I'm rambling...in my head.

"Jade..." Eden says, touching my arm.

"I want you," I blurt out like a lovestruck Neanderthal.

How is that helpful?

She smiles. "You just had me."

With a wince, I shake my head. "No, I mean…I *want* you. We want you. Not like as my mentor or as my friend. Like I think I love…you."

It feels like I just dropped a bomb on the floor between us. It's suffocating us with pressure and expectation, and I wish for a moment I hadn't said it.

But it's true, isn't it? I do love her. I can't stop thinking about her. I want her happiness more than my own, and I need her in a way I've never needed anyone.

"Jade," she says again. "Let's get dressed, and we can go talk."

My jaw hangs open as I stare at her. "You're shutting me down?"

Her expression turns serious. "No. I'm not—"

"Then what do we need to talk about? You either want me or you don't."

"It's not that simple," she argues.

"Yes, it is." I snatch my bra from the bedpost and pull it on with jerky, angry movements.

"Jade, will you just calm down?"

"No," I snap, turning toward her. "You want to go talk so you can tell me that you don't do relationships and that Clay and I are nothing but clients to you."

"Don't put words in my mouth," she replies angrily.

"Then put words in your own mouth. Say something. Anything. Stop running from your feelings. Stop running from us."

"I'm not running from anything."

"Yes, you are. Do you have any idea how terrifying it is to fall in love with you because you are so emotionally untouchable? It's like your heart is inside a cage, and for what? To protect Jack?"

"Jade," she snaps at the mention of her son, but I don't stop.

"Do you really think staying single and avoiding love your entire life is going to keep him safe?"

Her eyes are moist as she steps closer to me. I feel like a child having to look up to see her, but I'm already too hot and frustrated to stop myself.

"You don't know anything about me and Jack," she says. Her words are clipped, and her voice is low as if she's afraid to lose it at any moment. "You don't know what we've been through."

"Because you won't tell me," I argue. Seeing her get emotional for the first time is melting everything inside me. I have no weapons against that.

She turns away, walking to the corner of the room and hanging her head as she discreetly wipes her tears. "It's not that easy, Jade."

"I'm sorry—" I say, stepping toward her when the sound of a knock on the window cuts me off. I almost forgot we were in a voyeur room at the club, which is not the place to be having an argument or a delicate conversation.

We get dressed as quickly as we can, but it's Eden who reaches for the door first. I don't expect there to be anyone waiting on the other side, and I certainly don't expect it to be Clay.

Eden and I are standing frozen as he gazes back and forth between us.

Did he see all that?

Did he *hear* all of that?

When he sees the raw emotion on our faces, he reaches both of his hands out, one for her and one for me. Then he softly says, "Let's get out of here."

Rule #36: Sometimes, she just needs you to listen.

Clay

"How much of that did you see?" Jade asks as she buries her toes in the grass.

I brought them to one of my favorite secluded lookout points to talk. It's a pull-off from the road that leads to a rocky cliff over the water below. It felt like the perfect place to be alone—without a bed. As much as I love taking these two to bed, right now, we don't need the distraction of sex.

None of us said a word the entire drive, which I know was difficult, especially for Jade.

I pull a blanket from the trunk of my car and drape it over their shoulders, where they're both sitting together on a fallen log most people use as a bench. "I saw it all."

"Oh," Jade replies, risking a glance up toward my face. She must be looking for a sign that I might be mad at her, which I'm not. In fact, I'm glad they had their fun without me around. As jealous as I was to hear about it, they needed their moment to be about them, not my voyeuristic gaze.

Although…if that's the case, doing it in the voyeur room might not have been the right choice.

Eden and Jade were electric together. Far more than I expected. Nothing with them is ever soft or sweet. That was a full-out battle, and from the looks of it, they both won.

"We don't need to talk about that right now," I reply as I sit on the wooden log beside Eden.

I'm far more concerned with what I heard *after* the sex. Jade confessed her feelings, and Eden pushed her away. Or did she? It sounded as if there was so much more she wanted to say, and I know we're both ready to hear it.

Jade and I both look at Eden. She holds her head up high, keeping her gaze on the water as the waves crash against the rocks below. Her chin is raised, and her eyes are free of makeup, I'm assuming from when she cried. I could hear her sniffling in the car. It broke my heart into pieces to hear it.

"I'm sorry," Eden mumbles. It might be the first apology I've ever heard from her lips.

"You don't have to apologize," I say without hesitation. Because she doesn't. Not for anything. Not for what happened between us back in November or what happened tonight with Jade.

"Yes, I do," she replies quietly. "I thought I could push everyone out, but I've realized I was pulling you in at the same time. And that wasn't fair to either of you."

"I just want to understand," I mumble softly. My hand is on her back, and with every shuddering breath she takes, I feel something inside me crumble. I hate her pain. I wish I could take it away and carry it for her. I know she's strong, but I hate that she has to be.

"I'm ready to talk about it," she says, staring at the grass in the moonlight. "But only you two. No one else can know."

"Of course," I reply, leaning toward her. Then I press my fingers against her jaw and draw her gaze to my face. "Hey," I whisper. "It's us. It's okay."

"You don't have to tell us anything," Jade says, drawing Eden's attention to the other side.

"I know," Eden replies.

"But you *can*...when you're ready," Jade adds.

"I'm ready," Eden says, turning her gaze back to the water. My eyes meet Jade's for a moment, and we both put our arms around Eden, holding her between us.

Eden takes a deep breath through her nose and releases it through her lips. Then she starts.

"I was married to Jack's father for almost seven years. We both came from the same small town, and we left together right after high school. I saw marrying him as a way out," she says, taking a break to chew the inside of her cheek and compose herself.

Then she continues. "There was a time when I loved him and I thought he loved me, but it was never that simple. I figured once we were out of our town and on our own, it would be easier to leave him if I wanted to."

The air between us is so silent I can hear Jade breathing slowly as she watches Eden. My stomach gets tight and uncomfortable as Eden talks. I already know I'm not going to want to hear any of this.

"Things got worse gradually. I can't pinpoint a single day when it became a nightmare. Slowly, over time, shoves became slaps. Slaps became punches. Instead of yanking me by my hair or grabbing my wrist, he started choking me until I thought I'd die or throwing me down the stairs."

Bile rises in my throat, and I have to remind myself to breathe as she talks.

"He'd always apologize, of course. He'd grovel and beg me to forgive him. And I did...until the next time. And there was always a next time."

Her expression takes on a hard edge, anger and resentment spilling out as the memories resurface.

"Everything that happened to us was always my fault. He couldn't find a job and didn't want me working because it would have given me money and a sense of independence. Of course, he didn't say that. He just promised he would take care of me, and I found that chivalrous. Somehow, he would always find a way to make me forgive him and love him again. When he was nice to me, it was an act of mercy. Like not dragging me down the hall by my hair and slapping me off my feet was something heroic." She scoffs. "He wanted me to thank him for that."

My nostrils flare, and my face grows hot as her words settle over me. I can't keep my mind from imagining it. No matter how hard I try, I see it—Eden, alone and scared and hurting from the one person who should love and protect her.

I catch the moonlight glinting off the tears in Jade's eyes as one slips over the edge, running down her cheek. She doesn't wipe it away. She doesn't even move.

"I was always so good at staying on my birth control because he was on top of me about it. He never wanted me to get pregnant. He claimed it was because we didn't have the money to support another person, but I think it was because he was afraid I'd have someone to love. That I'd love that baby more than him.

"And I didn't mean to, but I ran out of the pink pills, so I just took the white ones I had stashed up from skipping them every month. I don't know why I did it. It was stupid of me because I didn't want to get pregnant. And then it had gone on so long that I couldn't bear to tell him. I could have easily gone up to the clinic and gotten more for free, but I didn't.

"By the time I did…it was too late. I was already pregnant."

"Eden," Jade whispers as she rests her head on Eden's shoulder, and I feel her hands beneath mine squeeze her closer.

I can't possibly imagine what that would have been like for her. To be in a situation you can't escape from. So stuck with a monster like that and now worried for another life more than your own.

I'm glad he's dead. If he weren't, I'd gladly kill him.

"I had enough money stashed away to afford about three weeks in a very shitty motel, but it was all I had. I knew that if he found out, he would make me abort the pregnancy, regardless of what *I* wanted."

Her eyes moisten with tears, and her voice shakes when she speaks again. "Jack saved my life. I never cared about myself enough to leave, but I cared about him."

"That's not true," I say, pulling her chin to face me. "You saved yourself, Eden. And you saved him. Don't discredit yourself. *You* did that."

Her sad face forms a small smile for me as she nods, tears falling down her cheeks. I reach my thumb out to wipe them away.

"Maybe it was because you didn't feel so alone anymore," Jade adds, holding her from the opposite side. "It doesn't matter why. All that matters is that you did it."

Eden sniffles and uses the blanket draped over her arms to wipe her face. "Well, after that, I met Ronan, and he gave me a place to stay until after Jack was born. I kept Jack a secret to protect him. I filed for a restraining order, and then I just...disappeared. A couple of years ago, I did some digging and found out he got himself killed in a drunk driving accident."

"Wait...is Eden St. Claire your real name?" Jade asks, lifting her head from Eden's shoulder.

Eden smiles. "It is now. This is who I am. I'm not that woman anymore. Who I was matters. I believe that, but I like to think she died so we could live. I may not have been born Eden St. Claire, but I was *reborn* Eden St. Claire."

My mind is reeling.

As much as I'm dying to know everything about her, including her birth name, a strange sense of relief washes over me, knowing that she's keeping that piece of information to herself. It's hers to keep. Almost like she's keeping her past self safe...as she deserves to be.

"Well, we love you, Eden. Regardless of what your name is or what happened to you," Jade says, reaching for her hand. Eden clasps it and holds it tightly as her smile grows.

"Thank you for telling us," I whisper, pressing my lips to the side of her head.

"It's been just Jack and me for so long. I was too afraid to bring anyone around him. I just wanted to keep him safe."

"And you've done a great job, Eden. You don't need to justify that," Jade says.

"She's right," I reply. "You've been carrying this alone for so long, and we know you can. But we also know how heavy it must have been." I turn her face to mine and kiss her softly on her forehead. "But you can take a break now. We've got you."

On the next exhale, she melts into my arms, and I clutch her tighter. Jade is still squeezing her arms around her when she looks up into my eyes and smiles. It's a soft, sad smile. But I think she's feeling the same thing I am.

I'm grateful it happened this way. I'm glad things between me and Eden didn't work out the first time, only for us to find our way back together with Jade. Everything feels right now. We are more complete than we were before.

And I no longer have to carry the guilt for how things went down.

"We should do something fun tomorrow. I think we deserve fun after this," Jade says, wiping her eyes.

With a sad smile, I nod. "I agree."

"Let's take Jack to an amusement park," Jade says excitedly.

Eden lifts her head and looks at her. "An amusement park?"

"Yeah, he likes rides, right?"

Eden shrugs. "We've never been."

Jade's jaw drops. "Then we *have* to take him!"

"Is that okay...with you?" I ask.

Eden sits up and turns toward me. She looks tired but not worn down and exhausted. She looks refreshed. Like she's been through a lot and she's come out the other side.

Then she looks into my eyes, and I see the fierce, confident person I met over a year ago. And my heart beats a little harder for her.

"Yes. I would really like that."

Rule #37: Enjoy the view.

Eden

JACK SHRIEKS WITH LAUGHTER, AND IT CAN PROBABLY BE HEARD on the other side of the park. He and Clay are on a ride that spins far too much for my or Jade's liking. So she and I are sitting on the bench near the ride's exit, enjoying the sound of my son having so much fun.

He was ecstatic this morning when I woke him up with the news that not only were we skipping school and going to Thunder Kingdom, but we were also going with Clay and Jade.

The smile on his face was worth everything. He practically hopped all the way in from the parking lot and hasn't stopped smiling since we arrived.

He'll remember this.

It's a thought that both excites me and terrifies me. If things don't work out with Clay and Jade—whatever that means—Jack will still have these memories for the rest of his life of when I gave him a family for a split second.

Jade reaches over and places her hand on mine, where they're folded in my lap.

"You okay?" she asks.

My spine straightens, and I glance at where the boys are still spinning on the ride.

I swallow. "Yes, I'm okay."

"I can imagine it's a lot," she replies. "Bringing new people around your kid. Lots of fear and anxiety and…jealousy."

I let out a clipped laugh. She nailed it on the head.

How is it going to feel when Jack always wants someone else over me? It's so heavy I can hardly wrap my brain around it. Still, it drowns my mind in anxiety.

"Yeah, it is a lot," I reply. "But how long could I really keep him to myself?"

"You're the most selfless person I've ever met," she says. "My mother never put me first."

My head snaps up. "That can't be true."

She shrugs. "Maybe when I was younger, but as soon as I graduated high school, she made it very clear she was done. And she just left."

I let out a sigh. "Being a mother is very hard," I say. "It literally requires more than you have to give. It's fulfilling, but it's also exhausting. And no matter how hard you try, you inevitably lose a sense of yourself along the way."

I watch her jaw clench as she chews on her cheek and stares out at the families passing us by.

Placing my hand back on hers, I squeeze it and then interlace my fingers with hers.

"I'm sure your mom loves you very much."

"Thanks," she mumbles.

"Your dad clearly does," I reply, trying to lighten the mood.

"Yeah," she says with a smile. "I've always been close with my dad."

"What does he think about Clay?" I ask.

Her smile fades, and she immediately looks away. Something about the way she's evading that question makes me nervous. That's not a good sign.

"Uhh…" she says as she scratches her leg.

Just then, Jack and Clay come bounding out of the ride exit, Jack bouncing with a wide smile.

"That was so fun!" Then he looks up at Clay, who looks like he's been through the spin cycle. "Can we ride it again?" Jack says with a shriek.

Clay winces, which makes Jade and me laugh. "Why don't we do something a little slower, buddy?" he says with a grimace.

Standing up, I smile at Clay. "What's wrong? Can't handle another turn on the Spin-o-Matic?"

He smiles, bumping me with his shoulder. The four of us make our way down the paved pathway toward the next ride.

"The Ferris wheel!" Jack says with excitement when he sees the giant ride up ahead.

"Perfect," Clay replies, and we laugh again.

"You look a little green, babe," Jade says, teasing him. I let out a laugh, biting my bottom lip and waiting for his reaction.

He looks back from where he's walking with Jack to glare at her when his eyes dart down to find my hand resting on the inside of Jade's arm. A smile crosses his face.

Then he faces forward and takes my son's hand in his own. "To the Ferris wheel," he calls.

"To the Ferris wheel," the rest of us echo.

The line is short, but we still have to wait about twenty minutes before we can get on. Of course, during that time, Jack steals all the attention, talking about all of his favorite parts of the day so far and all the things he'd like to do before we go home.

"Can we come back here on my birthday?" Jack asks excitedly.

"You just had a birthday," Clay replies with a laugh.

"I know. But my *next* birthday."

I ruffle his hair with a smile. "Yes, buddy. We can come back on your birthday."

"All of us," he adds. "I want *all* of us to come back."

Glancing up at Clay, our eyes meet, and I feel my skin breaking out in goose bumps. The future feels so distant and long, but
the possibilities of our future make it seem so exciting. Birthdays,
holidays, vacations. Could we really see that far together? Like
this?

"Of course, buddy," Clay replies, giving Jack a wink. "We will
all come back."

When it's our turn for the Ferris wheel, the four of us climb
into one pod together. Clay and I end up next to each other, and
Jade and Jack are on the other side.

He grabs her hand with a big cheesy smile, squeezing it excitedly as she smiles at him. The sight of them together makes the
inside of my chest warm.

I can't remember the last time I ever put my trust in anyone
the way I trust these two. Last night was a testament to that. I
told them everything and never worried once they would spill my
secrets or think of me differently after learning the truth.

And now, I'm trusting them with my son. And not just his
safety but his heart. He's falling for them the same way I am. If
they leave us, I won't be the only one left heartbroken.

But when the Ferris wheel reaches the top and Jack burrows
himself under Jade's arm in fear, I watch the way she holds him
tightly, comforting him when the seat rocks.

"Look at the hot-air balloon out there. Do you see it?" she
asks, distracting him from his fear.

His eyes are squeezed shut, and slowly he peels them open.

"And there's the roller coaster," he replies, pointing across the park.

"And there's the parking lot. Let's see if we can find Mommy's car."

The two of them hold each other as they scan the parking lot.

Clay's hands rest in his lap, and when I feel his fingers softly
brushing mine, I look down to see them. I want to hold his hand
so badly, but what would Jack think? What is the protocol here?
Would that be inappropriate? I feel so bad at this.

All my son would see is a show of affection between two

people. The only reason he'd think it's strange or weird is if we make it that way. But I still can't bring myself to link my fingers with Clay's.

So I rest my head on his shoulder and find comfort in the way his knuckle brushes mine.

Jack doesn't even notice. He looks right at me and asks if we can get popcorn after the ride and never makes a single mention of my head on Clay's shoulder.

———————

"He's out," Clay says as we pull up to the house. I turn around from the driver's seat to see Jack passed out in the back seat. The three of us giggle at the sight of him, head tilted back and mouth hanging open.

"He had fun today," Jade says next to me.

"Yes, he did," I reply.

When I climb out of the car, Clay is already carrying Jack, who's practically drooling on Clay's shoulder. Rushing to the front door, I unlock it and open it for Clay, who carries Jack all the way to his room.

I follow him, watching him place my son in his bed and delicately peel off each of his sneakers. Then, from the doorway, I watch in silence as he lifts up his comforter, gently tucking him in. My heart nearly stops when Clay runs his fingers through Jack's hair and leans down to place a kiss on his forehead.

It's like someone sucked the air out of the room. My chest is tight, and my eyes sting with the threat of tears. At that moment, I know he loves him. It's a discovery as significant as learning that he loves *me*, if not more so. There is no going back now. No tearing them apart or removing Clay from Jack's life, not without consequences or heartache.

But that fear is gone because I realize now Clay would never do that. I see the way he looks at my son, and I know...he will never leave him.

When Clay turns around and finds me watching from the doorway, he walks up to me, waiting for me to say something. But I don't speak. I just reach out and pull him in for a hug, resting my face on his shoulder and holding him tightly.

"Thank you," I whisper.

"For what?" he asks.

"For everything," I reply.

His arms squeeze tighter around me. "I don't just do it for him, you know?"

I force down the building emotion. "I know."

After a moment, I pull away from the embrace. Neither of us says anything as we walk out of the hallway and out to the living room. Then we pause at the entrance as we both notice Jade curled up on the couch, fast asleep.

I let out a laugh as he walks over to lift her from the couch. For a moment, I consider asking them both to stay. But even I know that might be too soon. It's one thing for Jack to see us together but another for him to climb into my bed in the morning to find two other people in there.

I know we need to introduce this slowly. And I need to have a serious talk with him before I start moving people in.

One step at a time, Eden.

Clay carefully wakes Jade from her sleep and kisses her cheek as he lifts her from the couch.

"I can walk," she says groggily.

"I know you can," he replies. "But I like holding you."

She glares at him. "Put me down."

With a laugh, he sets her on her feet.

"Thanks for a fun day," she says, putting her arms around me. I squeeze her tightly.

"Thank you for coming."

"I'm going to take her home," Clay says before looking at me. And I realize that he's telling me this for a reason. Because he's afraid I might be jealous of them being alone together.

"I'll see you guys at the club this week. Jade still needs her impact play lesson."

Jade's eyes widen. "I can't wait. Can we practice on him?"

"What did I do?" He puts his hands up and stares at her with confusion.

I laugh again as I walk them to the door. When they reach the driveway, almost to his car, I feel the need to say something. Like if I don't, I'll explode.

"I'll talk to Jack," I blurt out. They both turn around and stare at me expectantly. "And maybe next time you guys can stay...the night. I need to talk to him first."

Jade's lips part with a gasp as her eyes meet mine. "So you really...want to try this?"

"Yes. I do."

Clay bites back his smile, but it's Jade who bounds back to the front door, grabbing my face for a kiss. She moans into my mouth. "Oh my God, I'm so excited," she says after pulling away.

I force myself to smile, although inside, I'm feeling a lot of things. Excitement, fear, and everything in between. As I glance up at him, he seems to notice my apprehension.

This is hard. All of it. And no matter how much I want it, that won't change.

My heart is bursting for both of them, and I care about them both so much.

But do Clay and I still have things to get over? Because right now, he looks as afraid as I am.

Not to mention Jade and I never truly came forward with how long we've been seeing each other without him.

We can't start a relationship with secrets, can we?

Surely, we'll get past them. We care about each other enough. We'll make it work.

Rule #38: When in doubt, consult someone with experience.

Eden

"WILL YOU KNOCK IT OFF? I'M TRYING TO WORK."

"What's wrong? Is this distracting you?"

The door to Hunter's office in the back of the club is half-open, but as I approach, I hear him and Drake arguing, so I pause and gently rap on the door.

"Knock, knock," I say carefully as I peek my head around the corner.

"Come in," Hunter calls. He's sitting at his desk with Drake stepping away from him with a mischievous grin.

"I'm sorry to interrupt," I say carefully, my gaze passing back and forth between the two.

"You're not interrupting," Hunter replies, and then he glances back at his husband. "Drake was just attempting to make my workday more difficult."

"Successfully," Drake replies. Then he moves toward the door. "I'll let you work now."

I put up a hand. "Actually, I was hoping to talk to both of you."

Their brows arch in unison as they glance at me with curiosity. "It's…personal," I add, which only makes their expressions intensify.

Closing the door behind me, I take a deep breath as I move toward the empty chair in front of Hunter's desk. What once was a communal office has been designated to Hunter since he's the only one who works at the club anymore. An array of baby photos of their twin girls is scattered around the desk.

Garrett and Emerson have taken to working mostly from home, although they can often be found wandering around the club, tying up odds and ends. This leaves the other desk in the large office unoccupied and waiting for a new member of the team.

Yes, I've noticed how empty it is. And tempting.

"I have some questions about…your relationship," I say, feeling completely out of my element.

"What kinds of questions?" Hunter asks, resting his forearms on the desk and leaning forward.

"I'm…seeing someone," I say. God, this is uncomfortable. Just giving out one small personal detail of my life feels like walking naked through the grocery store.

When it's obvious they're both waiting for more information, I add, "Two…someones."

"Ahh…" Drake replies, now clearly interested in what I'm getting at.

"And you want our advice on being in a poly relationship?" Hunter replies, always the pragmatic.

"Yes."

"You're into both of them?" Drake asks.

I nod.

"And they're into each other?"

"They're dating."

I swear I notice him wincing for a split second.

"Is that bad?" I ask.

Hunter is the one to step in. "No. It's not bad."

"You're feeling like the third wheel," Drake says, not exactly a question but more a statement. Of course, he knows how it feels. It was just two years ago that he joined his best friend's marriage with Hunter's wife, Isabel.

"I'm used to feeling like the third wheel. How do I stop?"

"Chances are you're feeling that more than they are. When Drake joined us, we had a *lot* of conversations about that. More often than not, it was due to things we did unknowingly, so communication is key. Once Isabel and I were aware of that behavior, we stopped."

"Communication is always key, isn't it?" I reply with an uncomfortable grin.

"Unfortunately," Hunter replies with a scowl. He was never much for conversation, so I imagine he has as many hurdles as I do.

"Make sure you spend time with each of them on your own, too," Drake adds. "And then even more time all together as the three of you. That's a big relationship to take care of."

"Do you ever get jealous?" I ask, afraid I'm opening a can of worms they might not feel comfortable with.

"*Jealous* isn't the right word," Hunter replies. "What Drake and Isabel have is different than what Isabel and I have or what Drake and I have together. I'm never jealous of that. In fact, I love to see what they have. It's just different, not better or worse."

"We have the same relationship problems as everyone else," Drake adds.

"I'm not too good at relationships," I reply, rubbing my forehead.

Drake lets out a loud laugh. "You can't be worse than I was."

"So how do you go from no relationship to a relationship with two people?" I ask.

He shrugs. "Fuck, I don't know. We just...love the fuck out of each other. We get on each other's nerves and fight and fuck and laugh and then do it all over again the next day."

"Can I ask…" Hunter says. His brow is furrowed, and I appreciate the sincerity on his face. I've always related best to Hunter. He's serious and straightforward. A man of few words, he never beats around the bush or makes things complicated.

I nod at his request to ask more about my relationship.

"Is it serious?"

"No," I reply too quickly. "I mean…yes. A little."

Right? I don't plan on being with Jade and Clay forever. Do I? We're just having fun.

It can't be *too* serious. We're just dating. I'll never get married again. I'll never be so codependent with another person for the rest of my life. Living in a motel for three weeks will change a person.

So no. It's not that level of seriousness.

Although my feelings for them are serious. I care about both of them immensely. So much my chest feels full and almost painful at the thought of them. The same way I sometimes feel when I look at Jack. It's amazing and terrifying at the same time.

But things with Jade and Clay together just started. I only met Jade a few weeks ago. How could we be making a commitment already?

But it feels significant in the sense that nothing has ever completely flipped my entire life on its head—not since Jack was born, and that is certainly very serious.

"You sure about that?" Drake asks with a cunning grin on his face when he notices me reeling from such a simple question.

Hunter's expression is sympathetic. Surely that can't be a good sign.

Which can only mean one thing. Things with Jade and Clay are a lot more serious than I want to admit.

Fuck.

"You okay?" Hunter asks, but when I open my mouth to speak, I'm interrupted by a chipper voice behind me.

"Hunter, I just sent the VIP numbers—" Garrett stops when he sees me sitting in one of the chairs in Hunter's office. "Hey…Madame." He shoots me a wink and a mischievous smile.

"Hey, Garrett," I reply with a wave.

"Quite the performance the other day in the voyeur hall," he says flippantly.

I give him a snarky smile. "I fondly remember you giving a similar one last year."

He holds up his left hand, the gold band shining in the office light. "Turned out well for me."

I don't bother replying to that, not when Hunter and Drake just cornered me into realizing just how significant things might be with Jade and Clay.

Garrett steps into the office, taking the other empty chair next to me. "So…checking out your new office?"

My lips press into a tight line to hide my smile as I look toward the empty desk in the back. "I'm not really the office type…"

Garrett leans in. "But…"

I can't fight the excitement that's creeping up as I think about it. "But I doubt I'll be in here much anyway, right? I'm sure I'll be working more out there."

Hunter smacks his desk. "That means you're taking it?"

There's no hiding my smile now. "I'm still thinking about it."

"I'm texting Emerson," Garrett says with a smug grin.

"You have to take it, E," Drake replies from where he's standing behind Hunter, his hand resting on the back of his chair. "We need you around here."

"We should throw a party," Garrett says before I can respond to Drake.

"A party?" I ask.

"Fuck yeah."

"The anniversary party," Hunter replies. "Three years on the seventeenth. We'll celebrate the club and Eden's new position."

"We'll open the VIP level to everyone for the night," Garrett adds. "Waive all the room rental fees. I know Mia can fill up the voyeur rooms for a massive performance like we did before."

The energy in the room is electric. The guys are going back and forth, talking about big plans for the party and ways to draw in more members.

To my surprise, I love it.

For so long, I've felt like a bit of an outsider with them. Yes, I've been here for years. And yes, I've always been welcome and appreciated, but I never felt like *one of them*. Even when they gave me a room to run my business out of. I wasn't an owner or a founder. I don't get invited to their private parties and get-togethers.

And I'm not that petty or desperate. But I love the idea of being in the room where decisions are made. I like the idea of that office, even if I don't plan on using it.

"You're taking it?" Emerson's voice from behind me jolts me from my quiet thoughts.

"I thought you guys worked from home," I say with exasperation when Emerson Grant enters the room.

The other men in the office go silent as I stand from my chair and turn to him. He's wearing an expression of hope as he waits for my response.

"You'll take the job?" he asks again.

I swallow.

"If Salacious needs me…I'm here. Yes. Of course."

His face splits into a proud grin as he puts out a hand for me to shake.

"I'm so glad," he says.

The men behind me start speaking excitedly again as I stare at Emerson. I'm hit with a sudden flurry of emotions.

Right after Ronan, Emerson is the one person who helped give me a new start—and he doesn't even know. Emerson Grant took a chance on me. He saw something in me no one else did.

I wish I could tell him how much that means to me.

Then a harrowing thought comes crashing in my mind. I'll need to tell them about Jack. I'll need to tell them I've been keeping this secret from them for years.

One thing at a time, I tell myself, quickly calming my rising anxiety.

For now, I can celebrate. I just took a huge position at the greatest sex club in the country.

And the only thing I want to do at the moment is tell the two people who mean the most to me.

Rule #39: Sometimes, it's okay to lose control.

Clay

WHEN I GOT THE TEXT FROM EDEN THAT SHE WANTED TO CELEBRATE something at the club tonight, I knew that meant it was going to be a good night. Things feel different now. We're at the club, but I still feel as if Eden is really ours. It feels like the best of both worlds.

"What does this mean?" Jade asks excitedly.

Eden is sitting across from her in the large chair, holding a glass of red wine in her hands. "It means I'll be a manager here at the club."

"Like one of the owners," I reply with a smirk.

She shrugs. "I'm not an owner."

"You might as well be," I say.

Her gaze lingers on my face for a moment before she turns toward Jade and explains exactly what went down with her, Emerson, and Garrett. While she speaks, I think about how proud I am. How proud I am to be *hers*.

I was a fool for what happened before, for letting her go.

"So why aren't you out there celebrating?" Jade asks enthusiastically.

Eden reaches for her hand, petting the back of her knuckles softly. Then her eyes find mine as she says, "Because I wanted to share this moment with you." She turns her attention to Jade. "Both of you."

Jade's eyes grow soft and fill with affection as she leans forward, eagerly capturing Eden's mouth in a desperate kiss. They moan with their lips fused.

My cock twitches in my pants, and I shift to adjust myself as I watch them together. These two stunning, beautiful, brilliant women who I love so much. And they're both mine.

Out of nowhere, I'm blindsided by that rising guilt that seems to show itself whenever I dare to acknowledge how lucky I am.

I don't deserve this.

I've lied to Jade about my relationship with Eden. I've been keeping my relationship with Jade a secret from her own father.

What kind of man am I?

"Clay."

Blinking myself out of the spiral of dark thoughts, I look up to find Eden and Jade now on the bed, looking at me expectantly.

"You okay?" Eden asks with a flash of concern on her face.

"Yeah," I say, shaking off the shame as I stand from the chair and walk to the bed to meet them. They're both on their knees, facing each other as Eden kisses a trail down Jade's neck. I stroke the back of Eden's head and link my fingers with Jade's.

Eden pulls away for a moment as she bites her lip and stares back and forth at both of us. "I was thinking..." she says.

A thrill of excitement runs through me. I love when she gets ideas.

"I would love to watch you two," she says seductively.

"Watch us?" I ask with a smile as I glance at Jade to see her reaction.

"But I want us all to be together," Jade says as she reaches for Eden.

"Oh, we will be," Eden replies. "I have a couple of toys to add to the mix."

My heart beats faster. "What kind of toys?"

Jade and I glance back and forth at each other as Eden climbs off the bed and goes to the cabinet of toys along the wall.

"I bought these from the shop downstairs, just for tonight," she says.

When she turns around, I recognize them immediately. Well…I recognize *one* of them.

It's a sleek black silicone plug with a round part at the end. I know exactly how it feels rubbing against my prostate, especially when she turns it on using the remote she's holding.

The other toy, I don't recognize.

She walks toward us, holding both. "I want Clay to wear *this* while he fucks you," she says, holding up the plug. "Which I will control."

"What about that?" Jade asks, excitedly staring at the purple U-shaped silicone toy in Eden's other hand.

She leans forward, her face only inches from Jade's. Pressing a kiss to her lips, she pulls back and whispers, "I will wear this while I watch."

"And I get to control it," Jade replies, finishing her sentence.

"That's genius," I say. My dick is straining in my pants at the thought alone. All three of us will be connected and in control.

Unable to resist, I bury my hand in Eden's hair and drag her mouth to mine, kissing her hungrily as she fumbles for the buttons of my shirt. In the corner of my eye, I see Jade quickly undressing herself and then reaching for Eden's clothes. She's only wearing a simple tight dress tonight, so once Jade has the zipper down in the back, Eden's dress falls to the floor.

Pulling away from my kiss, she smiles at me. "You first."

I lick my lips and reach for the zipper of my pants, quickly undoing them and lowering them to my ankles with my boxers. "Jade, there's lube in the drawer by the bed," I say without taking my eyes from Eden's.

I want her to see how even the mention of lube and ass play doesn't affect me anymore. I'm not the man I used to be.

Kicking my pants away, I wrap my arms around Eden's waist and carry her to the bed. When I lie down, she lands on top of me, devouring my mouth with passion. Again, my hand finds its place in her hair. I pull her face closer, letting the long dark strands surround me, tickling my face and neck.

My lips drift from her mouth down her jawline to her neck, sucking and nibbling at her delicate skin. Inside my chest, my heart wants to beat its way out. All I can think about is how much I love her, how every kiss is my declaration to her.

I love you. I love you. I love you.

Reaching behind her, I find the clasp of her bra and quickly unsnap it. After she shakes it off, I toss it on the floor and pull her breasts to my mouth, devouring each soft mound with a growl.

While my face is buried in her tits, she reaches for the bottle of lube from Jade. They exchange a kiss, and my legs fall open in anticipation.

After her kiss with Jade, Eden crawls down my body, kissing her way across my chest and abs. When her hand wraps around my hard length and she strokes, I let out a low, raspy moan.

"Fuck, yes." I gasp.

When she licks my cock from my balls to the tip, I cry out again.

But then she leaves me there. Sitting on her knees between my legs, she uncaps the bottle and squirts a fair amount of gel on her fingers. Then she grabs one of my legs and lifts it, giving her room to smear the lubricant around my tight hole.

I hiss, throwing my head back.

Jade is sitting on the bed, watching Eden. Her bottom lip is between her teeth, and she's staring at Eden's fingers with rapt attention as they work their way inside me, stretching and thrusting.

"Does that feel good?" Jade asks in a sweet whisper.

"Fuck yes." I groan. At that moment, Eden hooks her fingers just right and hits my prostate. It feels like I've been hit by lightning.

"He's ready," Eden says with a wicked smile. After lubing up the butt plug, she slowly slides it in place.

I almost forgot how this feels. To be so full and hovering near the edge of pleasure. There is no other feeling like it. And she hasn't even switched on the remote yet.

My hand lazily strokes my cock as I force myself to take slow, deep breaths with the plug in place. I want this feeling to last forever.

"Your turn," Jade says as she leans in and kisses Eden on the lips. Jade is holding the purple toy in her hands. She grabs Eden by the hips and drags her to the edge of the bed.

Lazily, I sit up against the headboard, wincing when the plug hits my prostate again.

Then I watch as Jade kneels on the floor between Eden's legs, slowly spreading them as she stares up at her. Eden's lips part as she pets Jade's head.

I can't take my eyes off Jade, watching as she massages Eden's inner thighs, sliding her hands all the way up until she's running her thumb through Eden's soft folds.

A groan crawls up my chest when I see Jade lean in and drag her tongue along Eden's cunt, making her lean back and prop herself up with one arm.

"Do it, baby. Put it in," I mutter in a hoarse tone.

Jade leans back and makes eye contact with Eden as she slides the toy into place. Eden lets out a whimper and then smiles at her once it's in.

"Get the remotes," she says.

Jade grabs both of them off the bed and stares down at them with a curious expression. When she presses her thumb down on one, it's like having the wind knocked out of me. Electric heat climbs through every extremity of my body as I groan so loudly it practically shakes the walls.

"That must be for his plug," Jade says as she taps the remote again. The vibration stops, and I take a deep breath to stop myself from coming already.

"Wicked little girl," Eden says seductively as she drags Jade toward her and kisses her neck. "He's going to make you pay for that."

Fuck yeah, I am.

Eden takes one of the remotes and sits in the large red chair by the wall.

Completely naked, with her legs crossed in front of her and her hair draped over her shoulders, she looks like a goddess. Jade is watching her, too, the same expression on her face that I'm wearing on mine. *Desire.*

"Come here," I mutter darkly to Jade.

She bites her lip as she crawls toward me. I'm strung so tight I can't take another second. Burying my hand in her hair, I haul her mouth to mine, biting her bottom lip as I kiss her. She hums against my mouth, and I feel her smiling into the kiss.

Having Jade in my hands again feels like home. It's been a few days since I've been able to give her my undivided attention, and I didn't realize how much I needed this. And as much as I wish I could take my time with her, right now, I feel like a wild man.

Holding her by the scalp, I drag her mouth away from mine and aim her lips right at my cock. She swallows me into the back of her throat without hesitation. I love the sounds of her gulping and gagging as her head bobs up and down.

Suddenly, the vibration in my ass takes me by surprise. My hips thrust, and I groan with a slam of my head against the headboard.

Eden lets out a loud moan as well, which means while she's switching on my toy, Jade is switching on hers.

Once the plug quits, I work to catch my breath. Jade pops off my dick and smiles at me wickedly.

Feeling out of control, I dive toward her. Climbing onto my

knees, I fold her over in front of me, and she lets out a yelp with her ass high in the air.

I can't take another second without my cock buried deep inside her. So while I align the head of my dick with her pussy, I look at Eden. Her tongue peeks out and runs across her lower lip, and I keep my eyes glued to hers as I drive my cock into Jade.

She cries out, her fingers gripping the sheets on the bed.

"I want her to feel this too, baby. Let her feel it," I say, grabbing Jade's hips and thrusting hard again.

In her hand, Jade squeezes the remote. At that exact moment, Eden throws her head back on a cry. Her fingers are clutched around the arms of the chair as she slowly slides to the edge of her seat. Her legs are open, so we can see the purple vibrator as it pulses against her clit.

I know what's coming. A moment later, I feel my own vibrations.

It makes me fuck Jade even harder.

"Fuck, fuck, fuck," I say with a grunt as I fight the urge to come.

But I won't come before them.

"Harder," Jade says with her face pressed against the bed.

The vibration never really goes away from that point. Just as I pick up speed with my thrusts, the toy grows in intensity. Which must be the same for Eden because she's barely holding it together as she watches from the chair.

"Slap her ass for me," she says in a panting breath.

"Gladly," I reply. Rearing my hand back, I let it land against Jade's ass in a loud crack.

She whimpers loudly, so I do it again.

"Now pull her hair," Eden adds. She's writhing on her chair, her eyes glued to us on the bed.

Reaching down to Jade, I grab her by the scalp and drag her upward as I continue pounding into her from behind. My other hand slides down her front, and I pinch her clit between my fingers, making her scream.

"Just like that," Eden says with a smile.

"Let me feel you come, baby," I say in Jade's ear. She's clutching onto my arm as I move inside her. My finger is rubbing fiercely at her clit, and I'm spurred on by the sounds she's making and the way her body is tensing in my arms.

"Don't stop," she says with a squeal.

Eden and I are barely hanging on. I can tell by the way she's moving and the clipped sound of her breathing. And I've got a vibrating butt plug brushing my prostate that is making it very hard to keep from losing control.

When I feel Jade's muscles seize up and I know she's coming, I keep my fingers moving on her clit to ride out her orgasm. And when I know she's finally crested the peak of her pleasure, I let go.

"I'm fucking coming, baby," I mutter in her ear. My cock jerks as I release inside her with a roaring sound. I can feel it from the top of my head to the tips of my toes.

On the chair, Eden lets out a high-pitched sound, and I watch as her hips tremble through her orgasm. Her legs are pressed together, and her head is hanging backward.

We're so loud it sounds like we're about to tear down the walls of this whole building. It's a pleasure unmatched by anything else. And it feels as if this climax will never end.

Not that I ever want it to.

When we can finally breathe again, none of us move. I savor the sound of their panting and how incredibly beautiful they both look. Their skin is glistening from sweat as their chests heave for air. Their expressions are relaxed and sated. And it makes me feel so incredibly lucky to be a part of it.

When those menacing thoughts of guilt and shame try to creep in, I shove them away.

Right now, my only focus is them.

Rule #40: Bad things happen when you lose control.

Eden

THERE'S A CHANGE IN THE AIR.

Outside the club, the weather has taken on a chill that bites, but in here, we're warm and cozy.

But Clay seems restless.

I'd be a fool not to notice the way he's changed in the last month or so. And who could blame him?

I've kept him sheltered and secluded.

His head rests on my thigh as I stroke his head and ignore the fact that slowly over time, I've watched the light die from his eyes.

No amount of praise is going to change that.

When he rises from the bed, reaching for his clothes, I notice that his gaze doesn't reach mine.

"I have an early meeting," he mutters quietly with his back to me.

"You'll be back tomorrow?" I ask, trying to keep things light and normal.

He doesn't answer.

"Clay…"

Suddenly, he spins toward me. "What are we doing?"

My brows furrow in confusion. "What are you talking about?"

In nothing but his boxer briefs, he tosses his pants down on the mattress. He's angry, and I feel myself tensing up in fear.

"Eight months. Eight months I've been coming here, and I keep waiting for the day when you'll admit that what we have is real, but that day never comes. It's just the same, over and over and over again. How long can this possibly go on?" he asks, looking distraught. "What are we, Eden?"

My mouth goes dry, and I open it to speak, but nothing comes out.

"Do you care about me at all?" The pain and fear on his face gut me, but I feel so blindsided by this outburst I can't seem to form a response to anything.

Say something, Eden, a voice in my head screams at me, but no matter what I do, I can't seem to speak.

"Of course," I mumble weakly.

"Or am I just a client to you?"

"You're not a client," I say, which is implied by the fact that Clay no longer pays me, but I know that's not what he's talking about right now. For some reason, I'm so caught up in my own head I can't vocalize what I really need to say.

I love you.

I care about you.

I need you.

He walks to the opposite side of the room, keeping his back to me. And I feel the impending doom of his words even before he speaks them.

Rising from the bed, I cover myself with the robe draped over the chair, and I walk to him. But the moment my fingers touch his back, he says, "I can't do this anymore."

My heart falls to the pit of my stomach.

"What? Why?"

When he turns toward me, his eyes are red, and his molars are clenched. "If I asked you to come home with me tonight, what would you say?"

I'm so thrown off by the question I hesitate. "Tonight?"

"Yes, tonight. Come home with me. Sleep in my bed. Wake up with me tomorrow morning and just be real. Not my Madame."

"Clay…I can't tonight."

He lets out a huff and drags his fingers through his hair.

"Fine. Tomorrow, then. Or the next day. Next week. Fuck, Eden, don't you understand?"

"No. I don't. Help me understand, Clay," I beg.

I've done everything I can to show him how much he means to me. I take care of him. I praise him. I make him feel loved and wanted, but what he's asking for is not something I can give.

He reaches for my face, holding me by the jaw and stroking my cheek. "You called me yours. You tell me that I mean everything to you, but then you keep our relationship hidden in this room, and now I don't know what's real anymore, Eden. I just know that I'm in love with you, but I don't know if you feel the same. Or if this is all just a game."

"I–I told you, you are mine, Clay. You are," I stammer.

"I'm not talking about Madame Kink," he says softly. His eyes are pleading, and I want to erase every ounce of doubt, but I don't know how. I don't know how to do any of this. "I just want you, Eden."

Immediately, I think of my life as Eden. My house. My son. That life is a stark contrast to the one he sees me in every day. He has no idea who Eden is, and I know deep down that once he learns the truth, he'll never want her.

And there is no way for me to make him understand that without someone getting hurt.

"I can't…" I say with a shake in my voice.

He drops his hands from my face. It's like feeling the floor drop away from me.

And just like that, I watch the love and affection drain from his eyes as he stares right through me.

"I have to go," he mumbles, his voice full of pain.

"Clay, wait," I say, but he doesn't stop.

Brushing past me, he reaches for his pants, pulling them on with his back to me.

For fuck's sake. Say something, Eden.

"It's complicated. What happens outside this room doesn't matter," I argue, but it feels like I'm reciting something without emotion. I'm still talking like Madame. "When we're in here, you're everything to me, Clay."

He doesn't respond as he snatches his shirt off the stool and pulls it over his head. As he reaches for the door, I do the only thing I know how.

"Stop. Do not walk out of that door."

He pauses, his fingers resting on the door handle. Like a good boy, he obeys. And for a moment, I feel like everything will be okay.

Then, with a slight turn of his head toward me, he softly mutters, "No."

I watch as his fingers turn the handle, and he slips out of the room, letting the door slam closed.

And just like that, I'm alone.

My eyes peel open, and I stare out the dark window. I reach across the empty pillows beside me to check the time on my phone, *3:45 a.m.*

I have no calls or messages, so I drop my phone and turn over to try to fall back asleep. Of course, it's futile. My mind is still focused on the memory of that night with Clay randomly showing up in my dreams. I haven't thought about that night in days.

There was a time it would keep me up every night on end. The guilt of how I let him down plagued me for weeks.

But things are great now. Last night with Clay and Jade was amazing. Things have changed.

I've changed. I'm not afraid of commitment anymore. I'm ready to come out with our relationship, even to Jack.

So why do I still feel so weird?

Like something is off.

I never get back to sleep. Around four in the morning, I climb out of bed and check on Jack. He's sleeping peacefully in his room. The shark night-light is blanketing his room in blue and green light, and I stand there for a moment just watching him sleep.

I have to remind myself I'm doing the right thing. I'm not rushing into marriage or anything, but I am about to change a lot in my seven-year-old son's life. Even if Jade and Clay don't move in, they'll be around. Birthdays, holidays, milestones. They'll be there, making memories and carving out a place in our lives. Something like that isn't just easily undone.

This isn't a game. This is his life.

Am I rushing into this?

Is this truly what's best for Jack?

Turning away from his bedroom, I gently pull the door closed and curl up on my couch, staring into the dark void of my living room and letting every intrusive thought find its way into my mind.

From the moment I left my ex-husband, I have fought and struggled for control over my life. I worked hard to ensure that nothing would change, and for seven years, nothing did. When things change, that's when I feel the control start to slip.

And right now, so many things are changing. My life feels like it is in a state of chaos.

I have to have faith that it will turn out right. At some point, the dust will settle, and my son and I will be okay. Right?

There seems to be no fixing my mood today. Not even when Jade texts Clay and me a sexy selfie of her lying in bed in nothing but a pair of light-pink panties.

Good morning.

The picture makes me smile and think some very naughty things, but I don't respond.

Clay does.

> I'd like to crawl into that bed with you.
> Come on over. My dad is out.

The reminder that Jade lives with her dad isn't the reminder I need today.

She's so young. Is it really fair for me to drag her into my domestic life and tie her down with my child and me? Jade is still finding herself.

At some point, she's going to want to move out of his house. What if she wants to move in here?

Am I going to be ready for that?

Immediately my mind rejects the idea. Not because I don't love her because I do. I love her in a way that frightens me. But I also care about her enough to want her to be free of me and all of my baggage she certainly doesn't need.

The group chat goes quiet, and I figure it's better if I keep my foul mood out of the conversation today. I'll feel better tonight or tomorrow.

After Jack wakes up and eats breakfast, I promise him we can take his new electric scooter down to the paved trail along the harbor.

Maybe some fresh air will do me good.

And if I tire him out, there's a chance he'll take a nap with me this afternoon since I'm barely functioning on two hours of sleep as it is.

When we reach the trail, I find a nice paved area where he can zoom around on his scooter while shooting videos of him on my phone's camera to send to Ronan later. Jack loves to watch the boats leaving the docks and chase the seagulls that hover around, waiting for someone to drop their lunch.

It's peaceful and nice. Which means I'm immediately plagued with guilt for not inviting Jade and Clay. They would love this. Lord knows Jack would.

I can see Jade and me sitting on the bench to watch Jack ride circles around the park. And Clay would be out there with him, teaching him how to do tricks off the curb and tending to his wounds if he falls.

If the picture is so perfect in my mind, then what on earth am I so worried about? I must be really sleep-deprived because even I can tell how irrational I'm being.

Everything is going to be just fine.

"Eden?" a deep voice says from my left.

I take my eyes off Jack to see a stout, bearded man greeting me with a smile. It takes me a moment to recognize Jade's father.

He waves cordially. "Will Penner. We met the other day when you dropped off my daughter."

"Of course," I reply with a smile as I take a step toward him. "How are you?"

"Oh, I'm good. About to take the boat out for the day."

I look to the harbor. "You have a boat?"

"Yeah, just an old pontoon. If you and Jade would ever like to go out on the water, just let me know," he says, lifting the small red cooler and pointing toward the water.

"That would be fun. Thank you," I reply. He seems like a nice guy, and I can see the resemblance to Jade. Piercing blue eyes, button nose, cheerful demeanor. It makes me miss her.

"I would really love that," I add. "I'm sure Clay would love that too. Especially if he can bring my son. You can fit that many on there, right?"

His smiling face grows curious. "You know Clay?" he asks.

"Of course," I reply.

"Are you two…dating then?"

My smile fades as I stare at him in confusion. Either I missed something or he did, but right now, I'm too afraid to give something away that I shouldn't. There's no way Jade already told her dad about our relationship, is there? She would have told me.

"Who?" I ask. "Me and Jade?"

"You and Clay. He hasn't mentioned anything at the office, but then again, why would he tell me?" he replies with a laugh. Then he shakes his head. "I'm sorry. That's so forward of me. It's none of my business. Clay's a great guy. If you are seeing him, I'd be happy to take all of you out on the water."

He's rambling, but I don't catch a word. My mind is struggling to keep up. All it keeps repeating in my head is—if Clay is dating Jade, why would her father ask me if I'm dating Clay…?

Unless he doesn't know.

"It was nice running into you," he says as he carries his cooler toward the water, clearly oblivious to the way my mind is spinning. "Have a great day, and definitely let me know if you guys would like to get on the boat sometime."

Mindlessly, I wave and mumble something like goodbye to him.

Does Jade's father really not know about their relationship? Clay wouldn't do that. He wouldn't sleep with his coworker's daughter and lie about it for months.

Why wouldn't they tell me about this?

They've been keeping me in the dark this whole time?

Why?

When someone speeds past me on their bike, I blink myself out of my head. Quickly, I scan the area for Jack on his scooter. He was riding circles in the paved lot just a moment ago.

But all I see are people walking toward the pier to get on their boats. And families walking together along the harbor. And kids doing skateboard tricks.

No Jack.

"Jack," I call, trying to keep myself from panicking.

But after a moment and still no sign of him, my blood pressure starts to rise, and every terrifying thought creeps in. What have I done? He could be anywhere. This is all my fault.

"Jack!" I scream as I take off, running to every corner of the paved section of the park to find him.

It feels like hours before I hear his little voice. "I'm right here, Mama."

By that point, it's too late. Tears streak my cheeks as I gather him up in my arms and squeeze him tightly.

"I was just chasing birds," he says with his face muffled against my shirt. "I'm sorry, Mama."

His apologetic tone makes me feel bad for scaring him, but he scared me.

"It's not your fault, buddy. I just looked away. I never should have looked away."

"It's okay, Mama," he whispers, his tiny hand stroking my back as I hold him in a tight hug. "It's not your fault."

Everything inside me breaks on those little words.

He has no idea, but it is my fault. It always is.

Rule #41: Don't count your flowers before they've bloomed.

Jade

> Can we meet at Clay's tonight?
> 10 p.m.

EDEN'S TEXT TODAY LEFT A BAD FEELING IN MY MOUTH. EVEN after my nudie this morning, she didn't respond.

Then my dad came home from his solo boating trip and told me he ran into her at the park with her son. Why didn't she tell us she was taking Jack to the park?

What is going on with her?

I know something is up, but I have no idea what it could be. Things were amazing last night.

They've been amazing all week. I've never felt better in my entire life. I feel like I belong with them.

They are my home.

And I can't help but think about what my dad said that day on the boat about settling.

This doesn't feel like settling. I feel like I've found two people who I'm crazy about and who make me feel good. I'm not committing to forever, but the urge to build a life with them is stronger than I anticipated.

So maybe my dad was wrong, but maybe I was too.

Because I used to think falling in love was simple, but it's not. Falling in love costs a piece of yourself. It takes more than it gives. But with the way I feel for both of them, I would willfully give everything.

So when he warned me not to settle down too young, I didn't understand, but I do now. Because I know I will never be the same again.

When I show up at Clay's, Eden is not there yet. When I walk into his apartment, he greets me with a kiss.

"Everything okay?" he asks when he notices the heaviness in my expression.

"I'm a little worried," I say carefully.

"About what?" he asks, leading me into the kitchen. He makes me a drink while I talk.

"Eden was acting a little strange today. Don't you think?"

His brows pinch inward as he thinks. "She was quiet."

"My dad said he ran into her at the harbor today," I add, and Clay's head snaps up.

"Is it bad that we never really told her about him? That we were keeping our relationship a secret?"

He swallows. "It'll be fine, baby. I promise."

"How do you know that?" I ask, feeling uneasy.

He doesn't respond for a moment, but just as he opens his mouth to answer, his apartment buzzer goes off, jolting us both. Rushing past me, he hits the button to let Eden in.

Then he turns toward me, placing his hands on my arms. Kissing my forehead, he smiles. "It's going to be fine, baby. Relax."

A moment later, Eden walks in.

Immediately, I know Clay is wrong.

She's dressed casually, in just a pair of black leggings and a T-shirt. Not that she has to dress up for us, but normally, she's more put together.

"Hey," Clay says as he approaches her.

Everything is wrong.

When Eden doesn't reach for either of us and takes a seat on the solo chair instead of the couch, I know this is going to be bad.

"I was going to call, but I figured it would be better to do this in person." Her voice is low and quiet, and I have to fight the urge to start crying already.

I'm trying to get her to just look at me. I need her eye contact to ease my worries, but she won't look at me.

"What's going on?" Clay asks, still standing by the back of the couch.

Eden looks up. "I ran into Jade's dad today. He didn't seem to know that you two are dating."

"He's my boss," Clay replies, not taking his eyes off Eden.

"Since November, you've been lying to him about your relationship," she replies.

"It's fine," I say with a smile.

"It's not fine," Eden snaps. "How can we possibly start a relationship like this if we're still lying to each other?"

"We're not lying," I say, still wishing she'd just look at me.

"Yes, we are," she replies. This time her voice shakes, and I can see how hard this is. I wish she'd just stop fighting and let us love her. We don't need to ruin it just because of a few little secrets. We love each other enough to overcome that.

Then she finally looks into my eyes. "Jade, we never told Clay that we saw each other for weeks before he started joining us."

Her gaze turns to him. "And we never told Jade just how serious our relationship was. That you were more than my client. We were in love."

My lips part to say something, but it's all too much.

"I knew," I cry out, tears leaking into my lashes. "I'm not stupid. I knew you two had a relationship. So we can get over this. We don't need to end it."

"But don't you see, Jade?" she asks, her eyes pleading as they bore into mine. "I claim to hold honesty and trust so high, but I'm the one lying. I'm the one holding secrets. I'm the one who broke Clay's heart over six months ago. I'm terrible at this. I can't do this."

Her expression is pure anguish, and I want to run to her. I can't stand this.

"We love each other," I say as I kneel on the floor at her feet. I take her hands in mine and convince myself I can make her forget everything. "We can forgive each other, Eden."

She lets me hold her hands, but she doesn't clutch them in return. She just hangs her head. I see the bags under her eyes, proof of her tears.

"I'm sorry," she mumbles softly. "But I think we need to just…take a break. Rethink this. I have to make the right choice for my son, and I can't rush into things just because they're fun or they feel good."

"A break. It's not over, though," I say, biting my lip as I stare up at her with hope.

"It's over," Clay barks from behind me. The anger in his tone is obvious. "Let it go, Jade. When she says it's over, it's over."

Eden's gaze lifts. As she stares at him, I see the months of pain and regret etched in her features.

"You're in charge, right?" he says with bitterness. "At the first sign of trouble, you bail. You claim you do this to protect yourself and the people you love, but look at us, Eden. Don't you care about us?" he asks, looking hurt. "How long are you going to keep pushing people away? And what good is this to Jack?"

"Stop it," she snaps, glaring up at him.

"You've kept him so sheltered his entire life he latched on to the first person who gave him an ounce of attention."

"Stop fighting," I say as I climb off the floor and put out a hand to keep Clay from saying something he'll regret.

"Keep Jack out of this," Eden says heatedly. "Besides, do you really have any room to talk?" she asks. "Did you really love me at all, or was I just a woman who offered to give you the attention you were missing from your mother?"

He clenches his jaw and turns away from her.

"Eden," I call out, reaching for her to stop. "Don't say that."

"Let her, Jade. It's over anyway. She'll make sure of that," Clay mutters angrily.

"It's not over," I say with a sob.

I stare at Eden and wait for her to correct him. It's not over.

But when her eyes meet mine, they say everything I don't want to hear. She takes a step toward me, but I quickly step back, keeping distance between us.

I've never wanted distance from her.

"It's over, Jade. We can't even communicate. How on earth could we ever make a relationship work?"

"We try," I reply. "We work at it. We make mistakes, and we learn, and we try again. Because we love each other."

I expect at least one of them to agree or give in or accept what I'm saying, but they're both still so bitter and broken they don't move.

"I'm sorry," Eden whispers, but I shake my head, letting my tears fall.

"No, you're not."

As I grit my teeth and shove away the sob that's building in my chest, I feel something in me snap. Without a word, I grab my purse from the chair by the door. I've never been so angry in all of my life.

"You're both wrong," I shout. "You're *both* cowards, and now I'm convinced you deserve each other. Neither one of you can even bear to take a risk. So what if it eventually ends? So what if we don't make it forever? You can't even give us a chance now? Well, if you won't bother trying, then neither will I."

Without another word, I open the door and slam it behind me.

I run out of the apartment building, turning my back on them, on our future, and maybe on love altogether. I make it all the way home before I reach my bed and sob into my pillow until I fall asleep.

Rule #42: It's never too late to apologize.

Clay

SOMETIME LAST NIGHT, AFTER LEAVING THE CLUB, I FOUND THE NEAREST bar, *where I proceeded to get as drunk as physically possible. The last thing I remember is being shoved into a taxi by an angry bartender and somehow landing in my bed. Where I'm currently lying, wishing the last twenty-four hours never happened.*

But I can't undo anything. I can't undo that fight with Eden. I can't undo our entire meaningless eight-month relationship. I can't undo the damage she's done to my heart.

By some miracle, my phone and wallet both made it home safely, but my phone is currently dead under a heap of clothes on my floor.

It takes another two hours before I muster the energy to pick it up and plug it in.

I somehow manage to take a shower, make a cup of coffee, and shovel something cold and tasteless into my mouth so my stomach will stop growling. Then I go back to bed.

Tonight, I should go back to the club. I should be seeing her in just a few hours, but I won't.

Because it's over.

To distract myself, I pick up my phone and scroll through some meaningless sites. When I swipe them away and return to my home screen, I notice an unread text message notification.

Opening my messages, I read the one she must have sent me last night.

Clay, I'm sorry that it has to be this way. I wish I could take away the last eight months so you never had to feel this pain, but I promise you, it's for the best. I'm too broken to be anything more than your Domme. My life is a mess, and I'm afraid love will never be in the cards for me now. It was never about you not being good enough. You were always so good for me.

So now, I'm giving you one last command.

Forget about me.

Find someone who can give you everything you deserve.

Then love them even more than you loved me.

Do that for me. Please.

My throat is tight as I read her message. I must have missed this last night because I have no recollection of reading it. And reading it now feels like picking open the wound all over again.

I'm so angry at her for everything, for breaking us and every beautiful thing we built.

So, with a sense of bitterness and regret, I type out my response and send it.

Yes, Madame.

———————

"Clay, are you listening to me?"

My mother is sitting across from me at the restaurant, but I've zoned out as she speaks about something I wasn't paying attention to. It's been three days since Eden was at my apartment and my first time leaving it since. I've called out sick at work for two days straight. But when my mother invited me to dinner, for some reason, I couldn't seem to say no.

"No," I reply plainly to her question.

"Clay Edmund Bradley." She scoffs, looking offended and confused. "If you're going to be rude, you can just leave."

"I might as well," I say with surrender. "Unless…you'd like to know how my life is going."

"What are you talking about? You're acting strange." She leans forward, her diamond bracelet clanging against the glass table as she reaches for her glass of wine.

"You never ask about my life, Mother. Do you even care?"

She averts her gaze over the rim of her glass as she takes a drink. I can see the discomfort in her eyes. My family does not face discomfort. They brush it under the rug or pay it to go away. But right now, my mother has to face me. And for the first time in my life, I don't feel bad about that.

"I think you should just leave before you cause a scene," she whispers with desperation.

"I'd love to cause a scene, Mother. Because at least then you'd look at me."

"I look at you all the time. Are you on drugs?" Still, her eyes are around the restaurant.

I laugh. "No. I'm not on drugs. But I am sick and fucking tired of acting like this is the most I deserve."

"Deserve? I've given you everything, and you want more?"

Finally, she glances at my face. And it's enough to ignite a cannon inside me. One that's been loaded and waiting for *years*.

"You've given *nothing*," I reply. Tears sting behind my eyes, and for once in my life, I don't hold them back. My hand slams against the table, and she jumps. People around the restaurant start looking in our direction, and I don't bother whispering or keeping my voice down.

I just want her to hear me.

"I feel like I'm dying, Mother. Maybe of loneliness or anger or fear, but I'm tired of being so *alone*. I was a burden to you. I still am. The most I can do in your presence is sit still, be quiet, and exist without a sound. But now I'm in pain and I can't even get my own mother to look at me to let me express it."

When my mother blinks, I notice the well of moisture in her eyes, and it takes me by surprise. She glances around the room before leveling her gaze on my face again. Then she looks down as she softly whispers, "You were never a burden to me."

I lean back in my chair and quickly swipe away the tear that slipped down to my jawline. I feel the eyes of others on us at this quiet country-club restaurant. But I don't give a fuck.

Suddenly, I feel weightless. And fearless.

"You have no idea what loneliness is, Clay."

I'm shocked by her words as I stare at her with wide eyes. My mother has never been so candid or honest in her life.

"What are you talking about? You're constantly surrounded by people, and Dad—"

"You think a person has to be alone to feel lonely? You know nothing."

I lean forward. "But what about me?"

"You sit here and don't listen. I don't know how to speak to you, Clay. I don't know how to ask about your life. I know you don't care about me. And I don't know a thing about you. I assume you just show up for the money."

I blink another tear out. "I don't care about the money, Mother."

"Everyone cares about money, Clay. Don't pretend it doesn't rule our lives."

"It doesn't rule mine," I mutter angrily.

"Then why do you come? Why do you answer when I call? You clearly don't care about me either."

"I do care about you. You're my mother. You're all I have. Regardless of how angry I am at you or how much you've hurt me, I still love you."

This time, when she blinks, her tears spill over, and she holds my eye contact longer than I think she ever has before.

"I love you, too," she mumbles sadly, clearly embarrassed as she discreetly wipes her tears away. "And I'm sorry…if I ever hurt you."

I take a deep breath, letting out a heavy exhale as it feels like a thousand pounds have been released from my shoulders.

"Thank you," I whisper.

"So," she replies astutely, straightening her spine and trying to act as composed as possible. "Tell me what's going on in your life."

It's my turn to scoff. "We don't have enough wine for that."

When I feel her hand rest against mine, I glance up to see an expression of sympathy on her face. "I'm sorry you're hurting."

It's not enough, and even if it was, it's too late to undo the hurt that's been caused. But this is truly the first time in my life I've felt my mother's genuine concern. And while I won't give her a detailed explanation of why I'm in so much pain, it reminds me that anyone can change.

Anyone can try.

And while it is a little too late for my mother, it might not be too late for me.

Rule #43: You're never too tough to grovel.

Eden

LOVE IS NOTHING BUT A FORM OF CONTROL. MANIPULATION. Torture.

It's just another way for us to make each other miserable. As if life isn't hard enough, we have to put our hearts on the line. Offering to let others hurt us as much as they want. And for what?

What is the return for falling in love? There's no guarantee they'll love you back. There's no guarantee they won't cause irreparable damage.

Love is a mistake.

The only things in life that are true and real are sex and power. Those are undeniable. And love has nothing to do with them.

After canceling my clients for the third day in a row, I'm finally stepping foot in Salacious again after almost a week. But before I head up to my room, I need to have an important conversation with someone first. One I've been dreading.

"Knock, knock," I say as I tap on the office door in the back. Emerson Grant is sitting at Hunter's desk because I asked him to meet me tonight.

"Hey, Eden—" He looks up from his phone and reads my expression immediately. Standing up, he rounds the desk and comes up to me, placing a hand on my arm.

"Is everything okay?" he asks.

I swallow. I can't answer that question because, right now, nothing feels okay. I've ruined every ounce of happiness I might have felt in my life, and it's my fault. I can see that now. No matter how much I tried to make things right, I acted out of haste. I panicked. And it was stupid.

But there is no undoing what I've already done.

"I'm fine," I lie. "I just need to talk to you about the job."

"Of course. What's up?"

I look into his eyes and force myself not to feel anything. "I'm sorry, Emerson. But I can't do it."

"What do you mean?" he asks, motioning for me to sit. Instead of taking the seat on the other side of the desk, he takes the one next to me.

"I'm not taking the job," I say with conviction.

"Yes, you are," he says plainly.

I let out a scoff. "No, I'm not, Emerson."

"Why not?"

I straighten my spine and prepare myself for this next part. "Because I'm leaving."

He reacts like I've just slapped him across the face. "What are you talking about?"

"I quit. I mean…I know I don't work for you, but I'm going to quit being Madame Kink. I can't do this anymore."

He puts up a hand and blinks as if he's trying to make sense of everything. "Okay. That's fine if you don't want to work as a Dominatrix anymore, but why wouldn't you just take the job here then?"

"Because…it's too hard, Emerson."

My voice cracks, and I try to hide it by biting my bottom lip. I hate showing emotion, especially with him, someone I admire for being professional and composed. Emotion is weakness, and I won't let him see me break.

"What is too hard, Eden?"

He reaches out and places his hand on mine. I breathe in the comfort of his touch and try to force myself not to feel again.

"Everything. Balancing all of it. Trying to be in three places at once and somehow giving one hundred percent of myself each time. I don't want to be Madame Kink anymore because…"

My voice trails as I force down the rising emotion.

"Because that's not who I really am. Seven years ago, I looked in a mirror and I tricked myself into believing I was someone I'm not. And I'm just so tired."

His hand doesn't leave mine. And any hope of holding in the emotion is gone now. I came in here to quit my job and somehow ended up pouring my heart out instead.

Then for some reason, maybe because I am so tired or because I realize now how stupid it was to keep this secret, I let everything slip out.

"I have a son."

His expression doesn't even budge. He just stares into my eyes and waits for me to elaborate.

"He's seven. His name is Jack. I've been keeping that from you for years."

"Well, no wonder you're tired then."

I let out a laugh, which feels weird at such a tense moment. "Aren't you…surprised or mad or offended that I didn't tell you?"

At that, he lets out a sound of exasperation. "Why the fuck would I be mad about that? That's your life and your business. You're entitled to your privacy, Eden."

"I know, but…you can't possibly want me for that position now."

He leans back in his chair and stares at me for a moment as if he's sizing me up. "Is this because I said I was hiring more help because the others are starting families? Because that was all just an excuse to get you to take the job. You know that, right?"

I let out a chuckle as I wipe my face. "I figured."

"I think it makes me want you more, to be honest."

"Could I work from home?" I ask.

"Of course."

"And holidays with my son?"

"Naturally."

"If he's sick or I can't get my babysitter to cover me—"

"Eden," he says to stop me. "We'll handle it. I'm not just looking for someone to fill the hours of work. I'm looking for *you* to make this club better. Your talent. Your experience. Whatever your family needs for support, you've got it."

My lip trembles as I swallow down the burning building in my throat.

"Please take the job."

With tears in my eyes, I nod. "Okay."

"Thank you," he replies with a satisfied smile.

"I'm sorry for reacting emotionally," I reply with a shake of my head. "It's been…a rough week."

"Care to talk about it?" he asks.

"No. I'm too embarrassed to admit how bad I've fucked it up."

He winces before he stands, fixing his tie with a shift of his shoulders. "Well," he says as he reaches a hand down toward me. "If I've learned anything, it's that you're never too tough to grovel."

Rule #44: Growing up is hard.

Jade

"You didn't bother to discuss those things before jumping into bed with a married guy?"

"He's not a married guy. He's Dean, my Dean."

"He's not your Dean. He's Lindsay's—"

"Oh, fuck off, Lorelai." I groan. After clicking off the TV, I throw the remote control into the hamper and bury my face in my pillow. No amount of *Gilmore Girls* is going to distract me enough not to feel the pain of being not just dumped but double-dumped. Dumped by two people at the same time.

Technically, I walked out the door. But neither of them has called or shown up.

The urge to pick up my phone and text Clay is excruciating. We are both mad at Eden, and I want to talk to him about that.

But then I remember...he lied to me too. He had been in love with Eden since before I even came along, and all this time, they both had me convinced it was just a Domme-client thing. Deep down, I knew. Maybe it was denial. Or my eternal optimism.

All Eden does is keep secrets and lie.

We all do.

Maybe Eden is right. Maybe we are all so bad at relationships that we should just be alone.

But my heart aches just thinking about a life without them.

When I hear the door downstairs open and close, I wince. My dad greets his dog, Chief, and I wait for the inevitable. He will come up to my room and check on me like I'm still his little girl.

But I'm not. And it's dawning on me now just how much I enable him to look at me that way. I hide my boyfriend from him. I moved back into my old bedroom so he and I can live in the past and pretend nothing has changed.

This situation isn't helping anyone. I'm tired of bending over backward for the sake of others. I was more than flexible for Clay, never putting up much of a fight when he asked to keep our relationship a secret for a little longer. I didn't say anything when I suspected Eden and Clay had things about their past they didn't tell me. Now I'm living in my dad's house to help him deal with his own divorce after my mother left *three years* ago.

Who is bending over backward for me?

"Hey, Cupcake," he says from the doorway.

Sitting up in my bed, I curl my hair behind my ears and let out a sigh. "Hey, Daddy."

"Everything okay?" he asks, noticing my mood.

I hesitate before answering. Now is not the time to fill the silence with meaningless ramble, but I have no idea how to have any other kind of conversation with him.

I shrug. "Just dealing with some things."

He moves into the room, sitting on the end of my bed. He looks concerned as he sets a large hand on my shoulder.

"What can I do?"

I lift my gaze to his face. With a sad smile, I reply, "There's nothing you can do, Dad. I have to deal with things on my own."

He doesn't seem content with that response as his brow furrows even deeper. "Is this about a boy?"

With an exasperated sigh, I climb off my childhood bed. "Not a boy, Dad. A man. I'm twenty-three years old. I don't date *boys* anymore. I date men...or, well...adults," I stammer.

He stands from the bed and crosses his arms in front of him. "Cupcake, what's going on?"

"I'm not your cupcake!" I reply with a shriek. Then I quickly compose myself and focus on what it is I'm really trying to say. Looking up into his eyes, I force myself to do like Eden taught me.

Be clear. Be heard.

"Dad, I know I'll always be your daughter, and yes, to some degree, I'm still your cupcake, but I really can't keep living like your little girl. I'm grateful that you let me move back in after college, but I need to move out on my own. I'm going to experience heartbreak and pain, mess up, settle down, and make mistakes, but I have to. I can't learn from your mistakes. I have to learn from my own."

His eyes don't leave my face for a moment, and his expression is so serious that it makes me want to unspeak every single word that just came out of my mouth.

Then, on an exhale, he rubs his brow, and it looks like his shoulders melt away from his ears. Taking a seat on the chair in front of my small desk, he puts his hands on his knees.

"I know you're not my little girl anymore, Jade. I just thought you wanted to come back home and stay with me because...hell, I don't know. Growing up is hard. I wanted you to always know that no matter what, I'd take care of you. Especially since your mom..."

"Dad," I say, my voice cracking. "You can't always take care of me, no matter what. And Mom leaving had nothing to do with that. She's living her life, and so should you."

There's a wrinkle on his forehead as he lets that sink in. "I have a life."

My head tilts to the side, which makes him laugh.

"What?" he asks. "I do. I go out on the boat on weekends, which is nice, and I met this nice lady—"

"Whatever," I reply with a shake of my head, stopping him from oversharing something I don't want to hear. "I believe you. I just think…I'm going to move out soon."

He nods, but judging by the look on his face, he doesn't like it. But that's okay. He doesn't need to like it. He just has to accept it.

"I'll support you however you need me to…" His voice trails. "Cupcake."

I let out a chuckle as I roll my eyes. "Thank you, Dad."

"And if a *man* hurts you, I'll throw his body in the ocean."

"Dad!" I shout, shoving him on the shoulder.

"Okay, okay," he replies, holding his hands up in surrender. "I won't kill him. I'll just…rough him up a bit."

"Better." My shoulders feel lighter. Maybe we got somewhere. Even if he didn't, at least I did. This is what I needed. To pull myself out of the past.

"Or…" my dad says without looking into my eyes. "I could just fire him."

I shake my head. "No. You don't have to—"

My eyes dash over to my dad's face, and I feel the blood drain, leaving me in shock. Judging by the way he's staring at me with brows lifted and mouth set in a flat line, he knows more than I expected him to.

"Wait. You know?" I ask.

"Of course I know. I'm not blind or stupid. You two have been making eyes at each other since you came home from school."

I feel sick. This entire time, my dad could tell what was going on. Does Clay know this?

"You're not mad?"

"I'm mad that you haven't told me. And I'm *furious* at him, but…"

He takes a deep breath, looking very uncomfortable.

"You're a smart girl, Jade. And no matter how much I hate it, you're an adult now. You can do whatever you want."

It becomes increasingly difficult to swallow, and it feels like pins and needles are gathering in my throat, but I manage to at least nod without crying.

He closes his eyes with a wince and puts up a hand. "I don't want to know any details, but I'm serious when I say that if he ever uses you or hurts you, I will make him pay."

I force a laugh, not entirely sure how serious my dad is at the moment.

"I promise, Dad. He's been…a perfect gentleman."

Which is mostly true. My dad doesn't need to know that I was the one instigating the truly dirty things we got up to at that office. What he needs to know is that Clay is not the man he thinks he is.

"A gentleman?" he replies with an arched brow like he doesn't believe me.

"Yes."

"So what happened?" he asks.

I plop back down on my bed. "I don't know. It's very complicated."

"Was it…serious?" he asks with a wince.

Those pins and needles are back. When I look back up at my dad, my eyes are wet.

"I'll take that as a yes," he says with a sigh.

He stands from his chair and takes a seat next to me on my bed. Then he puts an arm on my shoulder and lets me rest my head against him, holding me in a tight hug.

"I can still do this, right?"

With a sniffle, I nod.

"I'm not trying to fix all of your problems or take care of you, but I'll still give you a hug when you need it. And offer my old-man advice, of course."

On my next blink, a tear falls. "Okay."

Then he squeezes his arm around me harder. "Nothing is perfect, Cupcake. Not love or relationships. And there is no guarantee that it will last forever, but not every good relationship needs to last forever. You can be happy with a person for however long it lasts. The best you can do is give love a chance."

Pulling my face away from him, I wipe away my tears as I stare at him in astonishment. This isn't the same man who told me not to settle down at all until I'm in my thirties.

When he notices my perplexed expression, he continues, "I was wrong for what I said to you that day on the boat. I was bitter about your mother leaving. But I realized that…I'm glad I married her. The twenty-four years we had were amazing. We kept each other happy, and we were never alone. Just because it ended doesn't mean there weren't great moments."

"But I don't want it to end," I say with a sob.

"Then talk to him. Don't leave anything unsaid. If he truly cares, he'll listen."

He's right. There is so much I want to say to Clay and Eden. And sitting here with my anger won't do any good.

And if it doesn't work out, then it doesn't work out. Part of growing up is getting my heart broken. Should it come down to that, I'll survive.

Rule #45: Come clean.

Clay

ON MONDAY MORNING, AT EXACTLY NINE A.M., I MARCH INTO the office. Jade is sitting at the front desk, and she glances up at me cautiously as I enter. Her lips part like she wants to speak, but I don't give her a chance.

I have to do something first.

Instead of going left to my office, I turn right. My heart picks up speed as I reach Will's office, pushing the door open and staring at him behind his desk.

I'm *not* a coward, I tell myself.

"I need to speak to you," I say in a low command.

His eyes lift to mine, and then I notice they slip past me for a brief second as if he's looking at where his daughter is stationed at the front desk.

"Come in, Clay," he says without any warmth in his voice.

I don't deserve warmth at the moment. This won't be comfortable, but I still need to do it.

I close the door behind me before waltzing right up to his desk. I don't sit.

"I'm in love with your daughter."

Letting out a secret is like jumping off a cliff. There is no going back. I can't climb up out of these lies I've been telling. So I just have to deal with the free fall.

Will takes a deep breath before he stands. His thick arms cross in front of his body. I'm struck with discomfort. This is my boss. We are not friends or family. We have a strictly professional relationship, and I just admitted to having very personal feelings about his daughter. "Go on."

"Jade and I have been dating secretly for six months, and it was wrong of me to lie to you. Wrong to you and wrong to her. She deserves better than that. So I'm apologizing now. I'm sorry. But I do love her. I love her more than anything. I've never met someone so strong and kind, and honestly, I probably don't deserve her, but I have to at least admit how much I care about her. She makes me unbelievably happy."

Will doesn't move, glaring at me with a furrowed brow, and I wait for him to blow up. Any moment now, he's going to tell me I've lost my job and my career in the industry altogether.

"Sit down, Bradley."

I take the chair across from his desk and wait. "I know she's your daughter. I *know* I crossed a line, and that was incredibly inappropriate of me. And I understand if you have to fire me—"

"Will you shut the fuck up?" he says, and my mouth closes immediately. "Jade already told me," he says with a hard expression. "Honestly, I figured it out a long time ago."

"You did?" I ask in shock.

"I didn't want to believe it. But I had a suspicion."

"Why didn't you say something? Why didn't you fire me?"

"Because you're a good investor, Bradley. And deep down— against my better judgment—I know you're a good guy. And there are far worse men my daughter could get tangled up with."

"Will, I—"

He holds up a hand to stop me.

"Don't thank me. I wanted to throw you off the side of my boat, but Jade wouldn't let me."

"I appreciate that," I reply, adjusting the tight collar of my shirt around my neck.

"You're not fired, and I won't hurt you. *Yet*. But if you hurt my little girl, Bradley, I can't make any promises."

"I would never hurt her," I say with confidence.

He tilts his head to the side like he doesn't believe me. "Well, she just spent the weekend crying in her bedroom and watching an ungodly amount of *Gilmore Girls*, so it would seem you have some more apologizing to do."

Thinking about Jade crying feels like being socked in the stomach. I take responsibility for that, but he's probably not ready to hear that I wasn't exactly the one who broke her heart. But that's a conversation for another day. "I will. I plan to," I stammer.

"We're getting a regular temp," he says, and it sounds like he's getting back to business. I can't help but wonder…is that it? "Not because I care about you two at the office but because I want Jade to get the job she really wants. She deserves better than sticking around here for us when she's qualified for more."

"I agree," I reply without hesitation.

"Good."

Then he and I stare at each other for a moment. There has to be more to this. Isn't he going to throw me out for doing filthy things to his daughter?

"Now get out of here. Go apologize. And if you hurt her, you die."

In shock, I stand up. "Yes, sir."

Halfway to the door, he stops me. "Bradley."

"Yeah," I reply on a turn.

His face has lost the stone-cold expression he wore a moment ago. It's a bit softer as he looks into my eyes. "You really love her?"

I swallow and straighten my spine. "Yes, Will. I do. Very much."

It feels good to tell the truth.

He takes a seat at his desk. Then he just…nods. He doesn't say another word, just turns back to his computer and lets me leave.

Even in the hallway, I'm struck silent.

This entire time I've dreaded this moment—Will finding out that I am the guy his daughter chose to be with. Not just because of the whole boss's daughter situation, but I have had myself written off as the sleazy asshole no one would want their daughter dating, and yet…he seems fine with it.

When I walk back to my office, his words echoing in my ear, I feel as if I'm weightless. The heavy burden of truth is off my shoulders now. Turning the corner into my office, I freeze at the sight of Jade standing in the center, tears in her eyes.

It takes me a moment to speak. I haven't said a word since she stormed out of my apartment, and I don't quite know what to say now. I can't fix everything. I can't get Eden back and make her commit to something she won't commit to. And I'm not quite sure where that leaves Jade and me.

But I'm willing to try.

"I'm sorry I didn't tell him sooner," I say softly.

She nods. "It's okay."

"He already knew," I say.

"I know," she replies.

God, I hate to see her cry. I want to hold her in my arms and keep her from pain for the rest of her life.

"I'm so sorry, Jade. I'm sorry I lied about my relationship with Eden. I'm sorry I kept us a secret from your dad for so long. I'm sorry I never told you how much I love you."

Her chest shudders with a sob. "I love you too."

"I never felt good enough for you," I say.

"I know," she replies. "But you were. You still are."

I can't take another second without her in my arms. Slipping my hand around the back of her neck, I haul her to my chest. She wraps her arms around me eagerly, and we hold each other close, both of us breathing in the comfort of each other's embrace.

"What now?" she whispers against my neck.

"I don't know," I reply softly.

"Do we just go back to the way we were before?" she says, pulling away to stare into my eyes.

"Is that even possible?" I ask.

Wiping her tears, she shrugs. "I can't bear the thought of losing both of you."

Holding the sides of her neck, I tip her head back and press my lips softly to hers. "I wish you didn't have to lose anyone." Then I put my lips to her forehead. "But if we're going to lose her, at least we can do it together."

She winces in pain as another tear squeezes its way through her lashes.

"I miss her," she whispers.

It's like the breakup in November all over again. Except now, instead of feeling the pain myself, I have to watch Jade feel it too. And it's worse.

"We take it one day at a time, baby."

Then I cradle her face and pull her lips to mine again, this time kissing her slowly and taking my time. It feels good to have her back in my arms, but it does feel like something is missing. I know she can sense it too.

With time, I hope we can be enough for each other. What choice do we have? I'd be a fool to hope for more with Eden. I've lost her twice now. I won't try again.

And I refuse to put Jade through that. For now, I'll focus on being everything she needs.

Rule #46: Sometimes, it is that simple.

Eden

"And the invites have been sent?" I ask.

"Invites have been sent," Garrett replies.

"What else can I do?" I'm standing in my laundry room, folding another set of Jack's pajamas with Garrett on speaker with my phone sitting on the washing machine.

"Everything is in place, Eden. Now we handle the inevitable problems that arise—and they will."

As I set the folded pajamas on the pile, I rack my brain for anything else that I can take care of for this event. Then I chew my bottom lip as I muster the nerve to ask what I want to ask.

"You sent those two extra invites for me, didn't you?"

He clears his throat. "Yes, I did."

"Thank you."

"Anytime," he replies softly.

"Talk to you later, Garrett."

"Bye, Eden."

The line goes dead, and I shove the phone into my pocket. Then I stare straight ahead, standing in my silent laundry room.

This still feels surreal. It's only been a week on the job at Salacious, and already it feels like everything has changed and nothing has changed at the same time.

I've sent notice to most of my clients, save for a few regulars who I promised to keep on if I can fit them in my schedule. I've changed my schedule with Madison. And I've set up my home office in the den so I can work from here as much as possible.

But no one at Salacious treats me differently. I don't feel like I'm taking on more work. It's just…different.

The three-year anniversary party is in three days, and I'm feeling sick over it. I'm nervous not only about the event itself but also because I'm holding out hope that *they* will be there.

To be honest, I have no idea what to say. Or do. I don't know how to make it right or prove to them that I was wrong and fucked up.

I need to suck it up, swallow my pride, and grovel my ass off, as Emerson suggested. But…I'm scared. Terrified. What if it doesn't work? What if they use their good judgment to never forgive me? I don't deserve to be forgiven, not just like that. I fucked up. I obliterated Jade's feelings to protect my own, and it doesn't matter how sick I am over missing them. If I don't make things right, then they will move on, living happily ever after, and I'll be stuck here alone. I can't bear the thought of getting my hopes up only to be disappointed again.

"I brushed my teeth. See?" Jack is standing in the doorway to the laundry room in nothing but his dinosaur underwear, his hair still wet from the bath. He's wearing a bright, cheesy grin as he shows me his sparkling white teeth—or what he has left of them. The front two came out on the same day last week, and I can't get over how cute he looks when he smiles.

Of course, it was bittersweet. Because we both wanted to share the news with Clay. He begged me to call him, send him pictures, and invite him over.

But because I'm a monster, I couldn't.

I shake off the sadness and give him a warm smile. "Good job, buddy." Then I grab the freshly folded pj's off the dryer and walk him back to his room.

"Arms up," I say as I slide Jack's pajamas over his head, putting one arm in each sleeve.

"Will Madison still come over for bedtime?" he asks as I ruffle his hair.

"Sometimes," I reply as I pull back the covers on his bed. "But I'll work during the day more. Which means I can be home for dinner and bedtime more."

He's wearing an excited grin as he crawls under the covers. "I like Madison, but I like when you put me to bed."

"Me too, buddy," I say, kissing his head. "What book should we read tonight?"

"The monster truck one," he replies with a yawn.

"Again?" I feign annoyance.

"Again."

Crawling into his tiny bed next to him, I lean against the headboard as I open the book and start reading. I could probably recite the whole thing at this point. Only a couple of pages in, he stops me.

"Mama?"

I pause reading. "Yes, buddy?"

"Is Clay coming back?"

My body tenses at the mention of his name. "Umm...I don't know, buddy."

"What about Jade?" he asks.

"I don't know."

"Why not?" he asks. "Can't they come over now that you'll be home? They can come over for dinner!"

I let out a sigh. It's been two weeks since the incident at Clay's house. I have to work up the nerve to reach out to them, but I won't do it until I have something to show. What good is trying again if nothing has changed?

But change is hard. And I don't know if I'm ready.

I nuzzle closer to Jack, lying on his pillow next to him. "You really love Clay, don't you?" I ask.

His tiny fingers play with the strands of my hair on his pillow. "Yes. Don't you, Mama?"

I swallow, but I hesitate with my answer. Love is so complicated. How can I possibly make a seven-year-old understand?

"Yeah, I do," I reply.

"Then he should come over."

"It's not that simple," I reply with a hint of despondence in my voice.

"Did you have a fight?" he asks, and my eyes dart over to his face. "Just say you're sorry and that you love him, and then him and Jade can come over for movie night."

How simple children are. Why can't adults be like this? Apologize. Love. Be happy. Like it's all that easy. I wish it were.

But instead, we have to deal with things like insecurity, fear, and trauma that seem to make simple things like love and forgiveness impossible.

Before I know it, I feel a tear slipping down the side of my face.

"What's wrong, Mama?" Jack whispers as he nuzzles himself closer, wrapping his tiny arms around my neck.

"Nothing, buddy," I reply softly. "I just get scared sometimes."

His tiny hand is gently petting my shoulder in his own little way of comforting me, and it makes my tears flow even more.

"What are you scared of?" he asks with a wrinkle between his tiny brows.

"I get scared when things change," I reply.

It's been Jack and me for so long, and I know, at the end of the day, that is why I pushed Clay away. I can claim it was for Jack's safety or my being protective of him, but I know the real reason is that bringing someone else into our lives would mean that it's no longer just my son and me. Our tiny world would change, and that's terrifying.

I sniffle as Jack leans in, pressing his little mouth against my cheek in a sweet kiss. Then he wraps his arms around my neck as he whispers, "It's okay, Mama. I'll protect you."

I let out a small laugh as more tears fall. Gathering him up, I hold him close to my side.

"Thank you, buddy," I reply.

We lie there for a while as I let my tears dry. In my mind, I'm rehearsing everything I'll need to say to Clay and Jade if I ever want them to forgive me. Before long, I hear Jack's tiny little snores.

Reaching over to his bedside table, I click his lamp off. But instead of crawling out of his bed to go to mine, I pull his covers over both of us, and I pull my phone out of my pocket.

I've composed this text a hundred times in the last two weeks. I can't seem to ever get it right. But if I don't send it, then they'll never know how I feel. And maybe Jack's right. It is that simple.

I'm sorry.

It's not some eloquent statement, but it's the only true thing I can say at the moment. I am sorry.

I just hope it's enough.

When there is no response after fifteen minutes, I close my eyes next to Jack in his little bed.

Before I drift off, I realize that I will never, ever be able to prevent things from changing in my son's life. And I think when I built this life for us, I did so thinking that it was something I could promise him forever, but it's not. There are no promises or guarantees.

Jack has people who love him and want to be in his life.

There are people who love *me* and want to be in *my* life.

And for some reason, I've been living in so much fear that I deprived us both of that love.

But not anymore.

Rule #47: It's never a bad time to respond to a text.

Jade

I WAKE TO THE FEEL OF SOFT HANDS DRIFTING UP MY THIGH. A smile creeps across my face when I feel his breath against my ear and his stiff erection grinding against my ass.

Who knew morning sex would be so amazing?

"I love waking up next to you," I say with a hum as he grinds against me again with a deep groan.

"Then you should stay over more often," he replies. "I could wake you up like this every morning."

As my eyes peel open, I slowly slip out of that space of euphoric and ignorant bliss and into the sobering realization that something is missing. This happens every morning. And I know he feels it too.

Because instead of pulling down my panties and fucking me right here in his bed, he pauses, kissing me on the cheek and squeezing my fingers in his.

This has to pass, right? Over time, Clay and I will fall back into the same rhythm we were in before. He makes me happy. I make him happy. I don't understand how one week with her could ruin all of that.

So we fell in love with a fantasy for a few days. So what? It wasn't real. She wasn't real.

Clay and I are perfect together, and we love each other, and that is real.

With that, I turn my head toward him and stare into his eyes. I sense the same heaviness in his expression, which means he's thinking what I'm thinking. But instead of facing it and talking about it, he presses his lips to mine, and we slowly roll away from each other.

I reach for my phone on the nightstand at the same time he does. Then we both settle on our pillows and scroll through our notifications.

But we both freeze at the same exact time.

There she is, in our group chat.

I'm sorry.

And just like that, she's back in the room. Not literally, of course. But her presence looms over us, driving a wedge between us and any hope of happiness in our future.

I glance at him and see that he's staring listlessly at the same message I am.

"What should we say?" I whisper.

"I don't know," he replies.

"Do you believe her?" I ask before biting my lip.

"Yes," he says with conviction.

"So what do we do now? It shows that we've read it. Do we just ignore her, or do we respond? I mean, is one *I'm sorry* really enough?"

He rubs my leg to stop me from spiraling. "You can respond however you want, baby."

I'm chewing my lip as I stare at her message. How do I want to respond?

I want more. I want her to prove she's sorry. I want to know if this is her attempt to reconcile what she broke or if she's just saying this for her own conscience. Has she really changed at all?

"I'm going to make coffee," Clay says before kissing the side of my head and climbing out of bed.

"Okay," I reply mindlessly as I stare at my phone.

Be clear about what you want. Her voice is still in my head.

So while I hear Clay in the kitchen, grinding the coffee beans and filling the pot with water, I compose my response.

What are you sorry for? You didn't want to be in a relationship, and now you're not in one. Are you sorry for lying? Or are you sorry for being selfish? If I sound angry, it's because I am. You thought you were so insignificant in our relationship that you could just remove yourself without breaking our hearts, but you did. You were never insignificant. We loved you. We still do. And, yes, we all had our secrets, but we loved each other enough to overcome those. We still trusted you. But you weren't even willing to try. So if you really are sorry and you want us back, we need more than a two-word text message, Eden. Prove to us that our hearts are safe with you, and they're yours.

As soon as I finish frantically typing it, I hit Send. I don't want to reread it and revise it and toil over it. I want it to come from the heart. She taught me to do that. She was the one who gave me the inspiration to speak up for myself. Not to mince words and stress over how they will be perceived. She wanted me to be unapologetic, and I am.

When I hear Clay's phone chime with the incoming text in our group chat, I wait. His movement in the kitchen stops, and I know he's reading it. My mouth goes dry as I worry that I was too harsh or too forward.

Then a moment later, he steps into the doorway. His expression is unreadable. Then he just softly mumbles, "I'm proud of you." With that, he crosses the room and crawls into bed with me. Draping his body over mine, he kisses me, and I hum against his mouth.

Lifting up, he stares down at me with sincerity in his eyes. "You still make me happy, Jade. We'll be okay, just you and me. I know you're worried, but I can try to be enough for you—"

I put my hand over his mouth to stop him. "You are enough for me. More than enough."

Pulling him down for another kiss, I spread my knees to allow him to settle between my legs. His mouth moves from my lips down to my neck, and I feel his cock start to stiffen between us. He grinds himself against me with a groan, and I work his sweat-pants down.

Taking one leg under his arm, he slips my panties to the side and thrusts inside me. I gasp when he slides in as far as he can go.

While he fucks me hard and fast, I quiet my mind and focus only on him. At least I'm not alone in this heartbreak. We can go through it together.

Our grunts and moans carry through his room when we're suddenly interrupted by the sound of an incoming text message on both of our phones. His thrusts come to a stop. We're both panting, frozen in place as we decide what to do next.

"We should ignore it," I whisper first.

"Yeah," he replies as he starts moving again, but not as fast or as passionate this time.

He lifts up so I can see into his eyes. "Or we can just check it."

Letting out a sigh, he nods. "You check it."

I quickly reach for my phone on the mattress while he's still buried inside me. Then I read her response out loud.

"'I intend to prove it. You should get an invitation this week. Please come. And I'll make it up to you. With a lot more than two words.'"

My heart is hammering in my chest as I read it over and over. Then I glance up at Clay for reassurance. Is this real? Should I be excited, or should I still be angry? Because I'm feeling a lot more of the former.

"An invitation?" he replies breathlessly.

"That's what it says. Should we go?" I ask.

"Do you want to?" he replies, his brow furrowed as he stares into my eyes.

Silently, I nod.

A subtle smirk tugs on the corner of his mouth. "Okay then, *Mistress*. We'll go."

Hearing him use that title makes my stomach flutter with excitement. So I drop my phone and wrap my arms around his neck. I press my lips to his ear.

"Now be a good boy and fuck me."

He chuckles into my neck as he pulls my leg up higher and slams hard, making me squeal.

It's amazing how much better I feel after getting that text message off my chest. I don't know the last time I ever stood up for myself before, but it feels good. I'm not as mad at her as I know I should be, but instead of forgiving and forgetting, I spoke up.

So now I can look forward to whatever this invitation is and how she plans to prove to us that she's changed.

———

The invitation is sitting on my bed when I get home later that afternoon. After leaving Clay this morning, I ran some errands and dropped off applications and paperwork for a few nearby schools that have open positions. My dad hired a new temp at the office and doesn't want me coming in anymore to help out. He says it's because I need to start looking for a job that *I* want, but part of me wonders if it's because he doesn't want to see Clay and me together.

Which, considering what Clay and I have done in his office, is fair.

I sit on my bed and look at the shiny gold envelope in my

hand. It's addressed to Mistress Jade Penner, which has me biting my lip and smiling. Carefully, I peel open the back and pull out the single matte-black card inside.

You are cordially invited to an exclusive party
at the Salacious Players' Club.
Your attendance is personally requested by our
new Madame of Operations, Eden St. Claire.
Should you choose to attend, you will have full access
to the club, including the VIP suite, the voyeur rooms,
and all other facilities the club has to offer.

At the bottom of the invitation, it says the party is this Saturday night at ten p.m. Immediately after reading it, I call Clay. He picks up on the first ring.

"I got my invitation," I say without a greeting.

"So did I," he replies.

"What should we do?" I ask while chewing on my thumbnail.

"It's your call, babe."

"No, it's not, Clay. It's *our* call. If we go to the club and we hear her out, then it affects both of us. I need to know how you feel about this. If we feel differently, we'll handle that."

The line goes silent for a second, and I wait with bated breath for his response. Deep down, I want to go. I want to hear her out, and I pray she really does apologize and make it right so we can have a second chance at something amazing. But if that's not what Clay wants, then I need to prepare myself for that.

"I want to go," he mumbles after a heavy sigh.

I smile as my knee bounces anxiously. "Me too."

"Good."

"Good," I reply with the same optimistic tone.

"Jade," he says.

"Yeah?"

"No matter what happens, I love you."

There's not a chance I will ever tire of hearing him say those words to me. I should feel bad that it took Clay having his heart broken to bring him to me, but in all honesty, I'm grateful for it. Not only did that heartbreak change him into the man I love, but if she had never lost him the first time, he never would have been mine.

This is why I'm not worried, because I know it's true. No matter what happens, we have each other. Falling back on my bed, I stare at the ceiling as I reply, "No matter what, I love you too."

Rule #48: Speak from the heart.

Eden

THEY'RE NOT HERE YET. IT'S TEN THIRTY, AND THERE IS ABSOLUTELY no sign of them.

Other than that, the night is a total success. The club is full, and people seem to be having a great time.

I'm surrounded by familiar faces, and everyone is stopping to congratulate me and welcome me as a member of the team. It's surreal.

I just wish I could enjoy it.

"Well, it's about damn time," a familiar female voice says from behind me. I spin away from the bar to find Maggie standing a foot away and smiling at me with a smug expression. She's holding a glass of white wine, and her hair is shorter than the last time I saw her. I let out a shriek as I throw my arms around her and pull her in for a tight hug.

"Oh my God," I cry out, not letting her out of my embrace. "I didn't know you were coming!"

"Like I would miss this," she replies with a laugh as I finally let her go and admire her new look.

"You look amazing," I say while I play with her wavy short hair.

"So do you," she replies, admiring my shimmery black pantsuit.

As I stare at Maggie, I can't help but feel a little emotional. I didn't realize how much I missed having her around until now. She was the timid businesswoman with a hidden Domme who was an absolute delight to watch her embrace and discover.

Then she and her boyfriend left to run the new club in Arizona, and I hardly kept in touch much after that. Have I always been such a bad friend? Always closing people off as often as I can.

"I'm glad you finally took the job," she says. "I've been telling Emerson to offer it to you for a while now."

"Thank you," I reply with a tight smile. "Where's Beau?" I ask, looking around the club.

"He's in time-out," she says with a roll of her eyes.

"Uh-oh," I reply with a wicked grin. "What did he do?"

"He likes to send me videos doing things he knows he isn't allowed to do. So now he's up in room twenty, waiting for me."

There's a blush to her cheeks, and it makes me so happy to see her so naturally acclimated to a role she once struggled with so much. It must be so fun for her to have someone so perfectly suited for her, who loves being a brat, so she can do the one thing I know she loves to do, which is tame him.

It makes me miss Clay so much it hurts. It's like a stabbing pain between my ribs, and it makes it hard to breathe.

I stifle my discomfort as Maggie takes another sip of her wine and glances around the room. "Although to be honest, if I really wanted to punish him, I should have made him mingle at this party with his dad and Charlie."

She laughs, and I force myself to laugh along, although I'm still swallowing down pain and regret because even now, as I look around, I don't see the two people I want to see more than anything.

"Well, I better go put him out of his misery," she says. Then she touches my arm with a warm smile. "It is so nice to see you, Eden. We should keep in touch more."

"We should," I reply before pulling her in for another hug. "It is so nice to see you."

When she pulls away, I stifle the tears that want to fall, and I wave at her as she makes her way toward the stairs that lead to the VIP rooms. I watch her, seething with jealousy. If I hadn't messed things up with Clay the first time, would we have ever gotten to that point she and Beau are at? No. I would have never swallowed my pride and opened up without Jade there to encourage me to. I'd still be hiding him in my room, trying to live two lives at once.

Now I have nothing more than some memories and the hard truth in the form of a text message from her. And that's all I deserve. Two people wanted to love me and give me more than most ever get in their lifetimes, and I pushed them away because I was scared. The secrets were a thinly veiled excuse for my own insecurities getting in the way of true happiness.

I'd say *live and learn,* but I know better. Love like that doesn't come around twice in a lifetime. The three of us were a perfectly timed enigma, and even if I wanted to wait for it to happen again, I know I'll never feel as safe or as accepted as I was with them.

Just then, there's a voice at the front of the room, and we all turn to see Emerson standing on the stage with a microphone in his hand.

"Good evening, guests," he says with a charming smile. "I'd like to thank you all for coming out tonight to celebrate three years at the Salacious Players' Club."

Everyone claps, and a few people cheer. When Emerson's eyes land on my face, my cheeks grow hot, and I know what's coming.

"It's been three amazing years, and I owe a great deal to my amazing team here at the club. But we are celebrating more than just the anniversary of our opening. We are also celebrating a new addition to that team."

I force myself to smile, and I feel Ronan winking at me from across the room.

"Eden St. Claire has been with us at the club since the very first day. She helped inspire so much of what we do but also what we strive to be. She helped shape our mission of equality and empowerment and has worked tirelessly as Madame Kink to help protect that mission."

When the crowd cheers this time, I feel my eyes prick with tears.

"Quite literally, Salacious Players' Club would not be what it is without her."

They begin cheering again, and I quickly wipe the inside corners of my eyes to keep from crying.

"We are beyond grateful that she has accepted a position on our management team, so please join me in welcoming Eden to the stage."

The crowd cheers wildly, but I stand frozen in my spot.

I don't know if I can do this. I can't get up there and give that speech if the people who I wanted to give it to are not here.

Looking up, my eyes find Charlie standing near the stage, and I remember fondly the meek and nervous girl who looked to me for guidance three years ago. I see Mia clapping next to her and remember the tour I gave her on her first trip to the club. For three years, I've been here helping these other women find love, but mostly themselves.

It's not about me.

Blinking away my tears, I set my glass down on the bar and walk toward the stage. Emerson smiles at me as I take the microphone, and I decide to speak from the heart.

"Thank you," I stammer into the mic. "I want to thank Emerson and his team—Garrett, Hunter, and Maggie—for inviting me to be a part of this amazing club—"

Just then, the heavy curtain at the front of the room opens, and they walk through. She has her arm looped through his, and my heart stops. He's in his dark-gray suit with his perfect hair slicked back like he always used to wear it. She's in a long dark-green velvet gown with her hair styled in curls.

They came.

The crowd claps sporadically as I finish my sentence, but then they wait for me to continue. I can't take my eyes off them, especially as they make eye contact with me.

Jade smiles but then quickly catches herself and wipes it from her face. I love to see her standing up for herself, just like I taught her to.

Putting the mic back up to my mouth, I continue.

"If I've learned anything in the past three years, it's that this place is about so much more than sex and kinks. It's about love and acceptance and…life. I've watched my friends find love here. I've watched young people learn to speak up for themselves," I say, glancing at Charlie.

"I've watched friends turn into lovers," I add, glancing at Drake and Hunter in the back with Isabel in front of them.

"I've watched my best friend find new meaning in life." I glance at Ronan and have to quickly look away to keep the tears from returning.

"This club has changed so many lives, and I've been so blessed to watch it, but I've learned things too." My eyes find Jade and Clay at the back, and they don't leave them for the rest of my speech.

"I've learned that people are capable of change, no matter how old they are or what they've been through. I've learned that no matter how many times you reinvent yourself, you are still the same person worthy of love. I've learned that love has many faces and comes in many forms, and all are equally beautiful and sexy. But mostly, I've learned that even a coldhearted Dominatrix can make mistakes."

I can see Jade's lip tremble from all the way across the room, and I fight the urge to jump from this stage just to hold her.

Somehow, I gather the strength to finish my speech.

"Three years ago, I met a pretty young woman in the bathroom on opening night, and I saw the fear in her eyes because she had stepped foot into a club that could have exploited her. But I knew what she didn't, that what these owners set out to create wasn't a place for people to find pleasure or even orgasms. They created a place for people to find themselves. That's what Salacious Players' Club has always been, and that's what I will work to ensure it always remains. Thank you."

As the crowd claps and cheers, I quickly hand the microphone back to Emerson. He manages to pull me in for a few quick photos before I escape his grasp and rush off the stage.

Then I'm bombarded by people. Friends and clients and strangers rush toward me to pat me on the back or thank me for my speech or offer to buy me a drink. I quickly lose sight of Jade and Clay, and I start to panic that they might have left already.

By the time I reach the other side of the room, where they were once standing, I'm frantic. But when I step out of the horde of people and come face-to-face with the pair of them staring at me expectantly, I'm so overwhelmed I let out a sob.

"I don't expect your pity or your forgiveness," I say, my eyes dancing between the two of them. "I'm so glad you came, and I'm happy to see you together. I had a whole speech planned, but then I got flustered, so now I don't know what else to say, but I'm sorry."

Jade licks her lip. I notice the way her arm tightens around Clay's. I really am glad to see them together. At least they still have each other.

"I liked your speech," Jade says sweetly.

"Me too," Clay adds.

I feel like a mess. Any hope of holding back my tears is gone now. I'm not supposed to be sobbing at the club. I'm Madame Kink. What the hell has gotten into me?

But I can't stop. The sight of them here for me when I asked them to come, the two people who see me more than anyone else does. The two people who make me *me*. They're here, and it's giving me hope.

I step closer to them as people move around us. I touch Jade's arm and brush gently against Clay. They don't back away or make me move. If anything, they lean closer. In a low voice, I say, "I told you I could prove I've changed. If you let me show you, I can take you to one of the rooms. If you don't want to, I understand. No hard feelings. I'm just glad you came—"

Jade touches my cheek. "Eden," she says, stopping me from talking. "Who's rambling now?" she asks with a smile.

Through my tears, I let out a laugh.

"We want to hear you out," Clay adds. He's a bit more guarded than Jade, but I can understand why. I've done this to him twice.

Then he cracks a small smile, and it gives me more hope than anything.

"Good," I reply. Then I reach out my hand, and he takes it. "Then follow me."

Rule #49: See things from a different point of view.

Clay

My guard is up. Of course it is. How could it not be?

But something is different about Eden. I've never seen her openly cry like that, first of all. And that speech? Judging by the vulnerability in that alone, I'd say she's changed. At least enough to open up and let us in.

But still…I'm guarded. Because now it's not just me at risk of getting hurt. I have to protect Jade too.

As Eden leads us through the club, she doesn't take us up the stairs to her private room. Instead, she walks us to the voyeur hall, and my blood pressure starts to spike. I already know where this is going.

I'm a mix of nervousness and excitement. There's a hidden layer of anxiety and fear that this won't work. Is she even capable of what I know she's about to do?

As she brings us into the hallway, I watch each window pass by, most of which are filled, and crowds are gathered. People will be watching us. Am *I* ready for this?

Jade squeezes my hand as Eden unlocks one of the discreet

black doors with her key card. Then she leads us into the room, and my eyes settle on the throne in the middle.

My mouth is dry, and I feel tense all over. I want this so badly I can taste it. This need to have her—no, *them*—back in my arms is overwhelming. We can't fuck this up. Not tonight.

As she leads us into the room, I stand by Jade and wait for her instructions.

While I wait for her to tell me what to do, like she normally does, she does something unexpected.

With her eyes on me, she lowers herself to the floor in front of the throne. Sitting on her knees, she gazes up at me, and I hear an audible gasp from Jade next to me.

Eden rests her hands on her knees. "I know now that I was unable to be vulnerable with both of you because I have struggled with trust for so long. The last person I trusted hurt me, but I know with all of my heart that neither of you ever would. So I want to prove to you both just how much I trust you. Tonight, I am yours. Completely and wholly yours."

My lips part in surprise. Just seeing her on the floor for me means more than I know how to express. For our entire relationship, I was at her mercy. I put my heart and my life in her hands. I trusted her more than I'd ever trusted anyone before.

That entire time, she felt out of reach.

But now, she's giving me back everything I gave to her.

My mouth waters at the very idea of having her like this. It burns inside me like wildfire, and I know that once we go through with this, there is no coming back.

I start to loosen my tie as I stare down at her. "You know your safe words?"

Her face relaxes as she nods and moves her gaze to the floor. "Yes, Sir."

"Good. I think we can have some fun with you tonight. What do you think, Mistress?"

Next to me, Jade smiles. "I think we can have a lot of fun with her. You want to please us, don't you?"

Eden bites her bottom lip. "Yes, Mistress."

"Good girl," Jade replies with a smirk.

"Then crawl," I say in a cold command.

Without hesitation, Eden transitions to all fours and moves across the floor toward where Jade and I are standing. When she reaches our feet, she sits back on her heels and waits.

Moving Jade in front of me, I place my hands on her shoulders as I stare down at Eden. "Go ahead now. Worship your Mistress. Kiss her shoes."

I spot a twitch at the corner of Eden's mouth as she fights her smile. "Yes, Sir," she replies.

Then she lowers herself to the floor and presses her lips to the tops of each of Jade's shoes.

"She listens so well," I say to Jade as I move her hair to the side, kissing the side of her neck.

"Yes, she does. Because she wants to please us. Don't you, pet?"

Eden nods. "Yes, Mistress."

"You exist only for our pleasure. Do you understand?" I ask, petting the top of her head.

"Yes, Sir."

"Good," I say calmly. Then I lean down, resting my hand on her cheek as I add, "Then take off my pants."

She lifts higher up on her knees and starts undoing my belt as I shuck off my jacket and hand it to Jade, who hangs it on a hook on the wall. Eden glances up at me, and our eyes meet as I unbutton my shirt and she gently pulls down my zipper. Just as my shirt slides down my arms, she tugs off my pants. My cock is half-hard behind the cotton of my boxer briefs, so after I slip off my shoes and socks and she helps me out of my pants, I smile at her.

"You want to get it hard for me, don't you?"

Her tongue peeks out to lick her lips. "Yes, Sir."

"Then go ahead."

Jade is standing at my side, her fingers drifting over my shoulder and chest as she watches Eden ease the elastic of my boxers down low enough for my cock to pop out. Then she grips the length in her hand and brings it to her mouth. Gazing up at me, she closes her lips around the head of my dick, and I let out a moan.

"That's it," I say with encouragement. "Get me nice and hard with those perfect lips of yours."

She hums around my cock as it slides to the back of her throat. My eyes roll back, and I hold on to Jade to keep from stumbling over.

"Fuck yes." I moan.

Jade softly strokes Eden's head, brushing back her hair and praising her as she sucks my cock.

Reaching down, I hold Eden on either side of her head. "You're doing so well, but you can take a little more, can't you?"

She gasps for air and wipes her chin. "Yes, Sir."

"Open for me," I say. When her lips part and her tongue slides forward, I ease my cock into her mouth as far as it will go. She gags when I reach the back, so I pull out.

"Hand on my leg, pet," I say. Her hand grips my thigh, and I know she knows the drill. If it's too much, she squeezes.

Tears stream down her face as I take control, fucking her mouth and making her gag. After every few strokes, I pull out to let her take a breath and to keep from coming too early.

"You are so fucking hot like this," I say as I fuck her throat again. There is saliva trailing from the tip of my cock to her mouth every time I pull out, and I love the look of her like this. "Look at you taking my cock like you love it. You love it, don't you, pet?"

She gasps. "I love it, Sir."

"Good. Take some more." Keeping up my thrusts, I stay mindful of her hand on my leg. "I want you to swallow every drop. Can you do that for me?"

She nods. "Yes, Sir."

As I slide my cock back into her mouth, this time, I don't stop. Just thinking about her swallowing my load has me wanting to blow. My hands stay firm on her head as I finally reach my release, coming hard with a few more thrusts.

I groan loudly as my body erupts in pleasure. And I watch her swallowing as I ease my cock out of her mouth.

"So perfect," Jade says with a hum from next to me. After Eden swallows, Jade leans down and buries a hand in her hair, smiling against her lips. "But now it's my turn."

"Take off her dress, pet," I say to Eden, who quickly moves toward Jade. Standing, she moves behind her to unzip her dress from the back. Then Eden slides Jade's gown off her shoulders.

"I want to see you on that throne," I whisper into Jade's ear. She smiles as she walks over to the chair in nothing but her high heels and a thin black thong. Eden is still standing near me, so I bury my hand in her hair and pull her mouth to mine. As I kiss her deeply, she moans into my mouth.

When the kiss ends, I stare into her eyes, still holding her by the back of her head. "Give me a color."

Her lips turn up in a gentle smile. "Green, Sir."

"Good," I reply softly. "Then let us see how beautiful you are."

With that, I slide her shimmering black jacket from around her shoulders. Beneath that is a light, silky black top with thin straps, exposing her delicate shoulders. Leaning down, I press my lips to her skin, trailing my mouth all the way up her neck to her ear. My hands move to her pants, sliding open the button and letting them fall to the floor. I have to break my lips from her neck to take off her top so she's finally naked.

"You are so beautiful," I whisper as my fingers dance softly down from her shoulder over her breasts to her stomach. "So beautiful and so ours," I murmur into her ear.

Her breath hitches as she leans into my touch.

"But first," I say, licking my lips. "Let me see you beg."

With her eyes on my face, she slowly lowers to her knees.

Grabbing a fistful of her hair, I gently guide her to where Jade is waiting on the throne. "That is your Domme," I say. "So worship her."

Jade looks so fierce in that large chair. With her arms resting on the sides and her legs spread, she exudes the same sense of confidence and power Eden normally does. My cock starts to stir back to life at the sight.

Eden must feel the same because she does not hesitate before crawling right to Jade and gently spreading her legs farther. Reaching to hook her fingers around Jade's panties, she swiftly drags them down Jade's legs until she's naked for her. Then Eden gazes up at Jade as she kisses her way back up her legs.

When she reaches the top, I watch as Eden drags her tongue through Jade's cunt, moaning as she makes her way to her clit and sucking so hard Jade starts to writhe. She reaches down and takes Eden by the back of the head and holds her there.

I move to the wall, leaning against it as I watch them. Lazily, I stroke my cock back to life.

Eden has Jade's legs draped over her shoulders as she devours her, loudly sucking and nibbling.

"Don't stop," Jade cries out. Eden plunges two fingers inside her, making her moan even louder. Jade looks like she's being slowly unraveled, on the brink of pleasure, as she holds Eden's head between her legs. When Eden pulls her face away for a moment, Jade smiles down at her.

Then she yanks her back as she mutters, "Give me more of that pretty little mouth."

With a wicked grin, Eden dives back between Jade's legs. By now, my cock has revived itself to a rock-hard state, so I make my way back over to the girls and lean down to kiss Jade on the mouth as she cries out with pleasure.

Moving behind Eden, I kneel on the floor and run my fingers down between her legs to find her soaking.

"I told you we were going to have fun with you, pet," I say as

I smack her ass hard. Eden squeals, fidgeting back and forth. So I lay another smack on the opposite side. "You like being ours to play with, don't you?"

She comes up for air long enough to mumble, "Yes, Sir."

"But you're not going to come when I fuck you. Understand?"

With a disgruntled moan, she nods. "Yes, Sir."

Lining up my cock with her soaking cunt, I grab her hips and ease my way in.

"You should see how good your pussy looks around my cock," I say on a strangled exhale. My hips take over, pistoning hard, and the three of us are all moaning and crying out together.

I don't even care that there is a crowd watching on the other side of the window. To me, they're not here. It's just me and Eden and Jade, all perfectly in sync and as one. Their pleasure is mine.

Jade's voice takes on a high-pitched tone, and I look up to find her seizing on the throne. Eden's fingers are thrusting hard just as Jade comes undone, convulsing and trembling through her orgasm.

Again, she makes one hell of a mess all over Eden, who is now holding tightly to the seat of the chair, holding herself upright as I pound into her from behind.

My second orgasm comes crashing against me like a tidal wave. Pleasure radiates through my body as my fingers tighten on Eden's hips.

The sensation pulses through my body like a cadence.

They are mine. I am theirs.

We are forever.

Rule #50: Good girls get rewarded.

Jade

"I'M NOT DONE WITH YOU YET," I WHISPER AGAINST HER MOUTH as I pull Eden's lips to mine for a blazing kiss. She smiles as I run my tongue along the seam of her lips.

Behind her, Clay is staring down as he pulls out and watches his cum leak down her thighs.

"Yes, Mistress," she replies in a sultry whisper.

"Can I still have fun with you?" I ask with a mischievous grin.

"Yes, Mistress."

This still feels so surreal. She's here, and she's surrendering herself to us. I never thought I'd see Eden like this, and it's not about her just being submissive, but it's really about her showing just how much she trusts us. She's letting us use her selfishly for our own pleasure, all the while knowing we would never hurt her.

Grabbing her by the back of the neck, I pull her ear to my lips. Then I mumble with a low rasp, "I'm going to fuck you now. So be a good girl and go get that strap-on from the cabinet."

I see movement in her throat as she swallows. Then her eyes

find mine, and they're dancing back and forth as if she's trying to decide if I'm serious. Which I very much am.

"Yes, Mistress," she mutters slowly. Then she rises from the floor and goes to the toy cabinet against the back wall. A moment later, she comes back with a black leather strap-on that suddenly has my heart racing.

I'm really going to do this.

Standing up from the bench, she helps me attach it around my waist, pulling it so snug my body shifts with her movement. Then our eyes meet, and I pull her in for another kiss. My body is practically buzzing with excitement. My teeth nip at her lips as she mewls against my mouth.

Taking her face on both sides, I pull her away and stare into her eyes. "Get it nice and wet for me," I say in a confident command.

Licking her lips, she drops to her knees and takes the shaft into her mouth, slathering it with her saliva until it's glistening. Then I drop back onto the throne and hold her gently by the chin.

"Get up here," I say.

As she climbs onto my lap, hovering over the length of the dildo, I stare down at where it's about to enter her. I can't explain how this makes me feel. She lowers herself, and I can't take my eyes off it. I've never been more turned on in my life.

Then I watch her face as it slides in. Her mouth hangs open, her eyes dilated and her body tense with anticipation. Once she's seated all the way, we both gasp for air at the same time. She grabs my arms as I hold her face.

"God, I've wanted to do this for so long. You have no idea," I say. She leans down and captures my mouth with a kiss.

"Me too," she replies against my lips.

With our eyes locked, she bounces on my lap, and I can't keep my hands off her. Her arms, her breasts, her legs. I need her so badly. I need to know she's here and she's mine.

Having her like this is like nothing I've ever done before. It makes me feel like I can give her everything she wants and be everything she needs.

She's moving her hips to a fast rhythm, and I watch her expression change as she finds pleasure in this moment.

Clay walks up behind her and stands against her back. Then he looks at me, and I feel the intensity in his eyes as if he's thinking the same thing I am.

We are whole again.

He strokes her cheek, and she turns to look up at him as she grinds her hips on my lap. He leans down to kiss her and wipe the sweat-soaked hair from her forehead. I love the way he's watching her—so tender and loving.

"She's been so good," he says with care. "I think she deserves to come. What do you think, baby?"

My hands on her hips squeeze tighter. I want nothing more than to watch her come. I need it, and I won't leave this room until I have that. Because she's proven that she trusts us, but have we proven that we will take care of her? Not entirely.

"Yes. She definitely deserves to come," I respond, without taking my eyes off her.

Reaching down between our bodies, Clay takes one of her nipples between his fingers and pinches until she lets out a sexy, needy sound of pleasure.

"She likes a little pain. Don't you, pet?" he says playfully.

She gazes up at him and nods. "Yes, Sir."

"Just a little," he replies as he leans down and kisses her again on the mouth. Then he releases his hold on her breast and walks across the room. When he returns a moment later, he's holding a thick black candle, and I watch with shock as he dribbles the wax onto her chest.

I let out a gasp at the exact moment Eden cries out in what sounds like pain and pleasure blended into one. Her movement on my lap picks up speed as if that little bit of pain made her closer to coming.

"Come here, baby," he says, looking at me. As he tips the candle again, the wax falls onto my breasts, and I let out a scream. At first, it feels like too much. Pure agony, but then in its wake, the pain blossoms into something different. It buzzes across my entire nervous system until it culminates in this erotic need deep in my belly.

"Oh my God," I cry out in a low rasp.

My eyes meet Eden's as I sit up a little straighter, pulling her chest nearly flush with mine.

"Do it again," I say to Clay. He moves Eden's hair out of the way, and we all look down to watch the wax drip over our pressed together breasts.

It might be the most beautiful thing I've ever seen. Or felt.

The sting of pain hits us both at the same time, and our grip on each other tightens. I suddenly feel closer to her. Right as the pain dulls and the arousal blooms, I grab her face and kiss her hard.

She moans into my mouth.

"I want to feel you come on my lap."

My hand is in her hair, and the other is on her ass. We are so close I can't tell where one of us begins and the other ends, so all I can taste and smell and feel is her. It's perfect, and I want to stay like this forever.

But first, I need to feel her pleasure. So I relax my hand on her ass, and I press my thumb to her clit. She rides the silicone cock on my lap even harder as I circle my thumb around her clit with determination.

"That's it, Eden. You're almost there," I say.

Clay comes back, this time without the candle, and pinches her wax-coated nipple again. His other hand grips her throat tight, so she is utterly surrounded by us, our touch overwhelming her body.

Her orgasm is a slow build, and I watch the way it climbs through every inch of her body. Starting with the way her fingers tighten on my flesh and the way her muscles contract. And then, finally, her breathing gets shallow and quick. Her moans fall silent just as she reaches the pinnacle of her pleasure. Then she is caught in an all-consuming orgasm. I feel it in the pulse of her clit and the squeeze of her hips around me. She lets out a desperate cry, and her body moves on its own, shuddering and jerking on my lap as she rides out every beautiful moment.

I've never seen anything more perfect in all my life.

It feels like minutes go by before her body falls limp, and Clay has to catch her from tumbling over. He strokes her face and kisses her forehead as she catches her breath. Then he takes her into his arms, lifting her from my lap.

Then he carefully sets her on her feet.

"Time for your favorite part," he says affectionately as he pulls her over to the chaise lounge opposite the throne. He's in his boxer briefs as he sits down first, pulling her into his arms next to him. Then he unscrews a bottle of water for her, making her drink as he wipes her neck and chest with a wet cloth.

Watching him take care of her makes me love him even more. Seeing what they have is special. It doesn't make me jealous. It makes me grateful to have them both.

Assuming that's what happens after tonight. This means she'll stay, right? She's proven to us that she trusts us, and we've proven to her that she belongs with us. That we'll take care of her and love her and give her everything she needs.

Standing from the throne, I find another washcloth and use it to wipe the dried wax from my chest. Then I grab my clothes from the floor and slowly pull them on. Then I take a bottle of water from the cabinet and guzzle it down.

"How are you feeling?" Clay asks Eden. She gazes up at him with a lazy smile. "I feel good." Her head rests softly against his chest, and her fingers lightly trace the ridges of his chest and abs.

"I don't know about you guys," I say as I take the seat on the other side of her. "But I could use a shower. Why don't I take her to the locker room and get us both cleaned up?"

Eden lifts her head from his chest. "Just come to my house. We can all shower there."

My eyes meet Clay's, and we're both staring in a bit of shock. "What about…"

"He's sleeping," Eden replies. "But then you can…both stay the night. If you want."

I can't keep my hands off her. Leaning in, I wrap my hands around her waist and kiss her on the cheek.

"Seriously?" Clay asks. "Are you sure?"

She nods. "Yes. I am sure. I'm not making this decision right now. I've had this planned for a while."

"This means that…we can try again, right?" I ask with hope.

She looks at me as she nods again. "If that's all right with you."

Grabbing her face, I kiss her lips. Then her cheek, jaw, and forehead.

I can't remember when I was ever this happy. Not only is she letting us back in, but she's letting us *all the way* in. We are a part of her life. Her real life.

"Yes. It's more than all right with me," I reply with a wide grin.

When she smiles back, I realize that everything might actually be all right.

We don't know how long it will last or what will become of us in ten months or ten years. What we do know is that we are safe with each other, and that's all any of us can ask for.

Rule #51: It doesn't have to be what you had planned to be perfect.

Eden

I WAKE UP MADISON, WHO'S SLEEPING ON THE COUCH. WHEN SHE opens her eyes and sees both Clay and Jade standing awkwardly in my kitchen, she doesn't even blink. She greets them politely, and when Clay introduces himself, she nods with a knowing smile.

"Jack talks about you all the time. And you must be Jade," she says, smiling at a blushing Jade in her dark-green ball gown.

I can see the pride on both of their faces to hear that Jack still talks about them to his nanny. I'm wearing a proud smirk as I walk Madison to the door, thanking her again for babysitting.

When I come back inside, Clay and Jade look so natural in my house. Jade is sitting on the countertop, and Clay is staring at the various school pictures and colorful drawings pinned to my refrigerator.

"About that shower," I say, nodding toward my master bedroom. They both follow behind me, and I shut us in as I move toward the bathroom. Then I twist the knob to turn on the water and pull three towels from under the sink.

It's not the world's biggest shower, but at least it's big enough to fit the three of us if we're comfortable being close, which we obviously are.

I help Jade out of her dress as Clay strips my jacket from my shoulders. Then I pull her into the shower with me. We both moan under the hot spray. She helps wipe the makeup from under my eyes while I lather up her hair with shampoo. Once we're both clean, I stare down at her. Her short brown hair is slicked back, and there are droplets of water on her nose and ears. She looks so incredibly perfect. I'm flooded with relief that she's here. I'm thankful she came to the club tonight, that she forgave me, and that she wants this as much as I do.

I wrap my arms around her neck and pull her tightly against me, hugging her naked body to mine under the hot spray of water. I've never been so intimate with someone in my life. Even after being married. Even after seven years as a sex worker. There has never been a moment as intimate as this one because we aren't just showing our bodies to each other; we're exposing our souls and our hearts. What could be more vulnerable than that?

The shower door opens as Clay steps in with us. Jade and I pull him into the embrace without hesitation. The three of us stand under the water together. It's not about sex, and that's not where this is leading. We're just holding each other and breathing the same air, as close as three people can possibly be.

At the moment, I feel like the luckiest woman alive.

How did I end up here? How do I deserve this?

There was a time in my life when all I wanted was the bare minimum. A safe place to live. A simple life for my son. A life without abuse.

I wrote off the idea of any kind of fairy-tale love. That would have been asking too much.

Then these two came along, and now I feel almost greedy accepting this. I clawed my way out of hell, and I never did it expecting to get to heaven. But here I am.

After pulling from our embrace, Jade and I wash Clay's hair, laughing as we style his long locks in different ways. He shakes them all out as we giggle at him. I think we're all delirious and high on the perfection of this moment.

Finally, we climb out of the shower one by one. I give Jade something to sleep in, and then the three of us stare at my king-size bed without anyone making the first move.

"Are you sure this is okay?" Jade asks.

"I can sleep on the couch," Clay adds, but I just shake my head.

I nod. "Yes, I'm sure. I'll talk to him in the morning."

Clay nods with a tight smile as I move toward the bed and pull back the covers.

"But you know...keep your clothes on," I add sternly.

At that, they laugh a little. Then we climb in. Jade is in the middle, and I take the side I normally sleep on. After we're all settled, I click the lamp on the bedside table. The room is bathed in moonlight. Under the covers, our legs are all touching, slightly tangled. On top of the covers, our hands are linked. Jade's back is pressed to my front, and she's using my arm as a pillow.

I love the way they feel in my bed. It feels like a dream, and I'm not even asleep yet.

———————

I wake up first. It's only seven thirty when I carefully roll out of bed. Standing next to it, I stare at the two of them in my bed, and I smile at how *right* it looks.

We're not rushing into this. They're not moving in or anything, but I wanted them to both know how serious I am about this. We will do things people in relationships do, like sleeping over at each other's houses.

Throwing my hair into a bun on the top of my head, I leave my bedroom and cross the house toward Jack's room. He's still sleeping peacefully in his bed when I enter. I don't wake him, but I know he'll start stirring soon.

So I go to the kitchen and start making a pot of coffee. It feels so normal, and yet nothing feels normal at the moment. Or maybe it's like a new normal.

While the coffee brews, I walk to the window that overlooks the yard. The sun has risen, painting the sky a warm orange and blue along the horizon. In quiet moments like these, I think about her—the version of myself that lived in agony. The one who endured daily nightmares for far, far longer than anyone should.

I've been telling myself for so long that I'm not that woman, but that doesn't feel true anymore. I did not escape some tragic past version of myself. Just like I can't run from my past. I carry it with me every day.

I was always the woman in the mirror.

I didn't save the woman I once was. I saved myself.

I am Eden St. Claire *and* Madame Kink.

And to some degree, I'm still *Nina*—the woman from a small town who refused to be defined by her birth or her fate. The woman who looked in the mirror one day and decided she wanted more.

"Mama?"

Blinking the tears from my eyes, I spin away from the window to see Jack shuffling out of the hallway, one eye open and scratching his head as he slowly wakes up. When he puts his arms up for me like he used to when he was a baby, I use all the strength I have to hoist him off the ground and hold him in my arms.

He rests his head on my shoulder as he slowly wakes up. Standing by the window, I rock him gently. I try to memorize this moment so I can carry it with me when he's far too big for me to hold anymore.

"Jack, I have to talk to you," I say softly while stroking his back.

"Yeah, Mama?" he replies with a sleepy rasp.

Deciding this is a conversation we need to have face-to-face, I carry him to the sofa and set him down next to me. Then I take a deep breath and do what I've been too afraid to do for well over a year now.

"I wanted to tell you that Clay is going to be my boyfriend." I stare into his eyes and watch as his expression instantly lights up. He shoots me a beaming smile as he starts to bounce in his seat.

"Is that okay?" I ask, although it's pretty clear that it is.

He nods emphatically. "Yes. Is he going to live with us?"

"No. Not right away, but he'll be around more. And we can do things together," I say as I play with one of his unruly curls.

"What about Jade?" he asks, his brows folded inward.

I love that he thinks of her. I love that after only a couple of days together, she's found a place in his mind. I take a deep breath, my stomach growing heavy.

I know Jack will be accepting of this, and I've always taught my son to accept love in every shape and form. But there's no denying that the world around him has taught him there is only one right way to be in a relationship. Every day, as his mother, I have to fight that heteronormative brainwashing. And he will have to fight that battle with me, *with us*.

But at the end of the day, it's still love. And my son deserves nothing less.

"Well," I say, reaching for his hand, "Jade will be my girlfriend. *Our* girlfriend. Mine and Clay's."

His beaming smile doesn't waver. He doesn't even look surprised. "Will she live with us too?"

I let out a soft chuckle. "Not yet. Maybe someday."

He's wiggling in excitement as he kicks his feet.

"Are you happy about this news?"

"Yes."

"Do you understand that your family might look a little different than your friends' at school?"

He shrugs. "London's mom only has one boyfriend. And there's a girl named Victoria who has two dads. But my mom has a boyfriend *and* a girlfriend."

"If you ever have any questions, you know you can ask me, right?"

"Yes, Mama."

"And no matter what," I say, leaning toward him to press my forehead to his, "you will always have me. You and me, forever. Okay?"

"Okay. I love you, Mama," he whispers, putting his arms around my neck.

"I love you so much, buddy."

We're still hugging when I spot someone walking out of my room. It's Jade in a set of my pajamas that she's practically swimming in. Her hair is tangled and messy, but she smiles at me when she spots Jack in my arms.

When he spins around to see her, he's beaming with a blushing grin. She walks over and sits next to him on the couch. "Good morning," she says, ruffling his hair.

"My mom told me," he whispers with a blushing smile.

Jade glances at me curiously. "She did? What did she say?"

"That you're her girlfriend. And Clay is her boyfriend. And that maybe someday you can come live here."

She lets out a laugh, and I roll my eyes. "Jack…"

"Maybe someday," she replies sweetly. "Are you excited about me being your mom's girlfriend?"

He launches himself into her lap. "Yep. Wanna watch TV?" Then he reaches for the remote while nestled between Jade's folded legs and clicks on one of his favorite shows.

Jade's eyes meet mine for a moment, and I can see the contentment on her face. Then she smiles at me before Jack starts telling her all about the show they're watching.

Standing from the couch, I touch her shoulder. "I made coffee. Want some?"

"Yes, please. Cream and sugar."

"You got it." Then I lean down and press my lips to her forehead.

Just as I reach the kitchen, Clay emerges from the bedroom. He didn't have a lot of clothing options here, so he's wearing his pants from last night and a white undershirt.

"Morning," he says, his eyes glued on where Jade is holding Jack in her lap on the couch.

"Morning," she chirps brightly.

As Clay looks at me, there is concern and curiosity in his wide eyes and furrowed brow. As I pass him by, I kiss him on the cheek. "I told him everything."

"Everything?" he asks with a chuckle.

"Well, I told him that you are my boyfriend and she is my girlfriend."

"And maybe someday you will live here with us," Jack adds without taking his eyes off the TV.

Clay's face stretches into a smile as he glances at the two of them on the couch.

"Sounds like a plan," he replies as he wraps his arms around my waist from behind and presses his lips to my neck with a rumbling growl. I squirm out of his grasp.

"Stop it," I whisper, swatting his hands away. "You want coffee?" I ask as I pull down three mugs from the cabinet.

"Sure. What's for breakfast?" he asks, looking around my kitchen.

"Pancakes!" Jack calls from the couch.

"Pancakes?" Clay replies jokingly. "You know how to make pancakes already? You're only seven."

Jack giggles loudly. "No, *you* make pancakes!"

"I've got bad news for you, buddy," Clay replies as I hand him a cup of coffee. "I've never cooked a day in my life."

"I guess it's time to learn," I reply with a smile.

"Yes, Madame," he mumbles under his breath. Then I show him where the skillet is as I pull the mix from the pantry and the milk and butter from the fridge.

I show him how to stir the ingredients together and preheat

the stove. As I watch him attempt to flip his first one, making a mess of batter all over the pan, I can't help but laugh. Then I take over as he stands by my side, watching me work.

It's not exactly as I envisioned, but nothing ever is.

That doesn't make it any less perfect.

Rule #52: Savor every moment.

Eden
One month later

"WELL, I'M TELLING YOU, IF FEMALE SIGN-UPS ARE DOWN, THEN IT doesn't matter where the retention numbers are. Getting them in the club should be our number one priority."

Emerson Grant furrows his brow at me on the other side of the conference table. "Any ideas then?" he asks as he leans back in his chair and crosses his leg over his knee.

I take a deep breath and roll back my shoulders. "Yes, I do."

"Hit us with it," Garrett says from the side of the table.

"Well," I say, hitting the button on the computer to show this quarter's numbers on the slideshow. "As of right now, our main female demographic is being pulled through mediums geared toward single, childless, wealthy businesswomen. And I believe we're missing a huge target."

"Who?" Emerson asks.

"Moms."

"Moms?" Hunter asks, looking up from his laptop.

"Yes. Mothers. Wives. There is an entire demographic of

women underrepresented in this community. The married ones won't come without their spouses, and their spouses won't come without them. The single ones have no outlet and wouldn't feel welcome, so I think we should extend an invitation."

Garrett chuckles. "What do you suggest we do? Drop flyers at the library during story time?"

I glare at him as I roll my eyes. "No, but they're online. If we target our ads and pull in a few of their trusted influencers, I think we can entice them to visit the club. It's not like I'm suggesting we open a day care. But I know these women. They are no different from the ones we already serve. Just because they spend their days at home with kids and cartoons doesn't mean they don't have the same dirty, kinky desires the rest of us do."

The three men at the table are all staring at me, and they're making it very hard to read their expressions. Part of me feels like I did just suggest we open a day care because it feels insane, but since coming out to them as a mother myself, I feel like I have an obligation to speak up for others like me.

Emerson is the first to crack a smile. "I like it."

Hunter nods as he contemplates the numbers on the screen. "What about a casual night at the club where we lay off the dress code to make it a little more inviting and less intimidating?"

A smile creeps across my face. "That's a great idea."

"And we can get Mia in here to show us what she knows about social media influencers to reach out for this. We can offer them a month's free membership for an outreach collaboration."

"I like that," Emerson replies.

Next to him, Charlotte is typing furiously on her laptop. Then she looks up at me. With a warm smile, she says, "You should be the one to reach out. Do it as Madame Kink. You have the following."

"Me?" I ask. "You're not afraid Madame Kink will scare them away?" I add with a laugh.

"Then do it as Eden. They'll relate to you."

Tapping my pen on the desk, I smile to myself.

"We can circle back to this on Monday," Emerson says as he stands from his seat. "Garrett, talk to Mia about a marketing plan. Hunter, run through the ad budget and see what we can spend on this. And, Eden…nice work."

As everyone rises from the table, I let the praise wash over me. It's only been a month, but I already feel suited for this job. I see the club from a new angle now. I come into the club with a new sense of purpose.

"You coming, Eden?" Garrett asks, pulling me from my thoughts.

"Huh?"

"Thursday nights we go to the bar down the street. It's sort of a tradition."

I quickly shake my head. "Oh no, I don't want to impose on your traditions."

Garrett rolls his eyes and walks up to put his arm around my shoulder. "You're stuck with us now, E. And being part of the team means you're not imposing. Also, I owe you a drink after my smart-ass comment during our meeting, so call up your boyfriend and girlfriend and tell them to meet us at the bar."

Charlotte is smiling across the room. "You have to come."

With a sigh, I shrug. "Fine. I'm in."

Garrett releases my shoulder as he walks away to make a joke with Hunter. Alone in the boardroom, I pull out my phone and open up the group chat with Clay and Jade. They're both at his place tonight since I had a meeting. Jack is home with Madison.

The team wants me to go to the bar with them down the street.
Will you two come?

Jade replies first.

You're part of the team! I'm so proud of you.

Then Clay adds:

Of course we'll come.

Smiling down at my phone, I shoot them the address and type out my response.

See you both there soon.

When I arrive at the bar, nearly everyone is already there. They've pushed together two large tables so everyone can fit around them. Garrett calls me over to the bar when he spots me walking through the door.

"Her drinks are on me tonight," he says to the bartender. "Because I was an asshole in our meeting."

I laugh as I shake my head. "A smart-ass, not an asshole."

"Same thing," he replies.

"Vodka martini, please," I say to the bartender. When I turn around, I spot Ronan and Daisy walking in together. Waving to them from the bar, I wait for my drink as they approach.

"I didn't know you two were coming," I say as I hug Daisy.

"Emerson told us," Ronan says as he holds his young wife close to his side. "I'm glad to see you here," he adds.

"Thanks. Feels good to be here," I reply. I'm fully aware that *here* no longer means at the bar. *Here* means in this position, in this place in our lives. And when he nods at me with a wink, I know he gets it.

Ronan and Daisy get their drinks as I watch the door. When I spot Clay and Jade walking in, I feel instantly at ease. I love everyone in our party tonight, but these two are mine.

Jade winds her arms around my waist and presses her lips to mine. I curl her hair behind her ear and kiss her again, letting my gaze connect with hers.

Then, keeping my hand on her waist, I lean toward Clay for a kiss.

We get our drinks and then carry them over to the table. Everyone greets us as we sit down. They've already been introduced to Clay and Jade, but it still feels good to see them accepted by my friends.

Mia leans across the table and admires Jade's floral dress. Drake and Clay share a laugh about something on the other side. This feels like a dream.

Emerson raises his glass as he calls out, "Cheers, friends. Ten years later, at the same bar that started it all."

"Without the shiner this time," Garrett adds, and the table erupts in laughter.

Emerson smirks at his friend before adding, "Look at how this table has grown over the years. I feel very blessed to have you all here with us now." Then he calls, "Cheers."

"Cheers," everyone repeats as we all tap our glasses together.

As we set them down on the table, I look at Emerson at the head of the table. "So what's with the shiner? Did I miss something?"

"Oh, I love this story," Hunter says, grinning over his beer.

"Wait, what story?" I ask. Emerson is wearing a mischievous grin. Everyone around the table laughs.

"You haven't heard that one? About Emerson getting a fist to the eye socket?" Garrett asks with a laugh. "It's how we came up with the whole idea for Salacious."

"No, but now I really want to hear it."

Emerson rolls his eyes. Next to him, his wife, Charlotte, is snickering to herself. Her arm is looped through his as she stares up at him with love in her eyes.

As the table of friends chatter with each other, I glance around at each of the people seated there. Mia is sitting proudly next to Garrett as they both recap something with Isabel across the table, who is sitting happily between her two men, Drake and Hunter.

Next to them, my gaze catches Ronan's. And there it pauses for a few moments as we stare at each other, having a silent conversation. If not for him, I wouldn't be here. If not for what these people started over ten years ago, I don't know if I'd even be alive. They may never know how much they saved me.

When Ronan smiles softly, I know he must be reading my thoughts. He reaches next to him to kiss the side of Daisy's head as if to show just how blessed he feels too.

How did we get so lucky to find this family and this home?

Under the table, Clay squeezes my fingers in his, and Jade rests her head on my opposite shoulder.

So *fucking* lucky.

"Okay, okay," I say, interrupting the commotion at the table. "Emerson, tell me the fucking story."

Everyone falls silent and turns their attention to him.

He picks up his beer with an amused smile as he starts, "Okay, so this woman was sucking my cock…"

Rule #53: Real family sticks together.

Jade's Epilogue
Five years later

THE WARM OCEAN BREEZE ON MY FACE FEELS NICE. MY EYES ARE closed as I rest my head against Eden's shoulder, letting the gentle motion of the boat lull me to sleep.

Her hand reaches down to caress my bare stomach, pulling me from my dreams.

"You're not feeling sick, are you?" she whispers against my ear.

I shake my head. "Nah. That was a first-trimester problem."

"Not even with these waves?" Clay asks.

"I've been coming out on the boat since I was her age," I say, nodding to Elizabeth, who is currently snoozing on Clay's chest. Her little lips are smooshed together, and her cheeks are red from the heat, but other than that, she looks perfectly content in her daddy's arms.

Eden's hand stays on my stomach. I swear she touches it more than I do.

"Grandpa, can I drive?" Jack asks from his seat.

"Sure, kiddo," my dad answers as he stands from his captain's chair and motions for Jack to stand at the wheel. Eden grabs her phone and snaps pictures of Jack as my dad stands behind him, showing him where to turn and what to avoid.

"He's a natural," Dad beams with pride as he rests a hand on Jack's shoulder.

Then Eden turns her phone toward Clay and snaps a few pictures of him holding Lizzie. He looks good enough to eat with that baby nuzzled against his chest like that.

"God, he looks good," I whisper to Eden as she glances up at her phone.

"It's the baby. There's something about a man holding a baby."

"I'm sure it's these hormones too. They make me feral," I say in a hushed tone.

She giggles quietly to me. "We can take care of that later," she replies, kissing me on my head.

"Too bad I feel like a cow," I reply, trying to stretch, but it feels like my body is already out of room, and we still have fifteen weeks to go.

"You're the sexiest cow I've ever seen," she replies before tweaking one of my nipples through my bikini top. It's a good thing my dad is preoccupied with helping Jack steer the boat through the open water.

When we reach a good spot to drop the anchor, Elizabeth starts to stir. She lifts her sleepy head from Clay's chest and gives him a cheesy smile.

"Dada," she coos, and he presses kisses against her cheek to make her squeal with laughter. Her tiny life jacket makes it hard for her to move, and she gets fussy pretty quickly about it, so he quickly passes her to Eden, who bounces her on her knee.

"Wanna go swimming, Lizzie?" Eden asks.

Lizzie smiles as she flaps her arms and starts screaming, "Swimming, swimming, swimming!"

Eden kisses her cheek. "Jack, will you hold her while I put some sunblock on her cheeks?"

Clay helps my dad drop the anchor and let down the ladder. And I watch contentedly as Jack entertains his little sister so Eden can slather her with sunblock.

It's moments like this when I wish I could stop time and keep things like this forever. But honestly, I've had the same thought through every phase. When we first started dating, it felt like Jack was the center of our lives. Then we decided to get married and try for a baby. After that, Elizabeth came along, and we got to watch Jack become a big brother. Next, we'll have a new baby to love and grow with.

Through every phase, our family has changed, but at the core, we've stayed the same. Clay, Eden, and I have built a life together, and it's never once felt like settling down. It's been exhausting and exhilarating and still incredibly sexy and fun.

I took a break from work to focus on the kids, and I've loved every minute of it. Just like I've loved watching Eden grow and prosper at work to the point now where she's basically running that club on her own.

My dad promoted Clay to co-owner at the firm. And it didn't take my dad as long as I expected for him to accept our relationship as it was. Once again, he claimed to have his suspicions when Eden showed up at our family functions for nearly a year before we finally came out to him.

Clay's family was less tolerant. His mother still calls from time to time, and she's seen Elizabeth and Jack a few times. But his parents didn't come to our wedding, and Clay has made peace with that.

If they can't see our family for what it is, then we don't need them.

Because what I see is love in all of its messy, misshapen, and perfectly eclectic form.

"You wanna go swimming with Mama?" Jack asks Elizabeth, getting her even more excited.

As Eden climbs into the water, Jack sets Elizabeth down on the edge.

"Come on, baby. Mama will catch you," she calls. We all watch with smiles, cheering Lizzie on as she launches herself fearlessly from the side of the boat. And just like she promised, Eden is there, arms outstretched and ready to catch her every single time.

Rule #54: You were not meant to live by someone else's rules.

Jack's Epilogue
Thirteen years later

"Yeah, I'm almost there. I can give you a call back later. After I tell her."

"You've got this. Good luck."

"Thanks," I say with a chuckle just before the phone line goes dead.

Pulling up to the house, I feel my palms start to sweat. I park in front of the two-story in which I spent my teenage years. Once my youngest sister was born, it was clear our family of six wouldn't fit in our little three-bedroom anymore.

Parking behind my dad's Audi, I take a moment to compose myself before opening the door.

I can do this.

I want to do this.

Climbing out, I walk up to the front door, and even before I open it, I hear the very recognizable screech of my sisters fighting.

"Scarlett, stay out of my room!" Lizzie shrieks from her bedroom.

"I was never in your room," Scarlett replies from down the upstairs hallway.

As I stand on the landing, I can't help but laugh. I do not miss this.

"Girls!" Jade shouts from the kitchen. When she emerges to find me standing on the landing, her face lights up. "Jack's home!" she shouts as she jogs up to wrap her arms around my neck.

"Hey, Mom," I mumble as she squeezes my neck without letting go. Calling Jade Mom had been a somewhat interchangeable thing since she and my mom and Clay got married. Then when my sisters came around, it started to feel more natural. I know she loves it when I do, and since she's by far the sweetest person in this house, I like to make her happy.

Her hugs seem to last forever, but I don't mind. She has to stand on her tiptoes to hug me now. I shot up past her by the time I hit thirteen.

My littlest sister, Scarlett, comes barreling down the stairs but stops halfway while she waits for Jade to let go of my neck. Once she does, I turn to see her smiling at me as I put my hands on my hips.

"I can't catch you anymore, Scarlett," I say with a laugh.

"You can try!" she replies.

She's still so small, taking after Mom, so when she launches herself off the middle stair, I catch her without falling over. This has been a tradition for as long as I can remember, but now that she's twelve, I don't think we can keep it up for much longer.

"I've missed you!" she says as I set her down on the landing.

"I've missed you too," I reply with a hint of shame.

"You never come home anymore," she whines.

From the top of the stairs, my sister Elizabeth adds, "Why would he, Scarlett? You're so annoying when he does."

"Elizabeth Nina Bradley!" Mom shouts from beside me. "Would you please be nice to your sister? And give your brother a hug. It's Christmas."

Lizzie rolls her eyes before begrudgingly walking down the stairs and giving me an obligatory hug. I laugh to myself.

Jade pulls me into the house, taking my coat and throwing it on one of the dining room chairs. Then she tries to get me to eat, heating me up a plate as if I've just finished some perilous journey, when the truth is it was only a ninety-minute drive from campus.

"Your dad is in a meeting, and your mom's on the phone, but I'm sure you want to see him first anyway," she says as she winces. Pressing my lips together awkwardly, I nod.

"You think she'll freak out?" I ask.

She quickly shakes her head. "I've never known her to freak out," she replies. "I don't think you have anything to worry about, buddy."

"Thanks, Jade," I reply. Her eyes meet mine, and there's warmth in them as she comes closer and rubs my shoulder affectionately.

"Now eat up. I have to take the girls to ballet rehearsal soon, but we'll make sure to catch up more when I get back, okay?"

"Okay, thanks," I say before quickly scarfing down the leftover lasagna she prepared. My sisters are still carrying on upstairs, and I pull out my phone to check my messages, but there are none.

When I hear heavy footsteps from down the hall, I quickly spin around to see my dad coming toward me. He's wearing a proud smile under that thick salt-and-pepper beard he's started growing.

"Hey, kid," he says with excitement.

I climb off the barstool and cross the room to greet him with a hug. When he pulls away, he places his hand on my shoulder. "How've you been?"

I shrug. "Doing good. Just working and...you know."

He laughs haughtily. "Yes, I do. Big change coming up."

My eyes dart toward the hall where I know my mom's office hides. He notices my nervous hesitation and guides me toward his own office on the other side. "Come on. You need a drink before you go in there."

Once we're closed into his cozy office with the high ceilings and tall bookshelves, he pulls out a bottle of whiskey he keeps hidden in the cabinet. It makes me laugh to see it, remembering the time my friends and I snuck it out and tried to replace it with sweet tea, thinking he wouldn't notice.

He did, and I was grounded for a month.

"How's work?" he asks.

I shrug. "The same," I reply. "Boring. Repetitive."

"Not for long," he says as he hands me a glass.

"I'm ready."

"I know you are." With that, he tips up his glass and takes a sip before I do the same.

A couple of years ago, I graduated with my degree in business management, but the only work I could find was lifeless and menial. I don't know what I was expecting with a degree like that, but I want more.

My parents never raised me to worry about money. They encouraged me to follow my dreams, but for some reason, when I hit college, I stalled out. I picked something safe and predictable.

I just kept thinking about everything my mother had sacrificed to give me the life she thought I deserved. I was terrified I would waste that on something trivial or indulgent. So I took the safe route.

I felt like I was reliving that day when I was twelve and she sat me down and told me everything. About my abusive biological father. How she had to hide me from him for years until he died. How she created an entire persona and a whole new life just for me.

What kind of asshole would I be if I took that opportunity and wasted it on one failure after another?

My life has been safe and predictable ever since.

"I think this is gonna be good for you, Jack. You need a change. A fresh start."

"You think she'll feel the same?" I ask without looking up.

"I know she will. Your mother only wants what's best for you. If you're happy, she's happy."

"Yeah," I mutter quietly.

"Hey," he says from where he's leaning against his desk. When I look up at him, his expression softens. "I'm proud of you, kid."

I force myself to swallow. "Thanks, Dad."

"Don't stress. It's going to be fine."

With a sigh, I nod as I throw the rest of the whiskey down, feeling the burn and praying it eases my nerves.

Then my dad opens the office door and ushers me out. "Just get it over with. She hates secrets, and this has been killing Jade and me since you told us last week."

"Fine." I groan as I hand him the empty glass and walk down the long hall to where my mom's office is.

The door is open, and I hear her on the phone before I reach the room.

"Yeah, let's discuss this again after the new year. Don't forget the franchise meeting at two."

When I spot my mom standing in her office, I stop and wait for her to see me. Her hair is still long and has been for as long as I can remember. The only thing that's really changed about her over the years is a few smile lines on her face and some crow's-feet around her eyes—proof that she's spent the last twenty-five years happy.

And I'm about to fuck that up.

I figured out what my mom did for a living long before she finally told me, well before I turned eighteen. I don't know how she managed to hide it for so long, but I had internet access and a teenage boy's curiosity. It wasn't hard to figure it out from there.

But I also never cared much where my mom worked. She was just…my mom.

She turns and spots me in the doorway, giving me a bright smile.

"Emerson, Jack just got home for Christmas. I've gotta go. Yeah, happy holidays to you and Charlie too. Bye."

Her smile is wide as she opens her arms for me. I feel that inane sense of comfort as soon as she wraps them around me.

"Hey, Mama," I mumble softly before she pulls away.

"How was your drive?" she asks.

My jaw clenches. I don't want small talk right now. I don't know if I can take another second.

"It was good," I reply, scratching the back of my neck.

"And work?" she asks.

"Mama, I have something to tell you."

Her mouth closes, and her brow furrows. "What's going on? Is everything okay?"

Deep breath, Jack. You can do this.

"Yeah, everything is fine. It's just…"

I look into her eyes and try to remember what my dad said. She just wants me to be happy.

"I'm moving to Paris."

She doesn't move. Her eyes stay glued on my face as her lips part like she's waiting for me to continue.

"Is that the secret everyone's been keeping from me?" she asks quietly.

"I'm sorry," I reply with a wince.

Her expression turns serious. "What are you sorry for? Don't apologize."

"I just didn't know how to tell you."

"Well…start from the beginning. Tell me everything," she says, pulling me to the two chairs in front of her desk.

"Uncle Ronan offered me a job."

Her eyes widen. "At the club?"

I shake my head back and forth. "Sort of. Not *at* the club. Just…for the club."

"Is that what you want?" she asks, leaning forward.

"Yes. I…need this. I need a change. I hate my job here, but I feel like if I leave you, then it's like I'm not grateful for everything—"

"Jack, stop," she says, putting a hand up. Then she places her hands on either side of my face. "My sweet Jack. I did not give you this life so I could keep you here with me. I gave you this life so you'd be free to live it however you want. Once upon a time, I felt stuck in my home, and getting out was the best thing that ever happened to me."

My eyes cast downward as I let the relief of exposing this secret wash over me.

She touches my chin, lifting my face until I'm staring into her eyes again. "I will miss you like crazy, and I'm going to visit a *lot*. But you were never meant to live by someone else's rules. You were meant for big things, my sweet boy. And I would never want to be the one to stop you."

"Thanks, Mama," I whisper as my voice cracks.

She pulls me into another tight embrace, and I try to absorb some of her courage and confidence. My mother is the strongest person I know, and I'm going to need some of that for the future I have planned.

Character Profiles

JADE BRADLEY

Current location: Briar Point, California

Occupation: Stay-at-home mom

Hair color: Brown

Eye color: Blue

Style: Sweet, feminine, colorful

Drink of choice: Anything fruity

Relationship status: Happily married

Significant other(s): Clay and Eden

Kink preference: Depends on her mood, switch, voyeur, role play

Hobbies: Going on the boat, traveling with her family, watching *Gilmore Girls*

Best friend(s): Eden and Clay

Sibling(s): None

Greatest fear: Jade's biggest fear is boredom. This is why she is always moving, talking, or creating something. Sometimes she's afraid she comes on too strong or can be "too much." Of course her husband and wife never laugh at her (unless she's trying to make them laugh) and if anyone is ever condescending or rude to her, her wife turns into a loyal bodyguard who isn't afraid of putting someone in their place.

Weakness: Sometimes Jade tries too hard to avoid big emotions or complex feelings. Why have serious conversations when they could be having fun instead?

Strength: Jade goes with the flow. She doesn't worry too much and is often the peacekeeper in her family. She is great at lightening the mood and making everyone feel special. Jade loves fiercely.

Greatest accomplishment: Owning her sexuality. Jade loves experimentation and exploration. She never feels shame or guilt for the things she likes and she ensures her partners have a safe and sexy place to express themselves physically.

Enneagram: 7

"Cruel Summer" blares in my earbuds as I slide the casserole dish into the oven. Even as I'm setting the timer on the stove for thirty minutes, I'm making a list in my head of everything I need to pack for this weekend.

> Passports.
> Lizzie's medication.
> Swimsuits.

I let out a yelp at the feel of someone's soft hand sliding over the round surface of my ass.

I quickly pull out the AirPods as I spin around to find Eden grinning at me flirtatiously.

"You scared me," I say, panting with my hand over my chest.

"I just couldn't help myself. I swear you wear these shorts to get my attention."

She backs me against the counter, and I bite back my grin as I close my arms around her waist. After the many changes in my body in the past decade and a half, it's reassuring that she still wants me the same way she used to. My ass isn't the size it was when we met, but that doesn't stop me from flaunting it for her and Clay. In fact, I do it even more now.

"I thought you were on a call in your office," I say with a whimper as her lips make their way down my neck.

"The meeting ended," she replies. Her hands scoop under my ass and my right legs lifts for her, allowing her more space to press her body to mine.

"Where are the kids?" I ask as her lips move lower. Digging my hand in her hair, I squeeze, making her hum from the slight pain.

"Clay took them to ballet lessons, and Jack is at the movies," she replies.

My lips pull into a wide grin. "Well, then we better hurry," I say just as her mouth finds mine. "We only have twenty-seven minutes left."

Pulling back, she hooks her thumbs in the elastic waistband of my shorts. With a wink, she quickly drags them down.

"Twenty-seven minutes? I'll have you screaming in five."

―――――――

CLAY BRADLEY

Current location: Briar Point, California
Occupation: Financial planner
Hair color: Brown
Eye color: Green
Style: Business, classy, tailored
Drink of choice: Vodka on the rocks
Relationship status: Happily married
Significant other(s): Jade and Eden
Kink preference: Submissive, praise, being a good pet
Hobbies: Running, baseball, hanging out with his son
Best friend: His father-in-law and business partner, Will Penner
Sibling(s): None
Greatest fear: Feeling insignificant or forgotten, although he never

has to worry about that anymore. His wives adore him, and he's often showered with praise from Eden and attention from Jade. He devotes himself to his children, so they never have to feel the way he did growing up.

Weakness: He often pretends that everything is fine when it's not. He struggles to speak up when he needs to because he hates confrontation or appearing weak or needy.

Strength: Clay always knows what everyone needs without them having to ask. He is a great listener and supportive husband/father. He is Jack's biggest fan.

Greatest accomplishment: His marriage. For a guy who never considered himself worthy of the love of one person or fit for long-term relationships, he managed to find two people, and he devotes himself to them every day.

Enneagram: 4

───────────

A feeling of calm settles over me as the collar clips at the front of my neck. It reminds me that I belong to someone. That I belong to *them*.

Even after fifteen years of marriage, that sound still does something to me—as if that reminder is still necessary.

"Such a good boy," Eden whispers as she leans down and presses her lips to my head.

Then, I hear the snap of the leash around the ring in my collar and arousal ignites in my bloodstream like a strike of lightning. My cock hardens against my thigh, rising upward. When Eden tugs gently on the leash, I feel my dick twitch with excitement.

I move obediently to all fours and crawl slowly next to her as she guides me to the beautiful woman sitting on the rug across the room.

Jade is kneeling, but not in a submissive way. She's kneeling because she's waiting for *me*.

"I brought you something," Eden says in seductive tone.

Jade's smile grows wide as she bites her bottom lip. Her eyes rake over me with anticipation.

"Can I use him however I want?" she asks, practically bouncing.

I struggle to hold back my grin. Even after all these years, she still treats each of our play sessions like actual play. Getting to explore everything with her is damn near the highlight of my life, and our always-attentive Eden is our guide.

"Yes, you can," Eden replies. "He's a very good boy and will do whatever you want him to. Won't you, pet?"

The corner of my mouth lifts. Jade leans forward and presses her lips to my neck, sending chills down my spine as I lift my gaze to the woman holding my leash.

"Yes, Madame."

EDEN ST. CLAIRE-BRADLEY

Also known as: Madame Kink

Current location: Briar Point, California

Occupation: Dominatrix, sex club manager, and kink educator/blogger

Hair color: Black

Eye color: Green

Style: Black, leather, sexy at work. Casual & comfy at home.

Drink of choice: Red wine or vodka martini

Relationship status: Happily married

Significant other(s): Clay and Jade Bradley

Kink preference: Madame, FemDom, BDSM, Exhibitionism, Voyeurism

Hobbies: Spending time with her family, shopping with Jade, going to the movies, and putting Clay in his place.

Pet(s): Clay

Best friend: Ronan Kade

Sibling(s): None

Greatest fear: Losing her family. She is protective to a fault. She encourages her daughters to be independent and teaches them to be

protective of themselves so they never end up in the same situation
she was in.

Weakness: Saying no to Jade. If her wife wants it, her wife gets it.

Strength: Eden is intuitive and wise. She puts her family first but is skilled
at finding a balance between work and family. She is able to separate
work (where she can be filthy and sexy) from home (where she can
be nurturing and loving). She works hard to make Salacious Players'
Club the best club in the world and knows exactly what it takes to
make it that way.

Greatest accomplishment: Raising three strong, independent, and
happy children.

Enneagram: 8

It's been a pleasure being your Madame. And while
I may not find the time to blog anymore, Westcoast
Escapades will continue to grow for all of your kink and
explorative needs. I hope you continue to find this space
as inspirational as it is educational. It will always be a safe
space for everyone to learn, experiment, and grow.

Signing off for now…
Madame Kink

As I type that last bittersweet line, I feel a sense of nostalgia wash
over me. This transition has been a long time coming. Twenty
years I've had this site, and while it's continued to grow over the
past two decades, finding time to contribute to it personally has
become harder and harder. Thankfully, I have a whole team that
runs the site now, but stepping back feels like saying goodbye to
the one place that helped nurture the person I am today.

"Hey, Mama. You busy?" The sweet voice from the doorway
pulls me away from my computer screen. Scarlett is standing in
her pajamas with an iPad clutched to her chest.

"Not at all, my love. What's up?" I ask, reaching an arm toward her.

With a smile, she crosses the room and plants herself on my lap. I press my nose to her hair, still wet from her shower, and inhale the strawberry scent. Out of the three, Scarlett is the most cuddly and affectionate. She is glued to one of our sides at all times, and I love it. It reminds me of when Jack was little, so I savor every moment.

"I want to show you my drawing," she says, clicking on her tablet to show me the sparkling blue dress on the screen.

"Scar, that's beautiful," I say, admiring how talented she is. She might only be ten, but I have no doubt, she has a bright future in design of some sort.

"Thanks," she murmurs. As she glances up at me with those dazzling round eyes full of innocence and joy, I wonder how I became so lucky. The blog might have started as just a silly place on the internet where I shared my experience, but somehow, in some roundabout way, it brought me here.

JACK ST. CLAIRE

Age: 25

Born in: Briar Point, California

Current location: Paris, France

Occupation: Business administration

Hair color: Dark brown curls

Eye color: Green

Style: Colorful and classy—bold colors and tailored at work. Graphic tees and jeans at home.

Drink of choice: Not a big drinker—will sometimes cut loose and have a bourbon with his dad or godfather.

Relationship status: Single

Significant other: None yet

Kink preference: Undiscovered

Hobbies: Going to the movies, travel, photography, quality time with his family.

Pet(s): None

Best friend: Phoenix Scott

Sibling(s): Elizabeth and Scarlett

Greatest fear: Disappointing his parents, especially Eden. Jack is a people pleaser, and he can't stand the thought of anyone being angry with him.

Weakness: Jack struggles with putting himself first. He's working on fixing that...

Strength: He is resilient and kind. He is constantly looking for love everywhere, and no matter how many times he's had his heart broken, he holds onto hope that one day he'll find his forever person.

Greatest accomplishment: Quitting his job and moving to Paris.

Enneagram: 6

"It's a good thing you didn't pack much," Phoenix says over the phone as I take her on a Facetime tour through my new apartment.

"No kidding," I reply. "The bathroom is literally a sink, a toilet, and a shower. Not one single cabinet."

She fakes a gasp. "Where on earth will you keep your massive collection of hair products?"

"Shut up," I say, propping the phone on the kitchen counter so I can pull a bottle of water from the fridge. On my way back, I check my hair in the reflection of the darkened window. I don't use *that* much product in my hair. I'd like to see her manage these curls.

"Ronan couldn't get you a bigger place?" she asks. I can tell by the way she's carrying the phone with the view of the sky that she's on campus.

"I didn't want Ronan's help. It's enough that he's getting me the job. I won't take his handouts and end up like *Julian*."

"Point taken," she says with a snort. "Speaking of Ronan, when do you start?"

"Not for a couple of days," I reply as I take a swig of the water. My face contorts in disgust as I realize I picked out bubbly water. I've made this mistake a few times already on our various trips out here.

"He wants to give me time to get acclimated," I add, once I recover from the carbonation. "But I don't know, Nix. I'm ready to get started *now*."

I can hear her chuckle through the line. "I still can't believe you're going to work for a sex club. My sweet, innocent friend."

"I'm not *that* innocent," I joke.

She lets out a sigh as she looks into the camera. And then with a laugh she adds, "Not for long."

Acknowledgments

Well, this is it. We made it.

grabs the tissues

All right, here we go.

If I could put into words what this series means to me, it still wouldn't accurately portray how grateful I am. I had no idea when I set out to write a kinky series about four owners of a sex club that it would become what it has. I never expected you to love these characters as much as I do.

Over the past two years, I've received emails, messages, and hugs from strangers because of what you found in these books. I am still blown away by the love and support you all have given me, Emerson, Charlie, Mia, Garrett, Hunter, Drake, Isabel, Maggie, Beau, Daisy, Ronan, Clay, Jade, and Eden.

So, as I hand them over to you, I know they're in good hands. Salacious Players' Club is all yours now.

Now for the good stuff.

Thank you to every single person who helped me pull this book off (and fuck, did they have their work cut out for them)....

My husband, Mr. Cate, for picking up a LOT of slack around the house while I locked myself in the office. Thank you for the encouragement and support and for talking me off of so many proverbial cliffs.

My assistant, Lori Alexander, for running everything behind the scenes so I never had to worry. Peace of mind is priceless. As are you.

My store manager and friend, Misty Frey. Even if I could do all of this without you, I wouldn't want to. You are such a gift.

My friend and alpha reader, Jill. Thank you for talking me through my impostor syndrome and for being my mental health ninja. And for the bathtub Marcos (obviously).

My betas—Janine, Adrian, and Becca. Thanks for taking the time to read through the messy versions one chapter at a time over the span of three months. You guys don't get enough credit for what I put you through. Your feedback is so important to me.

My favorite hype girl, Amanda Anderson. I couldn't do any of this without you, and I'm so blessed to have you on my team and as a friend.

My agent, Savannah Greenwell. Don't ever leave me.

My editor, Rebecca Fairest Reviews. You're too good to me. Thanks for holding my hand through this series.

My proofreaders, Rumi Khan (green eyes, got it!) and Rosa Sharon of Fairy Proof Mother.

Wander Aguiar and his entire team, for the quality of your work but mostly the kindness and love you've shown me and my girls. And, of course, the stunning model Dina, who I knew was Eden the moment I laid eyes on her.

Rachel Gilmer and the entire team at Sourcebooks Casablanca for bringing Salacious Players' Club to the world.

Becca & Shauna at The Author Agency for helping me spread the word about this release.

Sara's Sinners and Sara's Salacious Readers for creating such an awesome group of readers who support and encourage one another.

My amazing Shameless sisters for making me laugh and cheering me on.

And last, to you. Thank you for reading this book and this series. Thank you for visiting the Salacious Players' Club.

Thank you for the time of my life.

About the Author

Sara Cate is a *USA Today* bestselling author of contemporary, forbidden romance. Her stories are known for their heart-wrenching plots and toe-curling heat. Living in Arizona with her husband and kids, Sara spends most of her time working in her office with her goldendoodle by her side.

Website: saracatebooks.com
Facebook: SaraCateBooks
Instagram: @saracatebooks
TikTok: @SaraCatebooks